When Hearts Surrender

Victoria Lum

When Hearts Surrender

By Victoria Lum

Published by Eternal Hearts Publishing

Cover Design Copyright © 2024 Y'All That Graphic

Editing by Theresa Leigh and Amy Briggs

Proofreading by Virginia Tesi Carey

ISBN (Paperback): 979-8-9900169-3-4
ISBN (E-Book): 979-8-9900169-2-7

Author's Note

THERE ARE HEAVY TOPICS discussed in this book and your mental health is paramount to me. For a list of potential areas of sensitive content, please visit:

https://www.victorialum.com/sensitive-content-information

For interesting insight into the book (with spoilers), please read the acknowledgments at the end of the book.

For those of you who are in a dark place in life, please know that you are important and you matter.

United States:

988 Crisis Lifeline: If you or someone you know is struggling or in crisis, help is available. You'll be able to speak with a trained crisis counselor any time of day or night.

Call or text: 988

Chat: 988lifeline.org

SAMHSA Helpline: This Helpline provides 24-hour free and confidential help.

Call: 1-800-662-4357

TTY: 1-800-487-4889

Text your ZIP code to: 435748

SAMHSA Website:

https://www.samhsa.gov/find-help/national-helpline

DEDICATION

To my hopeless romantics and believers of soulmates, this one is for you.

RELATIONSHIP TREE

THE KINGSLEYS AND EXTENDED FAMILY
(LA HEARTS SERIES)

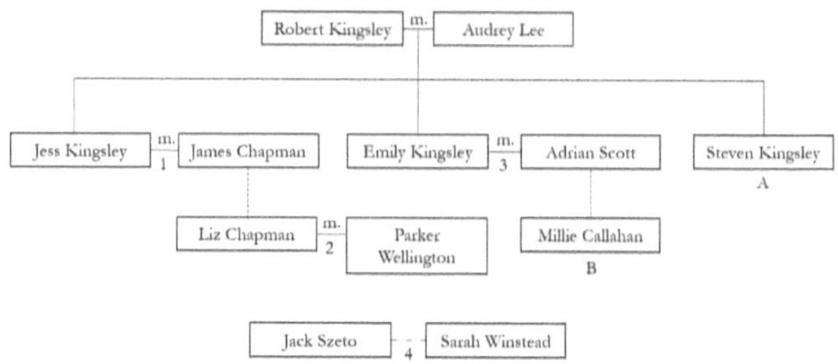

THE ANDERSONS AND FRIENDS
(THE ORCHID SERIES)

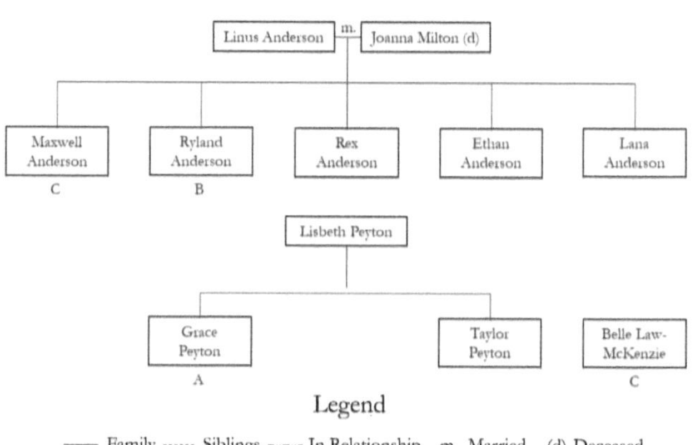

Legend

—— Family ⋯⋯ Siblings - - - In Relationship   m. Married   (d) Deceased

Books

1 – *The Sweetest Agony* 2 – *The Coldest Passion* 3 – *The Harshest Hope* 4 – *The Brightest Spark*
A – *When Hearts Ignite* B – *When Hearts Collide* C – *When Hearts Surrender*

Disclaimer: Only main characters are included. Awesome side characters including children are not in this tree.

Playlist

"Nessun Dorma" – Andrea Bocelli (starting at the 40-50 second mark)
"Past Lives" – Sapientdream & Slushii
"Work of Art" – Benson Boone
"Can't Help Falling in Love [Dark Version]" – Tommee Profitt featuring Brooke
"Arcade" – Duncan Laurence
"Nessun Dorma" – HAUSER and London Symphony Orchestra

PROLOGUE
THE CURSE

Wraithmoor Abbey, Manhattan, New York City
October 2, 1860

Emma

The dense fog reeked of death this morning. It was so thick, she could barely see the stone steps in front of her as she climbed the winding staircase to reach the top of the grand estate.

The mansion was built on hallowed grounds, atop the ruins of an old abbey that was burned to cinders years ago. Locals rumored the land was haunted by the ghosts of those buried here, who were exhumed and moved to other places of eternal rest before the great Anderson family rebuilt on top of it.

It was bad luck, they said.

She never believed the superstitions. But now, as the sorrow in her chest threatened to cleave her in half as she reached her destination, a place that once brought her joy but now only held a lifetime of regrets, she couldn't help but wonder if the superstitions were true.

She walked toward the edge of the rooftop and glanced around, secretly wishing *he* were here. That he would stop her.

But there was nothing other than the eerie silence and the occasional cry of the black crows hovering nearby, her companions paying solemn tribute to her before she took to the skies—her final flight.

She brushed past the skeletons of wilted flowers, long laid to rest after a dreary autumn, and past the dark vines twined around a veranda, the lush green appearing black in the gloominess of early dawn. Gripping the railing at the edge of the rooftop, she slowly climbed over the ledge to the tiny sliver of stone separating this life and the next.

"Do you love me, Silas?" she whispered.

"Always, now and forever, this lifetime and all the lifetimes thereafter," he murmured, his intense gray eyes filled with warmth as he pulled her close and sealed his lips with hers.

It didn't matter they were forbidden. It didn't matter she was putting everything at risk by being with him, a man far above her station. A man who could ruin her.

They were tempting fate, but it felt like destiny.

A sob wrenched from her throat. Lies. They were all lies.

Clutching her last missive to him to her chest, she teetered on the edge and stared at the rose garden far below. Her eyes skated over the murder of crows standing silently by, over the new hedges the groundskeeper put in several months ago, which had now grown at least a foot taller.

Her favorite place.

A place where she would meet with him after the house went to bed, where they would stare into the dark nights, admiring the millions of stars glittering amid the inky backdrop.

He would take her hand then, far away from the prying eyes of his wife, a woman he told her he despised but was forced to marry because his family believed a duke needed legitimate heirs to be from a lady of good bloodline.

Not a lowly servant of the household.

Someone like her.

It was the way things were done—they were both trapped in their stations, unable to escape.

But nonetheless, her life irrevocably changed the first time their eyes met in the estate's library. She was picking a book for her new employer, his wife, to read the next day, only to find him there, flipping through a thick volume by the roaring fire.

He never minded her status. He was curious what she had chosen. The curiosity burgeoned into a discussion on philosophy, which became nightly meetings where he'd tease her as she read her romantic novels after her chores were done. He'd flash her smiles she'd never seen him wear before, his hand grazing hers when they passed each other in the halls.

"I never knew love until I met you," he whispered in her ear months later.

He'd take her in his arms and press his lips to hers as they danced under the sliver of ghostly moonlight in the rose garden. The night chill pierced her flimsy work garments of gray wool, but every inch of her was on fire, her heart alight for the man in front of her, who, in those stolen moments, appeared to be giving her the world.

They moved to the haunting rhythms of nature, the foreboding night wind howling and the falling leaves rustling from the trees nearby, as if begging them to stop before it was too late.

But naively, they ignored the ominous signs. He'd murmur instead, "Emma, my love, my all."

Her heart fluttered a dying beat at the memories—the warmth in his charcoal gaze, the gentleness of his fingers trailing over her cheek, the slight quirk of his lips, dimples showing.

"Silas."

She closed her eyes and remembered how she melted into his embrace. His lips took hers and plundered everything away from her—her heart, her soul, her mind. They would spend endless hours in the gardens, forgoing sleep, coming together as man and woman, not as a duke and his servant, obliterating a thousand lines they were forbidden to cross.

He used to say he was a duke, and he could do anything.

One day, they would be free to be together.

But that was a lie too.

And now, she paid the ultimate price.

She tore her eyes away from the garden. The morning light had barely penetrated the swollen, smothering clouds. A storm was coming fast, based on the severe winds and the darkened skies. She should alert the rest of the staff so they could begin preparations, as the manor was still in an active state of construction.

The streetlamps were unlit, but there was an eerie calm, as if she had already crossed the threshold to another world.

This wouldn't be her job anymore.

She wouldn't be here to see the storm.

The vaporous mist hid the terrifying heights from the rooftop to the grounds four stories down. It surrounded the abbey like a thick blanket, enticing her to take the leap into her eternal slumber.

"Silas," she choked out, her fingers tightening on the letter he'd no doubt find on her later.

His name was carried away by a chilly breeze.

Tears slipped down her cheeks and her other hand cradled the small bump on her lower belly, the one she couldn't hide anymore, the bump signaling her adultery, her shame for the world to see.

Perhaps, if she'd never fallen in love with him or if he'd done what he had promised and taken her away from there much sooner, his wife wouldn't have shoved her against the vanity table three nights ago in a fit of anger before dismissing her. She wouldn't be bleeding now, knowing the baby had departed the world before her.

Perhaps it was best for everything to end this way. After all, what a scandal this would be for the unblemished Anderson family.

She wetted her lips as she smoothed her hand over her belly, her heart pulverized.

Would it have been a son or a daughter? Would he have had his dark, mesmerizing eyes or her brown hair if he were to have survived? Would she have had dimples just like her father, or would she have had full lips like her?

Would *he* forgive her, her Silas?

Her heart clenched in throbbing pain as she breathed in more of the cloying stench in the air.

Perhaps he wouldn't. Or perhaps he wouldn't care. After all, he silently stood by as the duchess berated her for her loose morals, for daring to disgrace her, making her the laughingstock of society since the rumors of his affair leaked. She remembered how his jaw clenched tightly, his eyes not looking at hers even though she pleaded with all of her heart for him to acknowledge her in the daylight—just once, a reassuring glance, a gentle nod, anything to let her know things would turn out all right.

But he didn't, even though he knew he was the reason for her current state, even though he promised her he would take care of her and their unborn child.

They were lies. A thousand breathtaking lies from a beautiful man.

In the distance, thunder rumbled, the violent sound angry and foreboding.

She hoped Silas would find her when the rain descended.

Her thoughts trailed to last night, before she'd gone to her room to pack her bags, when she'd first felt the painful cramps in her belly.

The elite gathered in the sitting room, eager to have an audience with the duke and the duchess, not caring the title held no merit in America. After all, royalty was royalty, and Silas, a staunch supporter of the Union, had important things to say about the war brimming around the corner.

She stood in the shadows of the second-floor landing, her heart clenched when the duke met his duchess at the bottom of the stairs. He stood tall and proud, his dark navy waistcoat, the one she once told him was her favorite, molded to his figure like a glove.

Lord Silas Anderson, Duke of Westfield in the British aristocracy, head of one of the most illustrious families in America, was a sight to behold, a man who stole her heart even though he couldn't protect it.

His glittering eyes had cut away from his duchess and snared on hers, as though he could see her hiding in the shadows.

But of course he could. He had always seen her, even when she was invisible most of her life.

His throat rippled, the previous placid expression on his face quickly slipping away as he dropped the hand he offered to his wife, who looked up at him in confusion, before following his gaze to her.

Her features hardened. "You pathetic *whore*. I don't want to see you here a minute longer. Go to the whorehouse where you belong."

She flinched and shrunk back, her mistress's words echoing in her mind.

Silas stood at the bottom, unmoving, staring at her. His slate-gray eyes flashed with the same passion she had seen when he met her in the gardens at night, or in the study, or the conservatory. His hands formed into tight fists as they stared silently at each other, a great divide between them.

"You coming, Silas?" the duchess asked from somewhere out of her sight line. "Our guests are waiting."

He took a deep breath, his eyes never leaving hers as he replied in that low, gravelly voice of his, "Yes, my duchess."

A reminder. For himself or for her, she'd never know.

He stepped toward his wife before pausing and turning around. Her heart skipped a beat as he took a few steps up the stairs toward her.

But he stopped, his fingers gripping the ornate wooden railing, pausing at the carving of a lion, part of the Anderson family insignia. His fingers grazed the family heirloom ring he always wore—an intricate band with a beautiful black gemstone. He heaved out a deep breath, and she could feel his gaze cascading over her features, landing at her swollen womb carrying their child. Her abdomen cramped—she wanted to tell him she was bleeding, not only from her womb but also in her heart. But he never gave her a chance to tell him.

He paused at the foot of the staircase, the muscles in his shoulders bunched tightly.

"I'm sorry, Emma. I'm so, so sorry."

"Silas, are you coming?" the duchess called from a few steps away.

He sighed and took out a few banknotes from his pocket and set them on the ground. "I'm sorry."

Anger burned through her veins at the memory, how he carelessly stood by as her future was burned to ashes in front of him. His promises, words of love and eternal devotion were all lies, poison disguised as beautiful prose and haunting promises.

This was the end of the road for her, for society would never give a woman like her another chance. Her future as a fallen woman saddled with the debts of her father would be unthinkable. No one would employ her after she was cast out by the influential Andersons. She had little education growing up, no connections, nothing to her name. Soon, the debtors would arrive and she would have absolutely no value except for what was between her thighs.

"Go to the whorehouse where you belong." The duchess's words carved themselves inside her chest.

There was no other choice.

The frigid morning air penetrated her thin dress and straight into her heart, temporarily stemming the agony leaching out from the tattered organ. Despite everything, she couldn't stop loving him, even as she hated him at the same time.

"Silas." She gripped her necklace, her most treasured possession from him—a pearl and gemstone locket with beautifully carved flowers and his eternal devotion carved inside—and whispered once more, "Perhaps, in another life..."

She looked toward the heavens, hoping she'd experience the happiness she lost in this lifetime there.

With her arms spread, she stepped off the ledge, her dark brown tresses billowing like a halo around her head, an angel falling down from the skies just as the first raindrops descended.

Silas

Half an hour later, a thick branch broken off by the storm shattered the windows of the sitting room causing glass shards to scatter across the carpet. A scream tore through Wraithmoor Abbey, echoing in the cavernous foyer, before a groundskeeper dashed in and alerted the duke of the body found in the rose garden.

Silas dashed toward the doors, his thoughts in disarray, the mysterious pain he felt in his chest deepening into scything agony.

Icy dread slithered up his spine, curling around his rib cage. Whipping winds and pelting rain thrashed his face as he threw open the doors and stormed outside, not bothering to wait for the butler or the footmen to follow him.

A figure laid motionless in the distance.

It can't be. Please.

His feet hurtled desperately toward the woman sprawled on the ground in the rose garden. His clothes quickly became sodden from the turbulent storm, but he couldn't care less.

Silas's heart dropped to the floor, unfathomable pain carving through him when he recognized the unmistakable deep chocolate of her hair, the lithe and graceful frame of her body clad in her uniform, the dark gray wool worn by all the staff.

No. Please, I beg you.

Clutching his chest, he charged toward her, hoping she was still alive yet knowing from the stillness of her figure that she wasn't.

Choking back a sob, he knelt before her, his fingers shaking as he brushed a few wet strands from her face. Her body was twisted and broken, lying amongst her beloved roses. Her eyes were closed, but her face was unblemished, beautiful even in death, even when lying in the macabre river of red soaked to the soil below her.

"Emma, sweetheart," he rasped. He cradled her broken frame in his arms, tears slipping down his face. "Why didn't you wait for me? I told you in my letter I was going to find you... Why didn't you wait?"

He buried his face in the crook of her neck and sobbed, "I'm so sorry, my love. It's all my fault. I'm so, so sorry."

Crushing regret twisted around his lungs, robbing his breath. He was trying to do the right thing by his family—his legitimate family in the eyes of the law. He was going to find her when things were in order, when he settled his affairs with his younger brother to take over his duties and ended things with his wife, a cruel woman his father forced him to marry at a young age.

He was going to. He was going to do so many things...

And now there'd be no opportunities to do any of them, for what he'd done to her, to their child, was irreparable.

As he held her cold body in his crushing embrace, willing the lightning to strike him so he could go with her to the great beyond, his thoughts were filled with memories of her—them painting together under the moonlight in the rose garden.

She whispered, her hand clutching a paintbrush, "'Hope is the dream of a waking man,' and I'm living my dream every day with you."

His voice was rough. "Aristotle said that."

"And he would be right. I'm the happiest person with you."

How wrong she was. If he had known the ending of their love story, he would never fall in love with the woman who could see through the glamour of his wealth and estate and could see the lonely man living inside him.

Then she would be alive.

"My love, didn't you say hope is the dream of a waking man? Why did you give up on hope...on us?" His cries were loud in the garden as he held her tightly, her blood soaking through his clothes. His mind held tightly onto denial, even though he knew it was too late...much too late. "Don't leave me. Please...don't leave me."

He should've known from the desperation in her voice as she pounded the door of his study last night, the hopelessness in her beautiful eyes when he told her there was nothing more he could do for her, that he wouldn't leave his wife for her. They were all lies he spewed from his mouth because he knew his wife was listening in the next room.

And now, she and their unborn child were gone—her melodious laughter, her gentle touch, her warm heart, all vaporized into the rain, swallowed by the hallowed ground.

Something sharp scraped his forearm, and he looked up, finding a crow pecking at a crumbled cream envelope clutched in the hand of his beloved.

He pried the envelope from her icy fingers as the storm raged around them, his breath choking in his throat at the elegant swirl of his name on the front, the smudges from the rain blurring the words.

My Beloved Silas

With shaking fingers, he took out her letter, miraculously kept dry in her tight grip. Her last words to him.

My Beloved Silas,

If you read this, then I and our unborn child have already departed this world. I have risked everything and given you my all—my love, my dignity, my reputation. Being the foolish woman I am, if I could rewind time, I'm not sure I would've had the strength to stay away from you.

I want to tell you I understand the pressures of being an Anderson, of upholding your righteous family name to keep it untarnished from scandal. I want to tell you I forgive you and love you all the same so you can close your eyes at night in peace.

But I can never forgive you for depriving our child of a chance at life. As I bleed and feel his life snuffing out, I finally know what true agony is, and I wonder, had you been a man of your word, if things would've turned out differently.

You are a coward, Silas, and I can't help but hold both immense love and hatred toward you. Your love is poisonous, a taker of lives. As retribution for our child who was innocent in our affair, I leave you with this:

I wish for your family to learn not to give love so cruelly, so selfishly. To learn the meaning of true sacrifice. Should a firstborn son of the Anderson name fall in love and marry, the person of his affections shall fall to an untimely demise lest the lesson be learned.

Yours, faithful in death,

Emma

"My love. It's all my fault. I-I failed you. I should've acted much sooner. I'm a c-coward." She was bleeding and losing their child, and he never knew. She had no one to comfort her as she was cast out of this house. How devastated and hopeless she must've felt.

"I'm sorry, Emma." He pressed a kiss on her cold forehead.

The butler and footmen pried his arms off his sweetheart, but he held on tightly, not willing to let go of his soulmate, the woman who'd always hold his heart, even in death.

He shouldn't have loved her. *He killed her.*

"No! Let me go!" he screamed, his eyes wild with anguish.

Amid the struggle, the necklace around Emma's neck broke off from its owner. The storm carried it away in blood-tainted waters, but Silas barely noticed as he was dragged back into the estate.

I'll find you again, my love. Death cannot separate us.

CHAPTER 1

Split Rock Lighthouse State Park, Two Harbors, Minnesota
Present Day

"You know, there's a saying that goes, 'Lake Superior does not give up her dead,'" a wry voice comments from behind me, snapping me out of the semi-trance I find myself in.

The dreams were back last night—swirling dark visions of a faceless woman so vivid, I'd wake up bathed in sweat, my chest clenching in pain.

"What are you painting, my love?" I whisper as I cradle her waist from behind her in the rose garden, my nose dipping to her neck.

The candles flicker in the late night, but I sense these are stolen hours—forbidden and precious.

"The canals of Venice. I've never been there before, but I had read about them. So, I'm bringing them to life."

Someone clears his throat, jolting me back to the present.

Who is she? Why am I dreaming of her again?

The stranger next to me clears his throat again when I don't respond.

Glancing away from the easel in front of me, I turn toward the man. "Excuse me?"

He grins and pulls his black beanie further down his head before crossing his arms over his chest. "Sorry, I'm here with my family on vacation and they're around here somewhere exploring the grounds and I saw you sketching. Couldn't resist looking."

He motions to my easel where I've been trying my damned best to capture the scene in front of me for the past two hours since the park opened.

And I'm failing. Failing miserably. Distracted.

Acid churns in my gut as I stare at my creation—dark slashes of charcoal against a white canvas. The technique is there—the straight lines, the contouring, the play between the brightness and the shadows—a perfect example of the technique of *chiaroscuro*. It clearly depicts the scene before me—the gloomy waters so vast, it looks like it can swallow you whole, the lonely lighthouse perched on the rocky cliff, the dense fog obscuring the pebbly, gray shoreline.

But it's all wrong. It's missing something.

It's trash.

"And what does that saying have anything to do with my art?" I mutter, my fingers tightly clutching my pencil.

"It's a gloomy piece. I thought you might appreciate the morbid saying." The man chuckles. "And frankly, I'm just killing time while waiting for the fam. Ignore my bullshit."

I grunt and tug the lapels of my wool coat tighter to ward off the sudden chilly breeze sweeping in from the lake. A scent of damp earth and a faint whiff of harsh minerals permeate the air. Being from New York City, I'm no stranger to chilly temperatures in April, but fuck, it's downright glacial out here.

Befitting the frigid king. I shove the unwanted thought away.

"Anyway, the saying became famous after the tragedy of the sinking of SS Edmund Fitzgerald in 1975 during a severe storm out here. The entire crew was wiped out but none of the bodies were ever recovered," the man continues, oblivious to the displeasure running through my veins.

"The bodies are rumored to be down there still." He motions to the dark waters, the waves crashing against the rocky cliffs in the distance. "The water is so cold, there aren't many bacteria to help along the decomposition process, so the bodies don't float back up. I'm a historian, so this is interesting shit for me."

He laughs and prattles on. The man must be bored out of his mind to be talking to someone who clearly doesn't plan to respond.

I stare at the canvas again, then at the scenery before me, trying to figure out what's wrong with my art, which is an extension of me, of my soul. This is the sole purpose of my little getaway away from work and responsibilities at home. I'm supposed to sketch and paint and find my muse once more, something to fill this gaping hole of nagging want inside my chest before I have to head back to the real world, which includes preparing for my first press conference in a month.

What the fuck is it missing?

My life is everything a man should want. I'm the eldest son of the influential Anderson family, billions at my disposal, the CEO of one of the largest companies listed on the stock exchange.

I can have anything I want.

What the damn fuck is missing from my art?

I rub the phantom ache in my chest and heave out a deep breath, which crystallizes in a white mist before floating and melding with the eerie fog before me. Another icy gust billows against my face, followed by the louder roar of the crashing waves against the sharp cliffs.

The fog seems thicker now, merging with the foreboding clouds in the overcast skies. The dense forest of pine and birch just past the shoreline fades into nothingness, like an apparition, a hallucination of the mind. A chill seeps inside me as I look at the lighthouse in the distance, its light blinking slowly, warning sailors of the dangers of the rocks.

How much tragedy has it seen occur in these frigid waters before?

"Damn. The weather looks like shit. I miss the California sunshine. Anyway, I should go find the wife and the kids," the man quips before nudging me with his elbow. He waggles his brows. "I promised them pancakes and hot chocolate for breakfast. Don't want to disappoint them. Happy wife *and* kids equal happy life, you know?"

I wouldn't know, and I'll never know.

I sigh. I never enjoy talking to strangers, but it seems like my silence isn't a deterrent for this man. Slowly, I roll up the canvas, which will most likely be relegated to the back of my failure pile in my studio at home.

One of many of the past year.

Maybe Rex is right. Maybe I should spend some hours at the voyeur room inside The Orchid. Maybe a few hours with a beautiful woman will chase away the emptiness in my heart. After all, it has worked in the past.

But deep down, I know that isn't the answer. Not this time. Not for this dark chasm inside me.

Like I'm missing a piece of myself.

Just then, something hits the legs of the easel, shaking the frame precariously, and I grab it before it topples over.

Frowning, I bend down and pick up a bright yellow soccer ball at my feet as I hear the faint sounds of children giggling, and the gentle words from a feminine voice heading toward us.

My pulse kicks up at the strangers about to invade my personal space. *They are little kids and their mom. Harmless. Calm the fuck down. Breathe. You are thirty-fucking-six years old.* I twist the heirloom ring on my ring finger before wiping my sweaty palms on my pants and blowing out a deep breath.

A little boy no older than seven runs over. His younger sister, judging by their identical light brown hair and big blue eyes, follows suit.

"Jeremy! I thought I told you to leave the ball in the car!" the man still standing next to me grumbles.

"Sorry, Daddy! We were just going to do one practice kick." Jeremy pouts before turning his wide eyes toward me, uncertainty flickering in his gaze.

I look down and realize I'm still holding the ball in my hands.

I kneel and watch him traipse over carefully, his steps sure on the large pebbles, and an unknown warmth sparks in my veins. Such bright innocence shining from his eyes.

The innocence, once lost, can never be regained.

"Here you go, little man." I roll the ball back to him, my lips curving into a small smile. "Kick with your big toe knuckle. That'll give you the strongest kick."

"You play soccer?"

"A long time ago. Not anymore."

"Why?" Jeremy questions as his sister and mom approach us.

"Say thank you, Jeremy, and apologize for hitting the man's equipment," she says as she beams at her son.

The man next to me shakes his head and walks toward his wife before tugging her flush to his side. He presses a soft kiss on her hair and a small blush blooms on her cheeks as she melts into his embrace.

The spark of warmth douses in my chest, and in its place is a sharp twisting pain. My lungs rake in a shuddering inhale.

A happy family of my own. Little kids running down the halls of my mansion, their hands messy, toys all over the place, the woman I love shaking her head, trying to appear stern even as her lips twitch in a smile as she chases the little monsters.

It turns out I can't have everything. But I've long made peace with this.

"Thank you, sir. And sorry for almost knocking over your art," the little boy replies obediently.

He scrunches his nose and moves in front of the easel, his little finger jabbing at the canvas which has unrolled itself in the past few minutes. "You drew this? Wow."

Another set of little feet scampers in front of me and I chuckle, the familiar ache from moments ago fading into the background again. Backing up, I make room for Jeremy's little sister as she grabs the bottom of the easel and tiptoes on her feet.

"Careful there," I murmur, holding the easel in place so it doesn't fall down on the siblings.

"I don't like it. It's too scary," the little girl whispers to her brother in the way little kids do, which essentially isn't a whisper at all.

"Maddie! That's not nice to say," their mom admonishes, wincing in apparent embarrassment. "It's a beautiful sketch."

"It's angry and scary." Maddie shakes her head and backs away, but not before darting a glance at me. "Like those stories Jeremy reads to me at home before Halloween."

"Okay, that's it. Playtime's over. We're going to get hot chocolate and pancakes," the man announces, and the two kids squeal in glee, their laughter sounding out of place in this gloomy morning.

He looks at me apologetically. "Sorry. Kids have no filter. I'm no artist, but that's a damn good drawing. Missing something though, but what do I know? Ignore me."

My lips twitch. I have a feeling Jeremy's no filter is also inherited.

He takes his wife's hand and leads them toward the parking lot. He turns back and waves at me with his free hand.

"Nice chat, man." He cocks his head to the side and furrows his brows. "And you look familiar... You aren't anyone famous, right?"

I freeze, my jaw clenching before releasing. *Please don't recognize me.* I shake my head. "I have one of those faces."

I'm probably the only Anderson left in the world who isn't recognized on sight, and these are the last days of anonymity before the only thing I chose for myself—solace—will be taken away from me.

A lump forms in my throat as the beginnings of nausea curl in my stomach.

"Huh," he mutters before shrugging. "Well, have a good day and stay out of the waters. You know the saying!"

He winks and chuckles before turning around and disappearing into the distance with his wife and two kids in tow.

The smile slides off my face as I turn back toward the lake.

Lake Superior does not give up her dead.

Too bad. The dead have never given me up either.

CHAPTER 2

Excited murmurs travel in through the double doors separating the staff corridor and the largest conference room inside the Kensington Hotel, one of the hotels under our Fleur Entertainment umbrella.

I'm standing with my phone to my ear, half-hidden in the shadows in the corridor. The public is waiting for their first glimpse of the frigid king, as they like to call me. The overhead lights dim and flicker, a signal from the staff that the crowd of reporters outside is growing impatient.

I pinch the bridge of my nose as a headache forms at the base of my skull. The sharp pain stabs me repeatedly, and I wince. I try to focus on the conversation on the phone.

"You sure you got this, Maxwell? You don't need to force yourself if you aren't ready yet," Ryland, my fraternal twin, asks, his voice sounding faint over the phone.

"It's time. With rumors of you stepping down from the COO position, the public needs stability from us. For Fleur. They need to see the CEO." Not to mention, the stock price has been volatile. One wrong move and it'll plummet.

"But your privacy. Heck, that's why you don't let anyone photograph you at events or even at The Orchid," Ryland murmurs, referring to the exclusive establishment for the rich and the elite, the crowning jewel of our family's international conglomerate, Fleur Entertainment Holdings. "If you step out there, your privacy will be gone. You can't go back. And what about your anxiety? Aren't you worried—"

"Well, what do you expect me to do, dammit! If it weren't for you, I wouldn't—*fuck!*"

I stop myself, but it's too late. The poisonous sentiment is out.

Silence fills the line and I hear heavy breathing on his side.

"I...I'm sorry, Maxwell, for putting you in this position. If I hadn't left—"

"Ignore me. It's the fucking nerves talking. You know I've always supported you leaving Fleur to pursue your dreams of being a professor. And look at how it turned out. You're happy; you're smiling again."

For the past decade, with Ryland as the chief operating officer, he took on all the public duties of the Anderson family and Fleur Entertainment Holdings. Nicknamed "the Prince of the USA," he diverted the media attention away from me and faced the pressures of being in the primary focus of the media. We'd convene either at the estate or in the offices for strategy, decision making, day-to-day management of the company, but the press and the public relied on him for information.

As his twin, I sensed his discontent in recent years, saw his forced smile whenever we'd meet up with friends at the gentlemen's club within The Orchid, but he'd brush it off. Until recently, when I found out the depths of his misery and how he almost gave up the woman he loved to be chained to the job and abide by the rules of a ridiculous family trust, which we thankfully unraveled recently.

That has to stop now.

I take off my simple family insignia ring, an ornately carved band with a black agate stone on it, the ring passed down for generations to the firstborn son of the family.

The son impacted by the curse.

The son with the most responsibilities to uphold. The generations of illustrious Andersons. The legacy.

Taking a deep breath, I slide it back on my ring finger. *I came to terms with this a long time ago. I'm at peace. I'm as calm as the waters on the lake.*

The frigid air and gloomy skies at Lake Superior last month seemed so long ago. A lifetime away. My fingers twitch, every muscle inside me tense and ready to bolt back to the estate, where I can wield my paints and brushes and cast out the turmoil rioting in my mind.

I'm calm. I'm at peace. I accept myself.

The words from my childhood therapist ring in my ears. He died a long time ago, and I haven't seen anyone else since. *Maybe you should.*

I pinch myself, concentrating on the present.

They are just people. Focus on the speech, the words. Don't focus on them.

More affirmations tumble around my mind, phrases I've repeated to myself before I need to meet new people. They used to offer me a modicum of confidence, of the calm I so treasured, but now they are as useless as a simple fire extinguisher to a blazing wildfire.

"Maybe Steven can step in. He's no stranger to the press with his previous dealings at Pietra. Or even Rex. The press loves him."

I shake my head. Steven Kingsley, our good friend and soon to be brother-in-law, as he's engaged to my half sister, Grace Peyton, has announced his departure from his high-ranking position at Pietra Capital. He's planning to take over Ryland's position at Fleur.

"You know that isn't enough. Steven's plans to join Fleur aren't public yet. And Rex? He's the life of the party. A great chief marketing officer, but not what the press is looking for. They want the head of the company to tell them everything is fine at Fleur."

I stare at my dim reflection in the mirror by the doors, placed there for the staff and others to check their appearance before stepping onto the stage. I tug the navy tie around my neck in frustration. *The damn tie is crooked.* The pinstripes blur in my vision as I fix the offending article of clothing.

My dark brown, almost black, hair is carefully swept up, my face cleanly shaven, the gray suit carefully pressed and immaculate on my six-foot-four frame. I look like the powerful CEO the public believes me to be.

The calm, collected CEO who can make a fucking speech without throwing up.

But my gray eyes hold the panic I'm desperately trying to rein in.

"Ethan can do it too. Nothing like a serious CFO to calm the waters."

"Fuck, I'm sure Lana can do it better than me!" I shout into the receiver, referring to my sister, the youngest of the five Anderson siblings, our resident PR guru. "I won't repeat history again—having my younger siblings shoulder a responsibility that should've been mine in the first place. You did it for years for me, Ryland, and you were miserable. It's time for me to step into the spotlight and do the right thing. I can't hide anymore."

"I just don't want you to regret it later. It isn't worth it."

"I won't. It's time." I won't let three measly words define me anymore.

Severe social anxiety.

So severe I get auditory and visual hallucinations, which are extremely rare for the condition.

I was diagnosed after Mom passed away when Ryland and I were seven. I'm fine with people I know, well or in controlled environments where the spotlight isn't shining on me, but in situations such as this, I'd rather take a dive in Lake Superior in December than brave the crowds.

But it's been twenty-nine fucking years since I got the diagnosis. I'm done hiding.

I'm calm. I'm at peace. I accept myself.

I can do this.

"I have to go, Ryland."

I swallow the bile rising in my throat. Taking a deep breath, I square my shoulders, push open the doors, and step into the glaring light, my mind spinning a thousand rotations a minute.

The sizeable crowd of grays and blacks rises abruptly, their shapes quickly blurring. Their voices morph into a terrifying roar in my ears. My heart throws itself against my rib cage and the tie cinches my neck in a chokehold.

My feet stumble, but I quickly recover and stride up the steps of the stage to the daunting podium with a solo spotlight shining on it. Sweat drips down my forehead as my fingers dig into the edge of the stand.

I'm calm. I'm at peace. I can do this. The words are swept away by the tornado obliterating my focus, my resolve. I stare into the crowd, unable to see the faces, my mind imagining a venomous monster, rising from the ashes of the dead, jowls opened wide, fangs bared, murder in its eyes.

White spots dot my vision. Flashes of lights from cameras. That must be what they are.

But my mind can't compute as I lean on the solid oak podium, clinging onto it for dear life, a captain sinking with his boat, lost at treacherous seas.

My vision is washed in more brightness, more white lights, and I feel myself swaying. Acid makes its way from my stomach to my esophagus, and I want to dry heave onto the desk. My fingers fiddle with my insignia ring, a last-ditch effort to cling on to rationality.

It's imaginary. It's all in your mind, Maxwell. Snap out of it.

I hear laughter and screeches. Chaos, more chaos.

"Look at him," my classmates jeer and point to me as I stand in front of the altar at the church. "He can't even make a speech for his mom."

"He's stupid. That's what Dad told me. A broken Anderson."

My legs tremble as I remain frozen in place, feeling the spotlight above me melting away my skin and muscles.

They are wrong. I want to tell them how much I'm hurting right now, how there are no words to describe what I feel when I think about how Mommy will never sit with us in the gardens again, watching me paint and reading books with Ryland. How no one will play songs on the old phonograph in the sitting room again. How our large, gloomy mansion will no longer have music or singing.

But I can't speak. I'm frozen.

The people blur in front of me. Scary shapes of black. Their fingers pointing, their mouths moving, whispering behind their hands or their opened fans. I'm melting onto the floor, my skin and bones a disgusting mess in front of them.

Maybe it's better that way. If I die, I get to be with Mommy.

After all, I'm cursed. I overheard Daddy and Grandpa talking about it. Mommy died because of the curse.

Tears gather in my eyes and I look at Mommy, lying in the casket with a cold, unfamiliar painted smile on her face.

I can't even tell the world how much I love and miss her.

I'm a failure.

Subtle laughter and loud shouts wrench me away from my memory and back to the present.

"G-Good evening. I'm Maxw-well Anderson."

More screeches and shouts, more flashes of blinding light.

The world swirls as more sweat gathers on my upper lip. I clutch my ring, letting the sharp edges of the gem dig and slice into my hands. I feel wetness but no pain.

Nothing can save me from this madness.

Blurred sounds echo in my ears, but they are muffled, like I'm underwater.

A dark shadow looms before me—the monster has me in its grasps. My veins turn to ice as my breathing quickens. It clasps me on the shoulder and I fist my hand and turn, ready to swing at it.

"That's it. Mr. Anderson is feeling unwell today. I'll answer your questions about the recent changes to the company."

Another firm hand blocks my swing and pins my arm to the side of my body. He leans in and mutters in my ear, "Come, Maxwell. Your brother's got this."

The words are a gong to my panic, icy rain onto the blistering inferno, and I glance up, noticing the familiar blond hair and light eyes. My good friend, Charles Vaughn.

What the fuck happened?

My eyes widen as reality slowly shifts into focus and I finally take in the horde of reporters standing up, their cameras and microphones pointed in our direction, their eyes widening in shock, mouths agape, their pens flying across the notepads. They're no doubt jotting down the top headline for the next month. How the illustrious eldest son of the Anderson family, the mysterious frigid king, turns out to be a quack, not right in the head.

My hand clenches in pain as the late sensations from my ring carving into my palm finally make an appearance. A warm, wet stickiness draws my attention to the wound.

Tiny streams of red seep out from the gaps between my fingers.

Blood.

I sliced my palm with my ring and didn't feel a thing until now.

The bile that has receded makes its way back up my throat and Charles squeezes my arm in reassurance as he walks me down the steps of the stage.

I straighten and disentangle myself from my friend, clinging to the last shreds of my dignity, and turn back, finding the worried eyes of my youngest brother, Ethan, from where he stands behind the podium. He gives me a terse nod before turning to the crowd.

"Now, I'm sure you have questions..."

Charles and I walk through the double doors, the chaos rioting behind me.

Shit. Shit. Shit. What have I done?

CHAPTER 3

Belle

OH GOD, HOW CAN *I save him? I can't let him die.*

Sweat beads on my back as I stare at the adorable brown husky in front of me. Sure, most people probably won't call him "adorable," especially since he lost one eye due to significant abuse by his previous asshole owners, who I hope are rotting in jail or dying of a slow and painful death somewhere.

It also doesn't help that the little guy is currently destroying a dog bed I snuck into his cage at the beginning of my volunteering shift here at the Bronx Shelter for Unwanted Animals, known to us as BSUA.

Ugh, I hate this name. It reminds me of the gothic orphanages I've read about in the early nineteen hundreds.

Technically, we're forbidden to bring any toys or bedding to the shelter because they are "a mess to clean up" as some of the higher-ups have complained in the past.

He growls, attacking the bed with vengeance, spreading cotton stuffing all across his tiny, cold cell of cement walls and peeling plaster. He's in solitary confinement today for attempting to nip the leg of the shelter manager, a sleazy balding guy named Bob. That has probably earned him a shortcut to the lethal drip this evening when the murder squad, as Cole and I like to call them, comes in later tonight.

Oblivious to his dire fate, he settles down on the ground, a cloud of stuffing floating in the air. He sticks out his tongue and lolls his head to the side, clearly satisfied with his handiwork.

"Oh, what am I going to do with you, little guy?" I groan.

But I already know the answer to this. I need to break him out of his cell and steal him. BSUA is a pound. A kill shelter. It's the main reason I've volunteered here for the last three years as opposed to the fancy no-kill humane shelters in Manhattan. I figure if I hustle and get these poor animals adopted, that'll be one less pup or kitten on the chopping block.

This little terror is now peeing in the corner, despite the fact I let him out half an hour ago.

"Paying your respects?" a quiet voice asks from behind me and I jump and face the interloper, my hand fluttering to my chest.

"You scared me, Cole!"

"Sorry, you looked like you were deep in thought, and I didn't want to interrupt you. But I'm heading out now and want to check on you before I go. I know it's a hard day for you."

I gnaw on my lip and quickly release it. *High-society ladies do not gnaw on their lips in public.* My etiquette tutors from my childhood have drilled that into my mind, but somehow, my body has never gotten the memo.

Staring at my tall, blond friend, I let out a sigh. "It's okay. I think I'm a mess today."

"It's the little guy's turn with the drip. Of course, you'd be pissed. I know I am," Cole grits out, his nostrils flaring. "Fuck these kill shelters."

"Yes. Pieces of...shi-crap. Heartless monsters pretending to be do-gooders."

He smirks. "Or you can just say fuck them."

I blanch. Curse words are unbecoming in the elite circles my family runs in.

"Repeat after me, Belle. *Fuck them.* Come on, you can do it."

"F—fuck them?" I whisper, my heart pounding wildly in my chest.

Not today, Ms. Goodie Two-Shoes. Not today. Today, you'll be a rule breaker. It's your year of yeses.

"Fuck them," I growl louder.

Cole whistles and claps his hands in a mocking slow applause. "Damn, I think I can quit volunteering now. My work is done. I've corrupted the elegant Annabelle Law-McKenzie."

I roll my eyes. "Shut up, Cole."

He chuckles then quiets and looks around the empty hallway, filled to the brim with rotten cardboard boxes of stale food none of us dares to use, but Bob doesn't let us throw out because he thinks that'd be wasteful. But what good is moldy food that'll make the animals sick? Not that he cares. I honestly wonder why he's in this business in the first place. Rumor has it there's a grant he's getting from a bigwig pharma lab who conducts animal testing.

It's disgusting.

The florescent lights suddenly turn off, plunging us into darkness. The windows rattle violently against the hinges as the subway train makes its regular pass underground.

I let out a squeal, my heart in my throat once more.

"Guys, we're still here!" Cole shouts, his voice echoing down the corridor, followed by raucous barking and yipping. He bangs on the bars of the cage.

"Sorry!" someone responds from far away and the lights turn on.

Panting heavily, I try to calm the racing pulse in my ears. I love the animals but hate this place. The creaky windows, dank corridors, and strange cloying smells that have nothing to do with animals.

"You want me to stay with you for a bit? Cry it out? Graffiti the walls in secret? Then, I can take you to Milton's for your favorite ice cream." Cole stares intently at me with those bright green eyes of his.

"Don't you need to be with your family? You mentioned there is an event, right?"

His face falls, and he locks his jaw. "Yes. A memorial for the anniversary of a death in the family. Life is fucking short sometimes."

He looks away, clearly not wanting to talk about it.

I shake my head and squeeze his arm in support. I don't want to pry. "I'm good here. Go home, Cole. Be with your family. Thanks for stopping by."

He nods, hefts his gray backpack over his shoulders, and takes a few steps toward the exit. He pauses and turns back, a brow cocked in question.

"I'm fine, honestly. See you the week after next, Cole."

"I'm always here for you, you know. Anytime, Belle," he murmurs, not looking at me.

He swallows, his throat rippling, and turns around before striding out of sight.

I groan into my hands. Even the blind can see Cole's interest in me, and I wish I could reciprocate. Cole Whelan is the dictionary definition for tall, blond, and handsome. He's thirty-two, eight years older than me, some sort of IT genius working his way up a security company for the investment banks in the financial district.

He's kind, funny, sensitive, and heck, volunteers at the pound every other Saturday without fail. I've seen how the other volunteers stare at him, their mouths practically open and drooling like the dogs here when he walks around.

But I don't feel a thing. Not a flutter or a skipped heartbeat. No shortness of breath or flushed skin. No daydreams about his beautiful eyes or wondering how his hands will feel on my body.

He's more like the brother I wish I had growing up, instead of being the lonely princess locked away in her large, shiny new castle, talking to her dolls as her only friends, wondering what it'd be like to be a regular girl being smothered by her parents' kisses or getting a bedtime story before bed.

I sigh. Not that my feelings matter to anyone. I overheard my parents last month talking about candidates for marriage. I knew it was going to happen sooner rather than later. After all, most people in our circles treat marriage as a business merger. But I'll fight them or die trying.

I shake myself and straighten my back. I'm a lonely princess no more. Now I have my girls, my career, I'm a *fucking* twenty-four-year-old and the world is my oyster. I'm going to take control of my life. There's no way they can shove a random man down my throat and expect me to just take it.

As if sensing my changing moods, the little terror ambles toward me, rubbing his thick fur against my leggings, leaving a trail of white and brown hairs behind. Then, he trots back to wreak more havoc on his crime scene, his fluffy tail wagging, not knowing these are his last few hours on this side of the rainbow bridge.

Unless I do something about it.

He stares at me with the solo cute blue eye and sits obediently on the ground like a perfect dog.

My eyes water and I crouch down and stroke his soft fur. I bury my face in his neck and he softens against me and lets out a low whine. Why can't the world see how perfect he is, one-eyed terror and all? How much love he has to give? Why can't anyone see the true him, this sweet dog?

My chest aches and my nose burns, the stench of sterile antiseptic filling my nostrils, bringing me back to my appointment three days ago with my reproductive endocrinologist.

"Sorry, I've reviewed your test results. Your hormones are low, Ms. Law-McKenzie, and the ultrasound shows a very small number of follicles," Dr. Chen says softly, her brown eyes shining with sympathy.

"S-So you're saying?" A heaviness weighs on my lungs and I can't breathe.

"You're right. Diminished ovarian reserve. DOR. Much earlier than expected, to be honest."

Shaking my head, the lump grows larger in my throat. "I knew there was a chance I'd have DOR, with Mom having the same issue when she was younger, and now with my periods getting more and more irregular."

"It isn't a death sentence. There are options for fertility, you know."

"IVF. Egg freezing. Trying earlier? But time is running out, isn't it? My egg reserves are that of someone who is near menopause, not someone

who has years left." I've spent hours researching online, panicking that my biological clock is about to run out.

I thought I'd have at least until thirty before I had to worry about this. And I don't have a boyfriend or any candidate to even think about trying earlier. And now, I realize I'll soon lose the chance of becoming pregnant.

I have three goals in my life.

First, I want to protect Grandpa's legacy at McKenzie Atelier, the only American couture company going head-to-head with the famous fashion houses in Europe.

My nose burns and eyes prickle at the thought of my grandpa, the only family member who'd given me his free time and care when I was growing up and taught me everything he knew before he passed away.

I'm going to make him proud.

Second, I want to have kids of my own so I can shower them with the love I wish I'd received as a child. I don't even need to have a husband or a man in my life. I just want the kids.

Now, with the ticking clock inside me, there's a desperate need to experience the miracle of life myself before it's too late. I want to fill the yearning and restlessness inside me and find the missing fragments of my heart.

Third, I want to give back to humane societies, to eradicate kill shelters one by one, saving unwanted animals so they can be taken care of the way they deserve.

But two out of the three goals are vaporizing in front of my eyes, and I'm helpless to stop them.

The little terror nudges me with his nose and lets out a soft whine before he delivers a comforting lick to my fingers. The burning sensation in my nose grows stronger and I sniffle.

You're perfect—flaws and broken body and all.

I ruffle his fur and he wags his tail so vigorously, it thumps against the wall in a staccato rhythm.

I can't let him die. I just...can't. I'm in control of my destiny and I've decided.

Dog-napper it is.

Wiping my nose with the back of my hand, I poke my head out of the open cage. Spying no other personnel loitering about, I hastily dart back inside and take out my cell phone from my jacket pocket. I press a button and wait for an answer.

"Belle, this better be good. I'm taking a nap." Taylor Peyton's grumpy voice travels across the line.

"Psst. I need help."

"What? I can't hear you." She yawns.

I step to the far side of the cage, away from the hallway. "SOS. I need you at BSUA *now*!"

"What? Why?" More yawning. Seriously, the woman has the strangest sleep habits.

"Why are you sleeping at four p.m. on a Saturday?"

"I have a show at the Met tonight. The director has high hopes for my solo. I need my beauty sleep."

"Can you get your sleep later? I need help and Grace is on her date with Steven and Millie said her brother is in town. I don't know who else to call."

She snorts. I can imagine my raven-haired, gray-eyed ballerina friend rolling her eyes in bed. "Gee, thanks for being your last resort."

I bite my lip and smile. She loves her sister Grace, and our best friend, Millie, as much as I do.

"Fine, Belle. I'm up. What do you need me to do?"

"I'm going to steal him."

"Who?"

"Little terror." My voice thickens, but I steel my nerves. "I can't let him die today. I need you to come and cause a distraction so I can sneak him out."

"But yours and Millie's apartment doesn't allow pets," she murmurs. I hear rustling in the background.

"Fuck this. My year of yeses. You know, this is all your fault for giving me that stupid book last month. Now, I'm thinking I need to have my year of yeses before I turn twenty-five because I can't be complacent in my life anymore. I need to take control." Not to mention, with the possibility of an arranged marriage and my new medical diagnosis, I feel like time is really running out.

"Hell yeah, that's my bad bitch. And you're going to that street race next week, right?" She cackles.

"Ugh. Don't remind me. That is so not my scene. And you're ditching me!"

"Year of yeses, Belle. Last minute practice—can't be helped." She sighs. "But to make it up to you, I'll leave my comfortable apartment and break some laws with you. I'll even wear my purple devil nose piercing."

She's the grumpy rule breaker of our girl group, the dark eyeliner, nose piercing wearing, curse words loving ballerina at the top ballet company in the country. The walking contradiction.

"Be there in thirty." The phone disconnects.

My pulse races in my veins as a warmth spreads from my chest to my hands. My head feels woozy—fear? Excitement? A middle finger to the world? I have no clue.

I squat down and motion for the little terror to come over, and like the beautiful, perfect dog he is, he trots over and settles in front of me. He delivers a long, wet lick on my cheek, and I realize tears have escaped without me noticing.

Clutching him closely, I whisper, "You're coming home with me, little guy. You'll get to go on my year of yeses with me and we're going to change our destiny. We're going to show everyone who underestimates us how wrong they are."

CHAPTER 4

"SON, IT'S TIME."

I freeze, my fingers tightening around the crystal tumbler as icy foreboding slithers inside my veins. The silence would've been deafening in the study were it not for the loud pounding of my heart.

Turning away from my father, the great Linus Anderson, on the screen of my laptop for our weekly conference call, I toss back the remnants of my whiskey, savoring the burn of the alcohol as it washes down my throat. It's the best of the best from the MacGregor's Whiskey Library at The Orchid, but it's tasteless on my tongue.

If only I could get drunk easily, I could pretend I didn't know what he meant.

But unfortunately, I'm as sober as a foot soldier on the battlefield, and after my fiasco at the press conference last week, I have no excuses to put my father off any longer.

My horrendous, pathetic press conference. Having a full-blown anxiety attack in front of everyone. The headlines are still going strong: "Nervous Wreck Debut—Investors Jumping Ship from Fleur Entertainment," "The Frigid King Should Be The Mad King," "Anxiety Attack or Other Mental Illness—The Case of Maxwell Anderson."

Grimacing, I pour myself more whiskey from the decanter before striding to the towering bay windows behind my antique oak desk. I stare into the dark gardens far below, barely illuminated by a starless night.

Sinister shadows loom in the gardens, and tree branches bend to the wind. The dim lighting offered by the lone desk lamp flickers as the howling gale creeps in through an open window.

"Do you have a candidate in mind?" I don't bother turning around.

"I do. I've already spoken with her parents. I think our families are well suited. They're in an industry we aren't part of and they can use our funding and influence. Their daughter is well educated, no scandals or gossip to her name, and—"

"Fine. Set it up, Dad."

A few seconds pass by, the atmosphere heavy with tension I can almost taste.

"You know this was the plan from the beginning, Maxwell. As the eldest Anderson son, we don't have a choice in the matter. It's our job to continue the bloodline, and if you don't get married and have heirs, the curse will fall on Ryland. That's what happened to Uncle Nathaniel because Father wanted to cheat the curse."

I bite back a snort. Having heirs so I can give the curse to my son instead of my brother—a lose-lose situation. What a clusterfuck.

"I said *fine*. I know my duty."

I toss back my whiskey. The burn from the alcohol is relentless this time, churning in my gut, and each breath of air seems to fan the flames into a fire I can't contain.

Gritting my teeth, I turn around, faking a smile for my father. "I don't need to know anything about the woman. I trust your judgment. Just let me know when and where to show up for contract negotiations, and I'll be there."

My father's eyes soften with apparent sympathy. After all, arranged marriages for the eldest son have been a tradition for our family for generations. When our forefathers were in England, as part of the aristocracy, this was the way things were done amongst the *haute ton*. But after the curse, this was done from necessity.

It's the fate of the oldest son to be in a loveless marriage. Even when we have an heir, as eldest sons, we still aren't allowed to fall in love with our wives, because we will endanger their lives.

Simply put, *she will die.*

The rules of the curse have been passed down by word of mouth for generations, but Grandpa and Dad have put them down in writing in a handwritten letter tucked away in the safe. We try to add to it based on what we learn over time, so that future generations will have a guide to this mess.

These rules have been hammered inside me since I learned of the curse in second grade.

First, death only happens to the woman the eldest son loves if they are married and confess their love to each other. Ergo, we shouldn't fall in love and arranged marriages are the way to go.

Second, should we ignore the first rule, there will be a series of unfortunate incidents or accidents happening to the woman in question—warnings, if you will.

Third, should we ignore these warnings, something will happen to the woman, and she will die, usually within one year of the couple confessing their love to each other. Before then, a branch will shatter a window in the estate, serving as a final omen.

Fourth, should the eldest son not marry and have an heir, the curse will pass onto the next eldest son in the family, and we Andersons have always been blessed with an abundance of male heirs.

I fought hard against believing it until I couldn't, until I experienced the touch of death myself. Mom died when she ultimately fell in love with Dad after almost a decade of cordial marriage. So did grandmother, whose death my grandfather never forgot, the sorrow clear in his eyes until the day he passed away, lonely in bed in this very estate. So did all the women the firstborn sons loved in the generations before.

So did Sydney.

My mind flickers to the beguiling green eyes that twinkled in laughter, the silky blonde tresses fluttering in the wind. Our heated argument—our last conversation together.

Her lifeless body washing up on the shore.

I remember the guilt in my grandfather's eyes when he told me about his role in his brother's death while lying on his deathbed. He wanted to challenge the curse by staying single, but the deaths occurred anyway when his sister-in-law and two adorable children died in a horrific accident. Grand Uncle Nathaniel, overcome with grief, killed himself a few years later. It was the curse, and those deaths were punishment for Grandfather not following its rules.

He never forgave himself.

Our family is well educated, but after so many deaths, we were forced to face the ugly truth. Denial is useless. Our only hope is someday, one of us will find a way to break the curse.

Knock, knock.

"Come in," I holler.

Morris Coventry, our butler, slowly walks in with a tray of food. I glance at the grandfather clock by the fireplace. Eight p.m. I apparently forgot about dinner again.

The elderly butler, the closest thing I have to a grandparent after Grandfather passed away, smiles, his kind blue eyes crinkling at the corners.

"Sir, your dinner. Eat it while it's hot." He sets the tray on my desk and nods at my father on the screen. Stifling a groan, he straightens and rubs his lower back and right leg.

"Thank you, Morris." I quirk a grin. "Can I convince you to retire yet?" I motion to his leg. "That old wound has been acting up more and more lately. Let me hire help and you can rest and enjoy your retirement here."

He harrumphs and shakes his head. "Nonsense. I'll work until my last breath." He ambles out of the study and quietly closes the door.

Dad chuckles in the background. "Old Morris will never change. He's been exactly the same for as long as I can remember."

I smile before sitting down on my leather chair and facing my father.

Dad sighs as he redirects our conversation back to the topic at hand.

"An arranged marriage isn't as hopeless as you think it is, Maxwell."

He leans back in his armchair in our house in the Hamptons, where he has moved to recently. The estate seems more silent in his absence.

"Your mom and I had nine wonderful years together before she passed. She was a good friend, my closest confidant. She was e-everything."

His voice cracks as he looks away, his eyes glistening with unshed tears. "Just don't fall in love. Don't do what I did, what your grandfather did. You know the risks. You understand what happened with Sydney—"

"I don't need you to remind me how my wife died!"

Dad's eyes sharpen as he takes in my uncharacteristic outburst, and I close my eyes. *I am calm. I am at peace. I accept myself.*

I repeat the mantras. Ten times, twenty times, until I feel my heartbeat calming.

Dad's patient. After all, he understands the lonely path in front of me.

"You can do it, son. If there's anyone in the family who can abide by the rules of the curse, it is you."

I know that to be true. After all, I've had the shadow of death hanging over my head my entire life, and I've suffered its cruel consequences. It has to be me to bear it. What if I detract from the path, give the middle finger I've always wanted to give to the ancestor who started it all and say, screw you and your need for heirs, and this curse falls on Ryland? There's no way I'd risk Ryland's happiness and safety.

And you're going to have heirs and doom your son, you asshole. Guilt nags at me, but I shake myself. I'll teach him how to thrive and live, despite the curse. He'll be fine.

The thought isn't comforting.

"And a side benefit," Dad begins, "having a wife and, later on, children by your side, will show stability to the press. It's archaic and ridiculous, but it symbolizes you are mentally healthy enough to have a family. It'll put any rumors to rest and the stock will recover."

Our stock plummeted thirty percent the day after the disastrous press conference. It's holding steady now, but complaints from the investors are loud and clear. They aren't happy with me.

They think something is wrong with the CEO.

How interesting they've conveniently forgotten the ten percent growth per year I've brought them since I took on the role when Dad retired.

Pathetic idiots.

"I understand. I'll fix this. I'll bring Fleur's stock price back up, Dad. I'll get married and beget heirs and all that shit. You have no complaints from me."

I hang up the phone and stride into the empty hallway, ignoring the creaking and groaning of the place—it's just the house settling in for the night. A lone sconce is lit, giving just enough visibility for me. Despite the paisley runner on the dark wood floors, my footfalls echo like phantom companions in the dark.

It's eerie and quiet. In another life, perhaps the mansion would be ablaze with light, with little kids like the ones I saw at the lake running around, laughing and squealing, music blaring from the speakers. A woman I love would embrace me as I crossed the threshold to the living room and whisk me into a dance.

There'd be life.

My chest clenches, the abyss threatening to swallow me whole. It's a dream that can only come true in my mind.

In another life.

But in this one, I'll fix everything I broke—the stock price, the press. I won't fail this time.

I'm not broken.

CHAPTER 5

TWO WEEKS OF TRAPPING myself in my art studio on the fourth floor of the estate, listening to the classic arias playing from our vintage phonograph and ignoring my siblings' calls, did nothing to dull the sense of doom lurking inside me. The only times I've ventured outside were for urgent meetings at Fleur.

It's one thing to know my role, but another thing to actually go through with it.

Rain patters against the tall lattice windows. A few showers in May are nothing unusual, but this spring seems exceptionally dreary—a never-ending parade of charcoal, graphite, and blacks.

There's a permanent chill in the air, the cold burrowing deep into my bones.

I don't have the heater on. There's no need for it when it's only me living in the estate now, with my siblings having settled in their own apartments either at The Orchid or elsewhere in the city.

I suppose I could move, but an inexplicable yearning chains me here, this enormous building filled with ghosts and sorrows, but that also holds so much beautiful, haunting history. This estate has been in our family for centuries, passing down from the eldest son to the next, just like the way my ancestors have done it with the dukedom and entail in England.

My phone chimes and I set down my paintbrush and swipe at the screen.

Charles

> We're at the gentlemen's club in The Orchid.
> Rex is drunk already. Come, Maxwell. Save me
> from him.

Rex

> Audio message: "F-Fuck y-you, tattle-taler,
> pants on fire."

Ethan

> If you can't handle your alcohol, why are you
> drinking? You sound like you're five.

I smirk, staring at the exchange from my family and friends in our chat group.

My phone buzzes again. This time, it's a private message.

Ryland

> Something's going on with you. I can feel it.
> Don't bullshit me. You told me to rely on you
> and the family when I was going through my
> shit. Why can't you do the same?

A weight presses down on my chest. Damn twin-sense. Even if I haven't seen him in the recent weeks, Ryland knows. I helped him out when he was in the pits before he got his act together and went after Millie, the love of his life, and now, he's expecting the same from me. As he should.

My fingers pause over the screen as I mull over what to type, and another message pops up.

Dad

> The meeting for the negotiations is set for
> next month. I've met with the family and they
> are proceeding with the match.

A muscle twitches on my forehead as I set down the phone back on the side table.

I can't breathe.

Grabbing my paintbrush again, I stare at my art on the canvas, another attempt at purging a restlessness inside me. It's a silhouette of a woman in our rose garden—the same painting I've attempted many times over the years. Her face is blank as always, a vague outline I can't bring myself to fill in because somehow, I know I can't do her justice.

Failure. Another failure.

I have a feeling the answer lies in my recurring dreams—vignettes of me dancing with someone in the twilight, the smell of roses in the air.

In those haunting visions, I wrapped my arms around a slender waist as I fiddled with a paintbrush, trying to paint something on canvas. The faceless woman in my arms laughed and nudged me out of the way.

"Someday, I'll be a painter just like you, and your face will be my masterpiece," I murmured.

A ghostly whisper replied, "Hope is the dream of a waking man."

As always, I'd wake up breathless and disoriented.

It's like a forgotten memory, just out of reach; the lines blurred, colors muted.

My hands tremble, fury gathering strength, and I set the brush down and grab the canvas, my fingers digging into the white cloth.

I'm calm. I'm at peace. I fucking accept myself, dammit.

I set down the art next to the pile on the herringbone floors.

Piece after piece of fucking soulless trash.

Twisting my family ring on my finger, I stare at the dark gemstone, wondering if any of my predecessors ever felt like this, like they were fighting an unknown enemy they couldn't see, like they were running away from a monster who had a noose with their name on it, only to look back and find nobody there?

I can't keep this up. Being a ghost of myself. Heck, I tell Ryland to live for himself, to be happy. Why can't I do the same?

Grabbing my phone, I check the time. One a.m. on a Friday. Sleep eludes me, as always. The night is still young. An event notification pops up, one I've ignored for weeks: *The Spring Race—2 a.m.*

My mind made up, I type a quick reply to the invitation attached. Then, I press a button by the painting of my great-great-great-grandfather, Silas Ashford Williams Anderson the Third, hanging above the fireplace, and stare at the man with whom I share the same slate-gray eyes and brown hair, so dark it's almost black. He wears a serious expression on his face, but I've always thought his eyes were haunted by sadness.

I wonder what he saw in his lifetime and what he would do in my situation.

"Yes, sir?" one of the staff responds.

"Have Simon get the McLaren ready for the race. I'm going out."

"Yes, right away, sir."

I shrug into my black leather jacket hanging on the coatrack and head toward the door, but as I cross the threshold, I pause, staring at the family ring on my finger.

Letting out a ragged breath, I tug the heirloom off and deposit it on the gilded tray on top of a small table. The ring clatters onto the dish with a crisp *clang*, and I shut the door behind me.

Half an hour later, I rev the engine as I turn into the lineup at an underground parking garage of a nondescript building on Broadway and Grand in Lower Manhattan. I roll down the windows of my latest beauty, my chrome-colored McLaren 720 S, with all the works done—nitrous oxide system and suspension upgrades, aerodynamic rear spoiler modifications, bespoke, imported from Japan, lightweight polymer for the hood, trunk lids, and door panels.

It's the car of a victor, not a failure.

A rainbow assortment of sleek, luxury vehicles gather in an orderly fashion, all smooth lines and bright colors, and hordes of people fill the floor of the parking structure.

The smell of gasoline mixing with the damp, wet scent of the rain sparks a fire in my veins, my senses turning on one by one and I can feel my lips twitching in the beginnings of a smile.

Live for myself. Be happy.

In this moment, as my heart thumps to the heavy beats of hip-hop music straining from the speakers of the cars in front of me, I can almost feel that elusive emotion.

I feel alive.

Closing my eyes, I inhale the aggressive, pungent cocktail of gasoline and burned rubber. *This is more like it.*

These are common sights and smells of the monthly races organized by The Orchid for its rich and elite patrons who have nothing better to do than to risk their lives for a taste of danger. Along with The Lilith, the voyeur room inside The Orchid, street racing is the occasional break I give myself, a place where I'm not the eldest Anderson son haunted by a centuries-old curse.

Excitement sizzles from the large crowd of bystanders and other racers, the women wearing tiny articles of clothing showing more skin than runway models for the summer resort collections, the men in various sports and leather jackets I know cost more than a month's rent for any of the apartments in the area.

A few girls nearby have their phones in the air, the flashes illuminating their pouting lips and sexy poses as they take selfies. Several couples are plastered next to their cars, hands roaming over their clothes, mouths devouring each other.

I scan the crowd, noticing a few famous models and actresses, beauties of all shapes and sizes, but my body doesn't stir, my cock not even twitching in my pants, another unfortunate, regular occurrence for the past year besides losing my muse for my art.

Gritting my teeth, I start to turn my head toward the settings in the front panels of my car, my eyes skimming over the sea of naked skin, glittering gems, and dark fabrics.

Until I see *her*.

A woman, standing on the outskirts of the crowd, looking as uncomfortable as a patient right before a rectal exam. Pale, flawless skin, without a stitch of makeup on, large, doe-like eyes, the color I can't make out from the distance, and thick, shiny black hair tied up in a high ponytail. She's gnawing on her lip, her eyes darting left and right, a deer in the headlights, her feet tapping a nervous rhythm on the ground.

While she's wearing a short dress like many women around her, a slinky black number ending mid-thigh, she carries herself like she's wearing an elegant ball gown. She has an aura of sweetness I can almost see and taste.

My chest seizes, riveted by this woman in front of me. There's something about her that prevents me from looking away.

She's breathtaking.

A redhead nudges her and speaks into her ear. She shakes her head and the other woman laughs. They murmur to each other and suddenly, I see her straighten up, the little deer growing a backbone in front of my eyes. She frowns, her lips pressing into a firm line.

What are you doing here? What are you thinking about?

Someone raps the roof of my car, interrupting me from my perusal of the mysterious woman.

"Maxwell, I thought you couldn't make it tonight."

Glancing at the interloper, I smirk, my shoulders loosening. "Last minute change of plans."

I motion to the excited crowd gathering around us. "Great showing tonight. No complaints so far?"

Jack's eyes sharpen, the jovial smile sliding off his face as he leans in. "None. Attendance is up, and folks are excited about this new route. We've checked in with the commissioner and he's directed his officers to other areas of the city during our race."

It's no surprise Jack has everything handled, including making sure the NYPD won't give our members any grief. After all, the commissioner is a member at The Orchid as well.

Jack Szeto started as a club promoter but quickly climbed up the ranks by being excellent at generating hype and capturing the particular tastes of the capricious billionaires in our circle. He's now the Director of Entertainment at The Orchid and occasionally frequents the races to "get a pulse" for the events himself, as he says.

I nod, satisfied with the turnout, and rev my engine again, enjoying the smooth purring of the cylinders. "I'll see you on the other side then."

"Will do. Good luck tonight, not that you need it." He doles out a lazy wink, transforming into the party-hard playboy right in front of my eyes, which is now a costume he wears since he's head over heels in love with his girlfriend, Sarah.

My eyes rove to the spot where the alluring woman was standing moments ago, but she disappeared. A mysterious ache forms in my chest, and I frown.

After closing the windows, I press a button on the side panel, and the infamous aria, "Nessun Dorma" from Puccini's *Turandot*, erupts from the speakers.

I sway my head to the sweeping drama of the song and the lyrics, listening to the Italian tenor playing the main male character, Calaf, sing about his character's love for Princess Turandot and his desperation for her hand in marriage pushing him to challenge her to discover his real name by dawn. If she fails, she'll marry him, but if she succeeds, he'll be killed.

To experience such a desperate, tumultuous love for someone else. To be willing to die for this person.

I swallow, a fruitless attempt at dislodging the lump in my throat.

To love with your whole body and soul...

It's a thirst I can't quench and will never be able to.

Thoughts of Sydney drift into my mind again—her laughter when she won a game of *Scrabble* after we finished our papers for twelfth grade English class. But even then, I'd never felt a fraction of what Calaf felt for Princess Turandot.

Just then, I hear the announcer mumble something about racers needing a passenger.

Fuck. This again? They do this every so often to change up the races.

Memories of being the last kid standing when no one picked me for their sports teams in elementary and middle school flash to the forefront. The helplessness, the anxiety. Fuck, I hate this feeling.

My heart drops to my stomach as a heat flushes through me and I see the mad dash of excited patrons getting into cars.

The heaviness returns to my chest.

I have no one. Lonely as always.

Shaking my head, I dispel the morose thoughts. If they won't let me race alone, then I won't race at all. I've accepted my course of life long ago. *I'm calm. I'm at peace. I'm—*

Slam!

My head swivels to the right, finding the mysterious black-haired beauty sliding into the passenger seat. Her eyes widen comically as she listens to the aria, her full lips parted as she heaves in panting breaths, like she has run a mile to sit next to me instead of walking the dozen steps of distance between us.

She gnaws on her lips again as I find myself speechless while the tenor's voice erupts into a crescendo in the tight space of the car.

What the fuck?

She takes in a deep breath, turns to me, and holds up her hands. "Look, I know I don't know you, but this is my year of yeses, and the announcer just said for this race, every racer needed to have a companion to liven things up, and I didn't see anyone get into your car."

Her hands cover her cheeks, which are flushed and pink.

She rambles, "Then, Jamie gave me an ultimatum and I couldn't say no because it's my year of yeses. I said that already, didn't I?"

My voice continues to desert me as I stare at this vixen, my fingers suddenly itching to pick up a pen or a pencil, my sleep-deprived mind even contemplating opening a vein to capture her on paper. Fucking insanity.

But the life teeming in her eyes beckons me. Then, there's her smooth ivory skin, unblemished except for a small freckle under her right eye, her long lashes, her beautiful irises, which I now see are a dark, tawny green, the colors of the moors in Scotland in spring.

My jaw flexes and every muscle in my body locks with tension. The air thins in the space between us.

She blinks, her face turning bright red. "What am I doing? Oh God, this is so embarrassing. You know what? I'm just going to leave—"

She reaches for the door handle and I don't know what comes over me this instant, but all I know is I don't want this woman to leave my car.

Stay. Don't leave me.

Leaning over her, I cover her trembling fingers with my hand, flinching the moment my skin touches hers, a barrage of jittery sensations overloading my nerves. She lets out a breathy gasp, and a thousand shivers coast down my spine.

And my cold, impervious heart—the muscle I thought was long dormant—stirs to life.

CHAPTER 6

MY HEART SHAKES IN my rib cage as my gaze traps on his large hand on top of mine. This handsome stranger looks even more beautiful up close, like he could be one of the Greek statues displayed at the Louvre.

Those long, lean fingers, an artist's fingers—a painter, an architect, a musician, I don't know. It's a gut feeling, a truth I can't shake. The map of veins on the back of his hand, which trails up his muscular forearms, sprinkled with a light dusting of dark hair.

The lips that look so soft, I wonder, for a split-second, how they would taste. *What's going on with me?*

Then there's dark hair, the brown so deep it's practically black, the strong Roman nose and angular aristocratic jaw.

But it's the intense eyes, the gray almost iridescent, that stall my breath, the eyes that drew my attention to him in the first place when he arrived in his car.

I don't know what came over me when I caught sight of him moments ago, because I'd never done anything like this before. He looked older than me by at least a decade, and yet, I couldn't find it in me to care. I just had to meet and talk to him.

Every atom in my body is awake as I watch his fingers lightly trail from my hand to slowly encircle my wrist, his thumb settling there, alighting a thousand sparks across my body.

I'm afraid he can feel how hard my pulse is beating against my skin.

"Don't leave me."

I gasp at the possessiveness in his voice.

Three quiet words. A rough, deep voice, which sounds so familiar and yet unfamiliar, like a voice from a dream a long time ago.

Dragging my eyes away from where his hand is still touching mine, I look at him, finding him staring at me, his turbulent eyes flashing with surprise before darkening into something undecipherable.

"W-What?"

He grips my hand harder; the dominance sending a wave of warmth inside me, chasing away the cold from a moment ago.

"Don't go. Stay. You said the racers need a passenger in their car."

"I didn't say that. The announcer did."

"Right. I didn't come with anyone. So stay. Might as well be you."

I squint, trying to read him, not sure if I should be offended by the phrasing of his words, like I'm his last choice or something. I guess that's how Taylor felt that day when I called her up at the shelter.

"Well, if you put it *that* way."

His lips twitch, and the almost smile softens his cold, handsome face into something more approachable.

"Where are my manners?" He turns toward me again. This time, a smidgen of warmth appears in his eyes. "Will you do me the honor of sitting next to me for this race so I can be eligible to participate?"

"Are you a good driver? Any traffic tickets or accidents?" More worries occur to me—year of yeses, my ass. "What about alcohol or drugs? Did you drink or consume anything illegal before now?"

He snorts. "Shouldn't you have thought of that before you got into my car?"

"I wasn't thinking! I got caught up in my year of yeses and Jamie said if I got into your car, she'd consider giving me her family's collect—"

I stop myself. There's no need to tell him the sob story of how I'm begging for design collection opportunities from acquaintances in my circles. Any chance to prove to my horrible boss I have talent, that I deserve my place at McKenzie's.

It's the only reason I'm at this event tonight, when I normally avoid hanging out at The Orchid or events hosted by them. I grew up amid the rich and the elite, whose social media posts consisted of "look at this new diamond necklace I got" or "we just bought our new vacation *cottage*," which turned out to be fifteen-thousand square feet. I don't plan on hanging out with the stuffy elite...unless I have to.

"Collection? What do you collect?"

"Never mind."

The sweeping, romantic aria playing in his car fades to silence. "*Turandot*, huh? I didn't peg you as an opera patron."

His eyes sharpen with interest as he regards me. "You know your operas. Why do you think I'm not a patron of the arts?"

"Everyone else here is listening to rap or hip-hop or some top twenty song. And you..." I motion to the vicinity of his muscular torso, straining against the constraints of a thin white T-shirt, his black leather jacket giving him a bad boy edge, especially with the thick lock of hair falling over his forehead. All he's missing is a pair of aviators and he'd be a dark-haired James Dean.

"My what?"

"You look like *that*." I groan inwardly. *If there is a God, you have my permission to kill me now.* I feel my face getting hotter.

He smirks. "Look like what?"

"A gentleman would not push when a lady is clearly embarrassed."

"Who said I was a gentleman?"

"Ugh!" I throw my hands in the air and cross my arms over my chest.

He chuckles, then stops himself and frowns, like he's surprised to hear his laughter.

A few seconds of silence pass by before the opening strains of a song from *La Bohème* play from the high-quality surround sound speakers, which must've cost a fortune, since I feel like I'm sitting right in front of the orchestra and not inside a sports car in a random garage in Lower Manhattan.

"Scratch that. Maybe you aren't an opera fan per se, but a Puccini fan?" I arch my brow at his widening eyes. He clearly didn't expect me to recognize this piece as another Giacomo Puccini work.

"Impressive," he murmurs and slowly slides on black driving gloves, the movement masculine and sensual and a heat gathers in my core.

"What's your name? I'm...Anna." I decide to fib a little since I know nothing about this stranger.

He swallows, his Adam's apple moving up and down his corded neck. "S-Silas."

His eyes dart to my face as if searching for something, but a second later, he turns away.

He stares out the windshield and I follow suit, noticing the crowd dispersing to the side and a girl with a black and white checkered flag walking to the front of the cars.

The race is about to begin.

The collective roaring of the engines breaks through the classical music and my heart shoots up my throat. Sweat beads on my back.

I guess I'm doing this. Sitting in a hot stranger's car in an illegal street race. *Year of yeses, Belle.* Quickly, I buckle my seatbelt and tightly grip the handle on the car door.

"Puccini was my mom's favorite composer. She was the person who showed me the beauty of classical opera and musicals," he answers my question from moments before.

My brows furrow at his usage of past tense, but my attention is quickly drawn to the activity occurring in front of us.

The girl with the flag stands on top of a center divider. She raises her flag into the air. I blow out an exhale, my lungs desperate for more oxygen, and I feel my pulse speeding, careening off a cliff. I tremble in my seat.

His gloved hand reaches over and clasps my free hand, which is gripping the hem of my dress as if that'll save me if anything happens to the car. My gaze darts to him, finding his eyes still intent on the scene before us.

Somehow, he senses I'm terrified.

"I'm a good driver. No alcohol. No drugs. No traffic accidents or violations." He turns to me, his penetrative gaze settling the nausea churning in my gut. "You're in good hands. Trust me."

Trust me. The two words echo in the small space between us, and I don't know why, but I trust him, this stranger who I swear I've never met before, and yet feels so intimate and familiar.

My rapid pulse settles and I nod.

His lips twist into a half smirk, baring one dimple, and a shrill whistle sounds in the air.

Tires screech on the cement as the car lurches forward.

The race is on.

CHAPTER 7

I SWERVE THE CAR to the oncoming traffic lane as a delivery truck unexpectedly stops in front of us on Canal Street, my car handling the shift in gears and transition smoothly despite the rain splattering on the windshield.

"Oh my God!" Anna shrieks, her eyes squeezed shut as she grips my hand tightly on her lap, her fingernails digging into my skin.

Horns blare and bright headlights flash at us as I weave the car seamlessly between oncoming traffic.

"I'm going to die. I'm going to die," she mutters. "I don't want to die. This is supposed to be my year of yeses, not my last year on earth. Why did I do this? Why did I get in his stupid car? Because he's hot, huh? Are you *stupid?*"

I swallow a laugh as I hear her prattle with the fervency of a monk praying before his deity on judgment day.

Beeeeeeep.

With one hand, I turn the steering wheel sharply right, squeezing my car in between another racer's red Porsche and a semi.

Her nails dig in sharper and I wince. That one will bleed. "I promise I'll go to church and pray more. I won't order well done steaks at restaurants. I won't dog-ear my books anymore. Please, just let me survive this!"

Chuckling, I squeeze her death grip. "You'll be fine. I have everything under control."

I maneuver the car into another strategic position as I hang a sharp right onto West Street. The car hydroplanes and drifts, the burned rubber smell of the tires scraping the wet pavement fills the air.

This is where the fun begins.

Her eyes snap open as the world flies around us in a blur of lights and sounds.

"You're holding my hand! What the fuck? Why are you holding my hand? *Don't you need it to drive?*"

"Technically, you held onto it and never let go. I only meant to reassure you when the race started."

She drops my hand like she's burned and claws the center console.

"Careful there, that's the juice."

"What juice? Why are you thinking of juice right now?" She lets out a squeak.

Seeing a clear path with no cars, I hit the tiny red button her hand was close to and the engine's roar transforms into a thunderous bellow, my hands gripping on the vibrating steering wheel as we're thrown to the backs of our seats.

She screams, her hands covering her eyes. "Forget I asked! What's this smell? Is there an issue with the car? We're crashing, aren't we?"

"It's nitrous oxide," I holler above the noise. "That's the juice."

The dark waters of the Hudson River to our left blur into a sea of black as we speed past the High Line, Hudson Yards, and other glittering, iconic buildings, my car at one with my movements, handling the road, the unpredictable weather, the other racers, and the traffic effortlessly.

"I don't think I can ever look at juice the same way again. I'm going to throw up." She mutters something else under her breath.

"Open your eyes!"

"What!"

"Feel the speed, the freedom! Open your eyes!"

"No freakin' way! You're *crazy*!" She clenches the door handle, her eyes squeezed shut so tightly they appear to be glued together.

"Year of yeses, right?" I toss her words back at her as we whiz down the street and I see 44th Street ahead.

Adrenaline races through me as the car reaches maximum speed.

Almost there. Sweat gathers on the back of my neck and I fake a right to the racer next to me. He slams on the brake as I straighten the car, my hand shifting gears, listening to the engine sing its beautiful melody to me, the purring a masterpiece that's as lovely as classical music.

Fuck yes.

Anna is silent as I make the last right on 44th Street, minutes away from the finish line in front of Grand Central Terminal.

Glancing at her, I find her eyes wide open, her mouth forming a cute little "O." She's sitting up and clearly marveling the streaks of golden lights from the streetlights cascading with the neon colors of various signage—real life avant-garde art one can only experience in the thrill of the race.

Grinning, I spot the race girls holding up red flares in front of us—the finish line. An enormous crowd is gathered on the sidewalks and I speed right past them, my foot lifting off the accelerator, and the car slowly cruises to a stop as I hear cheers erupt behind me.

My body is on fire—a glorious high from the race, the beautiful woman sitting in my car, and me taunting my old friend, death. It's the feeling I've been missing this past year.

I'm a victor, not a loser.

I'm not broken.

"So, what do you think?" I ask.

I shift the car into park, watching the crowd running toward us in the rearview mirror.

Her panting breaths are loud in the silence. She turns toward me, her mouth still propped open. "You're *absolutely insane.*"

I bark out a laugh as she struggles to maintain an angry face. Her lips twitch and she gnaws on her plump bottom lip again. She's nervous, but in a good way.

Heat unfurls in my gut and travels south as my eyes zero in on her luscious lips.

So plump and red. I'd give anything for a taste.

My nostrils flare and I find myself leaning toward her despite the warning bells blaring in the back of my mind, a desperate reminder I'm going to be engaged next month to a woman I've never met. But my heart races, every muscle in my body rioting with the need to touch her and taste her.

Fuck it. I'm Silas tonight, not Maxwell. I'm free.

She sucks in a breath, a pretty pink flush creeping up her slender neck to her pale face. Her eyes flutter shut.

"We have a winner!" the announcer yells behind us.

I flinch, backing into my seat. Her eyes open and travel to my face and the shade of pink deepens on her smooth cheeks.

What am I doing? This can't happen. The curse. The arrangement. This is wrong.

Seeing the crowd closing in on us, I can feel the beginnings of suffocating anxiety seeping into the cracks of my psyche, polluting the glorious high I'm on right now. The prickle of nausea curls in my stomach.

She furrows her brows and rolls her lips inward, her movements drawing my attention away from the crowd.

I've hurt her feelings.

Somehow, that thought is unbearable to me.

Cocking my brow, I ask. "Ready for your next adventure?"

Her eyes bug out. "W-What? Where?"

I shift the car into gear again and drive off, leaving the fans behind in a cloud of dust.

It's then I realize I didn't have an anxiety attack next to this stranger. There's only the righteous pounding of my heart in my chest.

Ba-dum. Ba-dum. Ba-dum.

CHAPTER 8

Maxwell

Fifteen minutes later, I park the car in front of Nellie's, the hole in the wall, twenty-four-hour diner a walking distance from Hudson River Park. Before my photo from the press conference was plastered everywhere, I'd enjoy occasional sojourns here, where they had the best pastrami and rye I'd ever tasted.

As I step out of the car, a cool breeze sifts through the air, carrying the scent of the briny waters of the Hudson and motor oil from the slick pavement. A dense moisture clings to the air, but the rain seems to give us a break. I look up at the oppressive dark clouds lit up by the city lights, a sight, which, mere hours ago, felt heavy and dreary, but now doesn't bother me.

Because of her. A bright ray of sunlight cutting through the darkness.

I swing to her side to open the door. She steps out gracefully, her slender, model-esque legs sliding out of the car first, her hands pressed over the hem of her dress.

My eyes rove over her face—something about her is familiar, but I can't place it. I've never seen her at The Orchid before, but she comes from money and manners. I'd bet my fortune on it. Perhaps she's a new member?

"Where are we?"

"My favorite sandwich shop in the city."

I usher her in and take a seat at my usual spot, a corner booth with a view of Hudson Yards. She looks around and eyes the classic American diner decor of reds and whites washed in stark florescent lights, gleaming chrome interiors with white signs detailing the specials of the day.

A few tables are occupied by teenagers who are busy looking at their cell phones, but the diner is otherwise empty. The smell of freshly brewed coffee mixes with the mouthwatering aroma of sizzling bacon on the griddle.

Nellie, the owner, steps toward us, her hand retrieving a pad from the pocket of her white apron. She has her usual toothpick in her mouth, her graying hair a disheveled mess. She used to tell me people were here for her food, not to look at her.

Nellie smiles brightly as she spots me with Anna and she waggles her brows.

"Well, nice to see you, M—"

"Nellie, it's good to see you too." I cut her off before she calls me by my real name. "This is my friend, Anna."

Anna beams at Nellie, her smile sending a current of electricity down my spine. "Hello! Silas said this is the best sandwich shop in the city." Unlike some other women in my circles, Anna doesn't scrunch her nose at the location or the waitstaff.

She's beautiful and kind.

Nellie lifts her brow. "*Silas* did, huh? Well, whaddya know."

I roll my eyes and give her a quelling look. "Can we have a pastrami and rye to share, please? A coffee for me and…" I glance at Anna.

"The same, thank you, Nellie." Anna smiles warmly at the woman, who beams right back at her before walking back.

I like her, Nellie mouths to me before disappearing into the kitchens. Shaking my head, I hide my smile behind my fist.

Thunder rumbles in the distance, followed by a bolt of lightning swiping its tendrils across the sky. It appears I spoke too soon, and the malevolent weather is back full force. The windows rattle as rain pelts against the glass once more. An insidious weight crawls on top of my chest and settles there.

Ryland loves storms but they've always sent ripples of unease through me, a foreboding feeling of something terrible about to happen. Whenever the weather rages outside, I always feel out of breath and about to crawl out of my skin. Perhaps twins aren't always the same.

Anna appears unaffected. "So, Silas. Why have you brought me here?"

"Too lowbrow for your taste?"

"Of course not!" She rears back, clearly offended. "I'd take this diner over fancy dinners any day of the week. But you," she fiddles with her fingers, "you surprise me."

Her words send a jolt to my heart. Maxwell Anderson never surprises anyone. He's the frigid king, the cold CEO of one of the largest companies in the world. He's a rule follower, the dutiful first son of an illustrious old-money family. There's no room for surprises.

But tonight, you're just Silas, a man having a late-night meal with a beautiful woman he just met. You're a rule breaker.

A server delivers our coffee and I take a sip and smile into the cup.

"You know, I feel like I've met you before or seen you somewhere. But we haven't, right?" she asks.

I glance at her from above the rim of the cup, my fingers clutching the handle tightly. Any moment now, she'll recognize me from the press conference, and then things will be different. She'll think I'm insane or unstable, as the press has described me, or she'll see me as a man with unlimited funds and power.

"I don't think I'd forget a face like yours," I murmur.

A streak of white light flashes through the room and the diner plunges into pitch blackness.

"Ah!" Anna shrieks.

I grab her hand in the dark, and there it is, the curious zap when our hands touch, the same electrifying sizzle I felt in the car, the same feeling I attributed to the adrenaline and anticipation of the race.

Her breath hitches.

"Oh darn. The wind must've knocked down our power line again," Nellie grumbles from far away. "Lucky for you two, your sandwich is ready. I'll bring y'all candles from the back."

Moments later, Nellie hustles over and sets down a crystal votive, its lonely flame flickering and casting dancing shadows on the booths.

"God, I'm such a wuss," Anna mumbles, sounding clearly embarrassed at herself.

"A sudden power outage would freak anyone out."

I look at my hand, still intertwined with hers, and she does the same before hastily withdrawing.

I stop myself from reaching out and snatching back those slender fingers, keeping her tethered to me.

Frowning at the sentiment, I glance out the windows as another rumble of thunder pierces the silence, followed by a flash of lightning.

Dishes clinking against the table draw my attention as Nellie sets down two small plates and her famous pastrami sandwich.

"Thank you," Anna murmurs, her face still flushed prettily, and reaches out to take the plates.

I grab her hand, unable to resist the lure of her smooth skin.

"Let me." I motion to the sandwich before carefully portioning it and handing half to her.

She grins, her tongue darting out to lick at those luscious lips again.

My heart pounds in my chest, and I quickly take a bite of my sandwich. I groan at the taste of the tender meat blending with the spiciness of the mustard and the tartness of the pickles and the bread.

"This is sooo good. Excellent choice, Silas." Anna licks the juices dribbling from her lips.

The warm glow of the candlelight lovingly caresses the smooth planes of her face, and those wayward, inappropriate thoughts of mine drift back to front and center. I wonder how silky her skin would feel under my lips. Would she bloom under my touch? My blood heats and warmth gathers in my groin.

"What? Why are you staring at me? Do I have food on my dress?" She looks down.

I shutter my gaze and shake my head. "No, you look fine." *Perfect. Where are these insane thoughts coming from?*

"So, Silas, what do you do? You're at an event hosted by The Orchid, so you must be someone important."

"I can say the same for you now, can't I?"

She narrows her eyes. "Playing the dark and mysterious card, aren't you?"

"Why don't you answer a question from me and I'll do the same?"

Anna takes another bite and delivers another sensual lick of her lips, which I'm sure she doesn't even realize she's doing. "Fine. That's fair. I accept. I'll ask first. What do you do, Silas?"

"This and that. I'm in the upper management of an entertainment company. It's boring." The biggest entertainment and hospitality company in the world, but I don't add that, of course. "Tell me about your year of yeses. What's that all about?"

She holds up her finger as she chases down her half-gone sandwich with a large gulp of coffee. The woman can eat, despite her slender frame. It's refreshing, unlike the high-society women I've dated in the past, who'd poke around their salads like the thought of calories made them full.

"So, my friend, Taylor, gave me a book last year, *The Wonderful and Terrifying Year of Yeses*, and it detailed a cancer survivor who decided life was too short to be afraid of trying new things. So, she embarked on a journey to say yes to anything anyone offered—new foods, experiences, etcetera. It helped her gain a new perspective on life and instead of feeling weak or unlucky, she felt empowered."

She clasps her hands in front of her expectantly. "I want to do the same. I'm reaching the quarter-life mark and have followed the plan everyone has laid out for me until now. I'm tired of it and decided life won't change if I just sit here and do nothing. I need to create my own choices and make my own decisions. I just started a little over a month ago and while I call it the 'year of yeses,' it's really a mindset change I'm going after."

Quarter-life mark. She's not even twenty-five yet. I'm twelve years older than her and yet, she seems to have the courage I don't have to carve out a different path for herself.

"And how is it turning out? This year of yeses?"

"Terrifying." She gives me a droll look and I chuckle. "But also awesome. I tried skydiving two weeks ago—something I'll never do again. I got a pet, even though my apartment doesn't allow any. I nearly lost my life in an illegal street race. And now, I'm eating in a diner at three in the morning during a blackout with a strange man." She frowns. "Hey, that's two questions."

"I'm sneaky that way." I stir my coffee. "What else do you want to know?"

"If you get to do one thing for the rest of your life, what would it be?"

"Art—painting or sketching."

"Yes! I knew it. I knew you were an artist!" Her eyes light up and she unleashes a dazzling smile.

My heart skips several beats. "How?"

She waves her hands in front of my face. "You have this aura about you. Bad boy looks but a sensitive soul. Don't look at me that way. I'm just telling you my gut feeling."

"Bad boy, huh? And you still got into my car. That isn't very smart of you."

Anna grins, the tips of her white teeth flashing in the dim space. I rake in a ragged inhale. She's like a cup of hot chocolate and a roaring fire in the middle of a blizzard.

My fingers twitch with the ache to paint again.

"Definitely agree with you on that. If it weren't for the year of yeses, there'd be no way on earth I'd go anywhere near you. You, mister, you're bad news."

"Regretting getting in my car already?" I bite back my grin before polishing off the rest of my sandwich, finding her plate already empty. She shakes her head and smiles shyly at her plate.

"Your favorite artist?" I ask.

"Frida Kahlo. Her work is vibrant, her style is impeccable. She marches to the beat of her own drum with a courage I hope to copy someday."

"Favorite color?"

"Hmmm..." she murmurs, her forehead pinched as she considers my question carefully. "I don't think I have one. They're all beautiful shades of the world. Even brown, which many complain is ugly, represents nature to me—the soil, tree trunks, and branches. But if I have to choose one, I'll say it's *atrovirens*."

My brow flies up high. "What?" Even I haven't heard of that color before.

"It means dark green in Latin, but it's really more of a deep teal. You know what's interesting? Most people don't know there's actually five percent red in the color."

She looks up and grins. "It's like the red is a secret you'll only discover if you care enough to look past the blues and the greens." She sighs happily. "It's a beautiful, soothing color."

"You know your colors." The inner artist in me is pleased.

"I do." She frowns. "Hold on. Why has this conversation become a one-sided interview of me?"

"You are interesting. Far more interesting than me." And I'm a greedy bastard, wanting to absorb her warm rays of sunshine on this stormy night, bathing myself in brightness and warmth before I embark on my uninspiring, dismal future.

"What excites you about your future?" I ask.

She takes the hair tie off from her ponytail, and her thick, silky black tresses tumble over her shoulders. My fingers clench with an urge to wrap those strands around my hand and pull, baring her slender throat to me. *I'm going crazy.*

She lifts her eyes and stares at me as if knowing the insane thoughts in my mind. The tawny greens of her eyes glow in the candlelight.

Wild moors in spring. Wildflowers in bloom. Irresistible magic.

"Carving a future for myself. Saving unwanted animals one at a time. Creating sustainable clothing for the public that doesn't harm the environment. Making my own choices without worrying about what other people think. If I'm lucky, having a family of my own."

She frowns at the last sentence and my chest squeezes. *She wants a family too, just like me.*

Anna blows out a breath, excitement slowly seeping back into her voice. "Anyway, the avenues are endless, don't you think? At least, that's what I'm trying to tell myself. What about you?"

I pause, and the chasm that has receded in the background for the past two hours rises to the forefront. I watch the light from the flame dance on her face. This fairy must be a mirage of my swirling mind. Swallowing the lump in my throat, I want to find an answer for her, something as inspiring as her passionate speech, but I come up empty.

"To survive."

Beads of sweat form on my forehead under her scrutiny, and I have the strongest urge to look away from her inquisitive stare—I don't want her to see right through me, right to the deep, dark secrets haunting me, keeping me up at night.

Standing up, I toss a few bills onto the table and reach for her hand. "Come. One last adventure before your night ends."

CHAPTER 9

Belle

A DULL ACHE SETTLES inside my chest as I twine my hand with his, a motion that seems as natural as breathing even though I only met him a few hours ago. Normally, when men tell me to do something without asking, like going on adventures with them, I'll rebel. But there's a soulful gentleness that draws me to him.

He said he's taking me on my last adventure for the night, but I don't want tonight to end. I want to know more about this quiet man who seems to hold the depths of the ocean inside him yet unwilling to share his burdens with the world.

I want more adventures with him.

He leads me out of the diner onto the dark streets. The temperamental rain has now receded into a light drizzle, not heavy enough to drench my clothes, but enough to mist my hair and face.

Silas squeezes my hand and tugs me toward Hudson River Park. His stern face is unemotional, but I sense a deep sadness inside him. His jaw twitches before he glances back at me and smiles, the brief flash of pain in his eyes squeezing my heart.

I wish he'd tell me what was bothering him. I want to understand him, this mysterious man. I want to make him feel better.

I shiver from the night chill and Silas shrugs out of his leather jacket and drapes it over my shoulders before tugging me flush against him. His scent of amber and sandalwood wraps around me like a protective embrace. Walking beside him, I feel safe despite the empty streets, the strange sounds of critters roaming in the dark, the menacing shadows of lurkers standing next to alleyways.

Minutes later, he leads me to the railing at the far end of Pier 66 in Hudson River Park. Standing behind me, he curls his heated body against mine, and I no longer feel the light drizzle of the rain or the dampness of the air. Instead, my nerves are attuned to his quiet breathing puffing against my neck.

I fight every urge to lean back, to press my curves against his hardness as a sultry heat swirls between us.

"What are we doing here?" I whisper, staring into the glimmering dark waters of the Hudson, which are half-hidden in the thick fog shadowing the atmosphere.

"If we're lucky, and I have a feeling with you...we will be." A light murmur, the vibration I can feel down my spine and my breathing quickens. "We'll see the sunrise."

He presses against me, his hands wrapped around my waist, fingers grazing my dress, and every atom in my body comes alive with each gentle caress.

We talk about our greatest fears, with mine being departing this world without leaving an imprint behind and his being losing his loved ones. From the sorrow in his deep voice, I know he has experienced gut-wrenching loss before.

We share stories of our childhood—how I'd create imaginary friends to keep me company when my parents were jet-setting around the world, leaving me behind with an army of nannies. He says I must've felt lonely, and I deserve more. My chest clenches at his words. He recognizes the emptiness inside me.

He tells me about his mother, whom I've learned had passed away when he was young. She'd sit with him in the gardens, teaching him how to paint, taking him to museums to see great works of art.

She believed in him, much more than he believed in himself.

The minutes pass by, bleeding into hours, our conversation endless, and I'm afraid it's the beginnings of an addiction I can't quit. A few hours tonight with him isn't enough. I want more—conversations, sensual touches, late night pastrami and rye.

He tells me he wants the simple life—family, kids, wife. But somehow the sadness in his voice tells me he doesn't think he'll get it.

It breaks my heart.

Why does he feel this way? And why do I want to give him his dream?

I shake myself—*don't get ahead of yourself, Belle. This man is still a stranger.*

Eventually, the first rays of sunlight pierce the clouds, the ethereal light of dawn chasing away the mystic fog—the angels vanquishing the demons of the night.

Chuckling, as if sensing my awe, he slowly turns me around to face the city.

My breath catches as I watch the dark skies part above the tall buildings and give way to the golden aurora, each glimmer catching onto the droplets of the fog, cascading into a million minuscule, incandescent sunbeams bathing the buildings in brilliant swaths of pink.

"It's beautiful." I sigh out a deep exhale.

My heart flutters and my soul ignites. I want to capture this moment in my designs.

Silas's arm tightens around my waist and I feel a pressure on my hair, like he has pressed a kiss there. Goosebumps form on my forearms and I turn around, watching his gray eyes flare in the golden light.

He isn't smiling, his face austere as a vein pulses on his forehead. A few errant strands of dark hair have fallen over, covering half of his face in shadows. With shaking hands, I reach up and gently brush his silky strands to the side. *Why do you look so sad, Silas?*

I feel bereft for some reason, a desperate ache blooming in my chest for something I can't name. It's a deep yearning—a need as essential as air to my lungs.

My fingers release his hair, and he clutches my hand to the side of his face and leans into my trembling palm. He dips his forehead to rest on mine and rakes in a ragged inhale. A burgeoning emotion rises in my chest—one at the tip of my tongue, but I can't seem to name.

"Thank you," he whispers.

"For what?"

Lifting my hand away from his face, he flips it over before pressing a soft kiss on the back. The spot tingles—it feels like a brand. His eyes flutter open and he stares at me.

Intense. Swirling pools I can drown myself in.

A car honks in the distance.

"I've called you a car to take you to wherever you want to go next, to the next yeses in your adventure," he murmurs, a deep anguish in his voice.

"W-What?" I whisper as confusion fights with heavy disappointment. Why does this feel like goodbye? Why isn't he asking for my number or taking me home?

My questions must have shown on my face because he answers, "I'm sorry, Anna. These few hours are all the adventures I can give you. If I were to take you home, I'm afraid I wouldn't be able to help myself..."

His voice catches as his sentence trails off. He takes a step back away from me, the brisk morning wind crashing between us, a wall separating two worlds that cannot be breached.

"But why?" I ask.

I don't understand. I want to know him better. My heart has never beat like this for another man before. There is a connection I can't explain—why is he just giving up?

Silas shakes his head, unwilling to say more, and steps to the side.

Wetness prickles behind my eyes from a strange urge to cry, but I don't. I've only known the man for a few hours and I have my pride. This has to be a side effect of the adrenaline from earlier. I won't beg anyone to go home with me or to keep in touch with me.

Squaring my shoulders, I strain a smile. "Thank you for an unforgettable night, Silas."

I walk toward the black sedan, every atom of my body telling me to turn back, to run toward the imposing, mysterious man standing there. Raking in a heavy breath, I shake my head and quicken my pace toward the car.

I'm not looking back. I'm not—

Suddenly, pounding footsteps echo behind me and before I know it, a strong hand curls around my wrist. With a quick tug, he spins me around.

I see a flash of furrowed brows, intense eyes glimmering with a determined light. He clasps his other hand at the nape of my neck and crushes his lips to mine.

He's kissing me.

I'm swept away by a tsunami of heat and passion. And relief. Because he wants me just like I want him.

Silas kisses me like it's the last kiss he'll ever receive, the last meal of a condemned man before execution. His mouth moves against mine, his tongue dipping out to taste the seam of my lips and my mind blanks, my body a slave to the sultry sensations.

Moaning, I curl my hands around his neck, my fingers tugging at the dark strands, and he growls before he tilts my head to the side and plunges his tongue inside my mouth. His movements are dominant, his hunger palpable, and he bands his arm tighter around my waist such that I'm plastered to him from my chest to my legs, and I can feel every twitch of his hard muscles through the thin fabric of my dress.

An unmistakable hardness prods my stomach and I feel myself growing wet, wanting to rub against him, against this stranger whose last name I don't even know, but I find myself not caring.

A year of yeses.

Somehow, I have a feeling I'll always say yes to him.

I let out a whimper as his teeth nip my lip before his tongue laves the bite mark. I drag in a breath of air before he swallows my mouth with his again, his long fingers knotting my hair and tugging, the sudden pain a direct caress to my clit.

This is insanity, but I don't care.

I need more. I need him. All of him.

"Oh Silas," I moan, and he freezes.

He wrenches me away and staggers back several steps. His chest rises and falls rapidly as we stare at each other, my lungs burning with the need for more oxygen, my mouth craving for another taste of him. His face is flushed, hair mussed, eyes wild with the same inexplicable madness swirling in my veins.

My skin feels hot to the touch, my core pulsing, needing the virile man before me, who looks like he's a beast and wants to tear into me for breakfast.

And I want him to.

I take a step forward and he lurches back, his index finger shaking as he points to the car behind me.

"*Go.* Leave me," he commands, the warmth from his face seconds ago morphing into a fierce coldness.

I flinch, the backs of my eyes burning, and I swallow my retort.

I won't beg for his kisses. By why does everything hurt so much?

His face is remorseless as I turn away and dash toward the car waiting for me, my hand clutching the fabric of my dress at my chest, a sharp pain robbing me of my breath.

And it isn't until I'm in the car that I realize tears have drenched my face and I'm still wearing his leather jacket.

CHAPTER 10

Belle

"You're getting married. We've chosen the man for you."

Mom's announcement has the effect of a sudden plunge into the frigid waters of the Arctic Ocean.

We're sitting in my parents' living room, freshly redecorated with white Calacatta marble imported from Italy, the third renovation my parents have done in the last five years.

Heaven forbid they have decor that is older than a few years.

"What?" I don't know why I'm surprised they *didn't* involve me in the process. So typical of them.

"Honey, you knew this was going to happen eventually. And with your condition..." She trails off, eyeing pointedly at my stomach.

"What? Because my biological clock is running out, I'm losing value to you guys soon? Marry me off while you can still barter for something?"

I stand up and fist my hands to my sides. *Nope. Not today. New and improved Belle will rather beg on the streets than follow suit.*

"Sit back down, Annabelle." Dad finally looks up from his phone—he's no doubt texting one of his mistresses, judging from his slimy smile earlier. "We have indulged you long enough. Because of your privilege, you have—"

"A roof over my head, a fine education, more money than I'll ever need, a cushy job," I tick off his usual items with my fingers. "What else are you going to say? Because I have the unfortunate luck of being born to the two of you, I don't have a say in my life?" I shake my head vehemently. "I don't think so." *Not anymore. I'm in the driver's seat.*

While it has only been a few months, if there's something the year of yeses concept has taught me, it's that I have agency in my life. I get to make those choices—good ones or bad ones—for myself.

Images of slate-gray eyes and sexy dimples float to my consciousness and I shove the thoughts of *him* away, even though Silas has occupied my mind far too often in the last month since that magical night between us, after which he disappeared—a phantom or a hallucination. I tried searching for him online, but the first name of Silas was too common and without a last name, it was impossible to find him.

"What about McKenzie Atelier? Don't you care about your grandpa's legacy?" Dad glares at me.

"Of course I do. Why do you think I work so hard?"

"Well then, this marriage will bring more business to the company."

I cock my brow. "I'm not going to get married just to bring in more business. That's ridiculous."

My parents glance at each other, and something about the way they are fidgeting is getting my hackles up.

I narrow my eyes. "There's something you aren't telling me, isn't there?"

Silence. *Crap. This has to be bad.*

"I won't entertain the idea of getting married unless you guys tell me the truth." I cross my arms and sit back. The ball is in their court.

Mom clears her throat and sighs. "Look honey, we've made a few bad investments over the years and the truth is, we're broke."

"How are you broke?" I look at the spacious apartment decorated with new wallpaper, new lamps, new everything, then at the expensive jewels on my mom's fingers. "Don't lie. And you can sell your things if you're so hard up on cash. What does this have to do with the company?"

More furtive glances and my blood boils in my veins.

"I...I may have taken out funds from our corporate accounts," Dad mutters, his face reddening, finally looking ashamed. "The corporate loans we have at McKenzie Atelier are due soon, and we simply don't have the cash for them. The investments were supposed to pay off. They were supposed to—"

"*You embezzled from the company?* How could you? It's Grandpa's legacy! When were you planning to tell me this?"

I think back to the man who taught me how to sketch designs on paper, cut patterns for my own creations, sew on a sewing machine, the man who died when I was sixteen and I've been left alone and adrift ever since.

This company meant everything to him...and to me.

"Well, we're telling you now. And you want to have a family, right? You want children? I know we talked about IVF and egg freezing before, but with our finances, that isn't an option anymore. Not to mention, you've never reacted well to hormonal medication," Mom begins, her brown eyes softening as she tugs my hand. "Sit down, honey. Let me explain. This isn't as bad as you think."

Reeling from the revelations, I take a seat.

"Look, the family you'll be married into is well-connected, well educated, a fine family."

"Rich, no doubt." I snort.

She ignores me. "They need an heir and want to enter the fashion industry. We need their money. Like you, we want to keep your grandpa's legacy alive. After all, few companies can compete with the top fashion houses in the world."

I don't look at her, and she clearly takes that as a positive sign. "I know you want children of your own and you don't have a boyfriend or anyone you're interested in. Your fiancé is a good man, well respected."

Nausea bubbles up inside me. *Fiancé.* I haven't even agreed to marry him yet.

Mom continues, "You just need to be married to him for a minimum of one year and give him an heir. I'm sure he won't mind IVF or something like that. He'll provide the funds for our company and afterward, if things don't work out between the two of you, you can amicably divorce."

She squeezes my hand, her tone softening. "I know how hard it is to get the diagnosis of DOR. And if you end up getting pregnant, isn't it fate then? For you to become a mom? Isn't that what you want?"

Tears burn in the back of my eyes and I look up, finding her lips wobbling slightly in an uncharacteristic display of emotions. For a moment, I wonder if she too went through something similar when she left Hong Kong and her modeling career behind to marry my dad.

Thinking back, I don't think my parents were ever in love. My dad is a womanizer and Mom spends more time socializing and indulging in spa treatments than at home. They live separate lives.

But now, as she's looking at me, I see a glimmer of maternal love, that somehow, in her mind, she really believes she's doing this for my own good, and not just to save my grandfather's legacy.

I swallow the lump in my throat and murmur, "Who's the family?"

"The Andersons."

My head snaps up, my eyes widening at the name of the most influential family in New York. They're the family tied to my best friends, since Grace and Taylor recently found out they are half-Andersons from their dad's side and Millie is head over heels in love with Ryland, the second son of the family. I've met most of the Anderson siblings before.

"Fleur Entertainment's Andersons?" I ask, straightening up. I do like them. They are good people. It feels weird to be considering this like a business transaction, but the nausea in my gut settles a bit.

Mom smiles, as if knowing what I'm thinking. "Now you understand? We know you know them, and we aren't lying. This is a good match."

"Which brother am I supposed to be marrying? Not Ryland, since he's attached to Millie."

More thoughts of a dark-haired man in a leather jacket flash in my mind and a dull pain twists behind my rib cage.

It was a beautiful dream. A haunting, romantic dream. *Darn it, why am I still thinking of Silas?*

"Maxwell, the eldest. I know he has some press issues recently, but I've been reassured by Linus what they are reporting isn't true. He isn't crazy," Dad comments, and goes back to scrolling his phone like he's talking about the weather and not about marrying his only daughter off for money and connections.

"Crazy? I haven't followed the news." *What crazy?* The girls never told me about Maxwell being crazy.

While I've met the Andersons a few times in social settings, I've never met the eldest brother. He's a known recluse, always ducking out of most public events except for the famous Christmas Ball at The Orchid. It was said he'd grace the crowd with his presence for the bare minimum of one hour before leaving, and photographers were strictly forbidden to take photos of him there.

But still, he's an Anderson.

I think about Ryland, who, with his wry humor, seems to treat Millie like the most precious person in the world. Rex, who flirts with anyone with a vagina, but is always kind, and Ethan, the serious one who doesn't talk much, but is always there to be a listening ear, and Lana, the stylish older sister I never had.

Not to mention, ever since Grace and Taylor learned about their relationship with the Andersons, they've gotten to know their half-siblings very well and cannot sing their praises enough.

He can't be that bad, right?

"Honey," Mom says, "this is a good thing for you. Think about it. Your grandpa's legacy. Having a baby—time is running out."

A lump forms in my throat and I feel a tug in my heart.

"Belle, time is of the essence. Maxwell wants to meet you in a few weeks and we shouldn't keep him wait—"

"Albert, let the girl breathe. This isn't a new car purchase we're talking about." Mom snatches Dad's phone from his hand, and he rolls his eyes and harrumphs.

"Fine." He glances at me and murmurs, "We know we're asking a lot of you, but I trust you'll make a rational decision. And don't think I haven't heard from Gordon how you've mucked up the first run through of the spring collection. Our numbers are dropping because the elite are choosing designs from the other fashion houses. An alliance with the Andersons will shift this narrative."

Anger burns through my veins as I think back to the humiliating presentation yesterday, where Gordon Flair, my lecherous boss and the bane of my existence, berated me in front of the entire design department.

He rips my designs in half and I want to shrivel from embarrassment. The room erupts in snickers.

"Nepotism is alive and well!" Gordon sneers. "What trash is this? This is why McKenzie's is failing, because of talentless people like you!"

"But you asked for these specifications in the design, I told you they were—"

"Excuses! Only the weak blame others for their failures." Gordon leans in and pats my cheek—like I'm a toddler. Heat rushes to my face, and it takes everything in me not to give him a right hook. "Try again, princess."

It was embarrassing and infuriating.

Dad leans forward, his eyes sharpening. "Belle, this is a win-win for everyone, and we'll get to keep McKenzie Atelier afloat. I know you want that."

I hate what he's saying makes sense.

Chapter 11

I take a few deep breaths, a last-ditch attempt at calming my nerves before I meet with my fiancé at The Menagerie, a small cocktail lounge on the second floor inside The Orchid.

I'm going to do it.

Marry Maxwell Anderson.

After mulling it over the last two and a half weeks, I realize I need to be logical about this. My three biggest dreams: a thriving career in my family's company, creating a haven for unwanted animals, having children of my very own, all could be solved by saying yes.

All these dreams require capital, and with having children when your fertility clock is quickly running out, I need a man, a donor with good genes. I've thought about my friend, Cole, but considering how he has feelings for me, asking him for the favor of sperm donation would be too cruel. Plus, I don't have money for IVF right now.

And so, I will proceed with my parents' plan, including their stipulations.

"Don't tell Maxwell about your condition," Mom warns.

"But isn't this lying? If he wants an heir, shouldn't he know I may encounter fertility issues?"

Mom grips my hand tightly. "You don't have issues yet, just fewer follicles than other people. Don't let him know. We don't want him to back out of the deal."

My conversation with Mom last night echoes in my mind and a slither of shame creeps inside me. The way Mom spoke of me as if I'm broken, but I'm not. I refuse to believe it.

But deep down inside, I wonder if perhaps I am.

Broken.

I shake myself—these thoughts aren't helpful, and I put on my brave face as I step into the lounge fifteen minutes before our meeting.

In a terse email exchange, Maxwell asked me to meet him here to discuss terms for the marriage. We also shared health check results with each other—all clear on both sides. We haven't spoken on the phone before, but I figure it doesn't matter since I'm going to see him in person, anyway.

My eyes widen at the intricate and tasteful decor, from the pale pink sunken plush seating, the low-hanging pendant lights in the shape of tree branches, to the hand-painted gold vines and foliage on top of the blue-green wallpaper.

"Favorite color?" His deep voice is laced with amusement.

"If I had to choose one, I'd say it's atrovirens."

Atrovirens.

The wallpaper is atrovirens.

A sadness weighs on my chest as snippets of my conversation with Silas float to the surface. It's been almost two months since the night of the street race and if it weren't for the leather jacket hanging in the back of my closet at the apartment, I'd think that evening was a figment of my imagination.

If the fates allow, after I divorce from Maxwell, perhaps I'd bump into him again, the only man I'd ever felt a deep stirring for in my heartstrings—an inexplicable connection far transcending the short time we spent together.

Maybe we'd greet each other with smiles on our faces and he'd ask me to go with him to Nellie's to share a simple pastrami and rye.

Maybe I'd bump into him at the Met, watching one of Puccini's operas, and he'd ask the man next to me to switch seats.

Or maybe...just maybe I'd see him in the distance, his fingers intertwined with those of a beautiful woman, two little kids in tow.

He'd be living his dream life, and I'd be alone.

My heart clenches at the bittersweet images. A few of many that have sifted through my mind ever since I met him, a stranger who left an indelible imprint in my heart after only a few magical hours spent together.

"Ms. Law-McKenzie?" a blonde in a crisp gray sheath dress addresses me.

I nod.

"Mr. Anderson is in the room in the far corner. Do you want me to lead you to him?"

"I'm sure I can manage." I look around the empty lounge and ask, "Is it always this quiet here?"

She shakes her head. "Mr. Anderson secured the entire lounge for your meeting. He said he didn't want any disruptions or distractions," she explains.

My pulse is thready as I stare at the frosted glass room with the door ajar.

My fiancé is sitting in there.

I've tried searching for him on the internet at home but his photos from the press conference have been removed. There are gossip sites saying the Anderson family has paid sizeable sums to media outlets and IT firms to scrub his images off the internet. The photos are rumored to be unflattering due to his very public panic attack.

I could've asked the girls for photos or information on him, but that'd require me to tell them what I was planning to do.

And to be honest, until this moment, I wasn't sure if I was brave enough to do it, to agree to marry a man I'd never met before. I didn't want to worry them and I was sure they'd have strong opinions about our match, since they knew Maxwell and loved him dearly. Plus, they'd want me to marry for love. After all, I'd want the same for them.

Blowing out a deep breath, I walk toward the room. *Let's get the show on the road.*

The opening notes of Puccini's "Nessun Dorma" sounding from the speakers stop me in my tracks.

My heart hammers a staccato rhythm and suddenly, tears threaten my eyes as I remember listening to this aria in Silas's car.

The world of what-ifs and what could-bes.

The tenor's voice strains at the high notes, the chorus and orchestra melding into an unforgettable melody and I square my shoulders and walk into the room, my feet coming to an abrupt halt when I see the man standing in front of the floor-to-ceiling windows, his back turned toward me.

The bright sunlight renders his shape into a dark silhouette, but something about him causes my pulse to flutter wildly in my veins.

Everything about him screams power and prestige. He stands tall, his long legs spread a foot apart, his hands in the pockets of his trousers. He's wearing a black suit that seems to be tailor-made for him, the fabric stretching over his lean muscles as he hums under his breath, too softly for me to make out his voice.

His head sways gently to the music, and as the tenor sings the pinnacle of the aria, Maxwell's head stills, his deep, smooth voice raising in volume as he hums louder to the climax of the song that has graced cinema multiple times in the last century.

The hairs on my forearms rise.

That voice. The unmistakable deep voice that sends shivers down my spine.

It can't be.

"Silas?" The name escapes my lips before I can stop myself.

He stops humming, his entire being freezing at my voice.

The tenor belts out the ending lyrics when Calaf proclaims his impending victory at winning over his beloved Princess Turandot.

My hand flies to my mouth as Maxwell slowly turns around.

It's him.

Silas. My Silas.

Heady warmth rushes inside me, happiness flooding my body, leaving me disoriented.

His intense slate-gray eyes widen in shock, a muscle twitches in his jaw, and he slowly takes out his hands from his pockets.

"Silas, is it you?"

I can't help but ask for confirmation, because this man, this billionaire standing tall in front of me, his dark hair carefully swept back, his imposing figure filled with restrained power, doesn't resemble the soulful bad boy from that night, the one who teased me and held my hand when I was terrified as he sped down the near empty streets of Manhattan.

He steps toward me but halts midway, his hands balling into fists by his sides. A few deep, mirthless chuckles slip from his mouth, the sounds full of incredulity threaded with ridicule.

He shakes his head, his eyes roving over me in disbelief before hardening into a cold glint. He extends his hand.

"Maxwell Angus *Silas* Anderson, at your service, Ms. *Anna*belle Law-McKenzie."

I flinch at the icy expression on his face.

Where is the warm, charming man from that night?

CHAPTER 12

THE FATES HAVE A dark, twisted sense of humor.

The thought whispers through my mind as I stare at her in shock.

The beguiling woman who has stolen my focus during the day and haunted my dreams at night for the last two months is the woman I'm supposed to marry.

What the fuck.

She took a piece of me with her when she got into the sedan that night, a car I called for her because I knew if I took her home, I would never let her go. And that was before I, in a weak and impulsive moment, kissed her on the pier with the sunrise shining around us.

The kiss obliterated my soul. It felt like coming home after being marooned on an island or reclaiming something precious I'd once lost. Every atom in my body vibrated for the woman I held in my arms, attuned to her every breath, every moan, every gasp.

I knew then, as I know now, I have to stay away from her.

Because of the curse.

Because...if I fail, then she dies.

And *that* is unfathomable.

Now, *Belle*, as she told me to call her in our email correspondence, stands before me seemingly as shell-shocked as I am, her beautiful lips parted on a gasp.

I am to marry her.

Sydney's lifeless face shifts into my consciousness and I flinch, the coffee I consumed moments ago threatening to make a reappearance.

I can't marry her. She's the last person on this planet I can marry.

She's the only person I'd ever want to marry.

Madness. I don't know the reason for these insane thoughts. *You've been in her presence for only a few hours.*

Nothing makes sense. Logic doesn't seem to pierce through the dark veil.

"Silas, is it you?"

I shake myself, my eyes greedily absorbing every beautiful inch of her—her thick, black hair curled in luscious waves, draped over her shoulder, her petite body poured into a cream silk dress which hugs her perfect curves.

"Maxwell Angus *Silas* Anderson, at your service, Ms. *Anna*belle Law-McKenzie."

She flinches at whatever she sees on my face, and I knot my hand into a tight fist to stop myself from striding over and pulling her into my arms again.

Irrational impulses. Madness swirling in my mind.

I'm going insane.

I unclench my hand and extend it to her, watching as her fingers tremble slightly before she slips her hand into mine.

A sharp current sizzles between us at our point of contact, and I take a quick breath.

"Did you know who I was that night?" she asks as she quickly withdraws her hand and hides it behind her back.

"No. Had I known, I would've never let you stay in the car."

Her tawny eyes darken in apparent pain, and I want to punch myself for hurting her. She opens her mouth to ask more, but I hold out my hand to stop her.

"Ms. Law-McKenzie, I'm sorry, I cannot go through with this. I can't marry you."

Belle staggers back half a step, her face scrunched in confusion. "What? Why?"

Picking up my phone from the table, I stride toward the door, eager to flee from her, from this forbidden woman who makes me want to spend days upon days painting her face on canvas, dancing to Puccini in the halls of my home, marveling at strange, obscure colors, and saying yes to adventures.

"M-Maxwell. P-Please stop."

Her dulcet voice whispering my name has me halting. I turn around, finding her eyes reddening, a wet sheen in them.

She shakes her head, clearly bewildered. "I don't know what's going on or how you ended up being the man I'm supposed to marry. Or why you're treating me this way when that night we shared was the best night of my life."

My heart skips another traitorous beat at her admission.

She continues, "But I need this arrangement." She takes a deep breath, as if fortifying herself, and looks up. "My family needs it...for McKenzie Atelier a-and because I want to have—"

She stops herself.

"What do you want to have?" I want to give her everything. I want all her smiles and kisses. I want to know every facet of her.

But I can't. I have to say no.

Belle swallows, her skin turning into an alluring shade of pink. "Our family needs this arrangement, and I'd rather it be you than a stranger."

Blistering anger chars my chest at the sudden thought of her with another man, someone else getting to hold her in his arms, to taste those sweet lips I've been craving for ever since that night, to listen to her adventures as she grabs life by the balls.

"No."

I'll strangle anyone who lays a hand on her. Destroy him. The disturbing thought comes out of nowhere.

"What do you mean, *no*?"

"You can't marry anyone else. I won't allow it."

The hurt in her eyes recedes and is replaced with anger. She straightens and crosses her arms over her chest. "You won't *allow* it?"

"No. I'll ruin anyone who comes near you."

"*What!* That's ridiculous. So, you don't want to marry me, but no one else can either? What kind of sick, twisted person are you?"

Very sick. Very twisted.

Her eyes flash with fury. "For the last month, I've dreamed of our night more times than I can count, wishing...wishing I could find you again."

Her tiny body shakes with passion as she stalks toward me and jabs her finger at my chest. "Apparently, that night was a mirage, an illusion, and I don't really know who you are. But don't think you can control me, mister, or you'll be the one who's sorry in the end."

She spins around, moving toward the exit. "I won't beg for anyone to marry me. If it isn't you, I'm sure there are plenty of men out there willing to do it."

I reach out and snag her wrist in my grasp, my fingers tightening automatically.

Don't leave me.

The words haunt my mind, but what comes out of my lips is a simple, "No."

She whirls toward me. "What do you want then, Maxwell?"

Staring at my hand covering hers, watching the smattering of goosebumps appearing on her forearm, I reply, "Fine. You want to proceed with the arranged marriage for your family. So be it. Let's talk terms."

She wrenches her arm away and gnaws on her lips. "Fine."

"One year and one child, minimum." My cock, the fucking organ which has been lifeless for the past year, twitches in my pants as I imagine trying for a child with her.

"I can't guarantee that...the child."

"That's the entire purpose of this arrangement for me."

"You can't guarantee that with any woman!" Her face darkens and her hands are now fisted to her sides, her voice rising in volume. "Not everyone can have children of their own!"

The words echo in the room, the background music long muted by the staff since our meeting started. A suspicious sheen glimmers in her eyes and she looks away, blinking rapidly.

She looks devastated. A fissure forms inside my chest. I want to fix her problems and wipe that expression off her face.

But instead, I say, "The attempt at it is what I'm asking for."

She sharply inhales. "A-Attempt?"

"Where do you think babies come from? Divine intervention?"

She grits her teeth, her nostrils flaring. "Don't patronize me. I assume we can go the IVF route."

"No."

I'm a damn bastard, because if I'm going to do this, to put myself through this marriage while keeping her at arm's length, I want to wrench out every morsel of happiness and intimacy from this relationship.

I want an excuse to touch her silky skin, to feel her warmth against me, even if I have to shield my heart from her.

"I'm not opposed to using fertility treatments or adoption, but only after we've tried for one year."

She blanches, her pulse fluttering rapidly in her throat.

"I-If we get pregnant, I want custody of our children after we divorce," she says.

My chest squeezes at her words, but I ignore it. "No. No children of mine will be fatherless. Fifty, fifty custody, that's my final offer."

Her nostrils flare. "Fine."

I recite the terms I had my lawyer draw up last week. "You'll get a bonus for every heir you give me, a generous severance package upon divorce if we remain married for more than one year, in addition to the investment I'll be providing to McKenzie's."

Her face darkens with each condition I list out.

"We'll be sleeping in separate rooms, conducting separate lives. I will require you to accompany me to certain events and also to plan and act as hostess for our upcoming charity gala at the estate." It's the first public event I'm hosting—another attempt at winning over the press and the public.

"You will conduct yourself in a manner befitting the position of my wife. There will be no scandals and no affairs."

Belle snarls. "I see you've thought of everything, *Your Majesty*." The little kitten has sharp claws, and a flash of pride carves through the tempest of emotions rioting inside me.

She narrows her eyes. "What about you? Am I to sit back and be a *good wife* while you mess around?"

"I won't cheat. I *never cheat*. From the moment we say our vows, I will remain faithful to you."

The words hang in the silence between us. It's a somber oath that rings true to the depths of my soul, something I desperately want her to believe, even though she has no cause to think otherwise.

"Belle, fidelity is something I hold core to my values. I won't cheat, and neither will you."

Her lips tremble and I see the struggle she's trying to contain inside her.

Pulling her close, I relish the soft gasp escaping her mouth and blood pools in my groin.

"We'll be married in October. But make no mistake, this will never be a love match. It will only be a marriage of convenience. You *cannot* fall in love with me, and I will never, *ever* be in love with you."

CHAPTER 13

THE BRUNETTE SITS ON a wooden chair as she toys with a button on her shirt, her hair already mussed up from what probably was a long night here on the Rose floors within The Orchid. She looks straight at me as though she could see me, but I know she can't because the glass has a one-sided view unless I hit the button on the wall panel to turn it double-sided or even eliminate the glass all together.

But as I stare at her, I find myself shifting in my seat in discomfort. I'm removed from the situation, looking at her like an art critic would over a piece at a gallery—cold, dispassionate, objective.

My dick doesn't even twitch.

After the intense meeting with Belle, where I acted like a complete bastard and laid out my requirements as if she were a luxury property I was purchasing, she stormed out of The Menagerie in a fit of anger.

I couldn't blame her when every part of me wanted to chase after her, fall to my knees, and ask for her forgiveness.

To do anything to see her sweet smile directed at me again.

To taste those addictive lips again.

But I didn't.

Instead, I spent another grueling week at work and in the studio, attempting to paint the same portrait of the woman in the rose garden, but this time, the woman's silhouette was no longer blank and in its place was a very rough sketch of someone with a graceful, lithe frame, long, flowing raven hair, elegant nose tipped toward the sun, and a beauty mark under her eye.

When I realized what I had done—sketched her in the masterpiece I'd been trying to complete all my life, I recoiled in horror and came here to The Lilith, the voyeur and exhibitionist room within the Rose floors. It was a vice I felt comfortable in indulging once or twice a year in the past, where any sexual encounters, were it to happen, would be initiated only when I was comfortable, where I could otherwise sit in the shadows and just...watch.

For those lucky enough to gain membership at The Orchid, which includes forking over an obscene fee and enduring rigorous interviews, their every whim and desire will be met within these walls.

But my need will never be fulfilled here.

It was a mistake to come tonight.

The nagging want in my chest resurges, and with a frustrated growl, I stand up and pick up the phone in the suite.

"Mr. Anderson, how may I help you?" an attendant asks.

"Please give my apologies to the lady, but I'll be cutting my night short."

"Yes, sir."

Exiting the luxurious suite, I turn right and stride down a long corridor of rooms made of special, one-way glass, where one can watch the action inside the rooms.

The tie around my neck feels like a noose as I ignore the amorous displays in the rooms and make a left, past an open space filled with leather sofas, swings, and other structures. People are gathering in various stages of undress, the occasional moans and sounds of skin slapping against skin piercing through the sultry jazz background music.

I feel soiled and about to crawl out of my skin, like I've somehow violated my oath to Belle by being here, even though we haven't said our vows yet.

Huffing a deep breath, I push through the thick door separating the lobby of The Lilith and the play space.

As I exit The Lilith and step onto the marbled floors of the central floor, I hear the unmistakable voice of my brother calling out to me.

"His Majesty frequenting the Rose floors. That isn't on my bingo card for tonight. Either it's the end of the world or some other shit, or you've finally seen the wisdom in my ways?"

I look up and inwardly groan. Of course, I'd bump into Rex, or Mr. C, as he sometimes likes to call himself. My parents have alphabetized our middle names by age, with mine being Angus, Ryland being Benedict, all the way to Lana, the youngest of the immediate family, and our half sisters, Grace with Felicity and Taylor with Gianna.

He has a wide, shit-eating grin on his face as he saunters toward me with a grumbling Ethan and a smirking Charles in tow.

"Rex." I roll my eyes, unable to stop my jokester of a brother from waggling his eyebrows like a deranged clown and pulling me into a bear hug.

"Our fearless leader. Are you here to sample the forbidden fruits the Rose floors have to offer? In case you haven't been here in a while, allow me to introduce you to these five floors of heaven on earth." He's in his dramatic element. I roll my eyes as he slings an arm over my shoulder and leads me to God knows where.

"There's Noire, our indoor forest if you're interested in primal play or outdoor pleasures, Trésor, our tasteful, luxurious burlesque club, The Lilith, our exhibition and voyeur rooms. There's something for every kink. Not to mention our beautiful companions. I've sampled all the rooms and personally, I like—"

"Fuck, Rex. Do you enjoy listening to the sound of your own voice? Like Maxwell won't know what's on every single floor here when he approves all the financial reports and project plans." Ethan runs his fingers through his thick hair and shakes his head, acting like he's older than Rex, instead of the other way around.

Charles chuckles beside him, his blond hair glimmering in the dim light.

"I'm just saying. His dick is probably moldy and nonfunctional, living like the monk that he is. Thought I'd be helpful," Rex quips and winks.

"I'm fine, and my dick is not your concern." It just appears to only stir for the woman I'm not allowed to develop feelings for.

Rex leans in. "So, why are you up here today?" His voice quiets, no doubt so that other patrons can't hear us. "Is everything okay?"

"Fine. Everything is fine. Business as usual." Guilt prickles my chest. I haven't told them about finalizing my arranged marriage yet because they'd feel guilty for no reason or try to talk me out of it. My jaw twitches as I look toward the elevator bay.

Rex lets out a sigh and slings his arm back over my shoulder. "Sorry, boys. It looks like our evening of debauchery has come to an end. Let's go down to the gentlemen's club to find out what has ruffled the feathers of our fearless leader."

"Thank God. I didn't even want to be here in the first place," Ethan murmurs, and Charles barks out a laugh.

"Look, I'd rather be left alone—"

"Shut up. Even I can tell you need a stiff drink and I'm not even related to you." Charles shoots me a quelling look.

Ten minutes later, we are gathered in the spacious suite perpetually reserved for my family within the gentlemen's club. Like everywhere else in The Orchid, the furnishings are top of the line and luxurious, from the plush leather sofas and navy wingback chairs, the dark wood floors imported from abroad, to the thick, velvet drapes adorning the windows.

I sit in one of the navy chairs facing the fireplace, which isn't lit on this warm summer night. My mind is a mess, much like the black soot marring the brick walls of the hearth, layers of charcoal and grime no amount of scrubbing can erase.

"So, are you going to tell us what's going on?" A glass of whiskey is thrusted in my line of sight and I turn toward Ryland, who has just arrived.

He sits on the sofa and unclasps a button on his shirt, no tie to be seen. He's eschewed ties since deciding to become a full-time professor.

I survey the room, noticing Charles propped up against the floor-to-ceiling windows, a pensive glimmer in his blue eyes, Ethan playing with his wallet by the dining area, Rex sprawled on the other sofa, a lazy grin on his face that is belied by the sharpness in his eyes.

Steven Kingsley, our other good friend and soon to be brother-in-law when he marries our half sister, Grace, takes a sip of alcohol from his tumbler, his brows furrowed. He came in with Ryland.

"I may get married soon," I hedge, not ready to tell them I've decided to get married...to someone I can't stop thinking about.

"What!" Rex exclaims from his corner.

Ryland is silent, his identical gray eyes searching my face, no doubt trying to figure out what I'm not saying. As my fraternal twin, he has the uncanny ability to read me sometimes. Fucking twin-sense.

I take a sip from my glass and look away, not wanting Ryland to peer into my soul any more than he already does.

"We need the good press for Fleur after my..." My voice trails off as shame washes over me.

"You don't need to take on the public. I'm more than happy to do it for you," Ethan says. "Don't get married just for good publicity."

No. I'm done hiding and shirking my responsibilities. And they know I'm not marrying only because of the press.

Shaking my head, I reply, "Even without my fuck up at the press conference, you guys know it's going to happen eventually. That's the way things are done."

I don't mention the curse since Charles doesn't know about it, and it's something we try to keep under wraps within our family. We've only recently clued Steven into the situation, seeing as he's going to become part of our family soon.

"What if you don't need to, Maxwell? What if everything is just coincidence, a bad stroke of luck?" Ryland murmurs quietly.

"A bad stroke lasting centuries?" I snort and take another fortifying gulp of alcohol. "I don't think so. I'm not superstitious, but even I can't deny the facts."

There are simply no surviving female Andersons who are married to the eldest son in the family and part of a love match. Not since our family set foot on American shores in the eighteen hundreds. The only women in our family are Lana and our half sisters, Grace and Taylor.

Sydney's face floats to my mind.

No one is safe.

"But, what if—"

"You forget what happened to Sydney?" I turn toward my twin and his brows pinch, but the expression is quickly wiped away. I lean toward Ryland, clasping my hand on his knee, and squeeze softly. "Because I didn't."

CHAPTER 14

Eighteen Years Ago, Anderson Estate

I STRIDE UP THE stairs of the estate, my fingers lingering on the lion head carved into the banister. It's a symbol of loyalty and strength—what our family stands for.

It's fucking dreary outside—another New York storm drowning us in torrents of water. The antique Tiffany floor lamps are turned on but do little to brighten the gloomy atmosphere as I take the stairs two steps at a time.

But nothing can dampen my spirits today.

I smile, thinking of Sydney...my wife, the beautiful girl I somehow convinced to elope with me after we walked across the stage for high school graduation at Broadbent Academy.

How did I get so lucky?

I pass by an oil painting of my great-great-great-grandfather, Silas, on the second-floor landing—he's the most auspicious duke in our family—the one who left his duties behind in England and moved to the States for business opportunities.

He stands tall and regal, befitting someone of his station, his wife by his side and sons at his feet, the heirloom black agate ring on his index finger—the same one on mine.

"I got married to a girl I love," I murmur to him, needing to tell someone other than Ryland. "There is no curse. They are idiotic superstitions, old wives' tales, and I'm going to prove it to Dad."

Silas's piercing glare never wavers and I feel a shiver down my back—a distinct disapproval radiating from his gaze.

Ridiculous. It's only a painting.

Shaking myself, I continue down the hallway to my room. I just need to change out of my casual clothes, speckled with paint from my hours at the studio, then I'll meet Sydney for dinner.

Heated voices around the corner alert me to the presence of someone else.

Two people, to be exact.

I slow my steps, my footfalls quiet on the Persian runner on the floor and walk toward the shadows of two people clearly in an emotional discussion.

Thunder rumbles outside and the wind hammers against the windows, letting in a howl akin to someone in pain, but I barely notice. Instead, unease sifts through my veins, an icy chill wafting my back because of the conversation occurring.

"Ryland, please. You don't understand. I…I love him too. But we married too young. I don't think I realized, but I learn it's possible to love two people at the same time. I can't get you out of my mind, Ryland."

My breath wrenches out of my lungs. I stagger back a few steps, my hand braced on the fleur-de-lis wallpaper. *It's only been two months, Sydney. Don't blame this on our age. You knew what you agreed to.*

I thought she was happy.

Sydney is the only woman I've ever loved romantically. The woman who has brought back joy in the house.

I hear a sharp inhale, the taller masculine shadow backing away. Ryland. My twin is just around the corner with my wife, who apparently has loved him all along.

And from the looks of it, she loves him more than she loves me.

Blood rushes in my ears as their voices pick up in volume. Sydney pours her heart out to Ryland, telling him how long she has loved him, how she thought when they met at *my* first and only art exhibit, that Ryland was me, and how she lost her breath over him.

My lungs rattle, each sentence from her mouth a javelin to my heart. I hunch over and try to dispel the blackness dotting my vision.

She stood by me every single time I butchered a public presentation. She didn't jeer at me like my classmates, who were eager to knock down a privileged Anderson. She'd stay with me at the estate even though I knew she'd rather go out and party with her friends.

I let out a mirthless chuckle, the storm drowning my sounds of pain. Of course, she wants Ryland, *the perfect twin...the perfect man.*

The signs were there, weren't they? Her smiles always seemed brighter in his presence. She'd look disappointed whenever he wasn't around during game night. Then she'd insist on keeping the lights off when we had sex because she couldn't bear to see my scars.

The same scars on my torso throb and pinch, reminding me of my flaws—both physical and mental. Steeling myself, I straighten up, lean back against the wall, and listen...because I have to know what Ryland says.

Was I the interloper all along?

"You said your vows, Sydney. For better or worse." Anger seeps through my twin's voice.

"I regret them! Ryland, don't you see? I can't go on living like this. You feel something for me. I can see it in your eyes. This...this is right. The right thing to do. Stem the bleeding now before it hemorrhages. We can't help what the heart wants!"

A fresh wave of agony slices through me, my heart pulverized by her words, and a heavy silence fills the air...even the howling winds and pouring rain are giving us a reprieve.

Holding my breath, an oppressive blanket of dread smothers me. I peer around the corner, and the remnants of my heart are incinerated by what I see.

Sydney...my Sydney, pressing Ryland against the wall, her lips on top of his.

I choke back a gasp and clutch my dirty shirt, not caring I'm smearing the paint from my fingers on the soft fabric.

A second later, Ryland hollers, "Excuses. All of it. You *disgust* me!"

But it's too late.

I saw his eyes fluttering shut when she was in his arms and how his fingers tightly clutched her slender waist, touching what I thought was mine.

He likes her. He may not act on it, but he likes her.

I hurry back down the stairs, past a bewildered Morris, and step onto the pavement, letting the storm wash over me, the water pelting my skin like bullets to the chest, a chest flayed wide open.

Present Day, The Gentlemen's Club Inside The Orchid

But it was too late for Sydney then...I'd already fallen in love with her. Even if she loved Ryland more, she also loved me. We were married, and we confessed our love to each other.

That was enough for the curse.

"I just want you to be happy, like what you've wanted for me." Ryland clasps his hand on top of mine, drawing my attention back to the room. His eyes are somber. I wonder if he's remembering the same moment...the moment that changed everything.

The moment I kept from him, even to this day.

Sydney died a week later.

My love is poisonous. It's a death sentence. I killed Sydney by loving her. I'm a murderer.

I look at my twin, my best friend, and reply, "I'm happy because you all are happy."

I've learned my lesson.

After all, I'm flawed and cursed. I don't deserve to be loved.

Chapter 15

"Come on, Silas." I tug the leash, and the adorable husky cocks his head at me, his tongue sticking out before continuing on his merry way.

I wipe the sweat off my forehead as I stroll down the streets of SoHo with my friends and dog in tow. The sweltering heat mid-June almost feels like I'm held captive inside a sauna, unable to breathe, to think, to do anything other than to bear with the circumstances.

Like the joke that's my life these days.

Silas wags his tail and chases the shadows twisting under the glaring sunlight. He has been a bright spot in my life ever since I stole him from the shelter. Luckily, Taylor and I weren't caught, and no one asked about the little guy after he disappeared.

For the past two and a half months, I've called him many names, from Little Terror to Ranger to Scout, but nothing has stuck. He has never responded to any of them, usually opting to destroy another cushion or chew on the wallpaper of the SoHo apartment I share with Millie.

But the other day, after returning home from that infuriating meeting with Maxwell at The Menagerie, I stomped into the apartment and muttered, "Damn you, Silas! What was I thinking, liking you for even a moment?"

The little terror , his posture picture perfect, like he was modeling for a husky calendar.

He liked the name.

Good. I'll name my one-eyed husky after the fraud who almost stole my heart. And then I'll make him go fetch...and fetch again.

"I can't believe you kept this from us for months!" Taylor scrunches her nose, her skull nose ring glimmering under the harsh sun. She's not in a good mood—her nose piercings are like mood rings for her.

Grace nods beside her, her eyes narrowing at me. She may have said the same thing multiple times this week in our group chat.

"And we had to find out...*by accident*, at my graduation dinner, no less. Were you *ever* planning to tell us?" Millie walks in front of me and turns around. Her hands are on her waist and she looks pissed—rightfully so.

I sigh and draw the group into the shade offered by the awning of the stucco building next to us. We're shopping for my wedding in a little over three months. As expected, with the Anderson wealth, most of the wedding planning is done, with vendors begging to be part of our celebrations, some even offering their services for free.

Today, in particular, we're shopping for jewelry and picking up something His Majesty has ordered me to retrieve, based on his terse email I received yesterday.

Belle,

I saw this online and thought of you. A gift to seal our contract. Go to this address to pick it up. Don't think too much of it. It means <u>nothing</u>.

Maxwell

I growl under my breath—the infuriating, perplexing man who gives me whiplash.

I can't believe I'm getting married...to a man who has refused to see me since that disastrous meeting at The Menagerie, when he bulldozed over me, making all the decisions unilaterally like a misogynistic caveman.

Just like my parents, my horrible boss, and other authority figures in my life.

The thought has me knotting my hands onto the hem of my dress.

He's the complete antithesis of the charming and mysterious Silas from the race.

"Well? What's your excuse?" Taylor prods.

I had been working up my courage to tell my friends about my arranged marriage when everything came to a head at Millie's college graduation dinner, when Maxwell was forced to be in the same room as me and Linus blurted out our arrangement in front of everyone.

Needless to say, the girls have not been happy with me.

"I wanted to. I really did. I was going to," I mumble, my responses sounding pathetic even to my ears.

"You know, I don't care you didn't tell us." Taylor squats down and pets Silas's fur. Silas rolls over belly up and wiggles on the patch of grass on the sidewalk. "I just want to know if he's coercing you into this shit. Do I need to beat him up or something, because half-bro or not, I will."

Millie snorts. This is on brand for our hold-no-prisoners, badass ballerina, even though I find it hard to imagine her tall, elegant frame beating up someone as strong and solid as Silas.

Maxwell, dammit. Maxwell.

"He didn't coerce me." I sigh, looking around the street, mostly devoid of people on this late afternoon. "I'm going to tell you girls something, but you can't repeat it to anyone else."

The girls huddle closer and I briefly recap the conversation with my parents, my unfortunate health news in the fertility department, and my deal with Maxwell.

I keep the magical hours of my time with Silas to myself.

It feels sacred—a secret I want to hold inside my heart.

Grace's eyes widen into the size of dinner plates. "You what! But why would Maxwell want something like this? He doesn't need an arranged marriage. The man is a billionaire!"

It's something I still haven't figured out yet, and it certainly doesn't help that the man in question doesn't want to talk to me. He can have any woman he wants. Why would he subject himself to something as archaic as an arranged marriage?

"He said it was because Fleur wanted a stake in the premiere fashion couture house in America. That's an industry they don't have their hands in."

It doesn't sit right with me. There are plenty of ways to achieve that without this arrangement.

Millie purses her lips, no doubt thinking the same thing. Suddenly, she gasps and tugs both Taylor's and Grace's arms, pulling them closer.

She murmurs, "Do you think it's because of you know what?"

"What you know what?" I ask, but they shush me.

Grace and Taylor's mouths drop open and Taylor shoves Millie on the side. How this woman is one of the top ballerinas in the country has me questioning my eyesight sometimes.

"I bet it is. The entire family believes it to be real," Grace whispers.

"What's real?"

The three of them ignore me, apparently clued in on something I'm not privy to.

"Will someone tell me what's going on? I'm marrying the man. I deserve to know!"

The girls look at each other, passing silent messages. Millie nods and Grace turns to Taylor.

Taylor shrugs. "She deserves to know. She's joining the family soon."

Millie turns back to me and says, "I found this out recently from Ryland. Apparently, their family is cursed. Something about the women the eldest sons love and marry will die an untimely death."

The cold sweat beading on my back has nothing to do with the summer heat.

"A curse?" I shake my head, my pulse quickening. "You're kidding me, right?"

"Nope. I wish Millie was making shit up, but they told us a few months after we learned that our biological dad is Linus." Taylor picks the black nail polish off her nails. "That's why there aren't any women in the Anderson family, except Lana and, of course, Grace and me."

She looks up, her brow arched almost to her hairline. "Grace doesn't believe it, but I think there are many things in the world we don't understand. Life, death, where we come from and where we go when we leave this earth. I'm on the fence, but not ruling it out as the truth."

"And because of the curse, it's rumored a lot of the Andersons end up in arranged marriages...to avoid falling in love but to get heirs. Something about heirs being required in the curse," Millie supplies.

I strain a smile. *What on earth is this crap?* "This is a *curse* we're talking about, something that has no scientific basis. Come on, girls. I don't even need to know the details. This is *ridiculous.*"

It has to be.

Silas brushes himself against my ankle and I look down, finding his lone eye staring at me intently, his tongue not sticking out, tail not wagging.

He looks somber.

I flinch as the sweat drips down my back and a chill crawls up my spine.

This is ridiculous. Insanity. It may be my year of yeses—a new attitude and all that—but I won't lose my common sense.

Wiping my sweaty palms on my navy sundress, I shake my head at my best friends. "Well, I don't believe it. Someone will have to give me cold hard facts before I believe any of it."

Grace suddenly grins. "You know, this means we're going to be sisters for real!"

"Oh my God, you're right! That is, if Ryland and I..." Millie's voice trails off, her face flushed.

"Oh shut up. That man is crazy about you. You might as well be married." Taylor grins.

Warmth flutters through me as I look at my best friends. *Sisters. I like that idea.*

Blowing out a breath, I turn around to look at my reflection in the window of the shop behind me. I'm sure I look crazy with my hair sticking to my sweaty skin and the makeup melting off my face.

I freeze at what I see inside the window display.

CHAPTER 16

I LOOK UP AT the store sign. *Wraithmoor Antiquities.*

My breathing catches—this is the place Maxwell wanted me to go to pick up my mysterious gift.

I press my hands to the glass, not caring if I'm smudging the window.

"What are you looking at?" Millie asks from behind me.

"I found it. Something old and something blue." I point to the necklace displayed on a bed of white silk.

It's beautiful—breathtaking. It's a silver oval locket adorned with pearls, gems, and delicate floral carvings on the face, each petal adorned in gold, silver, or rose gold. Sparkling sapphires and tourmaline are interspersed between the flowers, the display light illuminating every glimmer of ocean blue and teal.

I can't look away.

My face presses against the window. My breath fogs up the glass despite the suffocating heat surrounding us.

A mysterious yearning grips my heart in a vise as my pulse scatters in a wild rhythm.

I need that locket. It's mine.

"The chain is long enough for me to tuck into my gown," I murmur, my fingers twitching, eager to touch it and fasten it around my neck. "And the silhouette and inscription inside," I whisper, my eyes glued to the shiny jewelry.

"What silhouette and inscription? What chain?" Grace shakes me and I draw in a quick breath, my eyes finally pulling away to look at my friend who's scrunching her forehead in concern.

"The silver jeweled chain, the silhouette of the woman, and—" I turn back to the necklace, and a gasp tumbles from my mouth.

Only the locket is displayed. And it's closed, no chain to be seen.

"I could've sworn..." I trail off as unease swirls inside me.

I wipe the thin mist of sweat on my forehead. It must be the heat wave, my overactive imagination, and all this talk of family curses and strange deaths.

"What on earth?" I whisper.

I thought I saw...I somehow know the inscription and silhouette painting will be inside. I'm as sure of it as I am of my name.

But how?

"Let's go inside, buy the necklace, and pick up the gift. It's fucking hot out here," Taylor grumbles.

My pulse flutters wildly and I'm strangely out of breath. I tie Silas's leash around the trunk of a small tree and he happily lies on the grass.

Pushing open the doors, I enter a place that could be a time capsule with its dark wood decor, glass cabinets with brass hardware, lit up oil lamps, and a smell of incense in the air.

There are shelves and display cases filled with vintage jewelry, handbags, and the walls are lined with oil paintings—stark portraits of somber people from bygone eras. The corners are filled to the brim with racks of silk scarves, hats, and other knickknacks.

"Welcome to Wraithmoor Antiquities. I'm Eleanor. How may I help you?" an elderly woman with wavy white hair and shrewd eyes asks.

"I'd like to look at the necklace inside the window display, please."

She stares at me, her dark eyes penetrating as if assessing something, and I fight every urge to shrink from her gaze and run away.

"The Eternal Devotion locket is reserved for someone else. I'm sorry."

My heart sinks as I gaze forlornly at the locket once more. "Eternal Devotion...what a beautiful name."

"It is. It's a rare, handcrafted piece from the mid to late eighteen hundreds. It was said when the locket was found, there was blood on the surface and the clasp was broken."

The air thins and for a second, the floor spins around me. I grip the glass case in front of me to steady myself.

The shopkeeper continues, "There are many stories about how that happened, but the most popular one was the wearer of the locket tragically passed away and the blood symbolized the last of her beating heart before she departed this world. And so, the locket earned the name 'Eternal Devotion.'"

"That's so sad," Grace murmurs.

"Shit, that's morbid," Taylor huffs. "I have a question for you. Why is the store called Wraithmoor Antiquities? It's a unique name."

Eleanor is still staring unwaveringly at me, her brows pinching. I gnaw my lip and look away. *Why is she looking at me like she's seen a ghost?*

She answers, "My ancestors have lived in the city since the beginning. They were caretakers of an old church on the Upper West Side—Wraithmoor Abbey. Sadly, the abbey burned down a long time ago, but it held a special place in their hearts."

Wraithmoor Abbey. The name sears into my ears...so familiar yet foreign, and a strange sense of déjà vu washes over me.

"Interesting," Taylor mumbles before nudging me. "Silas looks impatient. Let's hurry up."

I glance outside and see Silas pacing and barking at bystanders. Crap. Any moment now he'll chew off the leash.

Turning back to Eleanor, disappointment over not being able to buy the necklace still weighing heavily inside my chest, I ask, "Thank you for telling us about the locket and the shop name. Actually, I'm here to pick up an order—a gift from..." My voice trails off, thinking about Maxwell, who's almost like a stranger to me at this point.

"Her fiancé," Millie supplies.

"Of course," Eleanor murmurs. "Name on the order, please?"

"Maxwell Anderson."

The shopkeeper freezes and looks at me for a few beats.

I nervously tuck a lock of hair behind my ear. "Is something wrong?"

Her lips curve in an enigmatic smile and she shakes her head. "Nothing, nothing at all. I guess some things are fated."

Without further explanation, she walks over to the window display, retrieves the locket, and carefully places it into a red velvet jewelry box. She slides it over to me.

"This locket is meant to be yours, after all."

A gasp slips out of my mouth and the pulse tremors in my veins. I reach out, my fingers shaking as I touch the delicate jewelry. A somber ache and an unsettling calm, two contradicting emotions, wash over me at the same time.

Gently, I open the locket and Grace gasps.

"You're right, Belle! There *is* a silhouette of a woman and an inscription. How did you know?"

I shake my head, unable to answer her. Nothing makes sense.

I trace the inscription inside:

To E.

Upon you, my dearest, my love rests for eternity and beyond, for anything less would be insufferable.

Your servant,

S.

A flinch of pain spasms from deep within me, but I can't look away. It's the feeling of finding something you aren't aware you've lost.

"Eternal Devotion is a fitting name for it... It's so romantic," Millie murmurs, and I nod.

Somehow, Maxwell found and gifted me with the one thing that calls to me deeply, something equally beautiful and tragic at the same time.

"The Anderson family is filled with mysteries too...just like the necklace," Eleanor comments.

I look up sharply. "What do you mean?" My pulse quickens.

She gives me a cryptic smile and says, "Someday, when you're ready, come back here and find me. We'll talk more then."

What? "I don't understand—"

"When you're ready," she reiterates and looks away, clearly ending the discussion.

Mysteries. Curses. Superstitions.

I clutch the necklace tightly in my hand before slowly fastening it around my neck. I can feel its pulse, its energy...an ethereal brand.

I shake myself and pinch my wrist. It's the stories Eleanor was telling, along with the topics we were discussing that's impacting my mood.

Nothing more.

"But make no mistake. This will never be a love match. It will only be a marriage of convenience. You cannot *fall in love with me, and I will never, ever be in love with you."*

His rumbly voice echoes in my mind. The sharp, severe tone, the words that stabbed me straight in the heart.

The curse.

I refuse to believe it. There's no way this is true.

Am I denying this because I really don't believe in it or because...because I'm hoping for something more with him?

CHAPTER 17

STRIDING DOWN THE SIDE aisle quickly, I strain a polite smile at the hordes of people gathered in St. James Cathedral, my family's parish. I feel like an exotic animal on display, a thousand pairs of eyes trained on me.

There's no way I'm walking down the center aisle until I have to. As I pass by the wrought iron votive stands, the flames flicker and dance, casting ghostly shadows on the marble walls.

It's a chilly October evening. The skies outside are overcast, not a ray of sunlight to be seen. The bluish daylight pierces through the stained-glass windows and projects a kaleidoscope of muted colors against the walls and vaulted ceilings in this large, gothic-styled church.

I'm getting married today.

To the woman who has bewitched me like no other, for reasons I can't explain.

I haven't been able to get Belle out of my mind since that fateful night, and ever since I've decided to marry her, it's been slowly driving me insane. Even though I made it a point not to see her since our negotiations at The Menagerie, I still remember how I felt with her that night at the race—the feeling of coming home, of finding something I didn't know I'd been searching for. Then there was the way my body came alive in her presence at The Menagerie.

Shit. Shit. Shit.

An excited murmur travels through the crowd gathered here—the event of the year, as I've heard the wedding being described.

It's a nightmare for me, in more ways than one.

I'd rather have a quiet ceremony at a small chapel and be done with this...arrangement.

I can only hope God is looking down upon me today and blessing me with the strength to carry on, to survive whatever is in my future...my loveless future with the woman who has inconveniently awakened my heart.

Banking a left in front of the altar, I stand in the center next to my brothers.

"Waited until the last minute, huh?" Ryland murmurs as he straightens the cuffs of his tux. "You know, you don't have to do this."

I stiffen and shake my head. "I won't change my mind." I glance at the pews filled with people. "I hate these crowds. I'm sweating through this tux."

"You look fine, Your Majesty," Rex quips from his position. "You're probably breaking many hearts by getting married today."

I roll my eyes.

Ethan snorts and chimes in, "But never fear, Maxwell. Mr. C over here is here to heal those broken hearts one at a time or fuck, maybe even several at a time. I think he already got five phone numbers when he was walking up the aisle."

Rex scoffs. "Going back to the alphabet, huh? Not everyone can be as charming as me. Green isn't a good color on you, D."

"Like I want—"

"Boys, we're in public." A faint scent of roses sifts to my nose as Lana wraps me in a hug. "You look good today, Maxwell. I'm so proud to have you as my brother. And...you can do this."

I nod, and a lump forms in my throat—my little sister, the baby who used to follow us around when we were growing up, is now a beautiful woman and is trying to console me.

Ryland clasps me on the shoulder.

Despite how I've been telling them I've made peace with everything in my life—the curse, the tragedies, my role in the family—they sense how difficult this is for me.

And they don't even know about my feelings for Belle.

No. I grit my teeth. *There are no feelings. Silas had feelings for Anna in a beautiful dream that was a fog-filled mirage.*

Maxwell Angus Silas Anderson has no feelings.

"We're always here for you," Lana murmurs before pulling away and taking a seat in the front row next to Dad, Old Morris, Agnes, our housekeeper, and a few close staff members who are like family to us.

I scan the crowded cathedral, mentally thanking the wedding planner for adhering to the no cell phone and photography rules and see Charles laughing beside Steven in the second row, his gravelly voice traveling to my ears.

Adrian Scott, the infamous billionaire nicknamed The Shark, who is also Millie's older brother, is sitting next to his wife, Emily, who happens to be Steven's older sister. Emily flails her arms around, her face animated before she jabs Charles on the side, who mock scowls at her. But it's Adrian's gaze on Emily that has the lump in my throat growing in size.

It's utter devotion and fascination, even though they have known each other for years and have been married for a few of them.

An endless thirst dries my mouth. *I'll never be able to have what they have.*

Rolling my tight shoulders, I look away as the organist and string quartet strike up the soft opening notes for the bridal procession.

My palms grow sweaty and the air thins as the cathedral quiets.

I blow out one deep breath. And another.

The double doors open and a ray of light casting on the center aisle renders the bride in an otherworldly, ethereal glow.

I promptly lose my breath.

My heart hammers wildly inside my chest.

She's wearing a long-sleeve gown that is modest, yet sexy, the silk draping over every delectable curve of her body. A swirling heat makes its way down my spine, chasing away the chills from earlier.

A silver jeweled chain peeks out from the modest neckline and I know she's wearing the necklace I gave her.

I was approving the antiquities Lana planned to purchase for the upcoming charity gala at the estate when I saw the locket on the website. My breath stalled in my throat, and I knew no one else could have it...no one else other than Belle.

The music increases in volume as Belle glides down the aisle, her dad at her side. She stumbles but quickly recovers as she recognizes the enthralling melody of "Nessun Dorma," the instrumental version, reverberating in the vast interior.

Her eyes widen, her gaze ensnaring mine, and a sharp current, so tangible I can almost see it, locks between us, the world fading into a blur of shadows and whispers.

In this civil, unemotional affair, the selfish man inside me couldn't help but give Silas and Anna an ode of recognition with the song—*our song*—the one that began our story.

It's fitting for the story of Silas and Anna to end with this aria.

Belle doles out a trembling smile, one I can see through the sheer long veil she has on as she continues walking up the aisle.

Toward me.

Adrenaline courses through my veins and I feel breathless. My fingers twitch at my sides.

Mine. Finally mine.

A strange voice screams inside my head and I fist my hands, making sure my nails dig into the flesh of my palms to the point of pain. Anything to keep me from bolting down the aisle, taking her hand, and running away.

Far, far away from here, from everything.

Her dad places her hand on mine.

My hand closes on hers automatically, the simple touch eliciting shivers down my spine and I hear her quick intake of breath.

I don't look at her.

I don't give her an ounce of compassion or camaraderie as we stand in front of the priest. My sanity is frayed at the edges as is.

"Dearly beloved, we are gathered here today to join this man and this woman in holy matrimony..."

The next hour passes by in a surreal blur and I feel the heat of the audience's attention on me.

Don't think about them. Don't look at them.

I'm calm. I'm at peace. I accept myself.

"...join your hands and declare your consent before God and his Church," the priest instructs.

I wipe my sweaty palms on my trousers before turning toward her and taking her hands in mine. Locking my jaw, I stare at her, not smiling, not yielding an ounce of warmth.

I can't let her think this is anything more than a loveless arrangement.

The priest murmurs the next words to me as my throat tightens into a vise.

The church is silent—so quiet, I can hear a pin drop and the squeaking of shoes against the floors.

I open my mouth to speak, but nothing comes out other than my heavy, ragged breaths. My hands shake against hers as I stare helplessly into her soothing, tawny eyes. Wildflowers. Moors. Nature.

"I, Maxwell Angus Silas Anderson," I begin, my voice a hoarse rasp, "t-take y-you, Annabelle Charlotte Law-McKenzie, t-to be my wife."

Her hands tighten in mine as her lips part, a shuddering exhale escaping.

Blood rushes in my ears, and heat crawls up my neck. I feel the audience staring at me, their attentions foreboding and sinister, a monster waiting with bated breath for the moment to pounce and tear me into shreds.

"I promise t-to..." My breathing quickens, my lungs not working properly, and I see her beautiful face pinching at what she must be seeing on my face.

The beginning of a panic attack.

"I p-promise..." I try again, but the world swirls around me. I'm seasick on a sinking ship, staring helplessly at a wave threatening to capsize us at any second.

"You promise to be faithful to me," she whispers, her fingers gently kneading my hands, loosening the tight muscles. "Look at me, Maxwell, just look at me. It's only you and me."

She steps closer, far closer than respectable in such a conservative setting, and angles us so I'm facing her and the altar only, the audience out of sight.

Belle lifts her hand, her fingers trembling as if to touch me, but she stalls mid-air, uncertainty in her features.

Closing my eyes, I lean toward her, resting my face on her out-stretched palm, enjoying her warmth flowing to me, much like the night at the pier, before I succumbed to my desires and kissed her.

A soothing calm flows through my body after a few seconds of ripe tension and silence.

Opening my eyes, I clasp her free hand in mine and stare into those soulful, familiar eyes, the eyes I feel an undeniable kinship to, a deep yearning, a mysterious connection.

"I, Maxwell Angus Silas Anderson, take you, Annabelle Charlotte Law-McKenzie, to be my wife. I promise to be faithful to you." My thumb caresses the back of her hand and she shivers, her mouth parted, and a heat simmers in my veins.

"In good times and in bad, in sickness and in health, to *love you*," I murmur, my voice rough to my ears—and for a moment, I forget about my promise to her, about the curse, about why we are standing here today, and from how she sways on her feet, her eyes dilated as they lock on to mine, I'm guessing she feels the same. "And to honor you all the days of my life."

Her breath catches, a wet sheen appearing in her eyes. A clawing need digs into my chest and I swipe her tear away with my thumb. I want to ravish her, to push her away, to flay myself for causing the anguish on her elfin features.

Belle's lips tremble before she murmurs, "I, Annabelle Charlotte Law-McKenzie, take you, Maxwell Angus Silas Anderson, to be my husband. I promise to be faithful to you, in good times and in bad, in sickness and in health, to love you and to honor you all the days of my life."

Fierce possession fires through me and I tug her closer so she's a hairsbreadth away from me, half noticing the surprised gasps and murmurs from the clearly shocked audience.

The priest says something, and I barely notice Ryland walking up with the rings. I feel like I'm underwater; the words tumbling out of my mouth sounding muffled, the music of my heart and pulse overpowering everything else.

I only see her, my beautiful muse. Her large, familiar eyes, her soft, warm body, her heady scent of lilies and sweetness.

For the first time in my life, I don't notice the crowds. The monster lurking inside me is abated. She grounds me.

"I pronounce you husband and wife! You may kiss the bride."

In this moment, there is only one desperate need inside me.

To claim. To mark. To possess.

Mine. Mine. Mine.

Snaking one arm around her waist, I pull her closer, so that every inch of our bodies touch. My other hand grips her nape, my fingers curling into her thick, dark strands, and I tug.

Her lips part in an erotic moan and I bend her backward and kiss those pouty red lips.

The lips that have haunted me, that have ruined me for anyone else.

I forget about the curse, the crowds, about how I vow to never kiss her again, about the Grim Reaper hovering nearby all my life.

She melts under my embrace as I pillage her mouth, a mad pulse hammering inside my ear, a burgeoning fire gathering in my loins. She gasps as she feels my hard cock digging into her stomach and a desperate desire awakens and I slide my tongue inside her mouth.

Her fingers dig into my neck, the pain only adding to the erotic kiss, which is much more sexual and intense than anything I've ever experienced in my life.

Someone coughs in the background, but I barely notice. I taste, sample, and feast on her lips, needing her sweetness to survive. A shrill whistle and a few catcalls finally pierce the veil of lust and emotions.

Panting heavily, I haul her away from me, my hands dropping from her luscious body like I've been burned. My lungs heave in deep, rapid breaths, my muscles quaking with the need to haul her back to me and finish what we've started.

Her chest rises and falls quickly, her pale skin pink and mouth swollen, ravished by our kiss. She stares at me in shock.

And finally...finally, a thought enters my mind.

Fuck. She's so doomed.

CHAPTER 18

I've married a stranger.

The thought reverberates in my head as I stare at my *husband*, chatting with Charles, whom I've met a few times in the past, and his friends near the fully stocked bar during our dinner reception in the Hyacinth ballroom at The Orchid. True to form, he has declined a public speech and has told the wedding planner he's only staying for one hour.

Of that one hour, forty minutes have elapsed, and he hasn't spent a single one with me other than to eat a quick dinner in silence.

My heart twists as I stare at his handsome silhouette—dark hair carefully swept up, jaw clean shaven, his black silk tux fitted over his tall frame like a glove. He's playing with a large ring on his finger. I saw it earlier at the church and marveled at the craftsmanship. It must be a family heirloom.

He looks composed, every inch the frigid billionaire the press calls him, not the man who almost had a panic attack in the church. My heart squeezes at the memory—the fear in his eyes, the helplessness. I'm extremely glad I could help him out of it.

I sigh, missing the charming man from the race. In fact, if I weren't at the race myself, I'd question whether or not I had ever seen that side of him.

But then, there was that kiss, when the priest said he may kiss the bride.

The searing kiss that reminded me of that night at the race. The electricity sizzling through me when he ravaged my mouth, when he felt like the soulful man at the pier.

I miss Silas.

Snap out of it, Belle. This has never been anything more than an arranged marriage or a marriage of convenience. Get what you need from it and get out.

Squaring my shoulders, I tear my gaze away from him and scan the beautifully decorated ballroom befitting a royal wedding. Towering centerpieces of roses, crystal lamps and chandeliers light up the space in a soft glow.

Millie is waltzing with Ryland on the dance floor, the two love-birds acting much more like bride and groom than me and Maxwell. Grace and Steven are taking a picture in front of the feature wall covered with wisteria and millions of fairy lights.

It looks like a wedding among the literal stars.

"Congratulations, Belle," a quiet voice murmurs.

I turn toward Cole, who is dressed in a gray suit, his blond hair appearing gold in the dim lighting.

"Thank you. I'm glad you could come today."

"You look beautiful." His voice catches and pain flashes in his eyes.

I force out a smile and there must be something in my expression because he steps closer, far closer than any friend would in normal circumstances.

Leaning in, he whispers, his voice ardent in my ear, "I told myself I wasn't going to say anything, but then I saw you today and I've never seen you look so miserable before."

Blinking, I look away from his inquisitive stare, and he takes it as a sign to continue. "I've never told you this, but I've seen this look on the face of someone I cared about before."

My eyes snap back to his. He's never told me much about his family or love life before. "W-What happened to her?"

"Her husband killed her."

The four quiet words shake me to the core. "What?"

Cole gives me a sad smile. "I should've done more for her—she looked just like you after she got married, sad...miserable, like she made a mistake. All the red flags I ignored because she told me she was fine."

He takes my hand. "I'm not saying this to scare you, but I told myself then I wouldn't stand by and do nothing again. I-I'm sure you know I like you, Belle. You're beautiful, smart, funny, and kind. And if you were happy tonight, I'd keep my mouth shut and drown my sorrows at the open bar."

Wetting my lips, I try to wrench my hand from him, but his grip tightens. "Cole, this is inappro—"

"Hear me out. I don't know what's going on with you, but Belle, you deserve more. You deserve so much more than standing in the middle of your reception with tears in your eyes while your *husband* ignores you. You deserve more than *him*. Anyone but him." There's a hard edge to his voice I've never heard him use before.

My eyes burn at his words. How is it my feelings are obvious to others but not to the one man I can't stop thinking about?

Dammit.

"Just say the word. You don't even need to be with me, and I'll take you away. Anywhere you want. Belle...Belle, just look at me." Cole pulls my hand and I look up at him.

Shaking my head, I twist my lips in what I hope is a convincing smile. "We're only friends, and I appreciate your concern, but I'm fine. It's my wedding day and I'm happy."

"No. Bullshit. Your smile is fake, you don't look hap—"

"Get your hands off *my wife*."

His low, growly voice courses through my body like a caress. I feel his imposing presence behind me.

Cole's eyes harden and fill with a hatred so cold, I almost shiver. He stares at Maxwell, who's standing so close I can feel his body heat transferring to mine.

I tug my hand out of Cole's clutches and move back, just a smidgen, into the hard body of my husband.

Maxwell curls his arm possessively around my waist, his fingers kneading my stomach like a brand, and my core clenches at this blatant display of ownership.

Cole's eyes snag on the movement, his throat working as he swallows. A muscle in his jaw twitches, and he extends his hand. "I'm Cole Whelan, Belle's good friend from the shelter she volunteers at."

"Maxwell Anderson, *her husband*."

My useless heart skips a beat at his words.

Maxwell grips Cole's hand, the whites of his knuckles showing, and the men stare at each other for a few seconds, the tension so thick I could cut it with a knife.

An old man in a tux—I think he works with the family—steps up beside Maxwell and glares at Cole.

Cole's eyes narrow, his nostrils flaring, and he turns to me. "It appears I'm not welcome here. But Belle, remember what I said. You *deserve* more."

Without another word, he spins around and stalks away, the old man quickly following, clearly escorting him out of the ballroom.

Maxwell breathes heavily behind me and I finally turn and look at him. His slate eyes are almost obsidian and his lips twitch in barely restrained anger.

He leans in and seethes, "Is this how it's going to be between us, Belle? A few hours married and you're already cavorting with other men?"

Indignation chars my insides. "*Cavorting?* What are you, ancient? He's my friend, Maxwell. I'm allowed to have friends."

"He doesn't look at you like a friend."

"You're being an idiot."

"And you aren't holding up your end of our bargain. Or have you already forgotten our vows at the church," he sneers, his eyes cold.

I raise my hand and take a breath. "I won't stand here and let you accuse me of something I haven't done. If you have a problem with our arrangement, you never should've offered or agreed to it in the first place. So please, take your surly attitude and shove it!"

He steps toward me and I find myself backing up slowly until I hit the wall by the ballroom doors.

My pulse quickens as I lift my head up to look at him. I won't cower underneath him.

"Our deal is for one year and one heir minimum. I don't want to have to do a paternity test when you get pregnant."

My mouth drops open and I reach up to deliver a well-deserving slap.

He catches my hand in mid-air as he leans down, so close I can smell the mint in his breath mixing with the heady sandalwood of his cologne.

My traitorous body heats and my core clenches.

Maxwell's eyes sweep down my face to my chest and I curse myself for wearing a silk wedding gown, so thin I'm sure he's seeing my nipples saluting him.

"You're turned on," he rasps in my ear.

I shake my head. *No, no way.*

"So, this is how my wife likes it in the bedroom? To be dominated? Degraded?" Another slivery whisper and my pussy pulses...very much against my wishes.

My lips part as I stare into his dark eyes, his pupils blown. I finally find my voice. "In your dreams, Maxwell."

He chuckles, his low laughter holding no mirth. "You have no idea how depraved my dreams are." He leans in, and my eyes flutter shut. I can almost taste him—his passion, his darkness, the addiction that is Maxwell Anderson.

But the kiss never comes.

I open my eyes, finding his irises a chilly shade of gray once more, a pulse threatening to burst from the vein in his forehead.

He whispers in my ear, "Too bad. You'll never find out what my dreams are about. Because they'll *never* be for you."

"You bastard," I growl.

Spinning around, I take a few steps toward the lobby, eager to escape this domineering, insane man.

He grabs my wrist and whirls me around before letting go.

"I'm not done with you."

I snap back, "But I am, Maxwell. I. Am. Done. And now, I'm going to the bathroom to get away from my *deranged* husband, unless you want to control that behavior too. Now, may I leave your presence, *Your fucking Majesty?*"

I don't even feel guilty for cursing at this asshole. This devil in a tux.

He fumes, a muscle pulsing in his jaw as he steps back and mockingly sweeps his hand out and cocks his head. "Anything for my queen."

He stalks off and I watch him disappear into the crowd. I touch the aching spot on my chest, right under the locket nestled safely under the neckline of my gown.

What did I get myself into?

CHAPTER 19

THE AUTUMN CHILL WHIPS up a scattering of brown leaves as I walk up the main stone pathway of the Anderson estate to the grand double doors. I'm no stranger to money as my parents were wealthy before Dad's investment and embezzlement issues, but the Anderson wealth is on an entirely different level.

The carefully trimmed hedges in the gardens seem right at home, surrounding the only single standing mansion left in Manhattan, where every square foot costs an arm and a leg. We've just arrived at the estate after spending our wedding night in two separate suites at The Orchid.

Maxwell ended up drunk by the time the reception was over, surprising everyone because he stayed far longer than the one hour he promised.

I remember how I recoiled when he tossed me a key card to a guest suite.

He stumbled toward me, the stench of whiskey in his breath. His eyes were glazed, but he clearly noticed my reaction to his dismissive behavior.

"What? Does my wife want to consummate our marriage already? Want to start trying for a baby?" he slurred, but his eyes flared at his words, like he wouldn't mind acting on them.

"You're drunk off your ass, Maxwell."

"I can still pleasure you, you know." He dipped his nose in the crook of my neck and inhaled before pressing a soft kiss there.

I bit back a moan as my nerves lit up from his light touches. "Maxwell, stop." The refusal came out in a breathy whisper.

"Are you sure, my little muse?" he rasped at the tender spot on my neck. My heart fluttered at his nickname—such a sweet name. If only it were filled with love instead of derision. "The sooner you get pregnant, the faster you can l-leave me."

His voice caught at the last words, pain etched in every syllable.

It was enough for me to snap out of that strange trance, and I stepped back and looked at him.

His head was dipped down, his eyes refusing to meet mine.

"Maxwell, you aren't making any sense."

He chuckled at the floor, his head shaking.

I sighed. "You're drunk, why don't you rest and we'll talk tomorrow."

I pushed him toward his room, trying to fight the disappointment that I wouldn't be having a wedding night with my husband after all.

No, Belle. You don't want a wedding night with this asshole! You should be rejoicing right now.

The door beeped and opened and he stepped inside.

I turned toward the adjacent suite, but his voice stopped me.

"I won't fall in love with you, Belle. A-And don't fall for me."

His warning sounded ominous, and my chest ached at his words, images of my Silas still filling my mind. Somehow, I wondered if I was destined to fail at his demand?

Bang!

The trunk of the car closes, the sound shaking me from the unsettling memory. Silas barks in the background as he darts off to explore the expansive grounds—no doubt heaven compared to the SoHo apartment, where I couldn't let him run free for fear of him being discovered by the building manager.

As the driver retrieves my bags from the car, and Maxwell finishes a work call, I marvel at the massive structure—the white marble and tan limestone exterior, copper cornices oxidized into pale green, towering spires and soaring arches, all hallmarks of the Gothic architecture I've studied in college in an art and architecture core class.

The land it sits on must be at least an acre in size. If it weren't for the historical building designation and how powerful the Anderson family was, it probably would've been razed and rebuilt by some big developer.

Several crows lounge on the roof next to sculptures that are too far away for me to make out if they are angels or gargoyles. A curl of unease slithers down my back as their eyes seem to follow my every move.

I smell the scent of roses in the air, the cloying sweetness clinging to the moisture in the atmosphere, a desperate attempt by summer begging fall to stay away. Turning my attention to the rose garden, I notice the decaying flowers and a strange patch of soil that is barren. I shiver, a suffocating sadness gripping my throat. A gut feeling tells me to avoid that place.

The door opens, drawing my attention away from the garden, and out steps an elderly gentleman with kind eyes and a full head of white hair, dressed in *livery*, down to the bow tie and tailcoat. He's the man who escorted Cole away at the reception.

"Welcome to the Anderson Estate, ma'am. I'm Morris, your butler, and always at your service."

Smiling, I nod to him. "Thank you. Please call me Belle."

A middle-aged woman with a severe bob haircut steps to the side of Morris, her simple black dress swishing from the movement. She bows her head and dips her body into a small curtsy, and I almost startle in surprise. I feel like I've stepped into a *BBC* period drama.

"I'm Agnes, your housekeeper." Her lips are pressed tightly as she eyes me from top to bottom, and I can't help but frown at her cold introduction.

She motions to a blonde woman dressed in a similar black outfit behind her and says, "This is Melody. She'll be your lady's maid and we will assist you with any duties around the house and beyond."

I giggle before I can stop myself. "Wow, I didn't expect all of this, a lady's maid and everything. I'm perfectly capable of dressing myself, you know."

Melody laughs and says, "Just think of me as your personal assistant then."

Agnes shoots her a glare before turning toward me. "It is our honor to serve the Anderson family."

A foreboding tickle of dread wraps itself inside my chest.

Morris clarifies, "We have a small staff here on the estate, much smaller than it used to be in the bygone era, but our families pride ourselves on working for the Andersons for generations, even if it may seem outdated and stuck in the olden days, very much like myself."

He gives me a wink and I relax, the strange tension from earlier dissipating.

A waft of amber and sandalwood cologne alerts me to *him* and I feel a gentle press of his hand on the small of my back.

"I see you've met the staff. They're practically family. Mora, the chef, works here as well. She's Melody's mother. I'm sure she's puttering around the kitchen, crafting a welcome meal for the new mistress of the estate," Maxwell says.

He fishes out a black metal card and hands it to me. "I forgot to give this to you, but this has no spending limit and is for your use." His voice thickens as he adds, "What's mine is now yours."

My fingers grip the black Amex card—of course he has a black Amex card—but it's his words that have me losing my voice.

I really am married to the man.

We step into the grand foyer, and it's almost like stepping back in time as I marvel at the dark oak finishes and pristine black and white marble floors. After the door is shut, the space is bathed in darkness, lit up only by a few wrought iron sconces. I'm hit with a sense of comfort and home, even though I've never been here before.

"Morris, I'll be in the study if you need me. Please set Belle up in the Gardenia suite as we discussed." Maxwell disappears down the corridor.

"I'll get things ready," Agnes murmurs, leaving with Melody in tow, but not before shooting me a sharp glance.

The earlier unease makes a resurgence and I rub the goosebumps on my arms as I await Morris's instructions.

The butler smiles at me, his eyes crinkling. He strides down the main hallway and I hasten my steps to follow him. For an elderly man in his seventies or eighties, he walks quickly, and I have a feeling he'd be even faster if it weren't for the limp in his right leg.

"I'm sure Sir Maxwell will give you a tour later, but I can give you highlights." We make a right into a grand entrance hall that's at least two stories high, featuring a vaulted ceiling, ornate paneling, all in the dark wood of the foyer.

"Wow." I gasp. This place is a museum frozen in time.

A massive crystal chandelier hangs from the ceiling, illuminating a grand staircase with intricately carved railings and a spectacular Persian runner that's probably an art piece in and of itself.

The hall glows from the light let in by the stained-glass windows, adding a touch of eerie beauty to the space.

"The estate was built in 1850 but remodeled in the 1860s. It has withstood The Civil War, two world wars, hurricanes, and other natural disasters. The family has outfitted the building with modern amenities—electricity, plumbing, but mostly, they've kept the original decor. We're quite lucky—much of the furnishings here are well preserved and intact."

I follow Morris up to the third floor and turn left, my lungs huffing out rapid breaths. I clearly need to exercise more because Morris looks like he hasn't broken a sweat. Curiously, his limp also seems to have disappeared.

"There are fifty-two rooms, four stories, and two wings. The first floor is public space, with a living room, grand ballroom, two sitting rooms, dining room, indoor theater, and galleries. The second floor houses the gym, an indoor swimming pool, guest quarters, and a library."

"That's a city in and of itself."

He nods. "This floor, the third floor, is the master and mistress's rooms and a few more guest rooms, including the Gardenia suite Sir Maxwell mentioned."

"Sir Maxwell?"

"He has asked us not to call him by his honorifics, which would be 'my lord' for him with his marquessate and 'His Grace' for Sir Linus because of his dukedom." Morris clears his throat and continues, "The fourth floor houses a study, music room, studios, and an indoor conservatory. There's an abandoned garden on the roof, but it's in disrepair, so no one really goes there. This side is the east wing, which is the master's side of the suites and the other side," he motions to the darkened corridors on the right of the staircase, "is the west wing. It's currently not in used but historically features the mistress's set of rooms."

I blow out a breath, my eyes trying not to bug out from this lavish overview of my new home. Growing up, my parents only liked new, new, new—everything new, from turnkey apartments to brand-new appliances and gadgets.

The Anderson Estate is the complete opposite of it. I feel like the air I'm breathing in is steeped in history, so much history I don't even know how to understand it all.

And now I'm going to be the mistress of this house?

It's unfathomable.

Morris leads me down the corridor to the second door on the right. He opens it and gestures inside. "This is your suite. Please settle in. Sir Maxwell had it redone two weeks ago. I hope you like it. Agnes and Melody will come find you before dinner."

He motions to a small panel with a row of buttons and a tiny speaker by the door. "Each room has an intercom you can press. It connects to our phones and allows you to contact us at any time."

"Thank you." I smile, and he shuts the door behind him.

The drapes are drawn closed so only a sliver of daylight is seeping in. I flick on a light switch and gasp at what I see.

The most beautiful shade of shimmering teal wallpaper greets me, the crystal pendant light illuminating the delicate floral patterns, clearly hand-painted in silver, gold, and rose gold.

My hand flies to the locket he gave me, the one I can't bear to take off. The design on the wallpaper is so similar to the carving on the locket—the same coloring, similar flowers and golden touches.

The same uncanny feeling of déjà vu hits me in the face and I pull in a rapid breath to steel my nerves.

Old houses, romantic notions—reading too many gothic novels.

Blowing out an exhale, I look around, noting a platform king-sized bed, an elegant white rug and bedspread, two beautiful armchairs by the bay windows, and a small coffee table, also in the same alluring shade of teal.

Atrovirens.

He decorated the entire room in a palate of atrovirens, my favorite color.

My breath flutters past my lips as I admire the artwork hung on the walls—bright colorful prints and sharp lines, all unmistakable works of Frida Kahlo.

He remembered—he remembered everything I told him that night.

The thought sends a sharp current to my chest, and my heart skips a beat.

A bouquet of lilies sits atop the mirrored nightstand and on it there's a note.

BELLE,

I HOPE YOU ENJOY THIS ROOM. MAYBE THIS ARRANGEMENT ISN'T THE ADVENTURE YOU'VE BEEN SEEKING, BUT I HOPE YOU GET WHAT YOU'RE LOOKING FOR.

MAXWELL

My fingers clutch the note tightly as I reread his words. Who is this man—one who seems so cold and sensitive at the same time?

Creeeak. Seconds later, a ghostly moan echoes outside my door.

I startle at the noise, my pulse roaring in my ears, and I carefully open the door to peer outside.

There's no one there.

It's an old house and don't they say old houses settle? I shake myself at my silliness.

Just as I close the door, a hand snakes in and blocks it from closing fully.

I let out a shriek, leaping a back few steps before I hear a knock.

"Ms. Belle, I've brought you refreshments." Agnes appears in my room a moment later with a tray, and I let out a sigh of relief.

I'm such a wuss.

Straightening up, I smooth my damp palms over my linen dress. "Thank you. Please set it over there." I motion to the small coffee table by the windows.

She nods and keeps her eyes averted as she sets the drinks down and hurries toward the door. I frown. I may not be a mind reader, but this woman doesn't like me. I'm sure of it.

"Agnes?"

She stops and turns toward me reluctantly. "Yes, ma'am?"

"Belle, please. Ma'am makes me feel old." I let out a few chuckles, but she doesn't smile...not one bit.

After clearing my throat, I ask, "Was it you just now out there? I heard a loud creak and someone moaning before you came in. I wasn't aware there were guests here."

Agnes looks at me, as if debating how to respond. I fight the impulse to fidget under her intense scrutiny.

"Ms. Belle, that wasn't me before, but," her voice is soft and foreboding, and I can't help but shiver, "I may be speaking out of turn, but a house and a family this old are bound to have ghosts and...unwanted visitors."

Cold sweat forms on my upper lip as she leans toward me and whispers, "I'd be careful if I were you...and not go asking questions you may not want the answers to."

With that, she leaves the room and shuts the door quietly behind her. The beating in my chest intensifies and an icy chill sweeps over me. Stories of curses and the mysteries of the family float to the forefront.

What's going on in this place?

CHAPTER 20

IT'S WRONG. IT'S ALL wrong.

I set the paintbrush down on the easel and stare at my latest work, the painting rendered from the sketch I drew at Lake Superior months ago.

The frigid waters, white-tipped waves crashing against the hard rocks, the lighthouse, a lone sentinel warning sailors and lost souls of the rugged terrain. Every stroke, every swipe of color is infused with a piece of my soul. It captures the haunted loneliness, the restlessness I felt that day.

And yet, something is still missing, a riddle I can't solve, but the answer feels just within reach. I'm thrown back to my dreams last night.

I had my arms wrapped around the mystery woman whose face I still couldn't see, the one who was painting the canals of Venice. In this dream, she was running through the rose garden before the scene shifted.

Moonlight illuminated the canvas in front of her, the scent of roses lingering in the air.

She laughed, her voice blurry, but I remembered the way my heart skipped a beat.

"Someday, I'll learn to paint...so I can paint you," I whispered before pressing a kiss to her dark hair.

I woke up with heartache in my chest. *Fucking dreams.*

Puccini's "O mio babbino caro" plays from the phonograph, the song made famous by the classic movie, *A Room with a View*, from the eighties—a movie both my grandfather and Mom loved when they were still alive.

Rolling out my tight shoulders, I stare at the art I've spent the last hour on after a dreary day of meetings at Fleur, after which I'd made the mistake of reviewing news articles reporting the latest upheaval over my sudden marriage. Word has leaked that I drank too much at the reception and now the narrative has turned me into an unstable man.

Fuck. I was just trying to forget the attraction I felt toward *my wife*.

Our stock has marginally improved, but the public definitely isn't buying the image of a family man yet.

Twisting my heirloom ring on my finger, I regard the canvas.

The strokes are too heavy, the colors too muted. I frown. *This is what you get for not painting what your muse is asking you to paint.* It's still the best work I've done this year, and I don't want to contemplate why that is the case.

My fingers twitch, another impulse to get a new canvas and start on it...the one thing I want to paint but couldn't bring myself to.

A full portrait of Belle in the rose garden.

Gritting my teeth, I close my eyes, listening to the heartbreaking melody. I don't speak Italian, but there's something about art and music that transcend languages and touch the soul.

"Aarroooooo!"

The hurried sounds of paws darting down the corridor interrupt my thoughts, followed by, "Silas! Naughty dog! You aren't supposed to pee on the rug! You have an acre of gardens and grass to pee on and you decided to do it here. Come back here!" Belle's dulcet voice cuts through the gloom and I hear her sprinting down the hallway.

More barking is followed by a few yips and halting footsteps. I guess she caught Silas.

My lips twitch as amusement sifts through me.

Fuck. She named the damn dog Silas.

I can imagine her lips pursing as she enacts her petty revenge by naming the one-eyed terror after me. The dog, who has been a menace, not only bares his teeth whenever I talk to his mistress, but has also been scratching at the doors, stealing food from the kitchen, much to Mora's dismay, and wreaking havoc in the mansion.

But he makes her happy. I see it in her smile as she ruffles his fur. I hear it in her voice when she talks to him at night, saying God knows what as he howls in reply.

He also gets to curl up in bed with her, enjoy her sweet kisses, and be the sole object of her affections.

And damn if I'm jealous of a dog.

I guess I deserve it. For being a complete asshole to her for the past month she's been in residence. I've mostly stayed away from her. During the day, I'm sequestered in the study while she's at work, and in the evenings, I usually hang out at The Orchid with my siblings and friends or spend my time in the studio.

We haven't consummated the marriage—the whole fucking purpose of this arrangement—to beget heirs. Because every time I think about it, my cock hardens to a point of bursting like a horny teenager who can't get enough. I imagine whispering dirty words in her ear as I thrust into her wet heat, listen to her moans as I fuck orgasm upon orgasm out of her.

Fuck. There's no way I'll be able to control myself with her.

So, despite having the bluest balls in the history of mankind, I've stayed far away until I can figure out what to do. But my body is attuned to her, my ears perking up when she speaks, my eyes seeking her out whenever I walk into a room, and I have to remind myself to breathe and look away when she directs one of her smiles at me.

Because I can't fall for her. To protect her, I have to stay away; I have to make her hate me.

More images of Sydney's bluish skin, glassy eyes, her stiff body on the sand rise to the forefront of my mind, and a heaviness sits atop my chest.

I have to stay away. *So why the fuck did you marry her then, you asshole?*

Because the thought of her being with another man has me seeing red.

"Silas, if you don't behave, Agnes will have my ass and yours. Now, I'm going to scrub out your mess before she sees it," she whispers.

The dog whines, like he understands his mistake.

Only Belle would be afraid of the housekeeper who works *for* her. Only she would go out of her way to make sure she—or in this case, her dog—doesn't inconvenience others.

Because she's kind that way. Just like how she was as Anna all those months ago.

It feels like a lifetime ago.

Her footsteps slow and pause in front of the closed door of my studio. I hold my breath. *Knock on it. Come in.*

A few seconds pass by, my ears straining to listen to her movements above the soprano's voice.

"Let's not disturb him," she murmurs, no doubt to Silas, and she walks away.

Disappointment crests inside me and I fight every urge to throw open the door and chase after her, to be in the presence of her radiance and joy.

But I don't. *Ugh.* I want to bash my head against the wall.

Knock. Knock.

My heart skips several beats. *Did she come back?*

"Come in."

The door opens and the hope bubbling in my chest deflates when I see Morris striding in. Of course it's not her. *Why would she want to spend time with you, asshole?*

"Sir, I was wondering if you need anything from me before I head out." Morris rubs his leg again. I wish he'd retire and enjoy his remaining years instead of working so hard.

"I'm fine, Morris. Thanks for asking," I reply. "I ordered a bouquet of roses—white ones, her favorite, like you told me before. They should be here for you to take to the cemetery."

Something flashes in his eyes and he looks away before I can figure out what it is. "Thank you, sir, for remembering. Ruth would've loved you if she were here."

"You're welcome. I wish I had met your sister too."

What more is there to say to someone grieving? Even if it's been years, the event happened long before I was born. But then again, there's no timeline for mourning. And I wouldn't know what I'd do if one of my siblings was brutally murdered with the killer still at large.

Morris nods before leaving and heading to his family's burial plot on the anniversary of his sister's death.

My chest aches for the old man. We're all that he has left—the closest thing to family.

Perhaps I'm unlucky to live a life with death hanging over me, a curse banishing me into a lifetime of loneliness without loving another woman, but at least I have my family.

And her.

Even if I need to keep my distance for her sake.

Things could be a lot worse.

CHAPTER 21

I WAKE UP WITH a start, my hair stuck to my sweaty forehead. I was chasing him, but he was far away and sobbing, hunched over an easel in the rose garden.

"Why can't I draw you?" he cried repeatedly.

What? Hazy, unsettling images sift through my mind. My heart pounds and I rub the soreness there. I must've fallen asleep while I was working. Ever since I moved here, I've been having the strangest dreams, with the restlessness inside me growing.

My stomach growls as I stare at the piles of paper on my bed and on the floor—designs I'm sure the asshole Gordon would reject and make fun of.

How could he not? He has tasked me with the impossible—to create a fall and winter collection giving cozy, warm vibes but can't have black, brown, grays, wool, *sleeves*, and the fabrics used have to include linen and taffeta.

"That asshole," I curse under my breath as I step on one of my drawings on the way to the door.

I really need to find a place for my work studio. Somewhere other than the bedroom.

Quietly, I traipse down the dark corridor, the floorboards creaking and groaning beneath my steps. The door to Maxwell's master suite across the hall is closed.

It's like we are roommates instead of husband and wife.

But a roommate's heart doesn't pound whenever she's in his presence, her ears don't perk up whenever she hears his voice.

A roommate wouldn't wish to share a simple pastrami and rye with a bad boy with soulful eyes on a quiet night.

Eerie whispers slither down the halls, the hollow sounds writhing then vanishing, but I've been told they are just air coming out of the vents. I don't know if I'll ever be used to the weird noises and constantly feeling like I have invisible company.

My stomach grumbles again, and I quickly make my way to the kitchen on the first floor. Mora told me in the olden days, the kitchen was in the basement where the staff lived as well, but the family has since moved the kitchen upstairs, with downstairs functioning as an extra cooking space if needed.

I pad across the cool marble floors, not knowing why I'm sneaking around when I'm the mistress of the house. My fingers brush the black marble countertops before opening one of the two stainless steel refrigerators.

What am I going to eat? God knows I can't cook to save my life. Maybe I'll have some fru—

"What are you doing here so late at night?"

"Holy shit!" I yelp. "Are you a ghost or something? Warn a girl next time. You scared the crap out of me!" I close the door.

Maxwell chuckles as he turns on the under-cabinetry lights, illuminating the space in a soft glow.

My heart stalls in my throat.

He's half naked, wearing only an opened flannel shirt and a low-slung pair of gray sweatpants, his hair wet and haphazardly raked over his head like he just got out of a shower.

I gulp, diverting my eyes away from him before I do something stupid like ogle and drool over the well-defined muscles.

"You scare easily."

"Anyone would if someone snuck up on you at one a.m."

"Afraid of a little street race, skydiving," he ticks off his fingers, "strange noises in the hallway."

I frown. "Agnes told you that, didn't she?" I don't want to admit this because I try to find the good in everyone, but I'm starting to dislike her.

Maxwell huffs out a breath, a rare smile on his lips. My heart pounds at the sight, the lightness I haven't seen from him since that night at the race.

"I have ears. I don't need her to tell me anything. Last week, you screeched so loudly because the wind rattled the windows, I could hear you all the way from the study."

"I was in my zone and I swear that wasn't the wind!"

I was marveling at the gorgeous two-story library, with its ornate coffered ceilings featuring intricate medallions, the Tiffany floor lamps and vintage light fixtures on the reading tables. The inner nerd in me was jumping with joy at the towering bookshelves filled to the brim with books.

I planned to curl up by the roaring fireplace in the large armchair with a book as the winds howled outside. There was something especially cozy about being in a warm environment while nature threw a tantrum around you.

But just as I sat down and opened a tome—an original, first edition of Regency era fashions—

Bam! Bam! Bam!

Something slammed against the glass repeatedly.

I shrieked, turning toward the windows as terror seized me. A man in a dark mask stared back at me.

I screamed. Loudly.

Morris rushed in minutes later and when I told him what happened, he turned on the yard lights to investigate.

But no one was there.

"It must've been the wind," Morris murmured.

"It wasn't! I swear!" I let out a shuddering breath. *Was it really just the wind?* "Morris... Can I ask you something?"

The old butler smiled and nodded.

"Is the curse real?"

The smile slipped off his face. He rasped, "Generations of Andersons lived in these halls. And yes, there have been tragedies...multiple accidents and misfortunes leading up to the deaths of several Anderson women."

My blood froze in my veins and my fear had to have shone on my face because he added, "I'm an old man and I've found that humans are eviler than the supernatural. And it's best not to believe in rumors. After all, curses and ghosts can't be real, right?"

With that cryptic, unsettling message, he left the library.

I shiver at the memory and narrow my eyes at my husband. "It was scary."

"Right. It's the boogeyman out to get you." Maxwell smirks as he steps toward me, completely oblivious to his state of undress.

"I swear, I saw a person in a mask."

"Someone standing out in the dark?" He cocks a brow. "Morris told me your worries." He walks over and I shift to the side as he grabs a few items from the fridge.

"We have state-of-the-art security systems installed. I didn't see anything on the tape when I reviewed it," he murmurs as he hovers over a cutting board and begins slicing the items he got out of the fridge moments ago. "There was no one there."

He checked on it for me? The thought pleases me. I shake my head to dispel the jitteriness swimming in my gut, I focus my attention back on him.

His movements are sure and practiced, and my core clenches involuntarily. There's something really sexy about a man who knows his way around a kitchen.

Maxwell pauses and turns to face me, his face severe and half-cast in shadows. "Belle, you're one hundred percent safe here. I'd *never* let anything happen to you."

My pulse reverberates in my ears.

I believe him. Somehow, I know this man will hurt himself before he lets me get in harm's way.

"G-Good." I flash him a tentative smile even though butterflies have taken flight in my stomach.

Ding.

He pauses his motions and wipes his hand on a towel before pulling out his phone from his sweatpants.

"Shit." He scowls.

"What's wrong?"

He glances at me before turning his attention back to his food prep. "They want me to speak at the gala."

"The one in January here?" *The one I'm hosting? It'd be nice if people loop me in.*

He nods.

"Who's they?"

"A PR think tank out on the west coast. They work closely with Lana on all things press related."

Before we got married, Maxwell sent me an email saying the gala I'm overseeing is a charity ball benefiting depression and anxiety research. It'll also serve as a press event to open the doors to the elusive Anderson family, so to speak, which the PR team hopes will ease the public and investors' recent worries over Fleur.

"You don't want to speak at the gala."

It isn't a question, but more of an observation. I remember how difficult it was for him to say the wedding vows at church. The haunted look in his eyes, which only lessened once I turned him away from the crowds. Then there were the articles I found about his disastrous press conference when I was doing my research on him.

The thumping of the knife hitting the cutting board ratchets up in aggression and his jaw clenches.

"No. But I have to. For the company. There have been too many changes in management in the last few years. Then I fucked it up at the press conference." And the wedding reception, but we both don't mention that.

He grunts and hangs his head low.

"I need to fix this. To fix what I broke." He grabs the towel and whips it against the counter. "*Fucking pathetic.* It's only a fucking speech."

I step closer, my heart tugging at the anguish and frustration in his voice. "But you didn't break anything."

Gnawing my lip, I take in his tense frame, wondering if I should continue. "Few people know this, but my grandpa had anxiety. Severe anxiety. His was different than yours, but I recognize the signs. His mind wouldn't turn off about his worries—work, family, how the next collection would do. Sometimes, he'd lock himself in his studio and not see anyone."

Maxwell stills and silence fills the air. I wonder if I overspoke.

"What did he do?"

Sliding my hand over his back, I rub reassuring circles over his bunched muscles. "He'd try to tough it out and every time he came out of the room, he'd put on a smile and tell me everything was fine. But I knew that wasn't true until one time when I was sixteen."

I swallow, thinking back to the day that changed everything for me.

"I barged into his studio and found him curled up on the floor, sweat plastering his forehead. He was breathing into a paper bag. He'd had a panic attack."

My eyes tear up. "He started crying when he saw me. Loud sobbing. He told me he thought he was useless for being a mess. And it couldn't be farther from the truth. This was the man I looked up to my entire life. The man who created things from his imagination. The man who spent the most time with me. It was then when I realized how much Grandpa loved his company and how much beauty—his groundbreaking designs—came out of such a dark place." I swallow before letting out a shaky exhale.

"When he died a few months later, I promised myself I'd take care of his legacy, to make sure the beauty continues."

I clutch Maxwell's shoulder, but he still refuses to look at me. It's like he's ashamed. "Anxiety and panic attacks aren't weaknesses. They're just chemical imbalances and neurons misfiring and whatnot. Standing up and trying again is a sign of strength. Not many people can do that. Be strong enough to keep trying."

He trembles under my touch.

"It's easy to paddle in the water when the seas are calm. But to push through and survive when there's a storm? That's true power. There's help out there, and I'll be with you every step of the way."

A muscle twitches in his jaw as his eyes rove hungrily over my face. "T-Thank you," he whispers.

My skin heats from his intense gaze and in this moment, I see Silas, the man from the race. He's inside him, hiding from the public.

But don't hide from me.

"Have you considered getting help?" I ask.

His eyes harden and he turns away from me. "I can do this on my own. It's only a fucking speech." He goes back to slicing his ingredients before he stacks them together.

I don't press him. I know he needs the space to figure this out for himself.

"I'll help you practice then." I walk back to the refrigerator, my stomach grumbling again. *Darn it, I still haven't gotten my snack.* I mull over my options.

"That soup looks good. Ohhh, there's some deli meat. Maybe I can make a sandwich. Those blueberries are *huge*," I mutter.

He chuckles.

"Look at you scrunching your face like you're making a decision of a lifetime."

Spinning around, I narrow my eyes at him. The fridge door slams shut behind me. "It's one in the morning! If I eat whatever I want, I'll have heartburn later, not to mention what that'll do to my waistline." I point to my stomach for emphasis.

"You're perfect," he rasps, his eyes flashing before softening.

My pulse quickens, and the air thickens between us.

"Year of yeses, no? A new attitude toward life." He smirks. "Live life on the edge, grab the bull by the horns. Eat whatever you want at one a.m."

Slowly, he prowls toward me with an arrogant swagger, the tensed man from moments ago nowhere to be seen.

"What are you doing?" I whisper. He's standing a few inches away from me.

Maxwell's smile disappears as his eyes rove over my face, then my neck, and slowly rakes down my body. I'm breathing hard and know the silk pajama camisole and shorts set does little to cover my body.

The tension swells in the room as all my nerve endings awaken for this virile man, my fingers twitching with the need to touch him, to feel those hard abs and pecs, to bury my face in the crook of his neck and inhale his comforting scent of amber and sandalwood.

Unable to stop myself, I place my palm on his chest. He flinches and groans at my touch, and I feel an aching need pulsing between my legs. My hands slide underneath the flannel, fingers tracing his defined muscles until they reach his side.

His right side that's covered in thick ropes of scars.

My eyes fly to his face in shock, noticing a pained expression on his features, his lips tight.

"What happened?"

"A boar attack when I was in high school... Ryland and I were hunting and we disturbed the beast by accident. I pushed him away and got mauled instead. Almost didn't make it."

He shrugs as he stares at me with those intense gray pools. "The scars cover half my body. They're flaws. Ugly."

His words are light, but I sense the agony behind them.

Wordlessly, my fingers trace the raised edges, some deeper than others, the ropes of scars twisting over his skin like art, a tapestry of untold pain.

How it must have hurt.

My eyes prickle as my hand kneads the tensed muscles under the puckered skin. "Not flaws, Maxwell. They're one-of-a-kind art on a canvas. They tell me the story of someone who risked his life to save his loved one. Someone who isn't afraid of sacrifice."

I don't know what comes over me, but I lean in and press my lips over the scar closest to his pecs, and he hisses.

He reaches out and digs his hands on my shoulders, holding me close and urging me to continue, a tortured groan slipping out of his lips as I press one soft kiss after another.

"They're beautiful." I breathe in his scent, a sultry heat swirling inside me.

Maxwell lets out another shuddering exhale before dragging me up his body and pinning me against the stainless steel fridge door.

"What are you doing to me?" he murmurs, his hand cupping my face, his thumb sliding over the sensitive area where my ear meets my neck. I let out a whimper.

"What do you want from me?" He leans down as my eyes flutter shut and drags his nose along the side of my neck.

I want you. All of you.

I moan, wetness gathering between my legs. I need more. I need everything.

Tilting my head back, I bare my neck to him, my hands clutching the rippling muscles of his back. He trails heated kisses down my throat, his mouth laving at the pulse points, and I let out a mewl, my fingers digging into his muscles.

Everything is so sensitive, so achy, so taut.

Growling, he hoists me up and palms my ass, and I wrap my legs around him.

"Fuck, fuck, fuck," he mutters.

He nips my clavicles, his hands digging into my ass cheeks, but the pain only adds to the erotic sensations coursing through me.

I claw at his flannel shirt, wanting to feel every inch of his hot body pressed against mine. He sets me on the countertop and slides out of the flannel, baring all his muscles in their full glory.

My mouth waters at every chiseled edge, every hard ripple, the leashed power inside him.

"Yes," I whisper, raking my nails over every indentation, feeling his body harden and tremor at my touch.

He buries his face in my chest, his lips trailing over the sensitive skin of my cleavage as his hand slides one strap off my shoulders.

My breasts are heavy and swollen, nipples aching for him to touch them, to taste them. But I need his mouth on mine more. I need to taste him again, to kiss those addictive lips of his.

I grip his hair and drag his head up toward my lips. He lets out a pleasurable hiss, our labored breaths an erotic symphony in the dim room.

Maxwell pins my hands to the cabinets behind me, his eyes glazed with madness and lust as they snare on my parted lips.

Kiss me, I command silently.

I need him so, so much.

He stands as still as a statue, hovering over me, making me feel so small and yet so safe. But he doesn't move.

Impatiently, I shrug out of his hold and cradle his face to draw him toward me.

"Kiss me," I say aloud, feeling his breath fanning my lips.

He freezes, then hauls himself off me before raking his hand over his mussed hair.

"Fuck!"

His eyes are a wild, turbulent storm, and he shakes his head in anger—at himself, at me, I don't know.

"I can't, Belle. I can't. It's for your own good."

What?

Without another word, he spins around and stalks out of the kitchen.

My pulse riots inside my veins as the dull pain appears in my chest, similar to the mysterious ache that pulses through me whenever I open the locket around my neck and read its heartfelt inscription.

A barrage of emotions hit me at once—anger, sadness, the pain of rejection. I don't understand him, this frigid king who burns hotter than the stars in the nighttime skies.

Before I leave the kitchen, I look at the counter, and my heart hiccups.

On it is a perfectly plated sandwich—a pastrami on rye.

CHAPTER 22

THE FLAMES GIVE OFF a scorching heat in the traditional brick wood-burning oven as Mora bustles around the kitchen in the dim basement. Morris is whistling under his breath as he tidies up some items in the pantry. I asked him if he needed help, but he shooed me away.

"If it weren't for this beauty, you wouldn't be able to pay me to come down here," Mora mutters, referring to the oven, her blond hair fashioned into a bun at her nape.

She's in her mid-fifties and has worked at the estate for the last thirty years, ever since her predecessor passed away from a heart attack.

I chuckle before replying, "It is a bit creepy, huh?"

The traditional kitchen is well maintained, with simple gray walls, yellowed with age, well-used wooden cabinetry and prep island, and dark, vintage cast-iron stove and ovens, complete with a concealed grate.

A sole small window lets in the barest amount of dim daylight from the outside, the sun having long disappeared behind the clouds as the evening creeps in.

"Mom makes me come with her every time she uses the ovens down here." Melody snickers as she hovers over her notepad on the counter.

We are meeting here to start the gala planning—after all, Melody used to work for a large corporation as their event planner, so it makes sense for her to help lead the charge with the charity gala.

It's also a good distraction from the almost kiss that's replayed itself in my mind for the last two weeks since the night I bumped into Maxwell in the kitchen.

"There's nothing wrong with admitting you need company," Mora huffs and mock glares at her daughter, but her eyes shine with warmth.

My heart pinches at the obvious affection between the mother and daughter, wishing I had the same relationship with my mom.

But it doesn't matter. There's no use in pining over the past. I'm going to focus on the future—having children of my own so I can love them the way I wanted to be loved when I was growing up. This is why I'm doing this—this marriage.

But you can't have kids unless he sleeps with you, Belle.

I groan inwardly—part of me wants to jump his bones and another part of me wants to strangle him. This maddening, exasperating man.

A strange howl whispers down the corridor, followed by the rumble of doors banging and creaking against the hinges. I shudder, the hairs on my forearms rising. *It's just the air circulating from the outside.*

Mora says, "Tell me about it. I'm not one to believe in ghosts and curses until I started working here."

Her words give me pause.

I lean over the wooden counter and ask, "Do you believe it? The curse?"

Mora chooses her words carefully. "I think science can't explain everything in this world and this family has had a very tragic history." She strains a smile as she kneads the dough for the flatbread she's making for tonight's dinner. "But it's easy to blame misfortunes on a curse or the supernatural."

Her words make sense, but her tone sounds unsure.

"Why are you going about spreading rumors, Mora?" Agnes sweeps in and levels a scathing glare at the chef. The two women have a silent standoff before Agnes hands Mora a bag of flour.

"Belle is the mistress, and she has the right to ask."

"It's better not to know sometimes." Agnes shoots a glacial look my way. "Let the ghosts rest where they lie, Ms. Belle."

Just as I'm about to ask her to stop being so difficult to talk to, her phone beeps. She retrieves it and her face pales.

"Is it Andrew?" Mora mutters, her face darkening. I look at her for clarification and she adds, "Her husband."

"Is everything oka—"

"I'm fine, ma'am. It's taken care of." Agnes stomps off, her feet flying up the steps.

I turn my attention to Mora and Melody. They're shaking their heads, pity shining clearly in their eyes. "What's going on with her?"

"Don't mind the old grouch. She's been this way for as long as I remember. She used to be good friends with Ms. Julianna, Sir Linus's wife, but ever since she passed away, she's been like this," Mora answers.

Melody leans in and whispers, "Her husband is a hardcore gambler. And not a good one too. Always owes people money, and Agnes is constantly worried about how to pay them back. These loan sharks aren't kidding, you know?"

I wince, feeling bad for the poor woman. Maybe she has every reason to look pissed off all the time then.

"Anyway, about the curse, I think there's something fishy going on. Women have been dying in this household since the eighteen hundreds. I mean, that can't only be bad luck." Melody plops a cherry into her mouth as she scribbles more notes about the gala on her notepad—the floor plans, the food options we discussed.

"The eighteen hundreds?"

"Melody!" Mora glares at her daughter. "You heard what Agnes said. Don't spread more rumors."

"It's not a rumor if it's the truth. You can pretend nothing fishy is going on by not talking about it, but the facts are there. A lot of women died within these walls, all at a young age."

Acid churns inside my stomach as I take in her fervent expression. I've done some research on the Andersons and haven't noticed anything unusual, but then again, they are a private family with significant influence on the press.

"You're scaring Ms. Belle." Morris steps back into the room and gives me a tight smile.

"It's okay, I have been curious about the history. Melody, tell me more."

Melody nods. "I grew up here, so I've heard the stories—things the family doesn't share with the public. Have you been to the galleries yet?"

I shake my head. It's on my to-do list today, to finally visit the galleries on the first floor and to poke around the closed west wing. Those are the mistress's set of rooms, after all. There are so many rooms in this place, it'll probably take me another month to see them all.

"Want me to show you, give you a guided tour?"

I nod, and she gets up from her seat and leads me to the stairwell. I turn back to say goodbye to Mora and Morris, only to find the butler's eyes pinned on me, his brows furrowed with concern. My confusion must have shown on my face because he quickly smiles, but it seems forced somehow.

Melody takes me back upstairs, and we make a left at the hallway underneath the grand staircase.

"This door on the left is the art gallery—you know, Rembrandts and Monets."

I'm so coming back here later. I can hardly contain my excitement.

"We're going here instead—the family gallery." She opens an ornate door on the right and flicks on the light.

My mouth drops open at the opulence in the room. There's a vintage lavender tufted sofa, the intricate wood carvings gleaming under the early evening light filtering in from the large lattice windows.

But what has me most in awe are the rows and rows of family portraits lining the three walls of the room not occupied by the windows.

Melody strides toward a photograph on the nearest wall and points to it. "This is a family portrait taken shortly before Sir Maxwell's mother passed away."

I peer at the photograph of a beaming family standing in front of the rose garden, the garden I still can't bring myself to visit. It just feels too heavy.

A tall, striking man with dark hair, clearly a younger Linus, has his arm around a beautiful woman with warm eyes and a bright smile, who is staring at her husband with clear affection. She's wearing a glittering key pendant around her neck and holding a baby in her arms.

In front of them are four boys, the dark-haired twins—Maxwell and Ryland, and while they looked more similar back then, I can still tell who is who, with Maxwell being the serious child standing tall, his lips quirked into a half-smile, baring the dimple on his cheek, and Ryland laughing as he nudges his brother on the side. Next to them is Rex, who's smirking and pulling Ethan's hair, with Ethan trying to push his older brother away, all the while sucking his thumb.

"They look so happy," I murmur, smiling at the younger Maxwell while wanting to go back in time and tickle him or something—to do anything to make him laugh like Ryland in the photo.

"They were, but Ms. Julianna passed away a month later, and from what Mom told me, the house was quiet ever since."

"How did she die?"

"She fell down the stairs and broke her neck. They said it was because Rex was playing with his marbles and didn't clean up and she slipped."

"How awful!"

"It really is. And what's worse, Rex found her body."

I gasp in horror at the image of a young boy finding his dead mother, and Melody sadly shakes her head.

"You see that patch of soil on the side of the photo? How no roses grow on it?"

I squint. She is right—there is a section of the rose garden that is bare, a large clump of dark soil. *It's the same plot of barren soil I noticed when I first arrived here.*

"They said that nothing ever grows there—that it's a sign of the curse. No life can survive in that spot. No one knows why."

Goosebumps form on my arms as I stare at the area for a few more seconds, a niggling sensation in my mind—like a thought trying and failing to burst through.

Calm down, Belle. There has to be a reasonable explanation. Maybe the pH is off or something.

She moves on to another portrait, this one black and white, and explains to me this is Linus with his parents and siblings.

When I ask when Maxwell's grandmother passed away, Melody replies, "It was a few years after Sir Linus was born, from what I heard. She had a heart attack, but she was so young, so it surprised everyone."

Melody chats about the history of the family as she walks around the room, and I notice the photographs soon turn into oil paintings, the portraits clearly arranged in chronological order from the most recent to the oldest.

We move from portrait to portrait, Melody doing her best to tell me the stories behind them, and I'm fascinated by the little tidbits of history I'm learning and the changing fashions of the times, from elegant sheath dresses to the fringes of the twenties to the thick petticoats of the nineteenth century.

However, the levity of our conversation is dampened whenever she mentions the fates of some women in these portraits. There is an eerie pattern of seemingly random accidents culminating in their deaths, particularly the wives married to the older sons. Carriage mishaps, accidental drowning, influenza, tuberculosis, food poisoning—women dying after a series of events attributed to bad luck.

Melody whispers, "I mean, sure, everything could've been random, but then, what about the tree branch? No one can explain *that*."

I frown. "What tree branch?"

She slaps her hand on her forehead. "You need to know this stuff. So, apparently, before each of these unfortunate deaths, there's always a tree branch shattering a window in the estate. It always happens shortly before the deaths and usually during a storm."

My veins turn into ice as I shiver. *This stuff can't be real.*

Melody cocks her brow, as if she knows what I'm thinking. "All I'm saying is, it's a strange, specific pattern, and one can't help but think it's an omen."

Finally, we stand in front of a large oil painting of a family of four from around the late eighteen hundreds, lovingly preserved behind a glass frame. There are two boys who look to be around ten years old, their postures ramrod straight and faces unsmiling, common for portraits around that time. They're standing in front of a regal couple, a beautiful woman with blonde hair arranged in an elegant updo, wearing a lavender gown with sashes and adornments I assume were at the height of fashion back then.

But it's the man standing next to her who gives me pause, who lodges my breath in my throat.

He looks like Maxwell.

CHAPTER 23

I swallow my gasp as I stare at the man, dressed in all black except for a crisp white shirt and an expertly tied cravat of a similar shade.

He has the same dark hair and striking eyes I've seen with each generation of Anderson, but his eyes are more familiar. He stands next to his wife, his hands clasped in front of him, his thumb rubbing a silver jeweled ring.

His piercing gaze smolders with so much anguish and sadness.

It's a gut feeling, something I can't shake. *He has experienced something terrible in his life, I'm sure of it.*

The floor suddenly swirls around me and I place my hand on the wall for support, my body growing clammy. I may be coming down with something.

"Are you okay, Belle?" Melody asks.

"I'm fine. Give me a second." I breathe in and out a few times, and things slowly come back into focus and I stare at the painting once more.

My heart is still rattling in my chest. I can't tear my gaze away from him, this man who bears an uncanny resemblance to the frigid king in my life.

"Who is he?" I whisper.

"My great-great-great-grandfather, Silas Ashford Williams Anderson the Third. This painting used to be hung next to the grand staircase." Maxwell's deep voice rumbles in my ear, and I startle, finding him standing right behind me.

He looks at Melody and murmurs, "I got it from here."

She nods and turns to me. "Belle," I'm thankful she doesn't call me Ms. Belle like everyone else in the household, "I'll have the detailed gala plans for you to review next week."

Quietly, she exits the room and closes the door.

Maxwell stands next to me and regards the painting of his ancestor, his face solemn.

He's wearing a navy three-piece suit today, the frigid billionaire back in full force. A quiet intensity hums from his frame.

"You look like him." I turn my attention back to the painting, trying my best to ignore the fluttering of the butterflies in my stomach.

"And so I've been told. I was named after him, the first duke who settled in America a few years before the Civil War started. He donated a lot to the side of the Union during the war, much to everyone's surprise. Because of his wealthy heritage, people expected him to side with the South, but his father and grandfather were abolitionists in the British Empire in the 1830s."

"Do you know why he left England? I'd assume he had a lot of power with being a duke and all that."

"From what he wrote in his journal, it's because he wanted adventure and freedom. To break away from the shackles of peerage. To make something for himself." Maxwell stares at the portrait and shakes his head. "I don't think he got what he wanted, to be honest."

"Why?"

"He wasn't a happy man—at least that's what I gathered from his letters and journals. He and his wife were estranged, but that wasn't very unusual for the wealthy people back then. Divorce wasn't common."

"Do you know why?"

"No. I figured it must've been one of those loveless high-society arranged marriages." He snorts, glancing at me. "Not much has changed since then, don't you think? Our family is still steeped in tradition and I don't think you're ever truly free after escaping from a lifetime in a prison...unless you have amnesia."

A few more mirthless chuckles escape his lips, and I want to throw my arms around him and give him some warmth.

Maybe people call him the frigid king because he always looks so lonely, shouldering an insurmountable weight for his family.

Living in his prison.

"He looks so sad in the painting."

Maxwell sighs. "It's interesting how you feel the same way because whenever I asked my dad or my grandfather in the past, they'd say men back then always wore severe expressions on their faces. But maybe it's the artist in me, because I always thought he looked sad."

Turning away, he leads me out of the gallery. I guess story time is over. As we walk down the dark corridor, lit only by one sconce, he surprises me by opening the door to the art gallery.

"His journals are stored in the library, but we're missing a volume. If I were to guess, something happened in the 1860s, because afterward, his entries were angrier whereas the ones before were more hopeful."

My inner history buff makes a note to find his journals in the library later on.

As we step into the art gallery, my eyes widen at the carefully preserved art pieces from the great masters of the past. Fashion design is intricately linked to art and I've always enjoyed visiting museums.

I spot a few gorgeous paintings of lilies by Monet, a few portraits I recognize as the work of Rembrandt.

"No way!" Gasping, I run toward a painting of people lounging at a park.

Maxwell laughs behind me as he follows.

"You have a Seurat too?" I marvel at the thousands of tiny little dots that make up the painting—pointillism, a technique pioneered by George Seurat—something I've always thought is amazing because the art up close appears to be haphazard tiny little dots but from afar becomes a breathtaking masterpiece of something else altogether.

Broken pieces forming a beautiful whole.

"My family is a patron of the arts...including opera." He gives me a droll look and I snicker, thinking of our conversation in his car the night I met him.

"The Frida Kahlos in your room are from this gallery too," he murmurs, a half-smile on his face.

For a moment, the cold billionaire is gone and my heart flips.

"I never thanked you for that."

"You don't need to. What's art for if not to be loved and admired?" There's a thread of wistfulness in his voice. A deep longing.

"I'm glad you enjoy them," he adds, his half-smile turns into a full-on grin.

Heat unfurls from my chest and spreads to my extremities.

My eyes catch on a rough sketch—a silhouette of a woman, very much like the one in my locket. But this one has faded features on it—like the artist attempted to draw the face over and over again but left only the outline intact.

"What's this?" I frown, walking to the framed sketch. It looks old and doesn't seem to be in a style I recognize.

There's an aged parchment with masculine script on it inside the frame:

Your image dwells eternally in my mind. Though I could spend the rest of my life attempting to capture your likeness on canvas, nothing will ever compare, for my skills can never do you justice.

Yet I vow, one day, when we are reunited in another life, when my heart is made whole, I shall attempt to portray you once more, my love. Perhaps then, I will finally be able to capture your essence.

A sharp pain pierces my chest, my breath catching in my throat. The heartbreak in the words. The love in the sentences.

"It's from Grandfather Silas," Maxwell says quietly. "The one whose portrait we just discussed. I've always wondered who he was trying to draw. It's obvious it's not his wife."

My heart rattles behind my rib cage as I stare at the letter and the painting, suddenly overcome with a sadness I can't shake.

"I hope he got to finish his drawing of her," I whisper.

Somehow, I don't think he did. Swallowing the lump in my throat, I step back.

There's so much history in this house, with his family. It's so unlike my childhood, where I was taught the newer, flashier thing was better, where I saw my parents always striving to be in the forefront of the latest trends.

Perhaps it's part of being in the fashion industry, to stay on top of things, to be a trendsetter. But it has always felt empty to me. Soulless.

And shouldn't art, including fashion, have a soul?

"I love everything here. In the estate. I feel like I'm part of something and am about to write my story to add to the history books."

Closing my eyes, I spin around and inhale the comforting scents of oil paints and canvas.

"I wonder what will be written in my pages." I smile, thinking about my year of yeses mindset and how much I've already learned by making decisions for myself.

After a few beats of silence, I open my eyes, finding Maxwell staring at me, seemingly transfixed. His nostrils flare and he swallows, the muscles rippling in his corded throat.

"How do you see the positive in everything?" he rasps.

"I didn't use to be this way," I murmur, my voice shaky at the yearning I'm seeing on his face. "Until I started my year of yeses, I was complacent, always thinking about how I must follow the path my parents set out for me. But I realize, maybe I can't choose everything in life, but there are still many things I have control over."

I spin around once more, my chest feeling lighter. Being in the room with grand masterpieces of the past has given me some ideas for my impossible collection.

"What's the alternative, Maxwell? We have to live life one way or the other."

Grinning, I walk toward him, wondering if I should ask him a question that has been nagging me ever since the day when I went shopping for the wedding with my girlfriends.

"Maxwell, can I ask you a question?"

He grunts in the affirmative, his gaze unfocused and turned toward the sketch. He's clearly deep in thought.

"Do you believe the curse to be real?"

He whips his head in my direction, his gray eyes sharpening. "Who told you about it?"

"My friends, before we got married. It's interesting how you didn't tell me about it, the soon to be wife of the *eldest* son."

"If I told you, would you have believed me?"

I shake my head. "I still don't believe it. It's the twenty-first century and for a family as large as yours who can trace their lineage to the dawn of time, there are bound to be some unfortunate deaths."

We continue strolling around the gallery. "My family was in the lower middle class until Grandpa turned it all around with McKenzie Atelier. We lost touch with pretty much everyone other than Grandpa's younger sister and her family. I'm sure if I could trace my lineage, we'd probably have similar sad stories as yours."

"So why are you asking me the question then?"

"I'm curious." I stop and face him and take a fortifying breath. "I wonder where the Silas I met at the race went, and why the Maxwell in front of me is so different—opposite, like night and day."

Why do you pull away when you clearly want me? When I still feel this pulsing chemistry between us that has only grown stronger over time?

Why are you hiding from me?

Stepping closer, I watch the Adam's apple in his throat bob, the dark stubble dotting his jawline adding to a rugged appeal.

His breath hitches and a thought occurs to me.

"Are you trying to save me from the curse?" I ask. "Is this why you're telling me not to fall in love with you?"

"Nothing will ever happen to you, Belle. *Nothing*." His eyes flash with determination, as if it's unfathomable for me to become another victim in the family curse.

He stalks away, a dark cloud looming over his head, and I hasten my steps to follow him.

"That's why, isn't it? You believe in the curse so you're acting like a mercurial asshole to me. The curse can't be real, Maxwell! It's not scientific!"

"I don't want to talk about it."

"I want to, because this marriage has two people in it. This affects me!"

He spins around, his face mottled. "This marriage is only an *arrangement* for us to get what we both want. Nothing more, nothing less. You should remember that."

He stalks toward the door as I reel from his words.

"Well, I can't exactly give you an heir if we don't even share the same bed!" The words escape my mouth before I can stop them.

I don't know what we are doing, this marriage we agreed to. He saved my family's company and asked for nothing in return.

"Why did you marry me, Maxwell? Tell me the truth!"

What is he getting out of this? Didn't my friends say he's doing this to get an heir and circumvent the curse? But why won't he touch me? I can't help but be hurt by his rejection over and over again.

Maxwell pauses by the door and keeps his back toward me. "Fine. You want to start trying? That desperate to get rid of me?" he growls. "Be careful what you wish for."

With that ominous threat, he walks out the door.

CHAPTER 24

Fuming, I stomp down the corridor toward the grand staircase and climb it two steps at a time. On the third-floor landing, instead of turning left, this time I turn right toward the other side of the mansion—the west wing containing the mistress's set of rooms that have been closed off.

"That asshole," I growl under my breath.

Every time, just as I think we're about to get closer, he'll pull the rug from under me and morph into his icy king persona once more.

I won't let him get to me.

The arrangement is for a short time and I want a baby. And if nothing comes from this marriage on the fertility front, at least I'll walk out of it having saved Grandpa's business and getting the funds to do fertility treatments and maybe even the animal shelter charity work too.

This isn't permanent.

But despite my blistering anger, the thought of leaving the estate, of leaving *him,* causes the hollow ache to reappear inside my chest.

My Silas is trapped inside the frigid king and I want to free him.

A quick pitter-pattering sounds behind me, followed by an excited howl, and I smile, turn around, and greet Silas.

"You want to come with me to explore?" I ruffle his soft, brown fur. Nothing like playing detective to distract me from an infuriating man.

Silas wags his tail and gives me another excited bark, and my earlier dark mood brightens a bit.

Blowing out a breath, I turn to the first door on the left and open it. Poking my head in, I see a guest room very similar to my room—a large bed, two wingback chairs, the curtains are half drawn, letting in some of the evening light.

Clearly, despite the wing being closed, the staff have kept things tidy.

Returning to the corridor, I continue my exploration of the other rooms, finding much of the same—guest rooms not in active use, some having white sheets covering the furniture, no doubt to extend the period between cleanings.

I walk toward the last set of doors on the hall, the mirror image position of Maxwell's room in the east wing, turn the doorknob, and step inside.

My movements must have dispelled some dust.

Coughing, I fan my hand in front of me, shocked at the thick, musty smell in here. After drawing aside the velvet curtains, I fiddle with the stuck latch on the French doors and open them, letting in some much-needed fresh air.

The room is three times the size of the other guest rooms. The furniture here is also covered in white sheets. I make out the shapes of a large bed, a few chairs and tables, a tall dresser. But unlike the other spaces, this room is a still life painting—a dark coat gathering dust on the coatrack, a purse half-opened on the floor, a book flipped to a page on the nightstand. The space looks eerie, like it has been locked up because whatever transpired here has caused too much sorrow, but the owner still wanted to leave things untouched, a living mausoleum.

Silas lets out a mournful howl and I frown, turning to him. He's standing next to an oak bookcase, sniffing the shelves. He pulls out a few books and proceeds to gnaw on them.

"Oh no! Silas, drop that now!" I imagine Agnes's glacial expression if the dog damages the priceless heirlooms. Those might be first editions!

I hurry toward him as he moves his attention to another book on the lowest shelf. Growling, he sticks his snout deep into the space.

Reaching him in a few strides, I gently nudge him away and squat down, my fingers smoothing over the few unfortunate books that appear to have bite marks on them.

"Please, don't kill me," I mutter under my breath while stacking the fallen books back on the shelf—if no one sees them and I say nothing, we can pretend nothing happened?

Just as I reach in to adjust the last volume Silas touched—the one that had him howling with his snout buried deep into the shelf, I realize that book isn't budging.

Frowning, I lean down and try again.

It doesn't move.

What the...

My fingers trail over the worn spine—it's an old copy of Emily Brontë's *Wuthering Heights*—before they catch on something.

A small dip on the bottom of the front cover. My brows furrow as I explore that strange recess. It doesn't feel like a dog bite—

Rumble.

The floor shakes beneath me and the bookcase moves, revealing a gap between the furniture and the wall.

Gasping, my hand flies to my mouth. *A hidden passageway.*

A chilly breeze blows from inside the dark tunnel and I shiver. Every instinct inside me screams at me to run away, far away from this eerie dark house with strange noises and morbid secrets.

But the year of yeses mentality. Try new experiences. Control my life.

After the initial fear passes, a burgeoning curiosity rises inside me and, clearly sensing my shift in mood, Silas darts into the space, deciding for me.

"Silas! Come back here!" I call after him, stepping into the passageway.

It's pitch black, the same musty smell from the mistress's rooms stronger here.

Patting the walls, I look for a light switch or a candle, anything to give me some visibility. Unable to find anything, I take out my cell phone and turn on the flashlight.

The passageway is narrow with weathered stone walls and cobwebs lingering in the gaps. My pulse is thready as I follow Silas's sounds that are fading into the haunted silence.

I'm starting to regret my decision. There are some things I should never say yes to. *What was I thinking? This is such a bad idea.*

Reaching the end of the corridor, I turn left and see a faint light. A simple wooden door is cracked open and gingerly, I step inside.

"Wow," I murmur as I step through a similar door behind another bookshelf into a beautiful room, which seems to be trapped in time as well.

A wall is lined with bookshelves filled with knickknacks, old books, and scrolls of yellowed paper. My eyes widen when I notice vintage musical instruments lying in the corners of the space—a harp, violin, and a harpsichord, the predecessor of the modern piano. Next to a brick fireplace is a reading chair, and an ornate antique writing desk is nestled on the other side.

There's a thin layer of dust on everything, and I can only imagine this space has been hidden away and not in use for a long time. I wonder if I there are any secrets here for me to reveal.

The room is dim as the thick drapes are closed, but I can make out the wrought iron table lamps and an exquisite floor lamp atop a dark Persian carpet. My mouth tips into a smile as butterflies beat inside my chest.

This is it. This is the place for my work studio—my little slice of heaven inside the estate.

My heart thumps a righteous rhythm as I'm imbued with ideas for my impossible design collection, all of which I'll bring to life in this beautiful space that's calling my name. I'm stepping into history to create history of my very own.

Silas huffs around the room as I open the windows to air out the room. I spot a small stack of towels and a broomstick in one corner. Grinning to myself, I roll up my sleeves and get to work.

Time to make this oasis mine, and later tonight, after I've cooled down, I'll talk to that madman again.

Saving McKenzie Atelier. Animal Shelter charity work. Having a baby. My three goals in this marriage, the first two already in progress.

I won't let his surly ass attitude detract me from my third goal, from satisfying the hollow ache in my womb. And if somewhere along the way, I find the soulful guy I met at the races, I won't complain. Not one bit.

We're going to make this marriage arrangement work, whether he likes it or not.

CHAPTER 25

Belle

THE EVENING BLEEDS INTO the dark night and before I know it, I've worked up a sweat tidying up the secret room. Silas has long since trotted back to the main rooms, no doubt exploring the other nooks and crannies in the mansion. Or maybe he's terrorizing his master.

I snicker, remembering Maxwell's glower last week when he found Silas with one of his black leather dress shoes in his mouth. I'm sure that was a thousand dollars down the drain.

Standing up, I rub my aching shoulders and wipe away the sweat on my forehead. The room is coming together nicely. I've given it a name of my own, Belle's Elysium, from the Greek word, *Elysion*; a paradise after life on earth. This place will be my paradise while I'm in this arrangement with Maxwell.

I wonder what the story is about this hidden room and if there are other secret passageways in the mansion. Glancing at the antique grandfather clock by the open window, I noticed it's approaching eight p.m. I'm going to find Maxwell and talk to him. I'll extend an olive branch and see if he's had dinner yet. This arrangement where we're avoiding each other and him randomly blowing up at me isn't working.

Eyes on the prize, Belle. A baby and my Silas. He's hidden inside the frigid asshole.

Mind made up, I turn off the lights and make my way to Maxwell's room.

Knock. Knock.

No answer. I try again, but the same result. Maybe he's not there?

But to be safe, I creak open the door to check and I hear faint noises coming from somewhere inside the room. Blowing out a deep breath, I step inside and marvel at the masculine space lit up by a sleek lamp on the nightstand.

Dark wood paneling with wainscoting leads to an arched ceiling. There's a king-sized bed with a navy tufted headboard and gray comforter facing a black marble fireplace. A lounge area by the bay windows is set up with a modern table and gray wingback chairs.

The fragrances of sandalwood and amber permeate the air—his scent, and I draw in a deep inhale, a heady warmth spreading inside me. My body comes alive with awareness of the only man who has ever enthralled me. The unattainable man.

Light seeps in from a cracked open door and I hear the sounds of water and someone mumbling.

Holding my breath, I tiptoe to the doorway and my heart stutters and stops.

Steam fogs up the bathroom and I see his backside, all rippling muscles and restrained power, underneath a large shower. The hot water pelts his hair and body, but he doesn't appear to mind. His head is dipped down, one hand pressed against the dark marble wall. His other arm is moving quickly in angry motions, the steam from the shower preventing me from seeing what he's doing, but I have a pretty good idea.

I release a thready exhale and swallow, my skin feeling warm to the touch.

"Fuck, fuck, fuck," he mutters, his voice angry as his arm moves faster.

"Damn it," he grunts and lets out a tortured groan.

I should look away, but I can't. Every atom in my body is attuned to the sex god in front of me.

Maxwell turns around, dragging his free hand over his wet hair before slamming it against the glass door, the sudden movement drenching the door in a deluge of water, un-fogging it temporarily.

His eyes are closed, a vein pulsing on his forehead, his jaw locked as he works his hand up and down, up and down, his biceps flexing. I drag my gaze down his body, past all his glorious muscles and beautiful scars, to the glorious weapon between his thighs.

He's thick and long, much bigger than the two guys I've been with in the past. The tip of his cock is deep red as it disappears and reappears in his fist. It looks angry, furious, just like its master.

Liquid pools between my legs and my sticky clothes feel abrasive against my skin. I clench my pussy and press my thighs together, but it does nothing to stem the pulsing need inside me.

"Fuck, Belle! What are you doing to me?" Maxwell roars.

He's thinking about me and I shiver. *I have been here all along—why have you stayed away?*

He fucks his fist harder and I'm burning for him, wanting him to touch me. To ease his pain inside me.

A whimper slips out of my lips.

His eyes snap open and meet mine—the gaze of a villain—and those gray eyes turn impossibly darker and more intense.

He doesn't slow his movements but instead trails his gaze over my body, his nostrils flaring, and I look down, realizing I have a hand curled over my breast.

Maxwell steps closer to the shower door, his large hand dragging up and down his beautiful thick cock in agonizing slow motions, his mouth parting as he releases one raspy breath after another.

I'm so wet and achy and the intensity in his gaze only fans the flames inside me. My feet move, an invisible tug pulling me toward this man who has driven me insane ever since I've met him.

He pauses as he stares at me, his hand curling around his dick in a death grip and his entire body stills, as if he's making a decision.

The steam fogs the space between us as I walk toward him, my mind mad with need—the need to touch him, to trail my fingers up and down his powerful body, to feel him inside me, filling me up, owning me completely.

Suddenly, his body bursts with movement.

He pushes open the shower door and hauls me inside, and the hot water immediately drenches my body and clothes.

He looks at me in awe, his eyes dipping to my lips, his heavy breathing fanning my face. But the split-second reverence is quickly masked as his asshole persona slips into place.

Spinning me around, he presses my face against the cool glass, his arm curled tightly around my waist. His body cages me in as his teeth nip my ear.

"You're going to give me an heir, aren't you?" he growls, his words sending a tremor down my body.

I let out a moan. *Yes. I want this. I want you. I want everything.*

He presses his thick cock against my backside and I feel him thrusting slowly through my sodden dress, gyrating against my ass cheeks.

Wetness seeps through my panties. I'm on fire for him.

"You're going to let me stuff you with my cock and fill you with cum, aren't you?"

"M-Maxwell, yes." I whimper. The image of him pulsing inside me, filling me up, has me thrashing against him. I rub against his hardness, needing him to touch me, manhandle me, to ease the torture building inside me.

He growls, his hand tugging up my dress before he rips off my underwear and tosses it to the floor.

I gasp from the burn between my legs, which only heightens the climbing pleasure. *I need more.*

"I'm going to fuck you and breed you. But make no mistake, this is not love." His voice is heated and rough, like he's desperate for me.

Without another word, he thrusts inside me.

I cry out at the sudden intrusion, his thick cock invading my body in a delicious burn. He groans as he slides one hand between my legs and rubs circles on my clit. Pleasure lights up my pussy and I shake against him.

"Fuck, fuck, fuck," he grunts as he hammers inside me, his body pressing me harder against the shower door.

His dick swells and becomes impossibly bigger, his fingers working expertly on my clit as sparks gather in a deep place inside me.

I lean back, running my hands over any part of him I can reach, trying to touch him, to have more connection than just his naked body pressed against my clothed one, his cock spearing me in half.

"Hands on the door. Don't touch me."

I follow his instructions, my body bowing to his dominance. My gut clenches at his rejection, but the ache is soon swallowed by a tsunami of pleasure building between my legs.

"You came looking for this, didn't you?" he grunts. "Me to fuck you, get your belly full with my baby, mark you from the inside?"

My mind blanks at his possessive and dirty words.

"My wife is a slut for me," he rasps. "Elegant on the outside, but you needed a thick cock stuffing you full of cum all along, didn't you?"

"Oh fuck, Maxwell." I whimper, a heat sparking from deep inside my womb and I'm almost blind from pleasure, from all his degrading words which somehow sound like poetry to my ears.

His thrusts quicken, the sounds of skin slapping against skin mixing with the pattering of the water crashing against our bodies.

The sparks in my pussy coalesce into an inferno and my legs tremble and I part my lips in a cry.

"Fuck, yes, yes, yes!" he roars, his cock thickening before throbbing, releasing warm spurts of cum inside me.

He pinches my clit and the sharp pain along with the hot cum trigger my orgasm. I tumble into nirvana, my legs quaking, body trembling, and he prolongs the high by gyrating his hips in gentle thrusts, his cock still deep and pulsing inside me.

Our panting breaths are loud in the shower as the pleasure gradually ebbs and we slowly come down from our high.

Without another word, he withdraws from me and stalks out of the shower.

I hear his ragged breaths as he wraps a towel around his waist, his fingers fumbling, a few curse words erupting from his mouth.

He doesn't turn around, doesn't look at me. His back muscles are taut with tension.

"I'll see you in the dining room for dinner," he rasps.

Then he leaves the bathroom.

The world slowly spins around me as I stand under the hot spray, still wearing my wet dress and reeling from the best sex I've ever had—the cathartic release, the intensity like nothing I've ever experienced before.

Then I feel his cum streaming down my thighs and reality finally catches up to me.

What just happened?

How was it both the coldest and hottest experience I've ever had?

A burning sensation appears behind my eyes as a sobering ache blooms in my chest. I blink away my impending tears and remind myself this isn't about love. This is about getting what we both want out of this arrangement.

I want to get pregnant. Focus on that, Belle.

But my heart is splintering in half, the blood pouring out of the deep wound.

He didn't even kiss me.

CHAPTER 26

THE BITING WIND LASHES my face as I throw open the doors of BSUA and step into the dingy shelter, a trail of dead brown leaves following me inside and littering the wet floors.

A pipe burst a block away, sending grimy, malodorous water down the streets. The driver had to make a few maneuvers around the block to find a place to drop me off.

"I'm so sorry for being late!" I wheeze at my girlfriends and Cole, who are gathered in the lobby and have already started wiping down the shelter during the BSUA's quarterly volunteering day.

Because asshole Bob is too lazy to hire a proper cleaning crew to keep BSUA up to code.

One day, he'll get one too many violations and then where will these poor animals go?

"No worries. We've been getting to know Cole over here." Millie giggles as she ties her dark brown hair into a messy bun. "Do you know he and Tay both like carrot cake and horror films?"

Grace grins and nods. "They also both love ballet and prefer the mountains over the beach."

"Right. Cole thinks Tay's piercings are *fascinating*."

"Totally, Millie! I forgot he said that!" Grace squeals, a devious glint in her dark blue eyes that frequently appears violet under certain lighting.

Cole snorts as he mops the puddles on the floor, no doubt from the busted pipe. He shakes his head, clearly amused at the girls' antics.

Taylor rolls her eyes and sighs. "You guys need to stop trying to match make me with any available men you see just because you guys found your happily-ever-afters."

She throws her dirty rag over her shoulder, clearly not caring about ruining her gray oversized sweater. "I don't need men in my life. They're more trouble than they're worth."

Sneaking a glance at Cole, she shrugs. "Sorry, dude. No offense to you, but I hate blonds."

Millie and Grace let out a collective sigh, clearly crestfallen at their failure at matchmaking our remaining single friend in our girl group.

Cole snickers. "None taken."

Taylor turns around, her face twisted in a dark scowl, and mutters under her breath, "Plus, one fucking annoying blond asshole is more than enough."

Grace and I exchange a glance, and I cock a brow. Taylor's hatred of Charles Vaughn is very obvious. He's well-mannered, mature, and gets along with everyone, but for some unknown reason, he and Taylor have been oil and water ever since they met.

After putting my purse and coat inside a dingy metal locker in the back room, I rejoin my friends as we wipe down empty cages on the side of the shelter not currently occupied by animals. The acrid smell of dirty water mixing with cleaning agents is enough to make my stomach turn.

"So, how's life going, Mrs. Anderson...or should we call you, *Your Majesty,* since you've conquered the frigid king?" Grace nudges me and I feel a heat blooming on my face.

"You can call her Your Grace too. She's technically a duchess now." Millie cackles and the two give each other a high five.

"Hold on a sec," Grace muses. "No, not yet! Linus is still alive—technically, he's the duke and Maxwell is a marquess."

"Oooh, marchioness? So, what do we call her, my lady?"

"Beats me—I learn all my stuff from Regency romances and *BBC* shows."

The girls guffaw and Grace laughs so hard she wheezes like a banshee.

"Har. Har. Har. You two are stand-up comedians now, aren't you?" I mutter.

Cole sidles up next to me and helps me move a table so I can reach the far back of the space.

"But seriously, how are things going with you and Maxwell? With all your gala planning and work, we haven't hung out recently. Is he treating you well?"

"You're going to let me stuff you with my cock and fill you with cum, aren't you?"

My heart palpitates at the memory of his words in the shower three weeks ago. How he used my body for his pleasure. How he manhandled me to succumb to his will.

How much it hurt after the lust faded when I realized he didn't kiss me or caress me and how impersonal it all felt—like he was holding a big part of himself back.

Since then, he'd come to my room once a week, usually late at night, sometimes after I'd drifted off to sleep. He'd be coiled with energy and tethered power, the intensity radiating off from his imposing frame in spades.

He'd rouse me from my sleep with his hands on my ass or back me against the wall if I was awake. Then his talented fingers would find their way between my legs as he pinned me in place and surrounded me with his strength. He'd play my clit like it was an instrument he had mastered, getting me off in a matter of minutes.

Then he'd turn me face down, slide his thick cock inside me, and rut against me until he came, all the while whispering dirty and degrading words about breeding and getting me pregnant that felt like a love language.

He'd never look me in the eye.

We'd still have our clothes on the entire time.

And he still wouldn't kiss me.

It hurt more than I cared to admit as I laid in bed afterward, reminding myself to lie on my back, as if that'd help my DOR situation and getting pregnant.

Despite how impersonal the sex feels, I can't stop my body from coming alive near him, from wanting him, from craving him and the pleasure he gives.

I can feel the connection between us, even if he tries his best to deny it.

"God, look at that blush on her face. Revolting," Taylor mutters, but her lips are twisted in a small smile. Cole stiffens next to me and throws me a glare.

Guilt pinches me from the hurt and unsettling anger on his face. But what can I do? I'm not in charge of what comes out of my girlfriends' mouths.

Fanning my face, I let out a half-hearted chuckle. "You girls, it's not like that."

"You just got redder!" Millie squeals.

Cole whips his towel on the cage, the loud sound startling me, and abruptly stands up.

I furrow my brows and he returns my gaze with a glower, his nostrils flaring.

"Excuse me, ladies." He strides out of the space.

"What's going on with him?" Millie asks, her brows pinched.

Groaning, I bury my face into my palms. I've never told them I suspect Cole has a thing for me, so they've always assumed he's just a friend from the shelter.

What a mess.

"So, are things really going okay between you and Maxwell?" she asks softly, sincerity brimming in her voice.

"It's complicated."

He has a wall around his heart that's more fortified than Fort Knox. Intimidating. Impenetrable. But I know there's a heart of gold behind those stormy moods and fiery gazes.

"You know, Ryland was complicated too. I think as Andersons, they had a lot of pressure growing up. The world was watching their every move, waiting for them to make a mistake."

She pulls me up from the floor after I finish wiping down the scuff marks and helps me put the table back in place. "They also went through a lot of traumas when their mom died and with the curse and everything."

Millie gives me a sad smile, like she knows exactly what I'm going through. "We may think the curse is baloney, but they've been raised to believe it...for generations. It'll take time to get through to him, Belle. That is, if you want to."

My eyes burn and my nose twitches.

I do. I very much want to. I want the gentleman from the races, the blistering kisses we've shared before, the late night pastrami and rye.

"Aww, sweetheart." She pulls me into a hug as an errant tear slips out and I curse myself for crying over the infuriating man who gives me emotional whiplash and makes me feel far too much.

"My offer to kick his ass still stands," Taylor mutters, tossing her towel on the ground and patting my back.

"We're here for you whenever you need us. There's always a guest room for you at Steven's and my place if you want to take a break," Grace murmurs.

Swiping my arm over my tears, I dole out a watery smile. "I-I'm fine, really. It's just...trying for a baby with a man who makes me feel everything is so hard. Harder than I expected." I swallow and heave out a ragged sigh. "But I knew what I was getting into. He's keeping his boundaries, and I just need to work on mine."

"You don't need to continue the arrangement, Belle. If you need money, I can lend you some, no strings attached. I can also ask my brother to help too—I think I can persuade Emily to invest in McKenzie Atelier. We can fund your fertility treatments and everything," Millie offers, referring to her billionaire brother, Adrian Scott's wife, Emily

Kingsley, who is a powerhouse businesswoman and a fashionista on top of that.

I shake my head. I don't want to muddle our friendship with financial matters. Things rarely end well in those situations. And I meant what I told Maxwell in our first meeting at The Menagerie. My parents would've arranged a marriage for me to another man if I didn't marry him.

And even after everything, I still rather it be him.

The man who has given me unforgettable adventures, who has decorated my room in atrovirens and Frida Kahlos. The man who looks at me with reverence in the gallery, the man I catch sneaking Silas treats despite grumbling about the dog ruining everything.

The man who makes my heart flutter in his presence.

Deep down, I wonder if I'm in way over my head. If my traitorous heart can separate matters of the flesh and love.

"I have it handled, girls. Don't worry about me. Plus, my baby will have good genes. Those Andersons are smart *and* hot." I wink, hoping I sound believable and clear my throat. "Anyway, I'm going to run to the basement to grab some dog food for the kennels. They were running low when I checked earlier. I'll be right back."

Without waiting for their response, I walk past the girls, eager to escape the topic and the turmoil of feelings it elicits inside me.

The swirling thoughts accompany me as I reach the narrow stairs, dimly lit by a flickering florescent light. A fresh wave of dizziness hits me, very similar to how I felt when I saw Duke Silas's portrait in the gallery, and I grip the railing for support while the spell passes.

I've been feeling out of sorts these days. I don't know if it's the stress of the situation or a lingering illness I can't shake. If this keeps up, I'll need to call my doctor.

After a few seconds, I feel much better and continue down the stairs.

A cloying stench reaches my nostrils and I notice the floors are wet with bits of dead leaves and black sludge sticking to the cement steps.

Darn it, the flood must've made its way here too. I hope the food stocked in the basement is still good. If not, I'll need to make use of Maxwell's resources to replenish the supply because Lord knows I can't count on Bob to do that for the poor animals.

My attentions are so temporarily distracted by my thoughts that I don't notice anything unusual until the door suddenly creaks open behind me.

"Who's there—ahhh!" I scream as a solid mass knocks into my back and I lose momentum, my boots landing on the wet steps, only to slip and slide.

Everything happens in a blur and I tumble down the stairs, the impact wrenching the air out of my lungs as my body hits the cement.

A blistering pain explodes in my head, my vision darkening at the edges.

Everything hurts.

My ears ring and I taste a bitter, metallic liquid on my tongue.

So much pain.

I see a faint, tall shadow approaching me.

"H-Help me," I whimper. "P-Please."

My breathing feels labored. My vision is dizzy and my eyes are heavy.

"Stay away from him," a ghoulish voice rasps in my ear. "Stay away."

I succumb to the darkness.

CHAPTER 27

"Sir, Belle's been in an accident." Melody bursts into my study without knocking, her eyes flaring in panic.

Chills crawl up my back, and I stand up. "What do you mean?" Images of Mom, Sydney, and all their accidents float through my mind. *This can't happen again.*

"Belle. S-She...the hospital called. Agnes isn't here, so I picked up. S-She...She—"

"What? Tell me!"

Melody flinches and I would've felt guilty if it weren't for the clawing terror ripping my heart into shreds. "S-She was volunteering at the shelter and fell down a flight of stairs. They sent for an ambulance and took her to Mount Sinai."

Panic mauls me like a rabid beast, my heart lurching to my throat, and I quickly grab my cell phone and dart toward the door.

"Car? Where's Morris?" I bark out as I pass by her.

"I didn't look for him! I ran up to you after I got the call."

"Fuck!" I jab the intercom button and as soon as a voice comes on, I command, "Bring a car around—any of them, right now!"

Please be okay, Belle. I run down the empty corridors, my footfalls echoing in a thunderous beat. Flying down the stairs, I take several steps at a time, every inch of my body needing to be where my wife is, where a piece of my heart is.

I thought I'd protected her by being an ass. *Had I not done enough?*

Heavy regret smothers my lungs as I sit in the town car minutes later. I think back to how I've treated her these past few months—moments of intense passion peppered with cold rejection, the hurt in her eyes whenever I left her after we had sex, when I wanted nothing more than to peel off her clothes and worship every inch of her delectable body.

I wish she knew how difficult it was for me to hold back the impulse to kiss those pouty lips, the lips that had worshiped my scars and called them beautiful, instead of the ugly flaws they were. She saw the monsters lurking inside me, and yet she accepted me all the same.

But I keep telling myself I'm doing this for her own good. To keep our hearts intact. To keep her safe.

Did I not do enough? *Does any of this even matter to the curse?* Is it already too late?

And if it is, she'd die not knowing how much I care about her, how much I regret hurting her feelings, how hard it was for me to stay away from her. I didn't even get to apologize to her.

It's too late, Maxwell, a ghoulish voice whispers in my mind.

Too late, just like before, all those years ago.

"I want to annul our marriage." Sydney stared at me, her green eyes coated with moisture. The bitter wind beat against our bodies as we stood at the helm of the family yacht, the dark waters of the ocean pitch black around us.

The knife she hurled at my chest ever since I overheard her confession to Ryland twisted into my heart, severing an artery, leaving me a bloody mess before her.

A bloody mess she couldn't see.

Shaking my head, a few mirthless chuckles escaped my lips.

"For better or for worse, for richer or poorer, in sickness and in health, to love and to cherish as long as you both shall live," I spat out the civil wedding vows we said to each other on our elopement, my middle finger to the curse and the path laid out before me as the eldest Anderson offspring.

Because I refused to let a curse run my life.

She whimpered and stared helplessly at me.

"I overheard you and Ryland, you know," I seethed, burning rage sifting through my veins like a wildfire.

Facing the ocean, I let the harsh winds flay me in my face to dry the moisture in my eyes.

I may be a failure, scars and all, a socially awkward idiot who panicked in front of crowds, an eldest son who wasn't worthy of the Anderson name, but I still had my pride.

"I-I'm sorry. I made a mistake."

"Why? Why were you with me then, Sydney? Why did you give me hope?" I swallowed the growing lump in my throat. "I-I thought you were different than the others."

Thunder rumbled in the distance, followed by a streak of lightning snaking across the turbulent skies.

"You were so sweet to me. I was moved. I-I thought I could change you, bring you out of your shell. Maybe we could try different things, travel, meet new people, party it up. We're so young," she whispered.

"And then you could have your art exhibits at The Met and show off your talent to the world, and I could be your doting wife next to you. We'd be the power couple. You'd be the talent, and I'd be the socialite. No one could stop us. I thought...we're so young and I could change you and make you be—"

"More like *him*? Like Ryland? The charming, popular prince?"

"Maxwell," she cried, "I love you both! It's just, I—"

"Love him more, right? That's what you're going to say, isn't it?"

Shaking my head, I turned my face toward the rain, which started to fall moments ago. I hated the fucking rain so much, but its appearance seemed very appropriate now.

"The sad thing is, Sydney, I would've understood if you were honest with me. I would've understood if you chose him."

I heaved out another breath. "I-I would've stepped aside."

Who wouldn't love my charming, extroverted brother? My loyal, perfect, unblemished brother, whom I'd always be willing to give up my life for, like that time with the boar attack. He was the perfect version of me.

"I love my brother more than anyone in the world, and I would've wanted him happy, even if that meant stepping aside and seeing you with him, as long as you love him."

Slamming my hand on the railing, I screamed, "And now you've driven a wedge between us and I'm so fucking pissed at you!"

Because I gave her my feelings, emotions I had locked up tight because I was told I wasn't allowed to have them as the eldest son—the cursed son.

It was all an illusion. A mirage.

But you can't just make love disappear, can you? It's out there now—the feeling, the I love yous, the vows, and I'm the one left suffering.

Curling my hands into tight fists, I whirled toward her. She backed away, fear clear in her eyes. Rain was pouring down in a violence I hadn't seen before. I couldn't do this now. I needed to tell the captain to head back to the dock.

"Sydney, I feel *nothing* for you but regret." And betrayed and heartbroken, but I didn't tell her that. "Whatever you want to say, I don't want to listen. It's too late. God, I wish I had never met you. *Go rot in hell.*"

"Maxwell, please," she cried after me as I stomped inside the cabin and ignored her, the storm raging outside only a fraction of the hurt and pain I was feeling inside.

Later on, I'd wish I could turn back time and undo everything.

I'd wish I could hear the splash of a person slipping off the deck that night, a person I loved with all my heart then, not knowing I was capable of feeling so much more. I'd wish the Coast Guard could've found her before she drowned in the icy depths of the Atlantic.

I'd wished I never married her or fell in love with her. Maybe that would've saved her.

And if she were still destined to die, I'd wish I could've told her I forgave her because, ultimately, I cared about her and would've wanted her happy.

But it was too late. Much too late.

My breathing is shallow, sweat rolling down my forehead as the car slows in front of the hospital.

It can't be too late this time. It can't be. Not again.

I may have married Belle already, but I can't let her think I don't care about her. I can't let her feel how Sydney made me feel.

Unwanted.

I'll just not fall in love with her. As long as we don't fall in love with each other, we'll be fine. It won't be like Sydney. It won't be like my parents.

I jump out of the car before it stops and dash into the hospital, not caring as attendants and doctors try to stop me from running down the halls. I only pause to find out Belle's room number and in a matter of seconds or minutes, as everything feels exactly the damn same right now, I burst into room 508, my thundering pulse a frenzied rumble in my ears.

My wife is lying still on the bed, her eyes closed. She looks so fragile, so breakable. My heart freezes in my chest.

Her friends are gathered around her bedside, but I barely pay them any attention as I shove my way in between them to my wife. "Belle! Please tell me you're all right."

She opens her eyes and gives me a tired smile. "I'm fine. It was an accident, that's all."

She's alive. My shoulders sag in relief as I curl my body over hers, my hands clasping her clammy ones tightly but a taunting voice inside me whispers, *the accidents are starting again, just like before. Remember when Sydney nearly drowned in the swimming pool and—*

I shut down my thoughts—I can't think about that right now. My eyes rove over her body, noticing a bandage on her forehead, a few red scrapes over her face and arms, purple bruises already forming on her pale skin.

"Fuck," I heave, the nausea churning inside me still making me want to throw up my lunch. "Thank God you're okay. Fuck, you scared me, Belle."

"I-I'm fine, Maxwell," she whispers, her hand slides out of my clasp and curls around my face.

She gently wipes the sweat off my brows and upper lip as if she knows I'm hanging on by the thinnest thread.

A swift current of emotions floods up my spine, and I want to tell her how she's an indelible part of my life, how she's the sunshine in my never-ending night, the spring in my barren winter. I want to tell her I need her by my side, that I married her because I couldn't stand the idea of her being with another man.

Fuck. Fuck. Fuck.

Someone clears his throat, and I finally pay attention to the other people in the room. That bastard Cole is standing there, his arms crossed over his chest, his glare threatening to murder me on the spot.

Something dangerous glints in his eyes, but I couldn't care less. He can go fuck himself.

Blowing out a breath, I ignore him and turn back to Belle.

I murmur, "I'm glad you're okay, little muse." An endearing flush blooms on her face.

Standing back up, I see Grace and Millie with beaming smiles on their faces and Taylor with a sly grin on hers.

Taylor twirls a lock of raven hair around her finger and says, "Doctor said she's fine. Only some cuts and bruises. They checked her out and did a bunch of scans and everything. Not even a concussion. But they'll watch her for a day or two just in case. As soon as they found out she is *the* Mrs. Maxwell Anderson, they gave her the VIP treatment and pampered her like the queen she is."

"I told them they didn't need to," Belle mumbles, clearly flustered.

"I'm glad they took care of you." If they didn't, I'll sue the shit out of them.

"It was so weird…oil on the stairs? Who the fuck would spill oil on the stairs and not clean it up afterward? Bastards. You *should* sue them," Taylor snarls, and my head snaps up.

"Don't! If they go under, what will happen to the animals?" Belle sneaks a worried glance at me.

"It was probably that asshole boss of hers, Bob something. He's always cutting corners and making a mess of the shelter." Millie scowls.

"Thank goodness Cole found her quickly," Grace chimes in.

My gaze darts to the blond in question, only to find his frosty glare still pinned on me. Stiffening, I meet his gaze straight on. *She's my wife and she'll never be yours.*

"Thank you." I manage to utter the bare minimum.

He grunts and turns away.

I'm going to find this Bob and unleash my wrath on him. For every bruise I find on Belle's body, I'm going to give it back to him tenfold.

A growl slips out of my mouth, and I curl my hands into fists.

"Don't listen to them, Maxwell. It was an accident, that's all." Belle grabs my hand.

Fury boils inside me as I strain a smile at her, not wanting her to worry. I pat her hand and step away, my other hand reaching inside my pocket to take out my phone.

Accident or not, I'm looking into this Bob person.

Leave no stone unturned. The curse isn't taking Belle from me.

CHAPTER 28

TURNING MY ATTENTION AWAY from the rough sketches of my fall/winter collection—a collection I'm calling "The Disaster" because everything I'm drawing looks like trash; I look outside the windows of the Elysium. It was supposed to be a slice of paradise for me in the mansion, a place where my creative juices could flow and I could show everyone how wrong they were for doubting my abilities.

But instead, I'm hitting a designer's block. I sigh and stare at the dreary skies and the thin layer of snow outside. Murky fog has invaded the premises, swallowing all the life and light, leaving nothing untouched. Winter came early this year, and this November feels exceptionally cold, the kind of chill that burrows deep inside your bones.

A few black crows swoop down from the skies, their squawking adding to the desolate atmosphere as I turn back to the charcoal drawings in my hand—simple silhouettes of sleeveless turtlenecks and long trousers—beautiful, understated, and infinitely *boring*.

How am I going to save McKenzie Atelier? Maxwell's investment will keep things afloat for a little while, but if the elite and celebrities don't come back into the fold, we'll eventually end up back where we were.

Rubbing the fading bruise on my arm, I wince at the lingering soreness from my accident two weeks ago. My tyrant of a husband insisted I stay at the hospital for an entire week to make sure I didn't have a secret concussion or some other hidden ailment. He moved me into a luxury suite and made sure I got around the clock care, even though I told him I was fine.

I remember how worried he was when he first saw me in the hospital.

The doctor had just left the room after telling me he thought I was fine from the fall. He mentioned as an aside, I wasn't pregnant based on the standard blood tests they ran on me.

I was reeling from the crushing disappointment when Maxwell stormed into the room like a madman. I still remember his fevered eyes, his hair in disarray, like he spent the entire car ride tugging it, and how he barged past my friends and took my hand by my bedside.

Like I was the most precious person to him.

Like he couldn't live without me.

My heart twists inside my chest. I wish my thoughts were true, that somehow, my cold, mercurial husband was secretly in love with me the way I'm slowly falling for him.

Maybe one day this arrangement of ours would become a real marriage.

He came over to the hospital every day at dinnertime and would bring Mora's meals in a container. We'd sit in silence and eat side by side, but his attentions appeared to be preoccupied.

"What are you thinking about?" I asked one night as he packed up Mora's containers into a bag.

His throat worked but didn't answer me. Disappointment filled me. He was keeping me at a distance...again.

I sighed. "Why are you here if you're going to be silent?"

"So you don't have to be alone." His piercing gaze snared on mine and for a moment, and I could've sworn he meant more than what he was saying, that he knew how lonely I was all my life, growing up locked away in my castle.

I bit back a smile.

His eyes flickered away, and I reached out for him but winced from the soreness in my body.

His nostrils flared, his eyes alert. "Are you okay? Do I need to call the doctor?"

I would've laughed if it didn't hurt so much. "I'm fine. Stop worrying."

"*Never*. I'll find the bastards responsible." Violence seeped into his voice.

"You told me you wouldn't do anything to the shelter!"

He looked away. "I promised nothing. No one hurts what's mine."

"I'm not yours," I muttered, but my heart skipped a beat.

He gripped my hand, forcing me to look at him. "For the duration of this arrangement, you're mine. Mine to protect. Mine to care for. Don't you forget it."

Heat unfurled inside me, and my lips parted. My body couldn't help responding to the dominance in his voice.

I want to be his.

His eyes flared and snagged on my mouth, but then he dropped my hand and looked away.

Not wanting this distance between us, I whispered, "Should we practice your speech for the gala?"

Maxwell gave me a curt nod, and I smiled encouragingly at him. "You can do this. It's just you and me. Let's start from the beginning."

He took a deep breath and rolled out his muscles. Clearing his throat, he began, "Good evening, ladies and gentlemen. Thank you for coming to the ball."

It'd be a repeating cycle each night. He'd sit next to me and silently eat, then we'd practice his speech. He'd wait until I fell asleep before he'd disappear.

What's going on in that beautiful mind of yours, Maxwell?

I walk back to my writing desk and set my drawings and pencil down, ignoring the rattling of the tree branches against the building, the creepy creaking of the bones of the house, like it's restless, just like me.

Taking a seat at the chair, I close my eyes, exhaustion weighing heavily on my eyelids as I listen to the howling sounds of nature.

Moments pass by before I open my eyes. The skies are pitch black. I must've fallen asleep without realizing.

Stretching, I stare at the desk in front of me—it's my favorite furniture in the room. It's obviously an antique, well preserved and made of rosewood with gold hardware. I trail my fingers on the smooth surface, tracing the thin lines betraying the years of use before moving to the intricate scrollwork carving on the legs of the table and the drawers.

Judging by the items I found on the trays on the desk before, Maxwell's grandmother was probably the last person to use this space before the room was forgotten.

My elbow accidentally knocks into my drawings, and my pencil clatters to the ground in the gap behind the desk and the wall.

Squatting down, I move the chair out of the way and maneuver myself into the tight space under the desk. Pressing one hand to the inner surface of the furniture, my other hand moves around the floor to reach for the pencil.

"Almost there," I huff as I lean in, trying to grab it.

Click.

I freeze, my pulse quickening. *Did I just hear that?* Frowning, I crawl back out and look around, searching for the source of the sound.

A small drawer pops out from the side of the desk, previously hidden by the intricate carvings in the wood.

My eyes widen. *A hidden drawer!* I've heard about these contraptions in vintage furniture. The howling of the wind ratchets up, the clashing of the foliage outside more thunderous, but nothing can dim the excitement rushing through me.

Quickly, I look inside the compartment, finding one crinkled envelope, yellowed with age, the red wax seal of the Anderson lion already broken.

I carefully take it out, my fingers gingerly smoothing over the elegant script that says:

My Beloved Emma.

My breathing catches and a desperate ache gnaws inside my chest as I open the envelope and take out the letter. The paper is wrinkled, like someone balled it up before, and the penmanship is beautiful.

My Beloved Emma,

In the next few days, you will see me behave like the role I was born into, a coldhearted duke. But let me reassure you, the man you love is still here, still very much in love with you with all of his heart.

Louisa found out about our affair and confronted me about it. As your belly became swollen with our child, she grew suspicious, because she knew you didn't cavort with the men on our staff and you rarely go out, since you'd much prefer spending your free time painting or reading.

She asked the servants and under coercion, one of them told her about us. While our marriage isn't a love match, she has her pride, and I'm afraid she won't let this go and will hurt you. I'm afraid she'll thwart my plans of leaving her.

To protect you and our babe, I have to cut you off as would any man of my station do in such circumstances.

But fear not. After I settle my affairs here and hand over my duties to my brother, I'll find you.

We will escape and start a new life together. We will be free. While I won't have my wealth and influence, I know my life will be far richer because we'll be together. Bear with me and forgive me for the hurt I'm about to cause you.

I love you most ardently and fervently.

Wait for me.

Yours forever, this lifetime and all the lifetimes thereafter.

Silas

29th of September, 1860

The letter slides from my grip and flutters to the desk.

Noises travel in from the entryway and my heart thuds in a rapid rhythm.

"Silas! Please—"

"She's gone because of you!" A loud bellow and I jump in place. "She never saw it, did she? Because you took it! Louisa, you—"

Suddenly, the light from the lamp flickers off, plunging the room into darkness and I shriek.

I jolt awake, my eyes snapping open, my breathing coming out in quick pants. My face is drenched in sweat. The wind rattles the windows, but the room is bathed in afternoon light.

What on earth? Wasn't it nighttime? I blink a few times. Still daytime. *That must've been a dream. But it felt so real!*

I take a few deep breaths to calm my rioting pulse. Another strange dream, just like the others I've had. The tall man in the rose garden I've still not step foot in, how he has his back turned toward me, but his silhouette is infinitely familiar, like my imposing husband.

Blowing out a deep exhale, I wipe my face, finding my cheeks wet with tears.

My chest hurts from deep within, the swell of emotions leaving me mysteriously unmoored. My eyes burn with the urge to cry some more. *Why am I feeling so sad?*

Silas. 1860. The penmanship is still so vivid in my mind. It's so hauntingly real. My thoughts travel back to the voices I heard. *Silas. Louisa.* The duke and the duchess? I think about the portrait of the somber man, the one with the anguish in his eyes.

The man who looks so much like Maxwell.

The dream is about a letter from Maxwell's great-great-great-grand-father to a woman he clearly loved who was not his wife.

Did she get it? No, she mustn't have, based on what I heard. Where did she go? Why didn't they run off together? Seeing as Silas's portrait is hung in the gallery and there's no mention of him being a missing duke, I know they didn't get their happy ending.

And the thought, somehow, is unbearable.

Don't be so silly. It's a dream. It can't be real. That'd make no sense. But it feels so real—the love, the heartbreak, the stirring in my soul.

Unease swirls inside me and a thought occurs to me, one that has my lungs gasping for air.

What if?

I can't even bring myself to ask the question aloud as I kneel on the ground, my hand trembling, sliding to that spot underneath the desk, the one I remember from my dream.

Click.

My blood turns to ice and the room swirls around me. *It can't be. That's impossible.*

Getting back up, I look at the side of the desk. *This can't be happening.*

A small, hidden compartment is popped open. A compartment I wasn't aware was there before.

Inside lies an envelope, the same envelope I saw in my dreams.

My Beloved Emma.

Shaking, I fall into my chair, a chill settling into my bones. Quickly, I open the envelope, my mind swirling with thoughts, none of which makes sense.

Nothing is inside.

What on earth is going on?

CHAPTER 29

Belle 

THE NEXT AFTERNOON, I step out of my bathroom, a towel wrapped around my body, the hot shower doing little to warm me.

I can't seem to dispel the ice lodged inside my chest, and I wonder how much of it is because of the dismal weather outside or if it's something else. The room spins as the dizziness that has plagued me sporadically in the last few months makes a reappearance.

I've probably been working too hard, that's all. Or maybe those crazy dreams or visions or whatever you want to call them are impacting me.

I've wracked my brain trying to make sense of the dream in the Elysium—the hidden compartment, the letter which feels so real and yet there's no evidence of it ever being there, other than the empty envelope. Could I have come across their names before when I was exploring the library? Maybe saw a mention of a hidden compartment and somehow forgotten about it?

Many questions, but no answers.

I've spent hours in the library this morning reading Silas's journals, but like Maxwell said, there's nothing from the 1860s and the ones from later don't mention an Emma.

It's like my mind is spinning stories, just like the whispers and moans I hear in the house at night, the ones I attribute to the estate being old. I don't mention these dreams to Maxwell, because he'll think I'm crazy.

The answer will come to me. It has to.

A fresh wave of dizziness hits me and I close my eyes, willing it to stop.

Could I be pregnant?

My breath stalls, but then I remember I just had my period two weeks ago, and the hope deflates inside me.

We've only been trying for a few months, which is nothing for people my age, but with my condition, my ovaries aren't like those of someone in their mid-twenties. They are more like the ovaries of someone in their mid-forties or later. I don't have the luxury of time.

I may have buried myself under the covers and cried when I saw the toilet bowl filling with blood.

The strange spell passes, and suddenly, I feel fine again. I make a note to call my doctor to fit me into their schedule for a checkup.

Taking out a cashmere sweater from the walk-in closet, I hear a terse knock.

"Come in. The door is unlocked," I holler.

A heated, reassuring presence fills the room and I don't even need to turn around to know *he's* here.

"Belle, we need to talk." Maxwell sounds grim.

Frowning, I turn to him, finding his brows furrowed, his lips flattened, as he takes a seat on my bed. He's wearing a blue button-down shirt, his sleeves rolled up with the collar opened, looking much too good in business casual attire.

"What's going on?"

"You can't volunteer at the shelter anymore."

"What! Why?" My mouth drops open from shock.

"I looked into your boss, Bob, and I don't trust him. He's involved in some illegal activities and also has ties to a few gangs. It's not safe for you there."

Anger boils in my veins as I stalk toward him. "That's not for you to decide."

"Too bad. I already turned in your resignation."

"You *what?* How dare you!"

I'm going to hell for this. But Maxwell, you're already living in hell. The fruit of your temptation is dangling in front of you and you can't have it.

She storms up to me, a Valkyrie wrapped in a towel, looking like a wet dream come to life, and jabs me with her fingers. "You have *absolutely* no right to do this. I'm an independent woman. Just because I'm married to you doesn't mean you get to be a diabolical tyrant and control me, you asshole!"

Desperation scrapes inside me. Nothing came up in my cursory investigation of her fall other than her boss being involved in suspicious activities. Maybe he's behind this. Maybe it's the curse. Maybe they are one and the same. After all, before the women died in our family, there were always a series of unfortunate incidents—whether they be accidents or crimes.

And I can't protect her if she goes back to the shelter. She isn't safe there. She has already been hurt—it's too close of a call.

But Belle clearly doesn't care. She jabs my chest some more. "I won't do it. I'm going back to BSUA to ask them to take back my resignation, just you watch."

I snort and narrow my eyes. "Unless they want to piss me off, they won't dare to take you back. I've made that abundantly clear. If you try anything, I'll make a call to the mayor and get the shelter closed. Then what will happen to your precious animals?"

I'm definitely going to rot in hell for this.

I tower over her, but she doesn't cower. That fiery spirit, that strong backbone.

God, she's spectacular.

Heat swirls inside me and I lean down. "I've also hired you a body-guard. You're to take him with you at all times when you leave this house.

That's not up for negotiations. If you decide to disobey me, I'll pull the funding from McKenzie's, contract be damned."

She fists her hands by her sides and glares at me. If looks could kill, I would've died a thousand times over. "I don't know what I ever saw in you, Maxwell. Why I get fooled time and time again, thinking there's a sensitive soul inside you, thinking the Silas I met that first night is the real you buried deep inside the frigid billionaire the world knows."

I flinch. *That Silas is there. He's trying to protect you.*

But I don't say anything. *Hate me, Belle. It's better than you dying.*

She seethes, "A marriage doesn't work this way. You don't get to make unilateral decisions for me and expect me to obey, because I won't."

My blood runs cold. "Are you calling my bluff?"

"And what if I am? What are you going to do about it?"

My nostrils flare and I lean down further, watching her shiver, her eyes turning molten as if just realizing how irresistible her taunting made her. My gaze rakes down her body, scantily clad in the thin towel.

Her nipples are saluting me through the cloth and my cock rears to life. My mouth waters, wanting to taste them. She's clenching her thighs. *Fuck, she's turned on.*

"Watch out, *wife*. I might be a scarred, anxious freak, but I never bluff," I rasp, drawn to her heat, the lust in her eyes, until there's less than one inch of space between us.

"You're not a fre—" she begins but stops herself.

She was going to make me feel better, my beautiful, kind little muse.

My heart throws itself against my rib cage, the blood pumping hot in my veins. My hands tremble with the need to touch her, to kiss the living daylights out of her.

She grits out, "God, I *can't wait* until this arrangement is over. I hate you so fucking much."

I rear back, her words piercing my chest even though I know they aren't true, judging from the way her pupils are dilated, the pulse fluttering rapidly in her throat.

But they hurt, nonetheless.

I press my lips against her ear, relishing her half gasp, half moan. "Oh yeah? Not before you give me an heir, Belle."

Before she can respond, I spin her around and pin her to the bed, my foot kicking her feet apart. She thrashes underneath me, and I would've stopped if she wasn't rubbing her sweet ass all over my aching erection like she needs this as much as I do.

Fuck, I should leave this room. I'm too emotional, too mad at her, for her, with her. I'm so goddamn crazy about her I can't think straight.

But instead, I trail my hand down her luscious, towel-clad body and squeeze the firm globes of her ass. She arches up, clearly wanting me to touch her between her legs where her little wet pussy is waiting for me.

I can smell her arousal and it gives me the highest of highs.

"My little muse," I rasp, "you may say you hate me, but your body tells me another story."

I bite her earlobe and she flinches, but she lets out a lusty moan when I soothe the pain with a swirl of my tongue. Belle whimpers, her body still half-heartedly fighting me, but she spreads her legs some more, her hand reaching back, grabbing mine, and trying to move it between her legs.

With one hand, I pin her arm to her back, my other hand yanking up her towel in one smooth motion. Her slick pussy pulses and pre-cum drips from my cock.

"Fuck, look at this wet cunt, all for the man you hate, huh? I wonder how much wetter you'll be for a man you love?" My mind is in a crimson haze as I imagine another man seeing her like this. Writhing, moaning, whimpering for him.

He'd get to kiss her, love her, do everything I couldn't do.

And fuck if that doesn't make me want to burn the world.

I quickly unbuckle my belt, pull down my zipper, and take out my throbbing cock, the tip dark red and dripping for her, needing to be inside her.

Unable to help myself, I rub the tip between her hot folds and hiss from the sharp pleasure.

She mewls when I circle her swollen clit with the tip. I'm not going to kiss her. I'm not going to take off my clothes or her towel and make this any more intimate than it already is.

Because I know that'll unmoor me and my control is already so close to snapping.

She thrashes on the bed, clearly needing more. But it's no use. I have her pinned underneath me, her ass up, legs spread, arms behind her. It's a position that may be degrading to some, but my slutty wife likes it.

She likes it when I take control, and I want to be her master, fucking orgasm after orgasm out of her, so she'll be addicted to me, to my cock, to the pleasure only I can give her.

Because that's all I'm allowed to give her.

Nothing more. I need to protect her.

Groaning, I thrust into her to the hilt, her tight pussy clamping me in a vise and I nearly see stars. Unable to stop myself or slow down, I rut against her, the pleasure gathering rapidly in my groin.

The headboard slams against the wall in a loud, staccato rhythm. Moments later, the crystals from the lamp on the nightstand also shake, the clinking sound adding to the lewd symphony of hate sex.

"Maxwell, they'll hear us, oh my God!" she cries as I speed up, angling my cock deeper, gyrating it on my way out so it caresses her G-spot with each glide. Sparks gather up my spine.

"Fuck them. I don't care. Let them hear you scream for a man you hate."

Pistoning harder inside her, I bear my weight on her body, smashing her face against the comforter, but I'm too far gone to care. Belle moans with each stroke, her back arching like she can't get enough.

Fuck, she's taking me so well.

"You're a fucking good wife for me, aren't you? Now you're going to listen to your husband and do what I tell you to do."

"Never!" she whimpers, but she melts against me.

My cock hardens to the point of bursting as I feel more wetness drip out of her. My little muse likes it when I boss her around.

The pleasurable burning between my legs intensifies, my balls swelling, cock pulsing, my body ready to detonate.

"You like this, little muse? Me fucking your pussy because I own it like I own you?"

"Never!" she screams again, and I wrap her hair around my hand and pull, watching her eyes roll back.

The pleasure climbs to a tipping point, traveling from my heavy balls to my cock—the point between heaven or hell. Her body starts spasming underneath me.

"Come, Belle. Take every ounce of cum inside that tight pussy. Scream and show the world what a slut you are for me. This is what you want, right? My cum deep inside you, flooding your womb."

My mind is filled with visions of my cum dripping out of her and her belly swelling with my baby, and all rational thoughts leave my mind.

Letting go of her hands, I slide my thumb to the crease of her ass and dip it into her sensitive, puckered hole.

"Maxwell!"

She explodes, her screams of pleasure echoing in the room. I feel spurts of liquid dripping down my legs. *Fuck me, she squirted.*

My thrusts turn erratic and I clutch her neck in a tight clasp as nirvana overtakes me. I roar against her ear, my cock throbbing, unloading ropes of cum inside her tight, wet channel.

We're a mess of anger and lust, hatred and another emotion I don't dare name, our heavy breaths sounding loud in the quiet room. She and I are oil and water, explosives and fire, combustible and unable to stay away from each other.

I notice the moment she realizes I haven't kissed her, opting to fuck her face down in the most impersonal way ever. Again. Her nostrils flare as hurt flashes on her face. She grips her towel tightly, her muscles tensing.

I pull out before I can throw myself at her feet and beg her for forgiveness.

"You're an Anderson, and you're my wife," I growl. "You won't volunteer at BSUA, and you'll take your bodyguard with you whenever you leave the house."

I walk to the door. *Don't look back. Don't you fucking look back, Maxwell.*

I open the door.

"I hate you!" she screams and I flinch, my heart spasming in pain.

"Perfect, then you can hate me even more. *I don't care.*" I slam the door shut and lean against the wall outside her room.

I hate myself for hurting her, this angel of brightness.

I hate myself for being the eldest son, cursed to live a cold, lonely life, haunted by dark dreams and death.

I hate myself for being weak, for not being able to stay away from her, for not being strong enough to let her go to protect her.

I hate myself for wanting to once again throw caution to the wind, to tempt fate once more, because I want her for myself.

And I hate myself because despite everything—all the losses, the deaths, the fact she got hurt under my watch—I still want her to look at me with love in her eyes, like I'm everything she needs in this entire world.

CHAPTER 30

Belle

"IF THESE ARE YOUR concept drawings, then I might as well look for a new job now because McKenzie's will be brought down by you, Belle!" Gordon tossed my initial sketches of The Disaster into the trash can and sneered at me, contempt dripping from his beady black eyes.

Gritting my teeth, I fought every urge to give him a right hook because getting arrested for assault wouldn't do the company's image any favors. "You've given me an impossible task, Gordon."

He scoffed. "It's impossible because you aren't qualified to be here. You're only here because of your family, fucking nepo baby, and the elite have caught on. They aren't buying what you're selling and to think, your parents want you to lead the company one day."

Gordon pointed to the papers in the trash can. "Complete trash. Uninspiring trash that isn't even worthy to be in my trash can."

Fuck you, Gordon, I'll show you.

I blow out a frustrated exhale as I turn on the electric lamp I placed in the secret passageway a few weeks ago. Memories of yesterday's horrendous exchange with Gordon at work flood my mind. He purposely left his office door cracked open as he ripped me a new one because he wanted to undermine me in front of everyone at every opportunity.

I know it's because he's pissed his last name isn't Law-McKenzie and he won't ever get the chance to run the company.

Dammit. This is just what I need on top of dealing with my maddening husband. The frigid king has made no effort to find me since our hate sex encounter two weeks ago, and I've gone out of my way to avoid him as well.

But I have fired the bodyguard—after giving him a nice bonus for his troubles, of course. I told Maxwell I would move out if he insisted on assigning me a shadow.

I guess I should be pleased he backed off, since that meant he wanted me living with him more than he wanted to get his way.

These bastards in my life.

My footsteps echo in the narrow corridor and the familiar haunted howls of the draft keep me company as I make my way toward the Elysium.

It's the day before Thanksgiving, and I have a few hours to spare before I'm to find Melody and Mora in the kitchens to finalize the menu for the charity gala next month. The annoying wave of dizziness hits me again and I place my hands on the stone wall for support, waiting for the spell to pass.

Clutching the vintage locket around my neck, my fingers trail over each intricate petal and gemstone on the jewelry, a familiar melancholic hollow filling my chest.

I visited Dr. Chen last week for my strange symptoms, and she performed a checkup and ran some bloodwork, but everything came back normal. *Perhaps it was stress,* she said.

Normal. Not pregnant. Stress.

The dizzy spell passes, but the chasm widens inside me and my eyes prickle with tears. I swallow the lump in my throat.

What am I doing? Married to a man who enthralls me and infuriates me, a man who's determined not to love me and is downright cruel at times. I'm not pregnant, not saving any animals or even volunteering at the shelter because that bastard took that away too. And now, I'm failing at saving Grandpa's legacy.

A sob wrenches from my throat as I clutch the locket tighter in my hand.

Wiping my tears on my sleeve, I continue down the passageway and push open the secret door to the Elysium but the soft light in the room stops me in my tracks.

The antique desk lamp is turned on.

I freeze. I'm sure I turned it off before I left the room yesterday afternoon.

I must have, right?

It's then I notice the heavy drapes are drawn shut, the sounds of the wind moaning outside more muted than usual.

Someone has been in here.

My pulse quickens as I slowly approach the desk, wondering if I'm going crazy from the stress or if it's the house driving me insane.

Then I see the drawings.

Someone has modified them.

I started a new batch of designs yesterday after my meeting with Gordon—a collection of shawls and scarves to be made with biodegradable non-wool fabrics such as hemp, bamboo fibers, and organic cotton. I had a list of all the random, illogical "rules" Gordon gave me for this project—no wool, no long sleeves, and other idiotic restrictions—next to my drafts.

But now, instead of my original sketches, someone has merged my original and new designs together in an artistic rendition of a stunning tank top with a wraparound shawl that functions as *sleeves* without being actual sleeves.

Then I notice the masculine scribbles on the side of the drawing.

I'M NOT A DESIGNER, BUT I THINK THIS WOULD FIT THE RULES AND BE QUITE UNIQUE, DON'T YOU THINK?

A sweet warmth sweeps into my chest, chasing away the chills from earlier, and my lips twitch up into a smile. *Damn him.*

Maxwell. He was here, working on my drawings, *my disaster*. Somehow, he knew I was stuck.

Gingerly, I pick up the sketch and trace my fingers over the clean lines of the drawing, obviously rendered by someone who's an artist but isn't familiar with clothing design. But the concept is there.

It's brilliant.

All along, I was trying to color inside the lines, to follow Gordon's pathetic rules to a T when I should be bending them. If I want to be the head designer of McKenzie's one day and follow Grandpa's footsteps in creating innovative clothing the public can't get enough of, I need to break the mold.

Feeling invigorated, new ideas spark in my mind and I head to the bookshelf to pull out volumes on vintage fashion I found earlier.

Smiling, I return to the desk with a stack of three leather books. I flip through the pages to find what I'm looking for and begin jotting down ideas on a new sheet of paper.

I don't even bother opening the drapes or turning on more lights, opting to dive straight into work, the rattling of the windows from the elements outside and the creaking of the floorboards no longer bothering me.

The hours fly by as I work tirelessly at my designs, rendering sketch after sketch, ordering fabric swatches online, my mind brimming with new ideas and more questions. It's like I've finally smashed through an invisible barrier and can see the finish line ahead.

Riiiing.

The loud ringtone of my phone startles me and I drop my pencil before snatching up the offending piece of technology.

Bronx Shelter for Unwanted Animals.

I *really* hate this name.

Frowning, I stare at the ringing phone, wondering why the shelter is calling me after I "resigned."

Pressing a button, I answer, "Hello?"

"Is this Ms. Annabelle Law-McKenzie Anderson?" an unfamiliar woman's voice sounds across the line. I startle at my new last name—despite being married for a while, I haven't had anyone call me an Anderson until now. Then I remember what a bastard my husband is and I scowl.

"Yes, this is she. Who is this?"

"Hi! I'm Dr. Naomi Wong from BSUA. You don't know me because I just started last week, but I want to personally call you and thank you." Her voice is excited—a warm, audible hug.

"You're welcome? Um... What is this about?"

"Your generous donation! This is the largest donation the shelter has ever received since it opened its doors sixty years ago. We have enough funding to last us for the next five years and also to complete some much need renovations here."

"Donation?" My mouth drops open and I stare at the phone in bewilderment.

"Thank you so much for your generosity. As per your terms, we are now a no-kill shelter, and any animals with us can stay permanently even if we can't find their forever homes. The board has hired me on as the director to revamp this place. I assure you, I have plenty of experience working with animals and shelters as I'm a veterinarian at..."

Shock sears me and I barely pay attention as she chatters about how Bob has mysteriously left his position. She walks me through her resume, which includes working at some of the largest animal rights organizations and shelters in the world, and about the plans she has to shine more awareness to the cause. Her goal is to eradicate kill shelters too.

My heart sprints around my rib cage, her words echoing in my ears, and all I manage to do is to utter "you're welcome," and "of course" when she invites me to a luncheon next week.

"Thank you again, Belle, for your generosity and kind heart. We'll talk soon," she says and we hang up.

My pulse rings in my ears as I sit there, stupefied, wondering what just happened and who could've done this when my eyes snag on the masculine scribbles on my drawing again.

Maxwell.

He must have done this.

My heart jolts into a sprint, running toward an unknown destination, and I stand up, a sizzling current rushing through my body.

I need to see him, to ask him if this is all him.

Laughing under my breath from all the good news, my mood climbing back to an all-time high on this insane rollercoaster ride I find myself on, I run through the passageway, pass the mistress's bedroom, then out on to the quiet corridors of the house.

Morris strolls by with Agnes. His eyebrow is cocked high, and I grin at him but don't slow down. Agnes shakes her head as she mutters something under her breath, but I don't pay her any attention.

Exhilaration floods my body—no one can ruin my day now.

Dashing to his study, I heave out a breath before throwing open the door, but the room is empty. He must be in his studio then. Running past the staircase, I make a turn at the end of the corridor, barely noticing that Silas isn't around to bark after me as he usually does when he sees me sprinting down the halls, no doubt thinking I want to play with him.

I slow my footsteps as I approach the studio, my breaths sawing in and out of my lungs in rapid pants. *Act cool, Belle. Act cool.* Wetting my lips, I wipe my damp hands on my pants and knock on the door.

No one answers, but I hear the beautiful strains of "Nessun Dorma" streaming in from inside and I smile.

Our song. The music that'll forever remind me of him.

Turning the doorknob, I gently push open the door and swallow a gasp.

Maxwell is laughing, his deep chuckles sounding more beautiful than the tenor's voice, a paintbrush tucked behind his ear. He's kneeling in front of an easel, his fingers scratching Silas's belly.

Silas lets out a happy howl, his tail beating loudly against the floor.

"You like this spot, don't you, you little terror," Maxwell says, still not having noticed me, as he tends to a sensitive spot under Silas's collar.

Silas barks and stretches his body on the floor, giving Maxwell more access.

"You're insatiable. Give you a scratch and you want more. And more. And more, until I can't get any work done and you take over my time and my life...just like your mistress," Maxwell murmurs, his lips curving into a smile, his voice infused with warmth.

My heart stutters to a stop and restarts before careening past the finish line, and I fall, head over heels, madly into something I never want to admit to with this man.

This infuriating, frustrating, overbearing man.

This passionate, kindhearted, beautiful man.

Butterfly wings flap in my stomach and wetness mists my eyes. The gasp I was holding in finally comes tumbling out.

Maxwell startles and freezes, his muscles bunching up under his cream-colored turtleneck sweater. He slowly lifts his head, his warm eyes snagging mine.

For a few seconds, all we can do is to stare at each other, the ethereal music wrapping us in a tender embrace, the world slowly fading away until all that remains is a man and a woman, two kindred souls with too many secrets and unsaid sentiments.

Maxwell and Belle, an artist and his little muse.

"Belle," he whispers, awe-infusing his voice as his gaze rakes over me.

Slowly, he stands up, and I notice the vein in his neck pulsing, his throat rippling as if he wants to say something but can't find the words.

I know how you feel.

Blinking the wetness away from my eyes, I fly toward him, and he opens his arms wide.

"Thank you, Maxwell," I sob into his shoulder as he wraps me in his warm embrace. "Thank you so, so much!"

"Belle, I'm sorry," he whispers into my ear. "I'm sorry for hurting you."

His arms bind me tightly to him, his heat a fiery brand against my body, his scent of sandalwood and amber searing itself into my brain.

I shake in his arms, too overcome with emotions to say anything else.

I'm home.

It's an instinct, a gut feeling, a belief that transcends time or logic. I'm home...and stupid curse or not, I never want to leave.

CHAPTER 31

A SUFFOCATING PRESSURE SITS atop my chest as I pull open the drapes in the study and watch the snowstorm obliterate the world in a tempest of white. The wind is restless, a vengeful spirit battering against the windows, begging to be let in, to spread its deathly chill to the inhabitants of the estate.

The same restlessness lives inside me as I clutch the speech I'm supposed to make in a few hours in my hand. Lana and the PR think tank drafted the quick speech that should be easy to do. *Should* being the operative word. They might as well be asking me to climb Mount Everest.

I can feel the stirrings of another monster trying to claw itself out of my chest.

"Sir Maxwell, your family just arrived. Should I bring them here?" Morris asks from behind me.

"We're barging in, whether he likes it or not!" Rex announces seconds later, completely disregarding Morris's traditional efforts to keep them in the sitting room while he finds me to announce their arrival.

Smirking, I turn around, grateful for Rex and his usual antics as a distraction from my dark mood. "Rex, nice of you to show up on time today."

"It's too early for my taste. If it weren't for Ethan and Lana dragging me out of bed, I would've shown up later."

"It's five in the afternoon."

"On a *Saturday*."

"Did someone just say my name?" Lana exclaims before sweeping into the room with a sly smile on her face. Her navy gown billows behind her. She strides up to me and gives me a hug.

I feel Morris's intense stare as I return her embrace and I give him a nod, telling him it's okay. A flash of sadness appears on his face before he returns my acknowledgment and leaves the room. I frown, not sure what that's all about.

"I said you are a cockblocker, Lana. Hold on, is that what you say when someone stops you from getting pussy? Or is it pussy blocker?" Rex looks sincerely confused. It'd almost be funny if I weren't so distracted by my upcoming speech.

"Oh fuck. The Anderson manners are wasted on you, Rex," Ethan grumbles and rolls his eyes heavenward before helping himself to a drink at the wet bar.

"We aren't in the eighteenth century anymore! Live a little!" Rex waggles his brows.

"The term is still cockblocker, by the way," Lana chimes in happily as she slings her arm around Rex's neck. "You have horrible taste in women."

Rex has to lean down in order for her to loop her arm around his neck and the two squabble the way they've always had growing up, the duo as thick as thieves.

"I'm not marrying her! She's a supermodel, Lana. Emphasis on the *super*. Ten out of ten. Those perky tits. That round ass." Rex smirks and waggles his brows.

"Ew. How am I related to you? I guess you overlooked how she blackmailed three of her ex-boyfriends in the past. I don't want to bail you out from some PR scandal."

"Blackmail? Is there something I should know?" a deep voice sounds from the doorway.

Elias Kent leans against the frame, his fingers fiddling with an ornate lighter—something I've seen him carry around everywhere even though the man doesn't smoke. He lifts his head and turns toward us, his lips curved in a ghost of a smile.

"Rex and Lana are just getting into their usual fights, no blackmail. Your services aren't necessary," I reply, watching his attention turn toward my squabbling siblings, with Lana throwing her head back in laughter as she says something that's making Rex's ears turn red.

"I see." He stares for a beat longer than necessary and I frown, trying to figure out who he's focusing on with his lasered attention.

Elias straightens and cracks the joints on his neck before murmuring, "Well, I want to wish you good luck on the speech today. And I'm having the issues looked into. You should've contacted me sooner. The trail grows cold over time, but my men will update me as they get more info."

I was hoping I'd get to the bottom of things without his *services*. They usually come with a hefty non-monetary price tag.

"Thanks. I know I can count on you to get to the bottom of this."

Despite Elias being the ruler of the New York underground, the infamous mobster everyone is fearful of, he has been a friend of our family ever since he appeared in our lives a long time ago after a chance encounter when Ryland and I saved his life.

Ever since then, he's been a dark shadow lurking in the background, a silent sentinel who has helped our family out of a bind a few times, from assisting Steven with the hostile takeover situation of his father's company to supporting Millie and Ryland when the scandal of their professor and student relationship broke to the press half a year ago. He has even invested in The Orchid and handles the staffing of the people working on the Rose floors, *voluntarily*, of course. He abhors human and sexual trafficking.

A villain with morals.

He may be dangerous, but I trust him.

I walk to the man, who is preparing to leave, and ask, "Could it just be an accident?" The thought doesn't make me feel any better because of the curse, but it's better than someone actively out there trying to hurt Belle.

"Maybe, but I don't believe in coincidences. Oil slick on stairs? A burst pipe that happened in a brand-new building? And you obviously have your concerns or you wouldn't have called me."

"Nothing came up for Bob Heines? I didn't get too much other than suspected illegal activities in my background check." He's the former boss everyone seems to hate at the shelter.

Elias shakes his head. "Lowlife with gambling debts who has a few low-level politicians in his pocket. He's scum but doesn't know anything."

"You sure? Belle's friends seem to think he has something to do with the incident."

Elias turns toward me, a chill falling across his features. The vertical scar spanning one side of his face twitches. The silent, lethal assassin.

His lips curl up on one side and he murmurs, out of earshot of the others in the room, "Trust me. *I made sure* he was telling the truth."

I swallow, not needing any more clarification from him. I don't care what methods he used to get his information—I'll kill anyone who hurts my family.

Fuck. I'm thinking of her as my family.

"Thank you." I clasp his shoulder.

He nods and walks off, disappearing into the dark shadows of the corridor.

"The man is a phantom, I tell you," Rex comments, suddenly appearing behind me. "What were you guys talking about? It looked serious."

"Nothing." I don't want them worried about Belle...or me. They don't need to know I suspect something nefarious is going on.

Less than a minute later, Ryland and Steven walk toward us. Like us, they're dressed to the nines, and Ryland is laughing at something Steven is saying, whose tall frame shaking with mirth.

A warmth seeps into my chest as I see my twin happy—the type of happiness that can't be faked—a transformation I've witnessed ever since he's embraced his life's passion as a professor and gotten together with Millie.

My mind shifts to Sydney again, to that conversation a long time ago, the one I never told him I overheard. Like me, he was devastated when she died, and I've always wondered if he held any resentment toward me.

If it weren't for me, they could've been together. Perhaps she wouldn't have been on the boat that night.

She wouldn't have been subjected to the curse.

As if sensing my thoughts, damn twin-sense, his gaze flickers to mine, his brows pinching in concern. I shake my head and smile. *I'm fine.*

He grins and tugs the leather bracelet on his wrist, its matching partner on my arm, a present I gave him during a trip to Ireland. It has an inscription:

"Let all that you do be done in love."

- 1 Corinthians 13:4

We're brothers. We'll always be fine.

And he's so damn happy right now. The love and contentment radiating from him is almost infectious. It's everything I've ever wanted for him.

"Want to run the speech by us?" Steven asks, his black hair glinting almost blue under the bluish daylight.

"I don't think that's going to matter. I've already practiced with Belle." My lips quirk into a smile as I think of my wife and how patient and encouraging she was with me these last few weeks when we worked on the speech over and over again. "And frankly, I'm always comfortable around you guys. It's the crowd of vultures out there I can't predict."

"I have faith in you," Ryland says and pats my shoulder. "We're all here for you. Just focus on us if you need to stare at someone later on."

"Or you can look at my handsome face and all will be fine," Rex quips and waggles his brows, and we all groan.

Crash!

Glass shards explode into the room, followed by a thunderous roar. Lana's screams pierce the air as Rex shoves her behind him. I recoil from the noise, the mournful wail of the wind bellowing into the room, flinging torrents of snow inside.

Papers whirl off my desk and books topple off the shelves as nature's fury invades the study.

"Fuck! What was that?" Rex exclaims. He swipes his hand over a few small cuts on his jaw from the glass shards before tending to Lana, who looks shaken but otherwise unharmed.

We all stare at the room that was pristine a moment ago but is now a victim of the murderous snowstorm—the debris and wreckage strewn about in a random act of violence.

A thick, skeletal tree branch is lodged through one of the broken windows.

My heart lurches to my throat. *It can't be.*

"Shit, we should've refurbished these windows a long time ago," Ryland comments as he walks toward the mess. He snakes a nervous glance at me but doesn't say anything. I know he's thinking what I'm thinking.

The branch. The broken windows. The omen.

"Double panes like the ones at The Orchid," Steven adds, oblivious to the tension. He examines the large branch. "It must've been from one of the trees outside the window or something."

Ice fills my veins as I stare at the gnarly branch, unable to move, unable to breathe.

The curse, the winds seem to wail. *Stay away from her.*

The warmth from minutes ago is swiftly replaced by a bone-chilling fear, which is seeking my panic as its macabre dance partner.

I tug my bow tie. I can't breathe. I can't fucking breathe.

Stay away...

"Oh God, it's happening again," Agnes whispers next to me, her skin as pale as a ghost. She must've come in during the commotion. Beside her, Morris is standing tall, his face grim. A muscle pulses in his jaw.

"The curse." She moves her hand to her forehead and chest—a sign of the cross—and closes her eyes, her mouth moving rapidly and I hear her whispered words of prayer.

It can't be.

Sydney, her green eyes unseeing, her mouth parted as if opened in a silent scream, her blond hair tangled and her pale skin blue. Her lifeless body sprawled on the beach.

Sweat gathers on my forehead. I shake myself.

It can't be. I haven't fallen in love with her. I won't *fall in love with her.*

My heart seizes, the escalating pain in my chest eviscerating.

The staff struggle to block off the shattered windows with a tarp as the storm surges outside, battering against the centuries' old structure, the violence unrelenting, the outdoors a nightmare in monochrome white.

The image of Sydney transforms into one of Belle, her eyes brimming with tears, her lips parted in terror as she reaches for me. It's like my dreams of the woman in the rose garden, but this time I see her face clearly. A darkness lurks behind Belle, dragging her into a bottomless black hole as she screams for me.

And I'm helpless, my hands and feet bound tightly, unable to move even as my heart splinters into a thousand pieces.

"No, no, no, it can't be," I whisper under my breath, shutting my eyes.

I can't love her.

She can't leave me.

Not this time.

The thought materializes in the back of my mind, a ghostly whisper, like a wraith from a past I'm not privy to.

CHAPTER 32

Belle

"You've brought back life into the place," Melody exclaims, her voice awestruck as we admire the opulent ballroom filling up with guests for the gala. "Growing up here, it always felt like a mausoleum, no sign of life. But now...now we're talking."

There was a disturbance earlier in the day, and some of the staff went to assist while Melody and I helped to finish the setup for the event.

It's the first public affair the Anderson Estate has hosted since the early nineteen hundreds. The press is salivating at the event hailed as more exclusive than the Met Gala *and* the usual crème de la crème event of the year, the annual Christmas Ball at The Orchid. That Ball was unprecedentedly canceled this year for this occasion.

I smile, marveling at the soaring, intricate coffered ceilings, the two enormous three-tiered crystal chandeliers lit up by *real* candles, the flames casting dancing shadows on the walls and the ceiling. A towering twenty-foot Christmas tree is tucked away in the corner and the sea of stark white from the storm outside the windows acts as a backdrop.

"You did all the hard work—you and your mom."

"Under your impeccable leadership, Your Grace." She sweeps her hand in a mocking bow and I grin.

"Technically, you're supposed to curtsy. You're a woman. Also, I'm not a duchess, I'm a marchioness. So, it should be 'my lady' instead." *Thank you, Millie and Grace, for that interesting factoid.*

"Ugh! You'd think after growing up here for almost thirty years, I'd know this stuff."

Laughing, I nudge her on the side as Morris walks in, his eyes roving around the ballroom before landing on Agnes. He frowns as he stalks toward her.

"What's going on with Agnes and Morris? They don't look happy with each other. I mean, Agnes isn't exactly the warm and fuzzy type," I murmur, staring at the housekeeper and Morris in some sort of heated discussion in the corner, a flush creeping up the old man's neck.

Melody shrugs. "I have no clue, but my money would be on Agnes being the problem. Morris gets along with everyone—he's like the old grandpa we all want to have. Agnes, on the other hand..." She doesn't finish the sentence, but she doesn't need to. The woman is as cold as the Arctic.

Morris throws his hand in the air before turning around and stomping off, his limp much more pronounced.

"Why doesn't Morris retire? His leg looks like it's hurting him a lot," I ask.

Melody sighs. "Trust me, Sir Linus and Sir Maxwell have both asked him to retire, saying he can just stay here in the estate and enjoy his remaining years, but he refuses. I think he wants to feel useful. The Andersons are like the only family he has left."

"What do you mean?"

"His parents and older sister, Ruth, used to work for the family. Now, mind you, this was way before my time. But from what Mom told me, Ruth was ten years older than Morris and the two were very close, but she died young."

Melody looks at me and whispers, "They said she disappeared one day and was found dead. The killer was never found."

I gasp. "What? How horrible!"

Melody nods. "It gets even worse. Apparently, their parents were so overcome with grief that in a span of a year, they both died, leaving Morris alone. I think he was," she scrunches her brows, "fifteen or sixteen at the time?"

My heart aches for the old butler. What a young age to lose everyone you love. "So he's been here ever since? Never married?"

"Yeah. I think he's stuck—like he can't move on if his family can't either. It's really sad. Luckily, the Andersons are good employers. They treat him like family."

I nod. I should talk to him more, give him some company then. I know how it feels to be alone in the world…and my parents, as problematic as they are, are still alive.

We make our way around the ballroom and finish the final touch ups—adjusting the white tablecloths at the tables spaced throughout or relighting candles that have snuffed out in the twelve-candle candelabras serving as centerpieces.

The gothic atmosphere of the house lends to an air of mystery and romance, and I intend to play it up as a nod to the gala name: The Anderson Legacy Ball. It may have been a bit on the nose to name the gala after the family. However, Lana said that with all the swirling press about Fleur Entertainment's leadership and Maxwell's mental health, it'd be a good thing to associate a charity ball with the family name.

My phone buzzes in the pocket of my gown and I take it out, absentmindedly swiping it open.

Cole

> Merry Christmas, Belle. I'm sorry I can't come to your gala and it took me so long to respond.

The three dots appear and I wait for him to finish his thoughts.

Cole

> The holiday season is a period of mourning for my family because this used to be my cousin's favorite time of the year, but she's no longer with us.

Oh, Cole. My fingers fly across the keyboard as I reply.

I frown, unsure how to respond.

"Wraithmoor Abbey back to its former glory!" Melody whistles under her breath after making her way back to my side.

"Wraithmoor Abbey?"

The name echoes in my mind. Goosebumps prickle my arms as I remember what Eleanor, the shopkeeper, told me when I picked up the necklace I'm wearing around my neck now.

"You didn't know?" She quirks her brow. "I can't believe no one has told you before. This place used to be called Wraithmoor Abbey. They changed the name after Sir Linus's wife passed away."

Melody leans in, clearly noting the guests funneling in through the double doors. "They say the place is haunted because it was built on top of a torn down church."

It was burned. The church was burned down. I shiver, remembering what Eleanor said that day. I can't believe I've been living atop a graveyard this entire time.

Melody prattles on, oblivious to my quickening breaths and rising panic. "And you know what they say, don't tear down houses of worship and most definitely don't build on top of them."

Suddenly, everything makes sense. The groaning and creaking of the mansion at odd hours in the night, the cries of the wind, the strange sounds of doors slamming and windows rattling. Then there's Agnes's grim face when she told me not to ask questions I didn't want answers to.

Stop it, Belle. You don't believe in this stuff.

"Do you know why they changed the name?" I can't help but ask, even as my hands grow clammy.

"Well, from what I heard—"

"Belle, you've outdone yourself!" Grace squeals as she approaches us with Steven in tow. "Look at this place! Everything...sparkles!"

Steven chuckles, shaking his head at his fiancée's excitement, the love shining clearly in his eyes as he tugs her close to him. The two of them have endured some dramatic ups and downs worthy of a daytime soap opera. I'm so happy things turned out well for them.

"Belle, how are things going?" Steven asks. He sounds casual, but a muscle is pulsing in his jaw. Something has clearly unsettled him and he's worried.

"We're good down here. Is everything okay? There was a disturbance earlier, right?"

"A tree branch blew in by the storm and broke one of the windows in Maxwell's study."

I gasp. "Is everyone okay? Is Maxwell okay?" My feet move toward the ballroom doors before I finish asking my question.

"He's fine, Belle. They're cleaning up. Rex had some scrapes, all minor flesh wounds, and the staff is patching up the damage as we speak."

"Good, good." I blow out a breath. "Never a dull moment around here, huh?"

But then, a thought occurs to me, one that sends my frayed nerves haywire again. "Did you say a *tree branch* broke through the windows of his study?"

It can't be. That's impossible. I look outside the windows, seeing the winter storm surging around us. *A branch. A storm. Broken windows.* Melody's story the afternoon in the kitchen floats to my mind.

Steven nods.

Grace frowns, her eyes whipping between the two of us. "What's wrong?"

"There are no trees outside his study. It's on the fourth floor," Melody whispers, clearly rattled, her skin leached of color. "Oh God, it's happening again." Her eyes dart to me in panic. "Excuse me, I need to talk to Mom."

Without another word, she dashes out of the ballroom, leaving us in a tensed silence. Nausea bubbles inside me as my breathing quickens. Dread crawls up my skin. *Stop it, Belle. You don't believe in the curse. This is ridiculous. It's just a freak accident.*

"Uh, what's going on? Why did she run off when I arrived?"

I jump, my heart seizing, and turn around, finding Taylor staring at us in a glorious black ball gown, reminding me of the black swan in *Swan Lake*. "Geez! You scared me, Tay!"

"What the hell is going on? You look like you've seen a ghost or something."

"Not sure...something feels off." Grace pulls Taylor into our group and explains the events of the past few minutes.

"So, do they think it's a ghost? An apparition?" Taylor whisper shouts—she's not exactly known for her subtlety.

"Seriously, ghosts? What are you, five?" a gravelly voice asks and I see Charles sauntering toward us, his blond hair gleaming gold under the candlelight, the CEO of the Bank of Columbia who is perpetually single yet claims he's always looking for his true love.

"Only the ignorant mock things they don't understand." Taylor scowls at him and rolls her eyes.

"I swear, the age difference between us has never seemed greater. Do you need a pacifier?" Charles retorts before turning to Grace. "Millie just arrived, and she asked me to find you and Steven. Something about the Kingsleys calling to wish you guys a Merry Christmas."

"Shit!" Steven takes out his phone and groans. "Five missed calls." He tugs Grace toward the doors. "My parents and the video call. Adrian or Emily must've called Millie to remind us."

"See you guys later!" I holler at the two of them as they follow Charles out of the ballroom.

I walk to the windows and stare at the maelstrom of white, the faint shadows of twisted tree branches clawing against the strong winds.

Wraithmoor Abbey. Silas's letter. Broken hearts and lost loves. Grisly deaths spanning generations. The tree branch shattering a window. *Could it all really be pure coincidence? Or could it be...the curse?*

I shake myself, trying to dispel the slithering unease making its way up my spine. *You don't believe in curses, Belle.* There has to be a logical explanation for everything.

There has to be, right?

But in this moment, I'm not really sure of anything anymore.

CHAPTER 33

THE NEXT HOUR PASSES by in a blur as everyone takes their seats at the assigned tables. My parents have arrived and are sitting with Linus and some executives from McKenzie Atelier. Dinner is served by an army of staff members decked out in crisp black tuxes and dresses.

Mora outdid herself with the pan-seared *foie gras*, caviar with *crème fraîche* served on thin butter crackers, truffle deviled eggs, *canard à la presse*—a perfectly roasted duck breast with the creamiest bread pudding, and a swordfish dish that's perfectly tender and flavorful.

But I barely touch my meal, my mind on Maxwell, who still hasn't shown up yet. A flash of light temporarily blinds me and I see a press photographer discreetly taking a photo. Security is as tight tonight as it would've been at the Christmas Ball at The Orchid. While the press may send one photographer and reporter per major news outlet, the usual antics of the paparazzi are strictly prohibited unless they want to be blacklisted by the Andersons—an industry death sentence.

I put on the fake society smile I've spent years perfecting, fighting the urge to go and find my husband, who must be sweating bullets because of his upcoming speech.

"Is he coming down soon?" Taylor asks to my right, clearly thinking about the same thing.

"I think so. The speech is in twenty minutes. We've rehearsed it and I think he's ready, but the pressure is getting to him. What he needs is alone time and not us hovering over him, so I'm going to do that."

The answer is more for myself than for her because I want nothing more than to run up to his studio, where he's most likely holed up, and give him a big hug for support.

Since I found out he secretly invested in BSUA, fired Bob, and converted the shelter into a no-kill shelter, our relationship has thawed somewhat. I still don't appreciate his overbearing, domineering personality, but at least he knows he's in the wrong for resigning from BSUA on my behalf without consulting me beforehand.

But he still doesn't kiss me or undress me whenever he comes into my room once a week to fulfill his "husbandly duties." He still has me pressed face down on the bed, the room cloaked in darkness like he can't bear to see what we're doing even as he delivers the most efficient orgasm to me and slakes his lust inside my body.

And I'm still not pregnant. It's like adding salt to the wound.

My chest aches every time these thoughts cross my mind. I wish I could break down this thick wall between us.

I wish I could have my Silas back.

The sound of a chair scraping on the parquet floor and the whiff of sandalwood and amber alerts me to his presence as he takes a seat next to me.

"Belle," he murmurs. "The gala is going well. You've held up your end of the bargain."

The bargain. The pressure in my chest increases. I have to remember that's all there is to it. Only an arranged marriage that has turned into a marriage of convenience.

Swallowing, I brace myself and turn toward him.

My breath freezes in my throat as I take in his appearance, which reminds me of the first time I met Maxwell Anderson, the billionaire, at The Menagerie. He's certainly not gentle, soulful Silas from the race.

The candlelight dances on his features, the shadows caressing his face. His expression is severe, his gray eyes the color of a swirling tempest, his dark hair carefully combed and swept up, and jaw cleanly shaven. He looks so good in his tux, a design I recognize as McKenzie's, and I release a sigh even as I hurt deep inside. He's doing his part in promoting my family's business.

Because what we have is an arrangement. A contract.

I reply, "Thank you. Here, eat something before your speech. How are you feeling?"

I try not to be disappointed by the way he refuses to look me in the eye, or the fact he didn't even comment on my dress this evening—a crimson silk ball gown of my own design with a sweetheart neckline, tapering at the waist, and flaring at the hips in a dramatic fashion, inspired by the gowns in the Victorian era.

He's just nervous about the speech. Don't overthink this. Heck, don't think at all.

"Fine. Let's just get this shit show over with." He flags a staff member carrying a tray of champagne, grabs one, and downs the drink in one gulp.

It's not personal, Belle. Don't take it personally.

Maxwell Anderson is a Seurat painting—made up of millions of tiny little dots and actions, forming a breathtaking whole. He's a study of stark contrasts, the icy chill and blazing warmth, the indifference and quiet passion, the masculine beauty and thick scars, the infuriating asshole and...the man who claims not to know how to love, but secretly loves the strongest of them all.

His loyalty to his family, how he almost lost his life to save his brother, the way he silently takes care of me. He's the definition of actions speaking louder than words.

Another flash brightens our table and I try not to let the growing heartache dim my smile. We're on a public stage, and I know every little thing I do will be magnified and discussed tomorrow in the newspapers around the world.

Maxwell doesn't touch his food as he turns to Ryland, who's sitting next to him, and the two fall into a deep discussion. Despite being in a room full of people, surrounded by my closest friends, I've never felt more alone than now.

My gaze sweeps around the table and lands on Millie, who looks stunning in the silver gown I gave her from my personal design collection. She flashes me a sad smile, her eyes brimming with sympathy as if she knows how I'm feeling.

I look away, unable to withstand her penetrative gaze which seems to see through this farce of a marriage I find myself in, a whiplash rollercoaster ride I can't seem to bring myself to disembark, even if that means I'm dizzy and nauseous the entire time.

"And now, let's welcome Mr. Maxwell Anderson to the stage," the emcee announces.

Loud applause rings through the ballroom and I see Maxwell fisting his pants before smoothing out the wrinkles and standing up. A dark flush creeps up his neck. He nods to the crowd, lips flattened, jaw clenched, and strides up onto the stage.

He doesn't look at or acknowledge me.

Despite the pain of his rejection, my pulse can't help but ratchet up as I stare at my husband, who's about to attempt something so terrifying for him, he's opted to spend most of his thirty-six years in the quiet background.

The microphone emits a sharp piercing sound as he adjusts it. He stares at the podium and the room quiets as the spotlight focuses on him.

We wait with bated breath for the king to address his subjects, but he just stands there, as stiff as the gargoyles guarding the estate.

The seconds bleed into minutes, the awkward tension thickening. I see his throat working, the flush from his face minutes ago long disappeared and instead, his skin is leached of color. His eyes widen and his nostrils flare as he grips the podium for dear life.

Oh no. I can almost see the monster he once described to me as his anxiety lurking inside him, wrapping its tendrils around his neck, suffocating him in front of everyone. The image claws at my heart and makes me want to cry.

Low murmurs and hushed whispers rise from the crowd and the photographers furiously snap photo after photo, reporters quickly typing notes out on their phones.

A chair squeaks beside me and I turn toward the noise, finding Ryland and Charles frowning, clearly concerned for him.

It's then I make a decision.

The monster will not murder my husband, not if I can help it.

Pushing out of my chair, I slowly stand up, ignoring the whispers and furtive glances as the crowd's attention shifts to me.

I fiddle with the locket he gave me, and his fevered eyes snag on mine as I slowly make my way toward him.

Smiling, I whisper, "You can do this. It's just you and me," knowing full well he can't hear me but also feeling, deep in my gut, he can understand me.

Like he always has.

He shifts and straightens, his intense gray eyes pinned on me, tracking my movements as I stride between the tables toward him.

Good evening, ladies and gentlemen, I mouth, prompting him. He swallows, his eyes holding mine.

"G-Good evening, ladies and gentlemen. Thank you for coming to the b-ball." His voice is deep and thick, sounding unused, a thread of uncertainty woven throughout his words.

The flashes from the photographers intensify as the crowd settles into an eerie quiet, clearly riveted by him.

But he's only looking at me, like he's speaking directly to me.

My heart skips several beats and I wet my lips, pausing at the bottom of the stage.

"My family has been f-firm proponents of giving back to the community, of philanthropy, b-because we recognize the immense p-privilege of being an Anderson," he begins, a vein pulsing on his forehead.

Immense privilege, but also a curse, it seems.

He stares at me, his face unsmiling but his gaze burning hot as he says, "Our m-motto is, 'Valor and virtue, with honor, we stand,' and perhaps you may question the valor with me s-standing before you tonight, the inarticulate orator," the crowd chuckles at his rough attempt at humor, "but I strongly b-believe in the virtue and honor we hold ourselves to."

Maxwell pauses, the color slowly coming back to his complexion, but his face still shines with sweat. "A-Anxiety and depression are global mental health crises, invisible illnesses plaguing millions of people. Our family believes in philanthropy, in d-doing our part to shine a light on these two invisible afflictions that p-plague the lives of millions of people in the world. And we h-have the p-privilege..."

He trembles and lets out a shuddering exhale. And another. The connection between us breaks as his gaze darts around the room, his chest heaving rapidly. "W-We h-have the p-privilege..."

He bows his head down, the muscles bunching in his shoulder.

"Fuck." A soft whisper, barely audible from the microphone, but I hear him from where I stand.

He looks so terrified.

I blink away the tears gathering in my eyes.

Quickly, I climb the steps and stand next to him. The bright spotlight temporarily blinds me. "Easy there with the spotlight. I think I may get a heatstroke from it. No wonder Maxwell is sweating bullets up here in his tux. Can we dim it a little bit, please?"

The audience laughs, and a staff member dims the lighting. I can finally see the faces of the crowd—the rich and the elite sitting with amused expressions, folks whispering furtively to each other, their eyes darting to Maxwell. Charles and Ryland standing up, their faces stern, like they are seconds away from storming up the stage and rescuing us. Taylor is uncharacteristically grabbing Charles's forearm and Grace and Millie are standing next to her, concern brimming in their gazes.

Slowly, I take Maxwell's clammy hand in mine, twining our fingers together.

His breath hitches as he holds on tightly, his grip borderline painful.

I'll be his source of strength, his partner...*his wife.*

"Our family," I squeeze Maxwell's hand and recite the speech from memory, "believes in philanthropy, in doing our part to shine a light on these two invisible afflictions that plague the lives of millions of people in the world. And we have the privilege and platform to do so. In lieu of the Christmas Ball at The Orchid this year, we want to invite you all to join us and open your hearts, your minds, and your *wallets*, to the conditions that can affect people in all stages of life and from all backgrounds."

Turning toward Maxwell, I find his lips parted, his gaze firmly affixed on me. His eyes darken with so much intensity, passion, and what I can only describe as awe, I can't help but be swept up in the turbulent pools.

"It's a cause near and dear to my husband's heart," I murmur. This isn't part of the official speech.

His eyes flare at the words "my husband," and I feel him tugging me closer, his fingers disentangling from mine before he curls his arm possessively around my waist.

Heat rushes through me and I wet my lips, watching his gaze dip to the movement before raking down the rest of my gown.

I shiver and turn back to the crowd. "Thank you for being here tonight, for the cause, for my family, and for my husband. We are eternally grateful and we wish you all a very Merry Christmas."

Applause rings out in the ballroom as I grab Maxwell's hand and lead him down the stage where my friends and his family have gathered.

"You were a badass," Taylor says, and I grin.

Grace nods enthusiastically and Millie blinks, moisture clinging to her eyelashes. I smile at her and she nods—the invisible kinship of loving Anderson men.

Loving? My heart races in my chest. *No, I don't love him. I can't. That'll just set me up for heartbreak because he won't love me back.*

Ryland clasps his brother on the shoulder, the twins exchanging silent sentiments before he turns to me.

He pulls me to him and whispers in my ear, "Thank you, Belle. Thank you for being there for him. He needs you."

I look back at Maxwell, finding him standing quietly to the side, his gaze inscrutable, a vein pulsing on his forehead.

Does he need me? And is that enough?

"I will never, ever be in love with you."

His words all those nights ago echo loudly in my mind.

My heart twists as he meets my stare head on, unflinching, and I know...

This can't be enough.

CHAPTER 34

THE SILENT AUCTION IS wrapping up as I excuse myself from the table and head back to my room to use the bathroom and freshen up my makeup. The wistful strains of the violin accompanied by the soulful notes of the cello fade into silence as I make my way up the grand staircase. I hear Silas's faint barking in one of the guest rooms where a pet sitter is looking after him.

The ferocious storm continues to batter the estate, the windows shaking from the onslaught as the icy tendrils of the elements seep in through the gaps under the windowsills. Shivering, I quicken my steps to the bedroom.

I complete my business in the bathroom and attempt to fix my elegant updo, which has dislodged as I moved about the ballroom socializing with guests, taking photos for the press, and performing other duties as the mistress of the house.

Sighing, I stare at my hair in the mirror, realizing there's no way I can fix this quickly. I pull out the pins and let the silky black waves fall over my shoulders.

This will have to do.

My eyes snag on the locket lying over my heart. The necklace has me transfixed ever since I laid eyes on it and I usually wear it every day. I wish Maxwell could put it on me himself. It'd be more meaningful that way, having the man who occupies your heart put on a piece of jewelry that symbolizes eternal love.

I open the locket, admire the silhouette of a woman's face, and read the elegant inscription again:

To E,

Upon you, my dearest, my love rests for eternity and beyond, for anything less would be insufferable.

Your servant,

S.

A twinge of melancholy snakes its way inside my chest and I close the locket, wishing it would imbue me with the same type of love in the inscription.

Ardent. Everlasting. Eternal.

Then I think of him, Maxwell, his brooding eyes, a soul I can spend a lifetime exploring and not reach the bottom of its depths.

And I wish...

I swallow the lump in my throat.

I wish he'd feel a fraction of what the giver of the locket felt for the woman he calls his dearest.

Blowing out a breath, I dispel my gloomy thoughts and leave my room to go back to the ballroom. A sudden chill sifts through the air when I reach the staircase, and I take two steps at a time—cardio will warm up the body. As I make a turn to the ballroom, a hand reaches out and grabs my arm tightly.

"What on earth?" I turn toward the person who has pulled me to a stop.

Ugh. My asshole boss. Darn it. I forgot my parents allocated a spot to him at the McKenzie Atelier table.

My stomach turns and I try to shake my arm free. "Gordon, let go of me right now."

He laughs, a cruel mocking sound drawing the attention of a few ball goers who are lingering outside the ballroom. He lets go of me. "I see being married to an Anderson has gone to your head."

I scoff and roll my eyes. "What do you want?" He reeks of alcohol.

He tsks. "Just wanted to see how the design collection is going. Is it going to be as pathetic as the one you showed me last time?" I'm still finishing up my final revised designs and haven't submitted them yet.

"If you give someone shit to work with, they can only come up with more shit, Gordon." I give myself an inner high five for not flinching when I curse, because if there's anyone who deserves curse words, it's the man in front of me.

"Why don't you run to mommy and daddy dearest and tell them you give up before you run the company into the ground?"

"Never."

"Imagine being so stupid and stubborn you don't know when to quit."

I straighten and meet his glare head on. "There's nothing you can say that'll make me give up my position at McKenzie's. Just like there's nothing you can do that'll make my parents give you our family business. You may fool everyone with your fake smiles and compliments, but you aren't fooling me. And the moment I take control of the company, you're the first person I'll fire. So why don't you do us all a favor and quit now before *you* run the company my grandpa created to the ground?"

"You *bitch*," he yells and a few bystanders gasp. Then, I see several flashes of white light.

Dang it, the paparazzi.

Fury burns inside me, the inferno threatening to swallow me whole, but I fake a smile instead. I won't let him make a fool out of me and win. That's probably his game, anyway.

"Excuse me, Gordon, I have to go back to the ball I'm hosting with my husband. I don't have time for your petty and meaningless mind games."

Spinning around, I walk toward the ballroom when he chuckles behind me.

"You don't have the talent to make it, so you're sleeping your way up the food chain, huh? Man, I wish I were a woman and I could do the same. Find a rich, powerful husband, and *poof*, all my worries would disappear."

More shocked gasps echo in the foyer and heat rushes to my face. Curling my fist, I turn around, needing to give this man a piece of my mind, and maybe a knuckle sandwich—

"Apologize to her."

The deep, quiet voice promises blood and violence, and my breathing quickens.

Maxwell steps out of the shadows in the corridor, his jaw locked, lips twitching in fury as he slowly stalks toward Gordon.

"Apologize at once," he rasps again, his footsteps measured.

"I...I..." Gordon stutters. The lecher backs up slowly, clearly sensing someone whose control is about to snap.

Maxwell continues stalking toward him until he's backed up against the wall.

Gordon swallows, his pale face flushed red, and he tries to stand on tiptoes, a poor effort to appear taller than Maxwell, who towers over him by half a foot.

"I'm an artist who is uncompromising in my beliefs and I'm saying the truth. Nepotism is disgusting and you won't silence me."

Maxwell growls and fists Gordon's shirt, dragging it up until he lifts Gordon off the ground.

"How *dare* you disrespect her in *our* home at *our* party?" His voice is a lethal whisper and his fists clench the shirt tighter. Gordon dangles midair, the sniveling idiot turning redder and sputtering.

"How *dare* you fucking disrespect *my wife*!" Maxwell roars and the music inside the ballroom stops.

Flashes of bright lights erupt as the paparazzi have a field day.

I know I should stop him, should remind him people are watching and anything he says and does will be splashed all over the front pages tomorrow.

But I don't.

Instead, my heart careens off a cliff. The burning rage inside me blazes into a sweltering hellfire of too many emotions to name. I want to pull him away, to kiss him, to hug him, to crawl all over him in appreciation for how he's standing up for me.

The madman. The frigid king.

My frigid king. Beautiful scars and all.

"I don't care if you're the president of the fucking world. If you don't apologize to *my wife* right now, I won't be held responsible for choking you to death."

He leans in so no one can hear him but Gordon and me. "And I can do it, make you disappear, and no one will ever know."

A sharp heat travels to my clit and my core clenches as I take in Maxwell, his eyes wild and fevered, his biceps still bunched and flexed, barely shaking from holding up Gordon by the collar of his shirt.

"Maxwell," I finally find my voice. "D-Don't. Don't do this, not in front of everyone. Not for him."

Maxwell looks at me, his eyes flashing, a muscle pulsing in his jaw. "I won't let anyone disrespect you." He turns back to Gordon. "Apologize. Now."

Gordon, finally coming to his senses, grabs Maxwell's hands and utters, "S-Sorry, B-Belle. I'm s-sorry."

Grunting, Maxwell throws Gordon against the wall and a few guards step in and haul the asshole out of the hallway.

Melody walks around the foyer, her mouth opened in apparent shock as she ushers the guests back into the ballroom. Morris frowns at us, his eyes radiating disapproval and anger as he spins around and heads toward the east wing. Agnes furrows her brows and shakes her head at me, as if I displeased her. She then follows Melody and helps direct the paparazzi back into the room.

But I know the damage to Maxwell's image is already done.

"Annabelle! That was completely embarrassing!" Dad stalks toward me from the entrance of the ballroom and my heart sinks. I really don't want to deal with him right now. "Everyone heard your argument with Gordon in there! What were you thinking—"

"I wouldn't continue that sentence if I were you." Maxwell's voice comes out as a low rasp. "I don't care if you are my father-in-law. Anyone fit to be called a father should first care about his daughter's well-being over anything else after that asshole harassed her."

A lump forms in my throat as I drag my attention to my husband, who is glaring at my dad with murder in his eyes. He's defending me again—fighting for me when no man has ever done so before in my life.

"Maxwell, y-you s-see, I—"

"No. *I don't see.* And I don't care. Go, before I give you the same treatment I gave to Gordon." He points his finger toward the ballroom, his body vibrating with intensity.

Dad sputters, his lips twitching, but he's clearly intimidated by Maxwell because he spins away and stomps back into the ballroom.

I turn to Maxwell, wanting to thank him, to kiss him, to yell at him because what happened just undid everything he worked so hard for.

"Maxwell." I reach for him, my hand shaking.

His stare is mutinous as he swiftly brushes my hand away. "Don't. Touch. Me."

Without another word, he spins around and stalks off, leaving me reeling and completely stupefied.

CHAPTER 35

I'm unraveling.

Every carefully knitted stitch, held together by years of painstaking control, is coming apart in front of my eyes, and I can't stop it.

I can't stop the way my heart pounds for her, my little muse, and how I live to hear her laughter and see her smiles.

I can't stop my addiction to her and how I want to be the reason for all her happiness, how I want her to think of our marriage as the real thing and not a sham, not a contract, not an arrangement.

I can't stop my fantasies of her every night in my room when I fight my lust as long as I can, fucking my cock in my hand until I can't stand it, until I allow myself one night per week for relief, when I feel at home sheathed inside her, feeling her orgasm squeezing my cock.

I can't stop the burning rage coursing inside me, a cataclysmic eruption, when I saw that asshole boss of hers belittling her, doubting her, *hurting* her with his words. I want to strangle him, to kill him for causing my little muse pain.

And that's why I'm stalking up the staircase, fleeing to my room instead of wrapping her in my arms and kissing her luscious lips, getting a hit I've been craving ever since I saw her in that gorgeous red dress looking like a fucking goddess and felt her calming touch as she completed my speech for me when she saw me floundering. I wanted to worship her in front of everyone, to thank her for knowing exactly what I need, one kiss at a time, until I don't know where she ends and I begin.

"Fuck!" I take off my tux jacket and hurl it on the floor.

The bow tie follows.

I wrench open the French doors, letting a blast of cold air rush into the room, uncaring if the wind is bringing the snow indoors even though the storm is letting up. "Fuck! Fuck! Fuck!"

I'm unraveling. My heart is swelling, aching, yearning for her.

But the curse. The branch from earlier. The omen.

I can't fall in love with her. I can't put her at risk.

My love is a death sentence.

I won't survive if she dies. I. Simply. Won't. Survive.

The vision I saw earlier in the study, Belle getting dragged to the depths of hell, black tendrils snaking over her skin and tearing her away from me, rises to the forefront.

No. No. No. I can't fall in love with her. The curse. I can't. I can't—

The door creaks open and the scent of sweet lilies filters inside and every nerve ending in my body comes alive, my muscles coiling in tension.

Please don't come in. I don't know if I'm strong enough to withstand you.

My pleas go unanswered because Belle enters the room and walks toward me. She steps into the moonlight streaming in from the open doors; the wind billowing her dress and sending a thousand snowflakes cascading over her body.

She looks ethereal. An angel from the heavens. My salvation from eternal damnation.

My breath hitches, my heart seizes, and I lose the ability to speak.

She steps toward me, her eyes glowing with concern, with anger, with appreciation, and with so much affection I can't think clearly, the clawing need inside me growing, morphing into a beast of its own, needing to touch her silky skin, to kiss those plump lips, to claim her.

Mine.

"Maxwell," she whispers, standing a hairsbreadth distance away. "Why did you run off?"

My hands clench into fists so tightly, my arms shake from the restraint. "Go away, Belle. Please."

"No! I'm done with you and your insane moods. I'm not playing your games anymore."

"You think this is a game?" I growl, my breath fogging up the air before dissipating. "You think having the woman of my dreams living in the same house, taking my last name, infiltrating my entire life and turning it upside down is a *game* to me?"

She gasps, her eyes widening at whatever she sees on my face. I dig my nails into my palms, the flash of pain barely registering as I fight every instinct to touch her.

"You think having you in my life and not being able to touch you, to kiss you, to fuck and make love to you whenever I want, when that's all I ever think about, is a fucking game to me?"

Moisture gathers in her eyes, and she reaches toward my face, her fingers trembling.

"Don't. Touch. Me." I jerk back and repeat the command from downstairs. "P-Please, Belle. Don't touch me."

"Why Maxwell? Why deny this between us?" A tear rolls down her cheek and I want to whip myself for hurting her.

"I'm not in control of myself right now. I'm losing my mind over you," I rasp, my voice thickening. "If you touch me, I won't be able to stop...I won't be able to—"

"What? Save me from the curse?" Belle shakes her head, her voice ardent. "I don't believe in the curse, Maxwell. No matter how many times you guys tell me about it, I don't."

Her voice grows stronger, her tawny eyes darker, fiercer. "This is *my life*, Maxwell. *My choice.* You don't get to decide for me, because what we have...I might not be experienced in love, but what we have, I know, doesn't come around often."

She points to her chest, to the locket I gave her. "I feel it here. Deep inside me, and it's a risk I get to decide to take."

"But you'll die. I-I can't...if you die, there's nothing left for me." The words, trapped in the deepest crevices of my heart this entire time, slip out, unable to restrain themselves anymore in her presence.

The presence of the woman who makes me feel so much, who makes me feel...

Everything.

"I don't believe it, and I'll show you."

She pulls my head down and presses her lips to mine.

My body stills for a brief second until my mind catches up and it's the precious air given to a drowning man, a match dropped on gasoline, and all my thoughts shut down.

Growling, I grip her face, my mouth conquering hers, claiming what's always been mine. Our kiss is a mess of tongues, teeth, and passion. Her sweet taste is giving me the highest of highs.

I can't get enough of her. I grapple with her gown and her hands tear the shirt from my body. Zippers are wrenched down, clothing tears, buttons ping off the hardwood floors, but we don't care.

It's madness, a cyclone overtaking our bodies, our souls, our minds.

She moans, the sound a direct caress to my hard cock, already thick and swollen, dripping at the tip for her.

"Maxwell, please," she cries as I bite her neck, my teeth scoring the tender flesh before laving it with my tongue.

I rip off her lacy bra and panties, not caring if I'm ruining them, and palm her breasts—perfect handfuls, the smooth globes swelling in my hands. My mouth moves down her body, kissing, biting every-where I can reach, and she thrashes in my hold, gyrating her hips up and down my torso, rubbing her soft, delicious body over my cock.

"Fuck, Belle," I groan and bite my lip. "Keep moving that pussy over my cock. Feel it dripping for you, unable to help itself. That's what you do to me."

She whimpers when I tug her nipple into my mouth, and my tongue laves circles and flicks at the tip. So fucking sweet and hot, my little muse.

My cock spasms as a spurt of cum leaks and I haul her up my body, wrapping her legs behind me.

"Fuck me, Maxwell. Please, I need to come," she moans as she presses my face to her tits, her hips humping my cock, each movement causing the tip to glide into her slick folds and my balls grow heavy and taut.

I throw her on my bed. "Spread your legs, little muse. I've craved you for so long and now I'm going to feast."

She whimpers and throws her head back, her thighs spread, and I dive in and taste her sweetness at the source, my lips closing around her swollen clit. She screams.

"Look at this pretty little pussy," I slide my finger between her folds until it reaches her clit, "so tight and fucking wet...all for me, Belle?"

"Yes," she thrashes on the bed, her breathing coming out in quick pants, "only for you."

"Mine." I thrust two fingers inside her tight channel. *Mine. Mine. Mine.*

"Maxwell!" she cries, her hips arching up and away, but I pin her in place as I finger fuck her in earnest, the sounds of her wet pussy swallowing my digits lewd in the room.

I circle her swollen clit and feel her inner walls clench my fingers. "You want to come, little muse? Come all over your husband's fingers?"

"Yes, please. I need to come!"

I stop my movement and she cries out in frustration, "No!"

"Too bad, because I need you to come around my cock and milk all my cum out of me. Every single drop, because," I line up the tip at her entrance, watching in fascination her juices seeping out of her pussy, "because I'm going to breed you again. And again. And get your womb full of my seed."

The image of her pregnant sears into my mind. It hasn't happened yet, but I'll be damned if I don't make it my duty to put a baby inside her. It's something that hasn't turned me on before until her. And now, my cock hardens, about to burst. I want to make her mine, create children with her.

I want everything with her.

My pulse roars in my ears. In this moment, I can only focus on her, on claiming my wife, my muse, of making her mine forever so we'll never be apart.

In one harsh thrust, I slam into the hilt and a guttural groan rips from my mouth.

Home. I'm home.

"Maxwell!" she screams, her muscles tightening, her legs trembling, her back bowing to my movements.

Thrust after thrust we become one and I link my fingers with hers as a fire runs down my spine and spreads to my extremities, building, coalescing into a breaking point like I've never known before. This intimacy is so startling and earth shattering, I can barely breathe.

"You're mine, Belle. Tell me you're mine." My hips snap against hers, my vision darkening at the edges as I climb toward the pinnacle.

"I'm yours," she moans, "only ever yours."

And I've only ever been yours too.

Her body starts spasming and I feel her walls tightening, gripping my cock, and I know she's close.

"Fuck," I mutter and snake one hand between us, my fingers finding her swollen nub. "Come for me, Belle, drench my cock with your juices." I pinch her clit.

She screams, her voice probably traveling to other parts of the house, but I couldn't care less. Her pussy strangles me as wetness gushes out of her.

I swallow her sounds with my mouth, our tongues swiping, joining with each other like our bodies below, and I fall off the cliff, the pleasure an avalanche, wiping away every worry, every doubt as I release ropes of cum inside her, my orgasm never-ending.

My body covers her, flesh against flesh, every inch of us entangled as I rain a thousand kisses on her lips.

A kiss for all the kisses I've withheld in the past because I was afraid of what they'd do to me...to my heart.

And I was right.

My heart swells and collides against my rib cage, surrendering to the woman in front of me, the person who has always felt like a kindred spirit from the moment we met. The other half I never realized I was searching for.

We break apart for air. I gently brush her hair sticking to her sweaty forehead, and I stare into her beautiful eyes. I can't look away.

I want to stare at her forever.

Her lips curve in a breathtaking smile and wetness pools in her eyes until they overflow and slide down her cheeks.

I know how you feel. I want to tell her all the emotions coursing through me, a cathartic release I've never experienced before. But I don't, a tendril of fear for her safety unfurling in my mind.

But I know she knows.

She continues to smile, the whites of her teeth blinding.

"I'm home," she whispers.

Closing my eyes, I kiss her tears away, and I hope...I just hope...if the curse is real, if it needs to take a life, please take mine instead.

CHAPTER 36

I'M SO HAPPY.

The storm is simmering outside, the icy gale still wreaking havoc on the barren trees, but I barely notice.

Instead, a potent warmth spreads throughout my body as I lay there on the bed, curled up against him, my head on his chest.

My husband. My Silas. My *Maxwell*.

After our soul-shattering sex, Maxwell carefully tended to me before shutting the French doors and lighting a fire in the hearth, imbuing the dark room with a warm glow. Now, I'm listening to the reassuring rhythm of his heartbeat as he plays with my hair with one hand, his other hand trailing over my arm. It's like we can't stop touching each other now that the dam has broken and the walls have fallen.

"You know," I whisper, fighting a smile, "we totally bailed on our own party."

Maxwell chuckles, his deep voice rumbly, and I splay my leg over his torso and snuggle closer. "I'd much rather be in here, having a party with you. Melody and my siblings can handle it." He punctuates the sentence with a kiss on my hair.

"Me too." I prop myself up on my elbows and stare at him. I know we need to have a talk about what this means to both of us. "Just so you know, before you start overthinking...I don't regret this. Us."

His fingers still on my body and he rakes in a harsh breath. "Belle, the curse—"

I put my finger over his lips. "Shh... Let me finish, and you can have your turn, then. Maxwell, I understand you believe this curse is real, as does your family. It's hard to question something you've been taught since you were young. But I'm an outsider to all of this and let me tell you, there are no such things as curses."

Doodling my finger over his hard chest, I continue, "I think it's easy for us to create stories to explain the tragic events in our lives because if bad things happen for no reason, what hope is there for us? We could live our best life one moment, only for everything to be taken away the next second."

Maxwell's throat works and his lips part, heavy emotions clearly swirling in those mesmerizing eyes of his.

"I look at it differently. Because life is so unpredictable, shouldn't we try to live with no regrets during the short time we're here? Instead of trying to explain the tragedies in the past, shouldn't we try to create more joy in the future?"

Leaning down, I press my lips to his, relishing his soft inhale as he kisses me back, his hand trailing reverently down my back.

Breaking apart for air, I whisper, "So no. I don't believe in the curse, but I can understand that you do. All I'm asking is for you to be brave with me...*for me*. So *I* can live with no regrets."

Maxwell's eyes trail over my face, his hand cupping my cheek, and his nostrils flare. "Year of yeses," he rasps, and I smile.

"Yes. Year of yeses. It's a great attitude. You should try it sometime."

"I don't deserve you, Belle."

I grin. "Few people do, so you should be honored I want to have my next adventures with you."

He lets out a laborious sigh. "I can't promise anything, but I'll try."

My heart hiccups—he's going to try...for me! My lips curve into a big smile.

"That's all I'm asking for. The attempt at it." I watch his eyes widen, his lips twitching at my near verbatim response to what he said to me at The Menagerie when we were negotiating the terms of our marriage.

"Can you tell me more about the curse?" I ask as I lay my head on his chest again. He stiffens and I add, "I want to understand it better so I can understand you."

He doesn't reply for a few seconds. The room is quiet, other than the faint sounds of the wind outside and the snapping of logs in the fireplace. "We don't know when it started...this curse. But our guess was somewhere around the late eighteen hundreds, based on the diaries and letters we have from the family."

Maxwell resumes his stroking of my arm. "There were many stories as to how it began. Some people said it was because the fates didn't like the rich. And so, those who flaunt their prosperity were marked with death."

He presses a kiss on my shoulder, and my skin blooms under his caress. "That's one version of it, which sounds silly, I know. But the more popular version is that one of my forefathers betrayed a woman who loved him and since then, it's been bad luck for the first sons. Centuries of bad luck. But my father and I have looked into this, searched the archives...we couldn't find any proof of this betrayal."

"Then why does your family think there's truth to this curse? Deaths happen to all families."

"For every single generation of Andersons since the late eighteen hundreds, the only wives of the eldest sons to have survived into old age were the ones from marriages that weren't love matches. Bad things would happen unless the eldest son married and had children—heirs to pass the curse down to."

The guilt is heavy in his voice as he continues, "Some men would seek love outside of marriage, but it's just wrong, to cheat on your wife. It's something I'd never do." His eyes are solemn and I understand now what he told me at The Menagerie. Maxwell is a man of honor. Fidelity is a core value to him.

He continues, "It's a mind fuck, you know? To keep people from dying, I have to get married to have a son who I'm dooming to the same fate as me. But what's the alternative? Letting other people I love die? I'll just have to teach him my ways—teach him he can have a fulfilling life without a loving marriage. There's more to life than love."

My heart pinches at the forlorn expression on his face. If he truly believes in the curse, which I know he does, this must've been a hard decision to make.

Maxwell shakes his head and sighs. "Dad told me his marriage with Mom began as an arrangement as well. They respected each other's boundaries and became friends over the course of a few years. Things were wonderful here then. Mom loved art—operas, musicals, painting, literature. My classmates' parents would leave them with nannies or at boarding schools, but not Mom. Despite our wealth, she gave us all her love and attention, taught us so many things. But..."

His eyes take on a faraway look as his brows pinch.

"Oh, Maxwell." I throw my arms around his neck, hoping my body weight and heat will comfort him.

His voice roughens. "It's impossible not to love her, Belle. And she and Dad eventually fell in love. Dad told me, within a year of them confessing their love to each other, she died. A series of random accidents happened before then—a flowerpot from a trellis nearly falling on her head, taking the wrong medicine when she was sick. Things like that."

Maxwell's voice is thick as he pauses, clearly overwrought with the memories. "Eventually, one of these incidents killed her. A fall down the stairs. A freak accident with Rex's marbles. And life was never the same. You may look at Rex and think he's always happy, but he was the one who found her, the one who beat himself up. That's why he's always the one who acts out among us."

"But it's not your fault. Any of you. Rex, your father."

"Dad doesn't think so. He blames himself for loving her and for accepting her love, even to this day. And later, I found out these series of incidents, all of a different nature, happened shortly before the women died. It was a pattern. Dad eventually tried to find love again, but he wouldn't marry the woman, and we all know how that turned out."

I whisper, "Grace and Taylor's mom."

From what I'd heard from my friends who found out their lineage not long ago, their mom and Linus had a passionate affair, but she left because she refused to be a kept woman in the shadows. She was heartbroken for most of her life until she died in a car accident shortly after Grace met Steven.

Maxwell adds, "While I don't think their mom's death is because of the curse…so many years have passed, after all, but it's still shitty luck. Horrible things happen to the women loved by the oldest Anderson son."

How do I get through to a man who has lost so much? I can hear the conviction in his voice—the fear, the regret, the helplessness. How do I get him to step into the light with me and see reason?

"But accidents can truly happen without supernatural explanations." My response is feeble, even to my ears.

Maxwell sits up and faces me, his eyes somber. He clasps my hand in his, as if needing my touch for whatever he's going to tell me next.

"I was once like you. Trying to rationalize all these deaths in my family…the Grim Reaper hanging over me all my life. But there's something I never told you before." He pauses and takes a deep breath. "I was married before, Belle."

I gasp at the unexpected news—both surprised and appalled at how a surge of jealousy charges through me, at the idea of Maxwell giving his heart away to someone else before.

A heart he doesn't want to give to me.

"Her name was Sydney, and she was my high school sweetheart."

He toys with my fingers as he tells me about the girl who befriended him, a guy who was socially awkward. He tells me how she was outgoing, kind, fun, everything he wasn't, and he was drawn to her energy, even though he knew he probably couldn't keep up. He explains how they eloped after graduation and how ecstatic he was for thinking he could beat the curse.

Then, he finally tells me how he found out she was in love with Ryland, how Sydney also had a series of random accidents—a fender bender while driving, food poisoning, almost drowning in a swimming pool. He tells me how they had an argument on the family yacht on a stormy night and she fell overboard, drunk, and drowned before anyone noticed.

"I didn't even know she slipped on the deck. I was so mad at her for her betrayal, for wanting to change me, for not loving me for who I am, just like all the other people, I didn't even stick around to make sure she made it inside as we headed back to shore."

Maxwell finally looks up, and I see tears glistening in his eyes. "So no, Belle, I don't believe in the curse because of stories and superstitions. I believe in it because I've lived it before. I've touched death, and death has surrounded me. Even though I've learned long ago what I felt for Sydney was an imitation of deep love, a puppy love if you will, the curse still descended on her. *My love is a death sentence.* Don't you see what I'm trying to tell you?"

I sniffle as I wipe the tears gathered under his eyes. Shaking my head, I say, "They still sound like random accidents to me. Horrible, but accidents, nonetheless. I don't believe in the curse." I can't believe it because the alternative is unbearable.

Because if it's real, he can never truly give me his heart and my life may be in danger.

Closing his eyes, he leans into my touch. "Over the years, our family had tried circumventing the curse—not getting married, not having kids, but something horrible would always happen, like my grandfather's younger brother's entire family perishing when their canoes overturned. Grandfather was trying to outwit the curse by refusing to marry."

Maxwell takes my hand in his and presses a soft kiss on the back. "Too many accidents to be accidents. Too many deaths. I've accepted my role ever since Sydney died. I'm at peace with it. Until..."

You.

He doesn't say the words, but from the fervent expression on his face, his eyes penetrating, I know that's what he's thinking.

"You know, others said the land our mansion lies on is haunted because these are hallowed grounds from an abbey that was destroyed a long time ago. Grandfather Silas never believed in superstitions when he purchased the parcel and built on top of it. Maybe our family was doomed ever since we stepped onto these shores."

Goosebumps prickle my skin at the mention of Wraithmoor Abbey, and I reach over to the nightstand to grab the vintage locket he gave me.

I dangle it in front of us, admiring the way the gems and metals sparkle under the warm light. "I heard about the abbey. The owner of Wraithmoor Antiquities told me about it." But I don't tell him about how I felt a sense of déjà vu that day or how the necklace called to me, even though I'd never seen it before. It still feels too strange to say aloud.

Maxwell opens the locket and traces the words of eternal devotion inside. He's silent, his breathing heavy, and I turn to face him, finding his eyes glued to the writing, his jaw clenching before releasing.

"Maxwell?"

"I saw this and thought of you—I knew no one else should wear it. That it was somehow meant to be around your neck," he whispers, his fingers still tracing the writing.

He murmurs, "Upon you, my dearest, my love rests for eternity and beyond, for anything less would be insufferable."

The words echo between us, a sudden tension heavy in the air. I silently stare at him as his gaze slowly trails up to mine.

He gently takes the necklace from my hand and I hold my breath, my pulse clamoring in my veins. Gently, he brushes my hair to the side and clasps the necklace around my neck.

He touches the locket nestled between my breasts. "Promise me, Belle... Promise me you won't fall in love with me."

"But the curse isn't—"

"Do it for me, then. Please. I'll take care of you, worship you, give you everything I have, but don't fall in love with me...for me. And I won't fall in love with you."

A piercing pain jabs me in the heart, and I try to fight the sadness creeping in. I know he's not ready to let go of his beliefs. I know he's terrified. But it still hurts hearing him say these words to me.

Especially when I find my heart on the verge of being stolen by him.

But I know if I say no, I might not get the slightest chance with him. And so, with a heavy heart and tears prickling my eyes, I knot our hands together, and let the vows I don't believe in slip out of my mouth.

"I promise to not fall in love with you, Maxwell."

CHAPTER 37

DENIAL IS A POWERFUL thing.

The next two days passed by in a blur of lovemaking and pretending our troubles didn't exist. Every time I mentioned I wanted to check on the outcome of the gala and what the press was saying about Gordon's disruption, Maxwell would pull me to him and tell me he didn't give a shit.

He'd wake me up in the morning with his face between my legs, drinking from my pussy like it was his sustenance, or I'd feel him prodding my back as he curled me tightly against him, raining kisses down my neck.

"I promise not to love you," he groaned as he thrusted into me from behind yesterday afternoon, his thick cock slipping into my wet core as he plastered me against the windows of his bedroom.

Unlike the times before, where we were clothed, and he'd avoid touching me any more than necessary, we were both naked, our bodies writhing as he held me upright, my nipples pebbled from pressing against the cold glass. Even though he was still his usual gruff self, I could feel the palpable connection between us—the way his body would seek mine, his hands touching me, his lips kissing me as though he couldn't get enough.

It felt different. *We* felt different.

I remembered how he reached around and gripped my neck, turning my face toward him before he crushed his lips to mine. His hips snapped against my ass in a punishing rhythm, each pass of his cock hitting my G-spot.

I thrashed in his tight embrace, my legs trembling as he reached between my thighs with his free hand and circled my clit.

"If someone were outside right now, they would see you being well fucked by your husband, your tits bouncing against the windows, your tight pussy swallowing up my cock like it couldn't get enough," he whispered in my ear, his voice low and guttural.

Wetness flooded my core at the image he painted.

"My little muse likes it. Being taken in front of people. That turns you on, doesn't it?"

"Maxwell," I breathed, my pussy clenching against his punishing thrusts, the pleasure building and gathering from deep within. "I-I'm going to come, oh shit."

"Yes, little muse," he rasped. He pistoned harder such that our bodies slammed against each other and the glass window, the sounds lurid. "All your orgasms belong to me now."

Every muscle in my body tensed as I shook in his embrace, my cries uninhibited, which seemed to only drive him crazier.

"I'm addicted to you, Belle," he grunted, his fingers rubbing harder at my swollen clit and my body locked in tension, the pleasure reaching a peak.

He bit my neck, and the sharp burst of pain sent me over the edge.

I screamed as I fell over the precipice, euphoria flooding my veins, and I collapsed on his body.

"Fuuuuck," he roared, his cock lengthening and swelling, before unleashing ropes of cum deep inside me, the heat of his release prolonging my high.

He slammed his mouth over mine, swallowing my cries, his tongue tangling, swiping before he whispered, "I promise not to love you."

While my heart would flinch every time he said that, I couldn't help but feel the passion in his voice, see the piercing intensity in his eyes, taste the hunger in his mouth.

He's lying, I'd tell myself, *you're getting through to him.*

But it still hurts to hear, even if I understand his fear. I wonder if I'll ever be able to convince him to believe me, to believe in us, to believe that fate hasn't put us together only for a curse to tear us apart.

Now, on the third day after Christmas, I traipse through the secret passageway to the Elysium, eager to distract myself from my thoughts and finish my sketches before Maxwell seduces me with his kisses again.

Silas howls as he runs ahead, clearly excited about me venturing outside of the bedroom I was practically chained to by my sexy husband.

I enter the room and find a fire already roaring in the hearth, two mugs of hot drinks set on the writing desk, the tendrils of the steam twirling before vaporizing in the air. An easel is set up, and a few blank canvases are propped against the wall.

He was here.

Maxwell told me the other day there are two more secret passageways he discovered years ago in the blueprints, but we haven't visited them yet. One goes to a back garden. Rumors were, the Andersons would use it as an emergency escape route. Another one goes to the rooftop garden, a place I still haven't visited yet. He said there's nothing up there, that he himself didn't care for the abandoned garden.

I'm curious about it, but something holds me back every time I pass by the fourth floor stairwell. A strange feeling, a sadness which seems stronger whenever I approach it, and so I've avoided it altogether.

Maxwell said most people didn't know of these passageways, and the only reason he knew I discovered the Elysium was because of the light shining through the windows when I cleaned out the space.

I toss Silas a bone I got from the kitchen and he happily settles in front of the fire and attacks it vigorously.

Grinning, I walk over to the easel and admire the painting there—a somber piece of charcoals and blacks, of what looks to be a blistering sea against murderous skies, and a lonely lighthouse perched atop a cliff, the David against nature's Goliath. My breath catches as I marvel at the thick paint strokes. I can see the passion in them, the leashed down emotions, much like the artist behind the piece.

The lighthouse looks like it's fighting a losing battle. It's forlorn. Hopeless. A tiny beacon of light in a sea of gray. I purse my lips in contemplation.

I don't think so, Maxwell. Nope, not on my watch.

Excitement tremors inside me, my work temporarily relegated to second place in my list of priorities. Picking up a brush and the oil painting palate on the desk, I get to work, starting with mixing different colors to create the new shades I'm envisioning. Thank goodness I took enough art classes in college to know what I'm doing. After all, fashion is art.

"I knew you'd go crazy if you didn't work a little. And why are you smiling like that?" his voice rumbles behind me and I shiver, thinking back to yesterday when he had me pinned against the window.

Seconds later, I feel his heated body pressed against my back, his lips trailing soft kisses over my cheek and neck. My blood heats and my core pulses, my body obviously not satiated, ready for another round between the sheets with him, but I have things to do.

More important things than sex. Like convincing him there's hope in the world.

"Maxwell," I moan, pushing him away, "I'm trying to be helpful."

He growls and nips my neck. "Trust me, you're *very* helpful."

"Ugh, you are impossible!" I laugh, wiggling out of his grasp.

He gives me a flirtatious wink, and I melt a little bit more inside.

"What are you doing with my paints?" His attention finally catches on the palate I'm holding in my hand.

"Your painting—something is missing, don't you think?"

A troubled exhale escapes him and he frowns at his art.

"I painted this based on a sketch I did in April at Lake Superior. It always felt off, like it didn't have a soul. I still can't figure it out."

"Do you trust me?"

Maxwell's gaze flickers to mine, his frown softening. "Of course I do."

"Let me do something then... I think I know what's missing."

He quirks a brow, his lips curved in amusement, and he steps aside.

Grinning, I work on the canvas. Soft, feathered strokes to highlight the clouds and the morning light, shorter, precise strokes for the lighthouse beacon and the birds.

Soon, I find myself immersed in his painting, transporting myself to the shores of Lake Superior on a chilly April morning. I hear soft scribbles in the background, no doubt him making notations on my new sketches, as we work in comfortable silence with the crackle of the fireplace as companion.

"What do you think?" I ask twenty minutes later, stepping back, my fingers rubbing at an itch on my nose.

Holding my breath, I watch him step in front of his easel, his dark eyes piercing, assessing the changes I made. He crosses his arms, his muscles rippling in his gray cable-knit sweater. A muscle twitches in his forehead.

Unease circulates inside me. *Does he not like it?*

After a few minutes, he turns to me, his face flushed, his throat working as he swallows.

"Belle...this, what you did there..." He seems to be at a loss for words.

"Too much? Did I mess things up? I haven't been to the exact location you went to, but I have been to Lake Superior before. But it was during summer, in the afternoon, with my girlfriends. So maybe my memory is faulty. Or maybe—"

He pulls me to him and hugs me tightly, pressing my ear to his chest. I hear the thumping of his heart, sprinting, soaring like the birds I painted on the dark skies.

"It's beautiful. The soul...what was missing. It's breathtaking." His voice is rough. "*Thank you.* You fixed it."

I release a relieved exhale, pull back, and beam at him, thrilled I've solved his problem when he has taken care of many of my problems for me.

I can fix him. Save him from the so-called curse.

"I only did minor touches—the painting felt like it was missing hope. So I added a dash of gold and pink to the clouds. You can't really see it, but it brings in more light to the stormy skies. It's like the bit of red in atrovirens, which makes all the difference. Because," I glance at the painting, "even in the darkest storms, there's always light, you see? It's always there—it might not be sunshine, but that glimmer of light is lurking in the background, telling you the storm is just passing by."

I point to the lighthouse and continue, "I added some white and amber here. Just a tad, so it looks like it's a beacon of hope, cutting through the dark clouds. Because that's what lighthouses do. They give hope to sailors, protecting them and telling them the shore is near. Not huge changes, but I think they've made all the difference, don't you think?"

Hearing no response, I turn back to him and fall silent. Maxwell's dark eyes glitter, the gray pools iridescent, like the clouds I just painted. His chest moves rapidly, like he's struggling to breathe.

"Maxwell?"

"You fucking amaze me, Belle, my little muse. God, I...I lo—" He stops himself. He balls his hands into fists at his sides.

He's going to say he loves me. My heart leaps in joy.

But he says nothing and I can't help but feel the crushing disappointment in my chest.

Clearing my throat, I strain a smile and change the subject. "Your art is beautiful. I saw your paintings in the studio. They're full of passion. Have you ever thought about displaying them in a gallery?"

I don't ask him if he wants to put on a huge art show—it'd be a nightmare for him, dealing with the crowds, not to mention people critiquing the work that contains part of your soul.

I would know since my designs all have a piece of myself in them.

His gaze is somber as he replies, "I'm surprised you aren't asking me why I'm not touring the country with my art or having exhibitions at The Met." He bites his lip before releasing it. "That's what most people would do."

"I don't think you'd like it—being in the spotlight. And that's perfectly fine. But that doesn't mean your art can't be admired. Didn't you tell me, 'What's art if not to be loved and admired?'"

His body stills. "You wouldn't mind hiding away from the spotlight with me?"

I shake my head. "The only spotlight I care about is you. Everyone else doesn't matter." My lips wobble as I try not to touch him, because I'm afraid he'll bolt from the way his muscles are coiled tightly.

"Plus," I whisper, "I'm not hiding in the shadows when you're shining your light on me."

He rakes in a sharp inhale and for a moment, the world quiets and all I can hear are the sounds of our breathing.

"I promise not to love you," he rasps before pulling me to him and crushing his mouth against mine. His lips seek, taste, and drink from my mouth while I do the same.

A warm furry body slinks away to the passageway, Silas's mournful howl echoing into the room, like he understands the ache I'm feeling inside.

Maxwell's words still hurt, but his crushing embrace stems the bleeding. If this is all he can give me, perhaps I'll learn to be okay with it.

Because I can't foresee living a life without him by my side.

CHAPTER 38

"You have an eye for design," Belle says, her head dipped over her desk.

I look away from my canvas—a blank canvas I'm sure will be my greatest work yet. Because it's a portrait of her. My muse. The person I wanted to draw for the longest time but couldn't bring myself to.

She's staring at the notes I made on her newest sketches. She had questions on color combinations, silhouettes, sustainable natural fabric options, and while I'm no expert on fashion, I know art and composition.

"You have an eye for colors," I comment.

She used the smallest bit of paint yesterday to transform the painting of the scene I witnessed at Lake Superior, when I was standing alone on the rocky shores.

I was restless then, a dark hole in my chest, my muse long disappeared.

Belle blushes and smiles. She looks so happy here. With me.

A warm heat floods my insides, and I rub the spot over my heart.

I no longer feel that dark hole.

And damn if that scares me, because I tell myself it doesn't mean what it means.

I vow to myself I'll never love her.

I know she's trying to convince me the curse isn't real, but she hasn't seen what I've seen. Mom lying in the coffin, her skin ice cold. Sydney's limbs twisted on the sand, her fingers rigid as if she fought until her last breath.

So, I can't love her. I can only give her pleasure in my bed, save her family's business, buy out animal shelters she has her eye on, and fulfill her adventures one by one.

A clawing desperation boils me up from inside, panic taking root.

I'm calm. I'm at peace. I accept myself.

I repeat the mantra ten times, twenty times, but my pulse doesn't settle. My mind is flooded with Belle's smiles, her soft touches, her sweet kisses, only for the memories to be chased away by images of Sydney and Mom, Dad sobbing at the cemetery, Grandfather's eyes glazed over as he finally smiled before taking his last breath because he said he was going to be with Grandma again.

The images swirl and shift into the snippets of my dark dreams at night—this time, it's Belle in the rose garden laughing, telling me she wants to go to Venice one day. Then there are the visions of me cradling her broken body on the ground, the rain falling around us. Dreams that feel so real, I question my sanity.

I can't love her. I can't. I can't love her.

My breathing grows shallow and I walk to the windows and look outside at the thick snow and trees, still barren skeletons of black and brown.

Lifeless.

"Maxwell? Maxwell! Are you okay?"

Releasing a calming breath, I turn around, faking a smile.

Belle frowns, her pencil perched behind her ear.

Shaking my head, I answer, "I'm fine. Just thinking about work. I fucked things up last week at the gala, didn't I?"

"You were defending me. I think everyone saw that."

"That's what Lana told me. I owe her a box of chocolates because she worked the past few days to put out press releases."

After we emerged from my bedroom yesterday morning, I finally saw the text messages from my siblings. They'd ironically changed the name of our text group to: "Where is His Majesty?"

It's almost a routine for them now. Last year, it was "Save Ryland from Himself," and the year before was "Save Steven from Himself." Now the idiots have their attentions set on me.

Ryland

> If I didn't see Belle going after you and Morris telling me you are otherwise "occupied," I'd be worried.

Rex

> What's better than a quick fuck? A sex marathon. Ha! Old man Morris is probably traumatized by you two being so "occupied" with each other.

Ethan

> Seriously, C. Some things belong inside your mind. You don't actually have to say everything you're thinking.

Charles

> Can someone tell me why I'm in this group chat? I'm not even an Anderson.

Rex

> But you have your eyes on an Anderson. I see you, bro.

Ryland

> Who? Charles, who the fuck are you interested in?

Rex

> I'm thinking of a certain ballerina who is the grumpy to our golden boy's sunshine.

Maxwell

Guys, I'm here. Don't comment on my sex life if you want to live. And Charles, I'll be watching you.

Charles

You need to get your eyesight checked, Mr. C. There's no way I'm interested in that goth brat. No offense.

Taylor

Fuck you. I'm here too, you POS. If you were the last man on earth, I'd rather die alone than be with you, Vaughn.

Charles

I don't recall asking.

Lana

I swear, you guys put a lid on it. Maxwell, I got the press covered. Right now, they're spinning the story of an angry husband protecting his wife from her drunk boss. Gordon Flair has been canned. Will let you know if we need you.

Lana

Go enjoy your "honeymoon." Muahahaha. But seriously, take Belle on a real honeymoon.

"Lana did a good job when Ryland and Millie had their scandal," Belle murmurs as she stands next to me. "If she says everything is fine, then it is."

"I'm not sure this will hold for long. The press still hasn't seen me acting *normal* before." I thump my fist against the window and press my forehead against the cool glass. "Fuck. So fucking useless."

Belle rubs my back. "What's normal, anyway? We all have our own issues to deal with." She turns toward me and frowns at what she sees on my face. "But you look miserable. Have you thought about seeing a professional again?"

I bow over, my head knocking against the window in frustration.

I'm angry.

At the world. At myself. At the curse. At my life. At being the firstborn.

Belle lays her head against my back as she wraps her arms around my waist. "It's okay, Maxwell. We'll get through this."

She doesn't pressure me, doesn't shame me. Belle understands.

"Dad took me to a therapist soon after Mom's funeral. I was already an outcast at school. A loner with the fanciest clothes and an important last name. But I always had issues talking to new people. They said I was introverted, and I was fine with that. I liked playing by myself and reading or painting. Ryland was the sunshine between the two of us and I was happy being the quiet older brother."

I let out a sigh. "But at Mom's funeral, something inside me broke. I wanted to be brave and tell the world how much I loved Mom. My father said I didn't need to, but I wanted to do it for her. I guess I thought maybe if I could make that speech, that, if Mom was there watching over me, she'd see how brave I was and wouldn't have to worry about me anymore. But I couldn't face the crowds. I froze until someone rescued me. Then the jeering happened at school. The kids said I was useless. How my mom would be so disappointed I couldn't even say a few nice words about her."

"Those awful brats!" Belle seethes. "I know I'm not supposed to say mean things about little kids, but those are some crappy, shitty little humans who probably shouldn't have been born. I should feel bad for saying this, but I don't."

She huffs and I bite back a smile, a small ray of her sunshine brightening the trip down the dark memory lane.

"I became more withdrawn, and it got to a point where Dad took me to a therapist. Dr. Chandler helped me a lot. Taught me to express myself through art. Sometimes I couldn't find the words, but I could paint them out. Anything I couldn't say, I could sketch. It was therapeutic, and I felt connected to Mom because she loved art so much. But Dr. Chandler died when I was twelve and the sessions stopped."

Lifting my head up, I stare into the gray overcast skies, watching a raven spread its dark wings and soar, its silhouette lonely.

"By then, I had my small social circle. I was comfortable. Then, we dove into high school and college prep. Time passed by and I could cope by working in the shadows. I could tolerate minimal small talk. I thought Ryland was happy being the public face of the company. I thought I had things handled."

She wraps her arms tighter around me.

"I thought, 'Yes, Maxwell, you have anxiety, but who isn't anxious from time to time?' It had been years since I had severe panic attacks. Dr. Chandler used to tell Dad they weren't true hallucinations but were my overactive imagination at work."

I scoff and shake my head. "You're going to think I'm pathetic. I'm thirty-six years old, and I couldn't even make a speech without breaking into a sweat and panicking. You're twelve years younger than me and you have to save me. My brothers had to save me. I couldn't save myself, I couldn't—"

Save anyone. Mom. Sydney. And now Belle's getting hurt—her week in the hospital still haunts me to this day.

Belle wedges herself between me and the window. The cool daylight bathes her skin in flawless ivory, tears framing the lushest lashes I've ever seen.

Tears for me.

She cups my cheek and whispers, "You're *not* pathetic. You're *not* a freak. You are so strong, fighting this battle alone for so long."

Her lips tremble. "I'm here now. I'll fight alongside you. You'll never be alone again. And if you want to consider finding a therapist...I'll be there with you too. They helped my grandpa...I know they can help you. And finding help doesn't mean you're weak—it just tells me how strong you are to fight against the current."

She slowly lifts my sweater, her fingers tracing the raised scars and mottled skin. Ugly patches of purplish red. Her lips rain kisses over my flaws and my rough edges, just like she did that night in the kitchen.

But now she knows. She knows everything, and she isn't running away.

"Your scars...inside and out, are so beautiful," she kisses the biggest one from my abdominal surgery, "you're enough. Just as you are."

Growling, I haul her up, slam my lips on hers, and she melts in my arms.

My beautiful muse with her beast.

My heart tumbles and swells, every thump the most beautiful music to her aria. She's the flowers in the spring and I'm the soil underneath, quietly nurturing her, protecting her, giving her my all so she can bloom brightly for the world to see.

A lone tear slips out of my eye as I angle her face to the side so I can kiss her deeper, so I can steal any piece of her for myself.

I vow to never love her. I vow to never love her. I vow to never love her.

The words don't stick.

What a fucking liar.

CHAPTER 39

A KNOCK SOUNDS AT my bedroom door as I finish tying the sash on my black and gray sweater wrap dress for a date night with Maxwell.

My husband is taking me out on a public date. I can't stop grinning with glee.

"Come in!"

Agnes steps in, her face severe as always, her hands clasped together. "Ms. Belle."

I swallow a sigh. It's been months of the same strained treatment and nothing I do seems to make her like me. But she's good at her job, managing the day-to-day chores around the mansion so I don't need to be bothered with many things.

"How can I help you, Agnes?" I try to smile but am afraid I look like one of those scary clowns at the circus instead.

She narrows her eyes before clearing her throat. "I see you and Sir Maxwell have grown...fond of each other."

I arch my brow. She is walking on thin ice. Very thin ice.

"I was Ms. Julianna's lady's maid when she was alive." Her nostrils flare and she looks away. "She was a wonderful woman."

Agnes lets out a sigh before facing me again. "I know you think we're all superstitious about the curse. But you weren't here when she died. You didn't see how it tore the house apart. And now, Sir Maxwell seems to be smitten with you. But if you want him to be happy, I think you should keep your distance."

My mouth drops open and I stand up, anger bursting through me. How dare she talk about my relationship with Maxwell like we are friends or something?

"Agnes, that is way out of line and I'm not going to—"

"Sometimes, the truth is the hardest to hear. But someone has to say it." She spins around and walks toward the door before pausing at the threshold.

Her throat works as she turns toward me, her dark eyes piercing. "I apologize for overstepping, but I can't stand by and watch history repeat itself."

She closes the door with a soft click.

I grit my teeth, fury singeing my insides. *How dare she?* I won't put up with this behavior. I'm going to talk to Maxwell and we'll start searching for a new housekeeper.

Knock. Knock.

My gaze whips toward the door. It had better not be her coming back in here. I won't let her walk all over me, even if she grovels.

"Yes?" I grit out.

Melody traipses in, her smile slipping off her face as she takes in my expression. "What's wrong, Belle? You look like you want to murder someone."

Blowing out a breath, I reply, "It's Agnes. She drives me absolutely crazy. Do I have a sign on my forehead that says, 'walk all over me'?"

Melody snorts and sits on my bed. Even though we are still in a boss/employee capacity, she's become a good friend, and I'm glad I have someone who understands the family as well as she does to talk to.

She shakes her head. "It's not you. It's totally her. Mom and I were afraid she'd be like that with you when Sir Maxwell announced he was getting married."

"What? Why? I've never even met her before."

"You know how her husband has those gambling debts?"

I nod.

Melody sighs. "Well, Mom told me back when Ms. Julianna passed away, she left behind a nice fortune and a will. She was very kind and left everyone who worked here a nice chunk of change, but of course, most of her fortune was split between Sir Linus and their children."

Silas barks and scampers to my feet and the hairs on my forearms rise. I don't like where this is going.

She continues, "Well, Ms. Julianna understood what it meant to be the wife of the eldest Anderson son and she wanted to show her support to Sir Maxwell's wife in the event she wasn't here. As a small token of appreciation, she left a portion of her fortune to his wife. I think there were some time stipulations...I'm sure Sir Maxwell has forgotten about it since he's a billionaire and all that, but you can ask him."

"Okay...but what does this have anything to do with Agnes and how she treats me?"

"Well, Mom told me Agnes was drunk one night, which was very unusual for her. It was because her husband had put them in debt again. She told Mom if Sir Maxwell didn't have a wife, the portion of Ms. Julianna's fortune that would've gone to his wife would go to her instead because Ms. Julianna knew about her husband's gambling habits."

I fist my hands. "What the heck?" Reeling from this information, my eyes see red. "So you're telling me Agnes wants me to leave Maxwell so she'll get money?"

Melody shrugs. "I don't know about that. But I'm thinking that's why she's cold toward you."

I fume as I put the finishing touches on my makeup. *Calm down, Belle. Calm down. Anger won't solve the problem.*

But anger feels so damn good right now.

"Anyway," Melody stands up, "I wouldn't care too much about Agnes. As long as you and Sir Maxwell are happy, what can she do anyway? She should just leave her bastard of a husband instead."

I stay silent, still unable to calm the anger churning inside me. *Game on, Agnes. Game. On.*

I see Melody waving in the mirror's reflection. Her lips curve up in an unsure smile. "Belle? Did I say too much?"

"No, thanks for telling me. Things make so much more sense now."

"This is just speculation from my end. But anyway, I came in here to tell you the result of the charity gala."

My ears perk up and I spin around and face her, the excitement temporarily dousing the need to find Agnes and give her a piece of my mind.

Melody beams. "We raised ten million dollars for depression and anxiety research."

I gasp. "Ten million?" It's far more than I expected for one night of dancing and auctioning.

She nods and waggles her brows. "Just got the numbers from the accountant, so I had to tell you right away! I'll send the results to Ms. Lana so she can tell the press too. This is such great news!"

I squeal, leap out of my chair, and wrap Melody in a hug. "Yes! This is awesome! Thanks for telling me!"

"It's you, Belle! People loved how you stepped up on the stage for the speech and how Sir Maxwell came to your defense when your boss attacked you. Everyone is saying you two are the power couple and how brave Sir Maxwell was for stepping into the spotlight when he was obviously anxious about it."

She pulls away, grinning as she traipses back to the door. "Congratulations on being a *smashing* success." Her voice takes on a very posh accent, as if she's an amateur trying out for a British film. She gives me a thumbs-up. "And you look hot tonight! Sir Maxwell will absolutely *die*. Have fun! And don't mind what Agnes said. She's just an old grouch."

The floorboards of the hallway creak as Melody leaves.

I hear the now familiar moaning wails whistling down the empty halls and suddenly, a door slams in the distance.

I jolt, my fingers flying to my locket as I recall my previous conversations with Agnes, all her cryptic warnings and disapproving glares.

Silas whines and I look at him, finding him growling at the closed door, his lone eye fierce and teeth bared.

"It's just the air and the old house, Silas," I murmur, reaching down to pet him, even as an insidious thread of unease resurfaces.

Agnes is trying to scare me away. That has to be it.

Silas barks again, clawing at the door, his nails digging into the dark wood. I open the door and he darts out, disappearing into the eerie quiet, chasing an unknown phantom that has been lurking in the shadows.

It's Agnes trying to scare me. Curses aren't real. Goosebumps prickle my forearms, and the room swirls around me. Cold sweat dots the back of my neck and I grab the doorframe for support, my eyes closing until the black dots disappear from my vision.

Stress. That's what the doctor said. I'm so firing Agnes for putting me through this crap.

Another haunting wail echoes from far away, followed by a damp chill running up my spine.

I clutch the locket tighter in my grip, the metal flowers digging into the flesh of my fingers as I heave in deep breaths.

There is no curse. There can't be. But deep down inside me, a voice whispers, *what if?*

CHAPTER 40

I can't stop staring at her during dinner.

The creamy swells of her tits are taunting me in this deep V-neck dress she has on. My cock twitches as I stare at her placing a small morsel of food in her mouth as we dine in a private room inside Carlisle's, one of the restaurants we have within The Orchid.

She moans and the juice from her steak drips out. Then she dips her tongue to wipe it off.

That talented tongue of hers. My cock hardens when I think about the blow job she gave me this morning in the shower, the way that pink tongue of hers swirled around my sensitive tip while she sucked me like I was her favorite popsicle, her tawny eyes dilated, gaze drunk with lust.

I groan and clutch my steak knife and fork in a death grip. *What the fuck is wrong with me?* Before her, I could go months without sex and even when I had it, it was never this desperate craving I've had with her.

"What's wrong?" Her brows quirk up in concern. "You haven't really touched your food. Aren't you hungry?"

My little muse is oblivious.

"You," I rasp.

"Huh?" She looks adorably confused.

"Fuck yes, I'm hungry. Seeing you in that dress, your tits lifting and falling, taunting me, your lips and moans and everything about you," I swallow, my nostrils flaring as her eyes grow as big as the dinner plates before her, "I'm *ravenous.*"

"Maxwell!" A pink flush creeps up her neck and tinges her ivory skin. She gnaws on her sexy lips. I have her flustered. "Are you taking me on a date just so you can ogle me?"

"I wanted to take you out tonight because I realized I hadn't spent time alone with you outside the estate since the race and Nellie's."

Reaching over the table, I link my hand with hers, relishing the electric zap and her gasp the moment we touch.

This powerful connection—it's something I can't explain. We're two halves of a whole, the atoms in our bodies recognizing each other. As I look at her, watching her smile sweetly at me, the whites of her teeth blinding, I'm hit with an impulse, the same impulse that got me to elope with Sydney all those years ago, but this time, the need is ten times more potent, more desperate.

I want to love her. I want to give the middle finger to my old friend, death again.

But what if? You know your love is a death sentence. You know that.

The thought is a bucket of ice water dousing the fire burning inside me and I think back to how Elias's investigation on her fall at BSUA didn't yield anything, how Belle had been complaining about getting dizzy even though the doctors found nothing unusual when they examined her, and uneasiness crawls up my throat.

But even then, there's a kernel of rebellion inside me. What if Belle's right and all the accidents were random? What if there isn't a curse?

She must've seen something in my face, because she asks, "You're worried about something, aren't you? You thought of it just now."

Giving her fingers one last squeeze, I let go and focus on the medium rare ribeye in front of me, hoping the food will settle my suddenly frayed nerves.

"I never told you this, but I asked Elias to look into your fall at the shelter." I tug my tie loose from my neck—it was getting hard to breathe.

"What? Why? It was an accident. Do you owe him any favors? Why didn't you tell me before?" Belle clearly knows who Elias is, but who doesn't? Everyone in the city has heard of him and he has helped her friends before.

"We have a silent agreement and you don't need to worry about it."

She shakes her head. "Maxwell, we're married. You need to tell me these things so we can make these decisions together. This impacts me too. For the thousandth time, it was an accident."

She shifts in her seat, a frown on her face. "I can't believe you went behind my back and now you owe him a favor. Who knows what he's going to ask you to do later on?"

Anything. He can ask me to do anything and it'll be worth it to make sure she's safe.

"You think it's the curse, don't you?" She looks so crestfallen. I have a feeling she has been hoping the last few weeks between us have changed things. "I slipped and knocked my head. Saw and heard some weird things because I almost had a concussion. It was my fault."

"But what about your dizzy spells? And didn't you say you saw a man in a mask outside the window when you first moved in?"

My heart races as I think back to all the little things she complained about in the past—the masked man encounter that I brushed off after a cursory inspection of surveillance tapes, her asking if there were ghosts in the house because she kept hearing moaning and wailing and doors slamming. I grew up in the mansion, so those sounds were normal to me.

All these things seemed innocent when Agnes or Morris told me about them, but now, I'm not so sure.

Then there's the branch shattering the windows, a branch that came from nowhere since the trees are so far away from the fourth floor. The same omen before the other deaths. Signs I'm choosing to ignore because I want Belle to be right. I want everything to be some twisted self-fulfilling prophecy and perhaps if I don't think about it, the curse won't happen.

Cold sweat forms on the back of my neck and my stomach turns. A series of unusual events. If it wasn't the curse, what could it be?

An anvil sits atop my chest as my lungs fight for oxygen. *Why is it so hot in here?* Staring at the food in front of me, I watch it swirl, the scent of the semi-raw meat suddenly nauseating.

I'm calm. I'm at peace. I accept myself. I'm calm—

Her sweet scent of lilies hits my nostrils, followed by a soft, warm body wrapping me in a tight embrace.

"It's okay, Maxwell. We'll work on this. In time, you'll see the curse isn't real. It's okay. I'm here." Her soft words and gentle touches calm the turbulent swirl in my mind and I close my eyes, breathing in her fragrance, one that'll forever remind me of home, and listen to the calm beating of her heart.

Her thriving, healthy, living heart. One I'll protect if it's the last thing I do.

She makes room for herself and sits on my lap and uses a napkin to blot the sweat off my forehead and upper lip. "Everything will be okay, Maxwell, you'll see."

She smiles, then frowns, as if she remembers something.

"What?" I ask, straightening up.

"In the interest of telling each other problems, I want to talk to you about Agnes."

She tells me about the housekeeper's cold behavior toward her, culminating in her warning for Belle to keep her distance from me.

My lips twitch and I feel my face heat. *How dare she disrespect Belle?* While Agnes has been part of my entire life, if I had to choose between her and my wife, I'd choose my wife always.

Belle says, "My immediate reaction was to fire her, but now that I've calmed down, I think maybe we can talk to her. Put her on some performance improvement plan? After all, she has worked for your family for so long."

I sigh, cupping Belle's cheek. My wife is so kind. I don't deserve her.

"That sounds good," I murmur. "But if she mistreats you again, she's out. No more chances."

Belle leans up and presses her lips to mine. The kiss is gentle at first, but it soon changes flavor as she settles over my hardening erection, her wide neckline slipping to the side, yielding one creamy shoulder.

The unease inside me latches onto lust and I want to feel her against me, skin to skin, heart over heart. Growling, I fist a handful of her silky locks, winding it around my hand before tugging, her breathy gasp a direct caress to my cock.

I trail kisses over her face—her eyes, her nose, her cheeks—down to her slender neck, sucking her throbbing pulse as she mewls and thrashes in my tight hold.

"Fuck, I'll never get enough of you." My hand slides down her shoulder and cups her breast over the soft material, finding her nipple already hard. I twist the nub, plucking it, playing with it as fire courses through my veins.

"Maxwell, oh my God," she rides my shaft over my pants, "I'm so wet."

Fuck me.

I might be unable to give her the love she wants, but I can give her this.

Grunting, I haul her off me, my breathing harsh as I take in her mussed hair, swollen lips, dazed eyes.

Standing up, I grab her hand and drag her out of the private room into the main dining area, ignoring the pointed stares and hushed whispers directed toward us. Nodding at the manager who served us, I know he'll send the bill to my account.

"W-Where are we going?" Belle still sounds dazed, and before tonight ends, I'm going to have her even dizzier with desire.

"I'm going to take you on another adventure."

CHAPTER 41

WE STEP OUT OF the elevators, and I turn the corner and head into The Lilith, where an attendant in a formfitting red dress greets us.

"Mr. And Mrs. Anderson. Lovely to see you this evening."

Belle grips my hand tightly, her face flushed, and I bite back a smile.

My last name sounds so good on her.

"Sir, do you want me to take you to your usual room?"

I shake my head. "You don't need to take me there. I got it."

The attendant smiles and walks back behind her desk.

Stepping through the hidden door behind her, I lead Belle down the hall of dark gray and navy hues until we reach the large group space that is already half full of people tonight.

Moans and whimpers mix with grunts and growls, the smell of sex and lust heavy in the air.

Belle gasps and tugs me on my sleeve. "What's this place? Do you come here a lot?" She stiffens slightly, like she's jealous.

Chuckling under my breath, I turn to her and caress her cheek, watching her eyes widen and darken as she takes in the erotic activities around her.

My little muse is curious, just as I thought.

Leaning down, I whisper in her ear, "This is The Lilith, the voyeur and exhibition room on the Rose floors. I used to come here once or twice a year because I could watch and indulge without the pressures of people wanting more from me. Follow me. We won't be spending our time out here tonight."

There's no way I'm letting anyone witness my Belle in the throes of an orgasm. That sight is for me alone.

Pulling her behind me, I lead her down a long corridor. Her breathing quickens as we pass by windows displaying occupants in various stages of sex. There are two men kissing each other on a bed in one room, followed by a masked woman writhing on a sofa with two men railing her from behind and another man stuffing his cock into her mouth.

"Oh wow," Belle whispers as she pauses by the window with the three men and the woman. She presses her thighs together.

Stepping behind her, I curl my arms around her waist and plaster her to my front so she can feel how hard I am for her right now.

"You see," I rasp before biting her ear, "I seem to recall my wife likes to watch and gets turned on at the idea of being watched."

"I never said that," she moans, her eyes fluttering shut, her hips moving in a sultry motion, rubbing against my aching hard on.

"Remember how you watched me in the shower, you naughty girl? How wet you got, how you couldn't wait for me to make you mine even though you hated me?"

I slide my hand down her dress, inching it up until I expose her lace panties. My fingers swipe the tiny scrap of cloth.

Fuck. She's so wet right now. My cock pulses, and I thrust into her backside and groan.

"And when I made love to you against the windows, remember that?" My voice is rough as we move in unison, two people twisting their bodies against each other in a lurid dance.

"Maxwell," she gasps when I find her clit over her underwear and give it a pinch. "Fuck me."

My control is taut, my restraint about to snap, and with a growl, I carry her in my arms as I stride past the other displays and into the room I usually go in on the rare occasion I visit.

I toss Belle onto the king-sized bed, watching her tits bounce, her cleavage indecent from the wide neckline.

She's panting heavily, her face flushed, and she licks her plump bottom lip.

The fucking tease.

I yank off my tie, then my suit jacket and shirt, watching her eyes widen with appreciation as her gaze trails over my body.

My belt comes off next, the loud whipping sound echoing in the room and she flinches, but instead of fear in her eyes, I only see lust and intense affection.

I hit a button by the door and the shades over the wall of glass lift, revealing two couples on the other side—exhibitionists randomly chosen since I didn't state my preferences ahead of time. Belle gasps as her attention shifts to the scene behind me.

A tattooed man is making his way down a brunette's body, kissing and fondling her as she whimpers on the bed. On the sofa is a couple already in the throes of fucking, the woman bouncing on the man like he's her personal bull at a rodeo, her cries loud in the room.

These couples don't interest me as much as watching my little muse turn redder, her legs rubbing against each other as she squirms on the bed. Her hand travels between her legs.

"Don't you dare touch that pussy," I command, and her eyes snap to mine. She freezes and shivers. My little muse is so turned on right now. "You don't get to do anything tonight other than feel and watch."

Slowly, I take off my pants and underwear, my cock bobbing up and curling against my stomach, the tip already glistening with pre-cum. I give it a few hard tugs, my balls twitching with the need to come inside my wife.

She wets her lips and widens her legs, letting me see her soaked panties.

Grabbing her legs, I yank her to the edge of the bed as I bunch her dress up around her waist, too far gone to spend the extra seconds to take it off. I rip off the scanty lace and she flinches from the burn, but before she can say anything, I dive and taste those beautiful lips down there, already wet with her sweetness.

"Maxwell!" she cries. She arches up, her body trying to move away from my onslaught, but I hold her tightly as I swipe my tongue through her folds.

She tastes like honey and nectar, sweetness and sunshine. I can't get enough. "Let's see if I can make you cry louder than the people in the room."

I seal my lips over her swollen clit and suck, my tongue flicking it in quick circles as I insert a finger, then two into her tight entrance, groaning when I feel her clench around me.

"Maxwell, please, p-please, oh fuck," Belle mewls, her legs clamping my head in a vise as she undulates on my face.

I suckle her clit and hammer my fingers inside her, the wet sounds of my movements adding to the erotic soundtrack of the sex happening on the other side of the glass.

Her walls clench as she bows up, her muscles tense and rigid, and with a dark chuckle, I kiss those pretty lips of her pussy and take out my fingers.

"No! Maxwell, I need to come," Belle complains as she tries to pull me back with her legs.

I crawl above her and yank down her dress and bra so I can see the pretty brown nipples saluting me. Hovering above her, I grind my body on hers, my cock leaking and making a mess, but I don't care.

"Look at my prim and proper wife, begging for my cock underneath me. You're a cum slut just for me. Insatiable. You need to come, little muse? You need my cock inside your tight pussy because you're aching for me?" I rasp as I stare into her tawny eyes, the blacks of her pupils nearly eclipsing her irises.

"Yes," she pants out her answer, and angles her hips so my dick slides against her clit with every gyration. Her eyes roll backward as I feel her legs shaking.

"No one knows the real you, you tiny little thing needing my big cock and cum so I can get your belly full of me, because I'm putting a baby inside you."

"Y-Yes, please help me." She claws my back and I growl from the pain, which only adds to my pleasure.

"Beg me, Belle. Beg me to fuck you. Beg me to stuff you full of my cum." Burning heat races down my spine to my balls and a spurt of cum erupts from my cock, dripping over her pussy lips, adding to the slick lubrication as I fight the urge to come.

Her glazed eyes snap open, her mouth parting. "Fuck me, Maxwell. Use me like your whore and give me all your cum." The dirty words slip out of her mouth and I see her eyes widening in surprise.

Only I get to see this side of her.

Mindless with lust, I wrench her legs above my shoulders and slam inside her in one stroke.

"Fuuuuck," I roar, the heat from her core engulfing my cock in a vise and pleasure, overwhelming pleasure, chases away all the worries in my mind.

She screams and thrashes under me as I lock her hands above her head and begin moving in a quick rhythm.

I won't last long.

Each thrust sends us farther up the bed until we're by the headboard.

Belle is moaning loudly, incoherent words slipping out of her lips as I stare at her flushed face, the beauty mark under her eye, the connection in our gaze only adding to the inferno burning inside me.

My cock swells and lengthens, sliding into her pussy like my life depends on it, and I briefly register the quieting moans from the scene happening on the other side of the glass.

I slap a hand on a button by the panel, and I link my fingers with Belle's over her head, my gaze glued to hers, watching her eyes darken and smolder.

Belle's legs tremble before locking around my waist and I angle her further under me so I can enter her deeper, hitting a spot so far up that has her screaming.

"Come, little muse. They can hear you begging for my cum." They can't see her, but they can damn well hear my little closet exhibitionist.

Belle screams louder and she detonates.

I grip her hands tightly as her pussy strangles my cock in a chokehold and I go over the edge with her, flying into euphoria.

Release after release streams out of me, the madness disorienting.

Minutes pass by before either of us can move. The room on the other side of the glass darkens, the performers long having vacated the space.

I brace myself above her, so that every part of me is touching her body, and kiss those pouty lips, tasting her sweetness, savoring this intense connection that has been simmering in the background since the day she stepped into my car.

My heart swells as I break our kiss to stare at her.

This beautiful woman who sees all my scars and flaws and yet accepts me for who I am. The perfect yin to my yang.

"Belle, I," I swallow before pressing another kiss to her lips. "I...I..."

Her eyes mist over, as if she knows everything I'm feeling, my soul bursting with so many vibrant colors I don't know how to get the masterpiece in my heart out onto paper.

A tear slips out of her eyes and her lips tremble.

A flash of pain stabs me—I don't ever want her to cry over me.

"Maxwell, I...I can't tell you what you want to hear," she whispers, the tears falling down in earnest and my heart clenches because I know how she feels and what she's going to say.

And maybe it's because we are in this bubble, away from the mansion, an overwhelming elation sifts through me, smothering the curl of dread threatening to break through.

"I love you, I love you so much, you beautiful man." The words tumble out of her mouth as she stares at me with so much love, so much affection, I'm robbed of my voice.

My heart bursts with warmth, the exhilaration disorienting and I can't do anything other than to stare at her, this goddess beneath me I don't deserve.

Then, the fear sets in. *She just told me she loves me. The curse.* My breathing quickens.

"I'm sorry, Maxwell, I know you told me—"

"Shhh…" I hush her before I seal my lips with hers once more, kissing the only lips I'm going to kiss for the rest of my life. *It's okay, I haven't said the words back to her yet. It should be fine. Fuck, please let it be fine.*

Our tongues tangle with each other, my lips moving reverently on hers, our fingers clutching each other tightly so we'll never be apart.

"Don't say anything more, *please*." My heart pounds ferociously inside my chest. The sentiment inside me, the one that has been banging against my rib cage, begging to be let out, is at the tip of my tongue.

And it's taking every ounce of restraint I have to hold it in, to not say the three words I want to tell her aloud.

Instead, I kiss her like there's no past, no tomorrow, no curses, no deaths. I kiss her like the present is all that matters, like this moment can last forever.

And I pray…I pray the curse didn't hear her.

CHAPTER 42

Belle

I'm walking on cloud nine.

It's been three days since I told Maxwell I love him at The Lilith and he hasn't pulled away. He even mentioned this morning that he has a surprise trip planned for us. I bite back a smile, wondering if this is all a dream.

Even Old Morris noticed my good mood this morning before I left the estate. The butler handed me an umbrella by the door and murmured, "Have a good day, Ms. Belle. The weather looks dreary."

I grinned. "It can be thunderstorms for all I care." I did a little twirl in the foyer.

He chuckled. "You're a breath of fresh air, Ms. Belle. You remind me of my sister—she made everyone smile too." His eyes took on a faraway look, like he was reminiscing about better days from long ago. "She was the sunshine of our family, always positive no matter how life treated her. My parents loved her. I loved her."

My chest clenched at the pain in his voice and I remembered what Melody told me at the gala, how Old Morris had no one left in this world. Without another thought, I threw my arms around him.

Morris coughed, clearly surprised. "Ms. Belle!"

"She sounded wonderful, Morris. I'm so sorry your family is no longer with you." Disentangling from him, I gave him a soft smile. "But if you want, I'll be happy to be an honorary family member. My grandfather passed away when I was sixteen, and you, sir, you look like good honorary grandfather material."

Morris swallowed, his eyes reddening, clearly overcame with emotions. "T-Thank you, Ms. Belle. I'd be so honored," he rasped.

I smile at the memory, glad I get to make the old man happy. He deserves more love and companionship.

"Geez, that smile on your face is making me lose my appetite. You're turning into my sister," Taylor mutters.

"It's a compliment, Belle, because Tay loves us." Grace snickers as she loops her arm around mine and we brave the chilly weather and leaden skies.

A fresh flurry of snow falls as we walk down the streets of SoHo toward Wraithmoor Antiquities, because I want to know what Eleanor didn't tell me last time and if she knows anything about the curse. Millie is attending some event with Ryland and couldn't come with us.

Maxwell had a meeting at the Fleur headquarters this morning, and I asked him to meet us at the shop afterward. Maybe if we learn the origins of the curse, the mystique and fear will disappear.

I know the curse is still bothering him. I see the flash of guilt in his eyes before he pulls me into a deep kiss, like he's afraid I'll slip away. I feel the tension in his arms as he tethers me to him when we sleep at night in his bedroom, since we've long abandoned sleeping separately.

There's nothing in the library. I've searched high and low and while there are letters and diaries mentioning a curse, there's nothing about how it came about. I have a feeling Maxwell's great-great-great-grandfather, Silas's missing journal may hold the answer, but to date, we still haven't found anything.

The girls and I trudge along the slushy streets, the cement marred with icy clusters of gray sludge. The stench of wet asphalt and overfilled trash cans reeks in the air.

"I'll never let a man be the cause of my happiness," Tay grumbles, and I sneak a glance at her, finding her face pinched as if she's thinking about something.

"I think the key is ensuring your happiness isn't dependent on a man. But it's perfectly fine for a man to make you happy," I say. We make a turn at the street corner, merging with the crowd of gray and black puffer jackets as we cross the street.

Taylor huffs and scrunches her nose. One day, I'll find out why she seems to have a disdain toward men in general.

"Belle!"

I hear my name being called above the ruckus of honking cabs and screeching car tires. Turning around, I grin when I see a familiar blond man waving.

"Cole! What are you doing here?"

He runs toward us and pulls me into a hug. "I thought that was you. Long time no see."

Even though I've since returned to BSUA after their change in leadership, I've taken time off from the shelter when the gala preparation picked up, and I haven't seen or spoken to Cole other than the texts we've periodically exchanged.

He's holding on to me for a beat too long, long enough for the hairs on my forearms to rise and for me to feel uncomfortable. Clearing my throat, I pull away and step a few paces back.

Tay sneaks a glance at me, her brow cocked high, and she stands in front of me, as if sensing my discomfort.

"Hey, Cole. What are you doing out in SoHo on a Saturday? Don't you need to be at BSUA?" Grace asks. "Bronx is a bit far from here."

Cole chuckles, but his smile doesn't reach his eyes. "I'm taking some time off from volunteering too. Life got too busy. I'm just here to pick up an art piece I ordered for my mom for her birthday. Where are you guys going?"

"To an antiquities shop a few blocks up."

We start walking and he moves beside me, nudging Taylor out of the way, who is now openly scowling at him, but he doesn't seem to care.

I shiver from this strange tension hanging in the air and sneak a glance at my friend. He seems slimmer, his face more gaunt, dark shadows rimming his eyes.

Something feels distinctly off.

"Are you okay, Cole? You look like you haven't slept in days."

He flinches, as if my question jolted him out of a deep thought, and he curls his arm over my shoulder and squeezes. "Worried about me? I'm fine. Work has been hectic, that's all." He turns toward me. "How have you been doing?"

I shrug his arm off my shoulder. I'm not sure what changed, because he has always been affectionate toward me as a friend, but now, I feel a thread of possessiveness and I don't like it one bit. But am I overthinking this?

"Things have been great. Maxwell is doing well too." I feel the need to mention my husband, to remind him I'm taken.

Happily taken.

"Are you happy, Belle? Truly?" he asks, his eyes darkening at the mention of Maxwell.

"I told you I am. And I mean it." Perhaps last time we met, before Maxwell and I got close the night of the gala, I gave Cole the impression I wasn't happy—after all, Maxwell and I were in a shaky situation then.

But I have to nip this in the bud. Everything is different now, and I don't like Cole that way, and he needs to accept that.

Before I can say anything, Cole stops in his tracks, his nostrils flaring, and a muscle twitches in his jaw. "Do you know your husband was married before, Belle? Do you know what happened to his first wife?"

The unease from earlier flares back up, and my pulse pounds in my ears. *How does he know about Sydney?*

Cole looks at me, his green eyes hardening. "You should look into that, Belle."

Without another word, he stalks away, melding with the crowds, disappearing from view.

"What on earth was that?" Grace asks. "Something is off with him. He wasn't like this before."

"No shit. See? This is why I stay away from men. They're more trouble than they're worth," Taylor says.

I shake my head in confusion. "I always thought he liked me before, and I tried keeping my distance...but I think something else is going on."

An icy chill sweeps up my skin as the snow falls harder, suffocating the air in a fury of white. The world spins around me again and I bend down and clutch my knees, trying to heave in a few breaths as the girls walk ahead.

"Belle, you okay? You look green." Tay stops from a few steps away. Grace furrows her brows, clearly worried, and starts walking back toward me.

Closing my eyes, I breathe slowly, waiting for the strange dizzy spell to pass.

I need to find another doctor. A specialist. This isn't just stress.

Something doesn't feel right.

"I don't know what's going—" I begin.

Suddenly, a loud screeching of tires bellow in my ears.

"Belle, look out!" Grace screams and I look up, finding a car barreling toward me.

Just then, a hard body plows into me, slamming me out of the way of the speeding car, which careens off the sidewalk before taking off, and I feel the heavy impact of a body on top of mine as we land on the wet, hard pavement.

Oxygen wrenches out of my lungs as pain spirals inside me, the dizziness from a moment ago returning with a vengeance. My ears ring from the sudden motion and impact.

The scent of amber and sandalwood hits my nostrils, and slowly, I open my eyes.

Maxwell is staring at me, his face leached of color, his hand cradling my head as his breaths fan over my face.

He looks terrified.

CHAPTER 43

BELLE LETS OUT A satisfied sigh as she snuggles next to me in the bedroom of the family jet. I don't think my pulse has settled until we're in the air, leaving New York behind.

She almost died in front of me yesterday.

If I hadn't arrived just then, hadn't seen her from afar and asked my driver to drop me off so I could surprise her by being there early, she would've gotten hit by the car.

And she would've been gone. Once again, I would've been helpless to stop it.

Chills run down my body as I hold her tighter in my arms, needing to feel her warmth, her chest rising and falling.

I've gotten too complacent, too addicted to her love. I'm tempting fate again, and this is a sign from the curse. The Grim Reaper is lurking nearby, waiting for the right opportunity to strike.

But I don't want to give up what we have, this connection I've never had with anyone before.

Fuck.

"Maxwell," she mumbles and buries her face in my chest. She inhales deeply and sighs, "Home."

The backs of my eyes burn as my pulse wreaks havoc in my ears, my heart feeling like it'll explode and give up on me.

I can't lose her. I can't lose this. There has to be some way around this curse. Once we get back to the city after our trip, I'll search the library to see if there's anything I've missed over the years. I'll reopen the autopsy files of the most recent deaths and see if there's anything that was missed before.

Anything to give us hope.

Closing my eyes, I listen to the soft sounds of her breathing, the whirring of the jet in the background as we head to Innsbruck, Austria for a quick weekend trip I'd planned as a surprise ever since Lana reminded me I should take my wife on a honeymoon.

Before the incident yesterday, I was excited about the trip, about seeing her eyes light up when she sees what I'd planned for her, but now I'm just relieved.

She's alive and in my arms and we're escaping the city that has cursed my family. *Who said the curse is just contained in New York City?*

I shove the annoying thought away. For now, I'll hold on to this trip as an escape from everything haunting us.

I'm calm. I'm at peace. Everything will be fine. I repeat the mantras as memories of my conversation last night with Elias rise to the forefront.

"Tinted windows. That sounds suspicious," Elias murmured. "I pulled the camera footage and there were no plates as well. I have my team tracing the car's movements via traffic cams to see if we get lucky and can identify the driver. You'll be the first to know if anything comes up."

I swallowed, my hand fisting my phone in a tight grip. Fucking helpless again. A sitting duck.

"Elias, could it be the curse?"

He knew about the curse. He told Ryland and me before, not that we were surprised. Elias Kent made it his business to know the secrets of important people. Rumor was, he amassed his power through bartering information and eliminating threats.

The silence was heavy on the line before Elias replied, "I've long given up on believing in a higher power or supernatural entities. Curses fall into that realm for me. But I have to say between the fall at the shelter, the frequent dizzy spells, all the other seemingly unrelated events you've told me about, and now, with the car, something is wrong."

He heaved out a sigh, and I could imagine his brows pinched, his face hidden in the shadows. "If I were you, if this woman was important to me, I'd stay away. Do anything to protect her. Then I'd raze this earth to get to the bottom of this and kill anyone who tried to hurt her." His voice deepens, and for a moment, I wonder if we're still talking about my situation.

He clears his throat and continues, "Something or someone obviously has ill will toward Belle, and it all began after she married you. So, curse or not, until the threat is eliminated, I'd recommend leaving her."

Leaving her.

His words echo in my ear as I reflect on his sage advice. It's rational. Logical. The right thing to do. But why does the idea of leaving her make me want to claw at my scars, opening the outside wounds so it bleeds the way I'm bleeding inside? And what if we couldn't find a way around the curse? This separation would be permanent then.

The answers don't come, and I fall into a fitful sleep until the flight attendant rouses us a few hours later for landing. Soon, we're whisked off to a luxury cabin in the Austrian Alps two hours from the city.

Belle grins as she hops off the car in front of the cabin, her nose tipped pink from the brisk winds. Luckily, she didn't hurt herself yesterday, and other than a bruise or two, she's the picture of good health. She looks like a snow bunny, jumping up and down with an abundance of energy, all warm in her thick, pink puffer jacket, the kind with the faux fur around the hood because I know she'd never wear real fur.

My chest warms from looking at her. *God, I don't deserve her.* Shaking my head in amusement, I chuckle before unlocking the door and stepping inside the quaint space, already heated by the owners when I called them on our way over.

"This place is gorgeous!" she exclaims and immediately goes to the roaring fireplace to warm her hands.

The cabin is full of history and character. There are tall, arched windows in the living room, which let in some natural light from the winter skies. A vintage armchair and a plush sofa center the room, which is also lit by a large wrought iron chandelier with candle-like lightbulbs. The wood crackles in the fireplace, the embers lending an orange glow to the dim space.

She spins toward me and asks, "You never told me why you whisked me halfway across the world."

Smiling, I walk toward her and tug her to me. "I owe you a honeymoon."

Her tawny eyes flutter and her lips part. The enticing blush is back on her face and I laugh softly, dipping my head to kiss those sweet lips, savoring the softness of her skin and the addictive taste of her.

Perhaps here, far away from the estate and the city, I can pretend the curse doesn't exist.

Just for a little bit.

Just so I can carry these memories when we return, when reality catches up to us.

But the curse, aren't you afraid? The insidious voice asks the question that has been echoing in my brain on repeat.

The answer is yes, I'm deathly afraid, but I'm a weak man.

I just desperately want these stolen moments, these breathtaking fragments that'll keep me company when I have to lock away my heart again, chaining myself in the prison I was born in.

Unless I can find a way out of this curse. *I have to find a way to break the curse.*

"So, what are our plans?" Belle pulls away and asks.

I brush my hand over her hair, dusting away the snowflakes that have gathered on her dark tresses.

"Anything we want, really. Here, we are Anna and Silas again, just you and me. No press, no work, no worries."

No death. Or at least, that's what I'm trying to tell myself.

"There's only one place I'll take you the day after tomorrow, but the rest of the time is free for us to do whatever we want."

She beams, her eyes crinkling at the corners. "You, mister. You surprise me."

My heart jolts as I remember what she told me at Nellie's. I want to be the Silas she saw that night, the one who surprised her and made her smile like she had everything she could possibly need in the world.

But I know I'm just delaying the inevitable, that every moment she's with me, she's in danger. Until I find out how to break the curse, I have to do the right thing to save her, even if it kills me to do it.

"Do you regret getting into my car then? Since I'm *Mr. Bad News*?" I smirk, throwing her words that night back at her.

Belle grins, and I fight the urge to kiss her again. If only I could bottle this moment to keep with me always.

She winks. "No, Maxwell. Never. There's nothing in this world that can ever make me regret knowing you and being with you."

My breathing quickens and my resolve fails as I crush my lips to hers again.

I hope that'll still hold true later when we get back to the city.

I'd recommend leaving her, Elias's voice whispers in my mind. If I need to leave her to protect her while I find the answers, I know it'll still break her heart. I'll be taking the choice away from her again and she'll hate me for it.

And I don't know what I'll do if she ever looks at me with hatred in her eyes.

CHAPTER 44

THE NEXT MORNING, I wake up to wetness in my underwear and cramping in my stomach, followed by crushing sadness in my heart because I know what this means.

My period is here.

We've been married for half a year now, and he has never worn a condom when we have sex, which has been regularly even during our hate sex phase and now, it's almost daily, and sometimes even multiple times a day.

But I still haven't gotten pregnant.

My strange dizzy spells and cold sweats have never resulted in a positive pregnancy test—the ones I take secretly because I wish a miracle would happen and two little lines would show up.

Rubbing my aching abdomen, a sob chokes in my throat, and I turn on the faucet in the bathroom, not wanting to wake Maxwell up, who's still asleep.

Images flutter through me—one or two little children, maybe more, dark-haired, gray eyes like his, or perhaps tawny eyes like mine. The girl would have my thick black hair and pale skin and the boy would have his tall build and dimples. These dreams have become more real and precious now that Maxwell and I are together, even if he won't say those three words to me.

But I know he loves me, deep inside.

He's just afraid.

I wipe the tears from my face, my heart pinching as I flush the bloody water down the toilet. I wish my body can grant me this wish, to have a child with this man I desperately love with all my heart.

He still doesn't know. I haven't told him about my condition because I'm afraid he'll think I'm broken, just like my parents do.

Deep down inside, there's a kernel of shame threatening to spark, disdain at myself for not being normal like other women my age, for not being able to easily do what we were put on earth to do.

Why me? Why?

It's irrational, and I know I'm much more than a fertile womb, but anger and sadness don't care about logic and reason. These emotions are my constant companion when I lay awake at night, my stomach burning and cramping, my body telling me yet again, not this month.

It doesn't matter. I look at my face in the mirror and wipe away my tears. *There are options. You aren't broken, Belle. You're worthy of your dreams, even if they may end up different from what you'd imagine. Someday, you'll look back and be proud of how far you've come.*

The words feel empty, tiny specks of dust trying to fill a cavernous hole, but I persist. Because I know everyone is dealt with different cards in life, and these happen to be mine.

Once I feel my emotions settle, I venture to the kitchen, eager to find something to distract myself. I think back to the slumbering man in the bedroom, how he gave me so many adventures, some I didn't even ask for but ended up needing, how he saved my life two days ago, and I make a decision.

I'm going to cook for him. The way to a man's heart is through his stomach, or so I'm told.

He should be honored because I rarely cook for anyone...including myself.

Rummaging through the fully stocked pantry and refrigerator, I pull out the things I think I need, my earlier sadness temporarily chased away by a frisson of panic as I realize I have no idea what I'm doing.

Fifteen minutes later, I'm chopping vegetables for my Asian-inspired spaghetti, since they don't have vermicelli noodles here.

Maxwell's soft chuckles fill the air as I feel his heated presence behind me.

"You're a bad influence," I say.

Not bothering to turn around, I bite back a smile as I huddle over the cutting board, trying my best to cut the bell peppers without taking off one of my fingers.

"Why?"

"I'm over here, frolicking with you instead of working on my deadline."

"Frolicking?" He snorts. "Not showing up to work is your idea of breaking the rules? God, you're so cute." He snakes his arms around my waist and presses his warm body against mine.

"I called in sick! But I'm *not* sick!" I whisper, which feels silly because there's only two of us here. "And I still have a deadline to make the pieces for the collection before the fashion show. Gordon may be gone, but I have a new boss and the other designers are watching. I really want to prove to them I'm there because of talent, not because of my last name."

Twisting around, I look up, finding his gray eyes crinkling at the corners, a thick lock of dark hair falling over his forehead. "I can't just drop everything and play house with you, Mr. Bad News."

Maxwell chuckles, the light in his eyes reminding me so much of the day I met him. "It's only for a weekend...for our honeymoon."

"This better *not* be the *official* honeymoon, mister. I want at least two weeks off, preferably three, with advanced notice next time. I may be nice and easygoing, but not *that* nice."

"Fine, Your Majesty," he says. At my cocked brow, he adds, "You married the frigid king. You think you aren't going to have a fancy title?"

I snort.

"Where would you want to go?" he whispers.

There's really only one answer. It's a place I've always wanted to go with the person I love. So much I've resisted going by myself because I want to save that experience for when I meet *the one*.

"Venice."

His breath catches. A flash of something crosses his face.

"What? You don't like Venice?"

"No, it's not that." He swallows, a muscle pulsing in his jaw. "It's just...I had a dream..." He shakes himself and strains a smile. "Ignore me. I'm not fully awake yet."

Hm. That was odd. But we all have our moments.

"I think it's so romantic to go to there with your partner and listen to beautiful songs while sitting on a gondola." I grab his arm. "Maybe we can even listen to 'Nessun Dorma'...live." I waggle my brows and he chuckles.

"Anything you want, Belle. Anything you want."

He peers over my shoulder at the cutting board, and his lips twitch. I see him fighting against an impulse to say something.

I narrow my eyes. "What?" I ask flatly.

"Nothing."

"Your face isn't nothing. You forget, I can read you like an art critic can appreciate a Monet. Spill."

He wets his lips, his shoulders shaking...from laughter?

"Hey! Why are you laughing at me?"

Loud laughter escapes his lips as he bowls over and presses his head against my waist. The beautiful sound of his happiness would've sent my heart soaring if it weren't for the fact that his happiness is at my expense.

"Oh fuck...so there *is* something my little muse is absolute shit at." He stops shaking and straightens, his hand caressing my cheek, his eyes shining with tears.

The damn idiot is crying because he's laughing so hard.

"Belle, what on earth are you trying to make, you serial killer of vegetables?" His smile freezes briefly as if something nagged at him, but that swiftly disappears and he smirks at me.

My mouth drops open. *Serial killer, my ass.* I turn around and stare at the mess I made. Sliced onions and carrots, mashed garlic, and chopped bell peppers.

I mean, it kind of looks like a Picasso, but it's edible. The vegetables have been sacrificed at the altar for greater good.

"If Picasso decided to make his paintings into real life, it'd be your knife skills. Half your vegetables are on the floor, and the other half that made it under your knife has sizes ranging from microscopic to gigantic. And are those seeds in your bell peppers? You didn't take out the seeds? Please tell me you washed them beforehand."

"Argh!" I scowl and cross my arms over my chest. "You do it then. I was trying to make Singapore style vermicelli because it's a comfort food I enjoy. It's the only thing Mom cooks well and her favorite dish to eat growing up in Hong Kong."

I sigh, thinking back to the rare occasions when I was younger when Mom would fix us some vermicelli noodles as a random special treat. Those were happy times. "Anyway, they didn't have vermicelli noodles here, so I had to use spaghetti. And apparently, His Majesty isn't happy with my efforts."

Maxwell bites his lip, looking infuriating sexy as he nudges me aside. "Thank God we aren't doing this at home. Mora would have a heart attack. Step aside and let me save your ass."

I cock a brow and make room for him.

"Go, Belle...stop staring at me while I work." He shoos me away and gets to work.

Rolling my eyes, I saunter to the living room and walk to the tall, arched windows. I look at the dense forest of towering pine trees, blanketed with snow. A mist is rolling in, the distant peaks of the Tyrolean Alps shrouded in a ghostly fog.

It's beautiful and haunting, isolating yet comforting. It reminds me of the man in the kitchen who prefers the shadows and is cold under the spotlight, but has the sweetest, warmest personality he only shows to a select few who are lucky enough to see it.

Turning around, I spot a small rosewood table where a gold phonograph sits, and I smile, remembering how Maxwell likes to play his music on a similar one at home.

I turn on the phonograph and watch the needle glide over the record, and the familiar strains of Puccini's "O Mio Babbino Caro" sounds from the bell-shaped horn.

The wistful violins lead way to the beautiful voice of the soprano pleading with her character's father to let her be with the boy she loves. Humming under my breath, I walk back to the kitchen to check on Maxwell.

He has a towel thrown over his shoulder and is *twirling* a knife before he starts chopping. He sways to the music as he moves around the kitchen.

My mouth drops open when I see him slicing and dicing the ingredients like he's one with the knife. He takes out a pan from a cabinet, fires it up, prepares the eggs, and sets it aside. Then he preps the onions and garlic, then the rest of the vegetables, and finally the chicken and sliced pork.

He moves in practiced motions, tossing the ingredients in the air, his brows furrowed in concentration as I see the flames engulf the pan briefly, just like the cooking shows on TV, and he finally adds in the spaghetti and sauce.

My man can cook. I'm thrown back to that night in the kitchen when he made me the pastrami and rye. My pulse ratchets up and I clench my core—seeing him move about in the kitchen like he owns the space makes me want to jump his bones.

He puts a lid on the pan, steps back, and tosses the towel onto the counter.

Smiling, I launch myself at his back, and he staggers a few steps. His hands grab my ass as I curl my legs around his waist.

He spins me around and sets me on my tiptoes, my feet on top of his, before he wraps one arm firmly around my waist, the other clutching my hand. He chuckles as we sway to the strains of the music, his sandalwood and amber scent wrapping me in a bubble of happiness.

I place my head on his chest, listening to the reassuring rhythm of his heartbeat before looking at him.

"All we're missing are two kids and Silas running around," I murmur, referring to what he told me at the pier the first night we met when he described his dream of having a loving wife, happy kids, and maybe a pet or two.

My heart clenches at his vision, the same one I had this morning, and I bury my face in his chest so he doesn't see my sadness.

His breath catches. "You remember."

"I remember you thought it wasn't possible, and I remember feeling sad because I didn't know why you felt that way. I asked myself why didn't this beautiful man have any hope for his future? For something so simple?"

"And now you know," he murmurs.

"And now I do."

The lush aria fades in to silence but we keep dancing. He releases a deep exhale and says, "You'll make a wonderful mom, Belle."

His words prick a raw nerve, and unable to hold it back, a sob escapes my mouth.

Maxwell stops swaying and tilts my face up toward him. He frowns and wipes his thumb under my teary eyes. "Belle? What's wrong?"

I rake in a ragged inhale before releasing it. I need to tell him the truth. Even though he's fine with us using fertility treatments after a year, we are partners in this marriage and he shouldn't be left in the dark.

Year of yeses and doing things that are uncomfortable. I'll be brave.

"There's something I never told you before," I whisper and hold his gaze, fighting the urge to look away.

He stills as a pulse flickers on his forehead.

Taking his silence as a sign to continue, I push out the next words, "I have a condition called diminished ovarian reserve. It means I have fewer follicles than other women my age and I'll enter menopause early. It also means the chances of me getting pregnant naturally are lower. Much lower."

The house is silent except for the sizzling of the noodles in the pan, and he reaches back to turn off the stove, not taking his eyes off me.

His face is inscrutable, the same mysterious intensity boring into me, and I want to cry, to ask him what he's thinking, to ask him...

If he regrets choosing me as his wife, since his goal for this marriage is to have heirs.

My face crumbles and I blurt, "I know I shouldn't have withheld this information. Before we agreed to the arrangement, my parents didn't want me to tell you because they were worried you wouldn't want me then. And with our financial situation, I didn't have money for fertility treatments and I needed our arranged marriage to save Grandpa's company."

He stands before me, his hands twitching at his sides, and remains silent. I feel like I'm standing in front of my executioner as panic and fear swirl inside me.

"And when we got married, we always fought and frankly, there were days when I was wondering what on earth we were doing and it didn't feel like the right time to tell you. But now, I don't want to hide anymore. It's not right. I'm sorry for not telling you, Maxwell."

Wiping my tears away, I sniffle. "If you want to divorce because of this, I'd understand." My heart twists in a vise and I dip my head down.

Maxwell doesn't speak as he stalks forward, and soon, I see his feet in my vision. His hands cup my face and tilt my head up.

"Maxwell," I whisper, not looking at him. Fear tears through me because I'm afraid of what I'll see in his eyes. Pity? Anger? Resentment?

"Look at me." His voice is rough and commanding, leaving no room for disobeying.

Swallowing the lump in my throat, I slowly meet his eyes.

A wet sheen glimmers in his eyes as his nostrils flare. His chest moves up and down rapidly from his heavy breathing.

He crushes me to him, wrapping me tightly in his arms like he wants to meld our bodies together. I feel his heart pulsing, beating rapidly against mine, and the rumble in his voice when he starts speaking.

"My beautiful Belle. You're my muse, the person who brought back light into my empty mansion, who brought back joy into my life."

Slowly, he pulls up his sweater, baring his deep scars in the bright daylight.

"You told me my scars were beautiful...art on canvas. And I'm telling you, Belle, you're beautiful. Glorious. Shining from within. The fact that you're facing challenges in life with a smile on your face makes you all the more breathtaking to me."

His voice grows stronger, more ardent. "You *will* be a mom, Belle. Even if it's not from natural conception. We can use treatments, see doctors, or adopt."

I clasp my trembling hand over my lips, unable to stop the choking sounds from escaping.

He looks similarly emotional as a flush creeps up his neck. He pries my hand off my lips and presses a kiss at the center of my palm. "We can grow old together, just you and me, if that's what you want. We can adopt a few more dogs and cats, even though they'll destroy the mansion and drive Morris crazy. We can spend the rest of our years painting and sketching side by side, listening to music, and I can be the old man who scares his wife by taking her on joyrides."

"But the heir? Isn't that what you need for the curse?" When he first told me his reasons for needing an heir, I didn't believe him, but now, with everything going on, I'm starting to doubt my convictions.

If we have a child together, will I be dooming him? *I can't think this way. There has to be a way out of this mess, if there even is a curse to begin with.* And I can't imagine having a child with anyone other than him.

"We'll figure something out, I don't know what." He pulls me tightly against him, a frenetic energy threading his voice. "Everything I've learned about the curse is passed down through the generations. No one ever said the heir needs to be biologically related to me, or maybe we can use a surrogate. We'll figure something out."

He smooths his hand down my trembling back. "I'm here, little muse. I'll always be here for you. You're not broken. You're perfect in my eyes."

His words and his touch are bandages on my bleeding wounds, sutures to my broken heart.

"I love you," I whisper.

He doesn't respond but holds me tightly in his arms. I try not to let his silence cut into my bleeding heart, but I realize even if I'll never hear him say those words to me, it doesn't matter anymore.

Because I'm hopelessly, irrevocably, in love with him.

CHAPTER 45

Belle

"Where are you taking me?" I ask, my eyes blindfolded, as the car coasts to a stop.

"We're here. You'll see."

"It's not skiing, right? Because I haven't recovered from yesterday."

He laughs. The rich sound is something I'll never get sick of. "No, it's *definitely* not skiing."

Yesterday, after the delicious Singapore style inspired spaghetti Maxwell made me—which he credited Mora with for having the patience to teach him how to cook—he whisked me off to a ski resort nestled in the Alps.

It was my first time, because I'd somehow lived almost twenty-five years without having skied before.

My legs felt like jelly, my butt probably bruised, but it was fun watching such a tall, imposing man on the bunny slopes with me, holding my hand and not letting go as I screeched and fell a thousand times.

A few little kids giggled when they saw him flat on his back, absorbing my fall, and he laughed and pelted them with snowballs.

He would make such a wonderful dad.

Tears threaten again, and I shift my thoughts away. A dark voice inside me can't help but wonder if I'm holding him back. *Ugh! Stop it, Belle. You're a great person and he's lucky to have you.*

But still...

He'd be a wonderful dad.

I touch my empty womb and sigh. It's a bottomless hole nothing can fill and something completely out of my control.

A brisk gale blows into the car as the door opens, and I hear Maxwell murmuring a few words in German to whoever is standing outside.

My thighs clench—listening to him speak foreign languages is like an aphrodisiac to me. Too bad I'm on my period still.

"Careful, little muse, watch your head." He gently leads me out of the car and I step on to a soft surface.

He takes off my blindfold and I open my eyes and see…

Large empty fields blanketed by snow, the skeletal remains of plants poking out randomly from the slush.

I narrow my eyes and turn to my husband. "This is where you're going to tell me you're secretly a vampire or a serial killer and you've taken me here to dispose of me, right?"

Maxwell barks out a laugh, his eyes shining. "The things that come out of your mouth. God, I love it."

He wraps his arm around me and leads me toward a building to the side. "And no, I'm not—I can't believe I have to say this—a vampire or a serial killer. I'm here because I thought you might like to see how hemp and linen fabrics are made."

My eyes widen. *So, I can call this a work trip!*

He murmurs, "See? Mr. Bad Influence is helping you out even though you didn't ask for it."

I stand on my tiptoes and kiss his jaw, thinking how he has been helping me all along, with his scribbles on my drawings, his large donation to BSUA. The man has been watching over me, my silent, brooding sentinel, knowing what I need without me ever needing to tell him. So what if he doesn't tell me he loves me? Actions speak much louder than words.

Swallowing the lump suddenly forming in my throat, I whisper, "Thank you, Maxwell."

He smiles softly, his fingers tenderly grazing my cheek.

"Austria is famous for their textiles. In the peak season, these fields would be filled with hemp and flax, and they would harvest them to produce fabrics. These two farms here are famous for their high-quality, environmentally friendly, organic textiles, which I know you care about."

I beam, butterflies swooping in my stomach. This man has thought of everything.

We spend the next few hours with the managers of the farms, who walk us through the production process and show us swatches of fabrics. I pelt them with questions, asking if I could have specially made textiles that blend lighter fabrics with heavier fibers such as cotton, or if they can make double weave or thicker fabrics. I end up placing an order for a few bolts of custom fabric to be expedited to McKenzie's.

There are so many options for my collection now.

By the time we leave the farms, it's already five in the evening, dusk having settled in, the skies darkening to deep blue. He takes me back to the cabin, where a chef and his team of two assistants are bustling around the small kitchen, talking in rapid fire German.

"What's going on?" I ask Maxwell as I shrug out of my winter coat.

"It's our last night here," he rasps. "I want to make it special for you." His voice is deeper and threaded with melancholy.

My chest pinches and unease simmers in my gut.

It's like he's saying everything will change when we get back home.

"It already is special, Maxwell."

He gives me a sad smile, his hand cupping my face before he leads me into the bathroom, turns on the shower, and slowly takes off my clothes.

The steam fogs up the room quickly, and he opens the shower door and ushers me inside. The hot water feels so good against my sore muscles, I can't help but moan.

A few seconds later, Maxwell steps in and surrounds me with his masculine heat. My mouth waters as I stare at his hard muscles rippling with his movements, the water running down those indents like a scene from the movies. My gaze trails lower to the dark trimmed curls flanking his hard cock.

Biting my lip, I drag my gaze up and trace his scars with my fingers. I love every single one of them, just like how much I love this man in front of me. He hisses in pleasure before thrusting his cock toward me.

My pussy clenches and I wrap my hand around his hard shaft, relishing the guttural groan ripping from his mouth. My thumb swirls over the slit at the tip, finding it already wet with his pre-cum.

Looking up, I find his eyes intense and dark, his nostrils flaring.

"Maxwell, I'm on my period. It's not a lot of blood when we're in the shower, but…"

"I don't care." The words are rough, almost a growl. "Do you?"

My clit pulses at the possessive glint in his eyes, and I shake my head.

Without saying another word, he hauls me to him and wraps my legs around his waist as he steps under the shower. The hot water washes over us as his lips tangle with mine, his kiss tender, then rough, then smoldering, as if he can't get enough.

Our tongues duel with each other as our moans reverberate in the small space. He slams me against the marble tiles, his hand trailing down my body and cupping between my legs. He trails kisses down my neck and over my collarbone before he captures my nipple and I moan.

My eyes flutter open at the pleasure that coils sharply inside me as his fingers swirl around my clit, flicking it, pinching it, and he's doing the same with his mouth on my hard nipple, moving from one breast to the other, until the sensations become too unbearable and I shake against him.

He reaches for my neck and plays with my pulse, the slight pressure making me delirious with want as I throw my head back.

"You're my *everything*," he rasps before biting my pulse point.

I scream as he punctuates the sentence with a thrust of his hips and enters me in one stroke.

The pleasure builds at a rapid speed, the sounds of him slamming against me mixing with my moans and his grunts.

"Oh God, I'm going to come, Maxwell. I'm going to come so hard," I mewl, my legs tightening, clenching around his backside.

"Come for me, little muse," he pants in my ear. His hips snap in a punishing rhythm, his labored breaths loud. "I'm so addicted to you. You're my other half, the one I never knew I was searching for."

His words burn through me, adding to the fire racing down my spine and gathered deep in my abdomen. I'm standing on the precipice, the pleasure so intense I feel like I'll die if I don't get relief.

He presses his lips against my ear, his voice dipping down to a low whisper, as if he's afraid someone else might hear, even though it's only the two of us.

"I-I love you, Belle, so damn much."

My eyes snap open as I hear the words I've been craving.

He loves me. He loves me. He loves me.

Tears run down my cheeks, washed away by the water as my heart swells and multiplies in size, the joy and relief pushing me toward euphoria.

He loves me.

"I never knew love until I met you," he whispers urgently, like we're running out of time. He thrusts harder against me, but at this second, it feels like we are moving as one.

Those words. I feel like I've waited my entire life to hear them. We're two halves finally reunited.

He crushes his lips to mine again, his finger traveling between us to flick my clit and I explode into a thousand pieces.

"Maxwell," I cry, the blinding pleasure bathing my body as I melt in his arms, every inch of me belonging to this man who has stolen my heart, my soul...my everything.

He roars his release, his dick throbbing inside me as I feel the heat of his cum coating my insides, prolonging my high.

We move our bodies in unison, our lips tangling, our hands touching, molding, grabbing each other like we don't want this connection to end.

As we slowly come down from our high, he tips my head back, his stormy eyes staring intently at mine.

"I love you, Belle. Always, now, and forever," he whispers. "Please remember that. Everything I do is for you, and I'll do everything I can to protect you."

My heart swoops and falls, and a shiver travels up my spine. The words are an ancient melody I've heard of but can't place, haunting and achingly beautiful and true.

"Please remember that," he repeats, his voice hitching.

He holds me tightly to him, our hearts thudding in unison, and suddenly I'm gripped with fear.

Why does this feel like a goodbye?

CHAPTER 46

I'm trying to delay the inevitable.

Staring at the somber February skies outside the car window, the clouds hanging heavy, no sign of the sun to be seen, I think back to my confession to Belle two days ago in Austria.

When I told her I love her.

It was the most selfish thing I've ever done, but I couldn't stop myself even if I wanted to.

Seeing her being vulnerable with me, sharing her fertility diagnosis, which was a wound that clearly pained her, realizing how she dealt with all of her troubles in stride, in positivity—it was too much for me.

She asked me if I'd leave her because of her so-called flaws. How could I? They weren't flaws at all. They were the battle scars of a warrior. They only made her more beautiful in my eyes. And so, I let the vibrant colors inside me override the darkness in my soul. I couldn't keep the sentiment inside me anymore, one that had been beating against my rib cage, dying to be let out.

I deluded myself—we were far away from the mansion, from the city, from the curse. In a small cabin near Innsbruck, Austria, it was just Silas and Anna again, two people desperately in love with each other. I tried blocking off the guilt for breaking or ignoring almost every stipulation regarding the curse that my father and grandfather put together—falling in love with your wife, confessing your love to each other, the random accidents happening to Belle, the branch shattering the windows.

I told myself I'd do whatever it took to break the curse before she got hurt again.

I'd do anything so that we could be together.

Nothing could separate us.

When I returned, I ransacked the library after Belle was fast asleep. I searched for Grandfather Silas's missing journal or some letter or book that may give me more information about the curse. I came up empty. Then last night, I moved on to the study, where I kept all the family records.

The lone lamp on my desk flickered on and off as I poured through genealogy records, trying to identify anything I'd missed before. But there was nothing other than rows and rows of names, dates of births, deaths, and marriages. All the women who didn't die of old age had a cause of death listed next to their names—all seeming to be unfortunate events with no discernable pattern other than these women were in love with their husbands when they died, as cross-referenced with the related entries in the old journals.

"Fuck!" I brushed the records off the desk and buried my face in my hands. I felt so damn helpless, just like the little boy in front of the altar at his mother's funeral.

I can't give up. I have to save Belle. I have to find a way for us to be together.

A thought came to mind, and I picked up the phone and called my father, not caring it was close to midnight and he was probably asleep.

"Son, it's late. What's going on?" Dad sounded worried.

I took a deep breath and replied, "I need to break the damn curse, Dad. I want to see if there was anything that stood out to you when you looked into the curse before."

The silence seemed deafening.

"You fell in love with Belle, didn't you?"

A lump formed in my throat. "Yes," I whispered, afraid the curse would hear me somehow. "She loves me back too. S-She's the one for me, the person I can't live without. I can't just sit here and do nothing. I can't let what happened to Sydney happen to her."

"I was afraid of that after the gala. Even the blind could see the love between the two of you."

"I need to save her, Dad. I-I…" I blew out a breath and closed my eyes, exhaustion weighing heavily on my eyelids. *There has to be something we missed.*

"I assume you're going through the journals then?"

"Yes, the ones from the library. I just reviewed all the old letters and the genealogy records again. There's nothing! And I still can't find Great-Great-Great-Grandfather Silas's missing journal from the 1860s."

Dad sighed. "I did the same when I was falling in love with your mom. I tried to find the missing journal too. It never turned up. Did you review the autopsy records yet? I looked over the one for your grandmother and the ones before then were so brief they were practically useless, but I never examined the records of your mom and Sydney. I was too devastated to care by then."

I froze and pulled out the last folder in the pile I took out earlier. *Autopsy records.*

Flipping through them, I scanned the oldest records first, noting they were of no use. Then I got to the ones of Grandma, Mom, and Sydney, which were filled with medical jargon I couldn't understand. But there was a note at the bottom of each one.

Detailed records on file at the coroner's office.

"D-Dad, I need to go. Thanks for picking up."

"Son, I hope you break the curse. There's nothing I want more in the world than to see you happy and in love, and if your mom were here, s-she'd say the same." His voice thickened, and he cleared his throat. "Regardless, I'm p-proud of you for trying. For facing your fears head on. You're a braver man than me."

I let out a ragged exhale, my eyes burning. "I had a good role model with you, Dad."

We hung up, and I swiped opened my text messages to type a message to Elias.

Maxwell

Do you know a good medical examiner?

He responded almost right away.

Elias

For?

Maxwell

Accessing and reviewing old autopsy files. I want a fresh set of eyes. Someone who can work off the books. I don't want this to leak to the press.

Elias

I may know someone. Will contact you soon.

A car honks in the distance jolting me back into the present, and I lean back against the headrest, a headache quickly forming, most likely from the lack of sleep last night.

I loosen my tie, unable to breathe as my driver takes me to Fleur for a meeting to debrief on the financial performance for January. The stock price is still a third lower than what it used to be before my disastrous first press conference, even though the recent headlines are more positive.

Attempting to distract myself, I take out my phone and scroll to Lana's messages.

Lana

Look at these articles. I'm a genius and you're welcome. Don't tell Rex I said that.

Lana

CBC article link: "Drama at Fleur is No Longer?"

Lana

IBC article link: "The Frigid King Can't Make a Speech but He Can Make You Rich."

Lana

GossipTimes link: "How to Find a Man Who'll Protect You Like Maxwell Anderson."

Rex

I'm trying to figure out if this is a passive-aggressive attempt at gloating, Lana, or if you accidentally sent the messages to the group chat *again*.

He's referring to an incident last year when Lana sent some advice to Ryland regarding Millie but accidentally sent it to everyone under the sun.

Rex

I taught you everything you need to know, Lana. I take credit.

Lana

God spare me from the fragile ego of a rich white man.

My lips twitch at the bickering between the two when the phone rings.

Elias Kent

My pulse quickens. *Does he have news for me?*

I quickly answer. "Elias?"

"Do you know a Cole Whelan?" His tone is brusque. No nonsense.

"Yes," I grit out, thinking about the blond bastard I want to punch in the face for having the hots for my wife. Belle mentioned how he asked about Sydney the other day—the bastard had looked into me.

"You've never met him before Belle?"

"No." I sit up straighter. "Why are you asking this?" Something feels off...very off.

Elias pauses, as if he's mulling over something.

"He's your late wife's cousin."

"What?" My heart pounds in my chest. Given Sydney and I had secretly eloped, I'd never met her extended family, but this news still comes as a shock.

I think back to the hatred in his eyes at my wedding reception and in the hospital, the hostility in his voice, and how he has always been too close to Belle for my comfort.

He murmurs, "He's never told you he's Sydney's cousin. Interesting."

A sense of foreboding washes over me. I can't help but think I'm a participant in a game I didn't sign up for.

"He's never told Belle either. She was shocked when he mentioned Sydney." I rub my temples. "What does this all mean?"

"Don't you find it curious he was the person to find her when she fell down the stairs? And didn't the girls report seeing him before Belle nearly got run over?"

My veins turn to ice and a muscle twitches in my jaw. "You're saying you think he's the one behind everything? That he tried to kill my wife?"

I'm going to find the bastard. I don't care what his reasons are or if this is somehow all influenced by the damn curse, but I'm going to slice him with my palette knife and watch him bleed to death for hurting her.

My Belle.

Elias seemingly reads my mind. "Don't do anything stupid, Maxwell. I don't have all the answers yet. I have no qualms about ending a life, but only after I'm sure of the facts. But I thought I should warn you. Give some thought to what I said before you went on your trip. She's in danger and, curse or not, I'm pretty damn sure it has something to do with you."

He pauses and I hear a faint clicking sound on his end. He must be playing with the lighter again. "Also, I took the liberty to task someone with reviewing the autopsy records of Sydney, your mom, and your grandmother."

What the fuck? Is he a mind reader? How does he know those are the records I'm interested in?

At my silence, he continues, "My contact at the coroner's office tells me the records of your great-grandmother and before will probably be useless. There isn't as much documentation back then. This is what you wanted to do when you texted me last night, right? It's what I'd do."

"Elias, I swear I don't want to know what happens to people who get on your bad side," I murmur. The man can predict behaviors like no other. No one would ever escape him.

He lets out a raspy laugh. "They won't survive to tell the tale. Anyway, I'll have my contact call you when he finishes his review. Will be in touch if I learn more about Cole."

He disconnects the call before I can ask him more questions. I grip my phone, my fingers trembling from the bombshell that was just dropped on my lap. Cole's relationship with Sydney. Elias's contact re-reviewing the autopsies. My mind is a swirl of chaos.

Belle's face surfaces in my mind—her beautiful eyes, her beaming smile, the tinkling laughter in her voice. She's full of life and brightness and I've kept her selfishly by my side, basking in her warmth for as long as I could. But now, there's a sense of doom I can't ignore any longer.

Why did Cole hide his relationship with Sydney from Belle? What if nothing comes out of the medical examiner's review? Will she get hurt before I get more answers, *if* I even get *any* answers?

Am I running out of time?

My lungs heave in deep breaths, and I tug off my tie and fling it into the corner. I can't breathe. The dark shadows in my car seem to loom before me, clawing, slithering.

I can't breathe.

I open the windows and listen to the biting wind howling through the canyons of the tall buildings, the scent of wet asphalt and burned tires sifting into the car.

Leave her now, the wind moans. *Leave her now or she dies.*

I try to ignore the sinking feeling in my stomach.

My texts to Maxwell have been unanswered for the last few hours.

Belle

I'm thinking of getting some real Singapore style vermicelli tonight, you in? How's your day?

Belle

Love you.

He's a busy man running a billion-dollar company. Don't be one of those clingy wives, Belle.

I clutch the locket around my neck for reassurance. He put the necklace on me after we took the sexy shower in Austria together—who knew what orgasms could do for menstrual cramps?

Sighing, I turn my attention to more important matters, like the meeting I'm about to have with McKenzie's new fashion director, Fiona Kim, to see what she thinks of the designs I sent her before leaving Austria.

I bank a left at the hallway and nod to a few junior designers before pausing at Fiona's door.

Knock. Knock.

"Come in."

I step into the stylish office decorated in lavender, fresh flowers, and feminine touches—she obviously redecorated after Gordon left—and Fiona stands from behind her desk and beckons me to the couch.

"Hi Fiona, you want to talk about my designs?" I wipe my sweaty hands on my pants.

She smiles and adjusts her black cat-eyed frames on her face. "You're not what I expected."

"Is that a good thing? I think? I hope so. Being what someone expects is boring, don't you think—"

She laughs. "No need to be nervous. I know we didn't work together before because I was in high couture and you were in casual wear, but I promise I won't bite."

I sit still and pinch my wrist to keep from rambling.

"I was expecting a talentless designer who climbed the ranks because of her family." She looks at me and grimaces. "No offense."

I shake my head, thinking here we go again, my fingers twitching on my lap.

"But I'm glad to be wrong."

Fiona takes out a few sketches—final designs of my hemp and bamboo shawl sweater lined with fleece, a matching asymmetrical skirt, a draped coat using the same technique—all without official sleeves but can be rendered to have "sleeves."

"Now, I'm not sorry Gordon was fired. The guy was always an asshole." She smiles and I relax marginally. "But I have to say, I like to throw out impossible requirements for my designers as well. It's a good way of getting them to think outside the box."

She leans forward. "If people want average designs they can get anywhere else, why would they come to us? What would make McKenzie Atelier stand out from the other brands?"

I nod. I had the same thought after my breakthrough at the mansion.

Fiona holds up the sketches. "I like these three designs a lot. I've never seen anything like them before. Can you tell me how you got the inspiration?"

Excitement chases out my earlier dread and I sit up taller. "Actually, these designs were inspired by books I have at home."

The next few hours fly by as Fiona asks me questions about the composition and color choices. She tells me she wants these three items at the fashion show next month because they are unique and versatile and the environmentally friendly materials are a fit for what consumers are looking for right now.

I can hardly contain my joy as I step out of the building later that night after spending the rest of the day revising the drawings to her specifications and reserving time with the design construction team to help with the sewing once the custom fabrics arrive.

The brisk winds lash at my face. The dreary daylight has faded into gloomy dusk. The streets are unusually quiet for eight p.m.

I take out my phone to check my messages, my chest falling when I don't see any text messages from Maxwell.

It's nothing, Belle. He's probably stuck in meetings all day. You know how he hates these group gatherings—it's draining for him.

I begin to type another message when I sense the piercing stare of another person close by. The hairs rise on the back of my neck.

"Belle."

I startle, seeing Cole standing a few feet away, his blond hair mussed up, his hands jammed in his coat pockets.

"Cole? What are you doing here?" My pulse quickens as he walks toward me.

He runs a hand over his messy hair. "I want to apologize for what happened when we ran into each other in SoHo. I think I made you uncomfortable and I'm sorry. You see, there are some things you don't know about me."

My hackles rise as chills run through my body. *Why didn't he just call me? Has he been waiting outside this whole time?*

My vision blurs, the dizziness that has been plaguing me before making a reappearance. The doctors said I was anemic at my last checkup, but that makes no sense. I've never been anemic in my entire life.

I back up slowly, my body trying to tell me something my mind hasn't caught up with yet. I heave out quick breaths, but I can't seem to get any oxygen inside me.

I feel nauseous. Literally sick to my stomach. This feels different than before. The dizzy spell isn't letting up. It's getting worse.

"Belle?"

His tall shadow looms closer and I suddenly find myself backed up against the cold building, my vision spinning, darkening at the edges.

"Belle? Are you okay? Belle?"

He steps even closer. I raise my hand and open my mouth to tell him to back off, but nothing comes out.

Everything feels so heavy, the world blurring around me.

"Belle?"

The wet floor rises to meet me and darkness claims me in its grasp.

CHAPTER 47

I DASH DOWN THE halls of the hospital like a madman, Charles and Steven quickly following behind me. We were wrapping up a meeting at my office when the hospital called, saying they found Belle passed out in front of the ER and they got my number from her cell phone.

"Annabelle Anderson, where is she?" I bark at a nurse behind the desk, and she doesn't even flinch, but instead cocks her eyebrow at me.

"Sir, this is a hospital. Please lower your voice. And you are?"

Blood boils in my veins and I see red. I'm about to hop over the desk to type on the computer myself before Charles grabs me by the shoulder.

"He's Maxwell Anderson, her husband. The ER staff found her unconscious an hour ago," Charles supplies as I grip my hair in frustration.

I never want to be recognized on sight until this very moment. Now I want every perk of being an Anderson, all the privilege I grew up having.

I want them all now. I'd give up my anonymity, have the paparazzi breathe down my neck every day for the rest of my life for Belle.

The nurse's eyes widen in recognition as she quickly types on her computer. "She's in room 320 in the Intensive Care Unit on the 3rd floor."

ICU?

Terror curdles my insides and I break into a sprint, pushing people out of the way, not caring if they're going to sue me later and dash toward the stairwell because the elevators are too slow.

I fly up the steps as someone opens the door to the third floor and barrel past the man, dashing toward the room, barely hearing Charles and Steven murmuring apologies behind me.

Throwing open the door of room 320, I see her on the bed, the sight eerily similar to a month ago.

But this time, she isn't moving. She's wearing an oxygen mask, her eyes closed, face pale. Fuck, she's hooked up to so many goddamn monitors.

My legs tremble as I make my way to her. My hands are icy.

Mom's pale face in the coffin.

Sydney's stiff body at the beach.

Oh God, please. Not again. Bile makes its way up my throat.

"Belle," I rasp, taking her hand in mine. "Little muse, wake up. *Please.*"

She doesn't respond.

I collapse on the chair next to her and bury my face in her palm. She's still warm. She's still alive.

The thoughts don't make me feel any better. The Grim Reaper is still hovering over us in a dark, menacing shadow, and once again, I'm helpless and wracked with guilt.

I did this. I told her I love her. I let her tell me she loves me.

I did this. I'm killing her. The curse. Oh God, the curse.

How could I've been so stupid, so selfish? I shouldn't have told her I love her *until* I broke the curse, if the curse can even be broken. I should've left her when Elias suggested.

Wetness drips on to her hand, and I realize they are my tears.

"Belle, please. Please wake up. I-I'm so sorry," I choke out. My chest feels like it's being ripped to shreds. *Take me instead. Please take me. I'll do anything.*

A hand clamps on my shoulder and I whip my head toward the intruder, the person who dares to distract me from my wife.

"What?" I snarl, my vision blurry.

"The doctor is on the way." I make out gleaming blond hair and light blue eyes. Charles.

A darker shadow steps up beside him. Steven murmurs, "She'll be okay, Maxwell. You need to hold yourself together. Stay strong for her. She needs you."

A knock sounds at the door, and a tall man walks in, his dark eyes assessing before they land on me.

"Mr. Anderson, I'm Dr. Cavanagh, the intensivist on call today."

"How is she? What happened?" I grip Belle's hand tightly.

"My colleagues down at the ER found her unconscious outside the entrance. It appears someone dropped her off and sped away."

"I want all the footage."

His gaze roves over my face, but he clearly understands who he's dealing with, and nods. "I'll have our administration and security team contact you."

"Is she going to be okay?"

"We're running tests, but from the CBC panel, it appears her hemoglobin and red blood cell counts are low, which leads us to think anemia. But then her white blood cell counts are high, so that tells me something else is going on. She's unresponsive, so we're expanding our tests to include common toxins and other conditions, but the labs will take a few hours to a day to complete."

"Whatever you need, I'll get for you. Specialists around the country, donating a fucking wing to this place, just tell me. Save my wife, please."

My hands shake, the panic digging deeper in my chest as I stare at the man before me. I'll do anything I can to save Belle.

Dr. Cavanaugh nods. "Until we know more information, she'll remain here. She's stable right now. You're free to stay with her until she wakes up. But no more disturbances on the floor or you're out, Anderson family or not."

A muscle pulses in my jaw and I nod.

His eyes soften. "We'll take care of her. She's in good hands."

After the doctor leaves the room, I close my eyes as Charles and Steven settle into the guest chairs.

"Maybe it's not as bad as you think," Steven says. "We have to stay positive."

"I've texted the group. They're on their way," Charles comments.

Their words are meaningless to me.

My world is a wash of hopeless grayscale and I feel myself sinking back into the abyss Belle pulled me out of when she got into my car that fateful night.

Meaningless. My life is meaningless without her.

This has got to be the worst hangover I'd ever experienced.

A headache pounds in my skull, my stomach lurching like I'm seasick. Everything is so blurry and bright.

What is that annoying beeping sound?

I blink several times, the smell of antiseptic agents reaching my nostrils, and I groan.

"I don't feel so good," I mumble as I try to move, but my body feels too heavy, like I ran two back-to-back marathons.

"Belle!" Maxwell's panicked voice reaches my ears, his warm hand engulfing mine as I see the dark, blurry shape of him hovering over me.

Amber. Sandalwood. I heave in an inhale. *I'm safe.*

"How are you feeling? Fuck, you scared me."

Blinking my eyes some more, my vision finally clears and I gasp, seeing the haunted look on his face—sunken eyes with dark circles, his jaw scruffy because he obviously didn't shave, his hair mussed, shirt wrinkled.

"Maxwell, what happened? Why am I in the hospital?"

He clenches his jaw. "You were found unconscious outside the ER. They rushed you in and you were unresponsive. Fuck, Belle. I was so terrified."

The events from earlier start floating in. Meeting with Fiona. Cole on the streets.

Cole.

"I saw him right before I fainted. He said he had something to tell me..." My voice trails off as more snippets of the strange conversation I had with Cole stream into my consciousness.

"Who?" Maxwell growls, his lips twitching.

"C-Cole. He said there's something I don't know about him." I grip his hand tightly. "There's something wrong with him. He wasn't like this before."

"That motherfucker. I'm going to find him and end him."

"Don't do anything stupid." Another wave of nausea hits me and I dry heave, but nothing comes out. "What happened to me? Why am I feeling so sick?"

Maxwell wraps his arm around me, lending me his body heat. "They ran a bunch of tests on you yesterday. You know how you've been feeling random dizziness and nausea?"

I nod.

He takes a deep breath, his free hand knotted on top of my blankets. "You were poisoned, Belle. Chronic cyanide poisoning. The doctors have given you an antidote and they'll be monitoring you for a few days. They suspect it has been happening for a while, but not at high doses." He swallows, and whispers, "That's why you're still alive."

What? Poisoned? Why and how? Hairs rise on the back of my neck as fear grips my lungs in a vise. *Why would anyone want to kill me?*

The curse.

I shake myself. That isn't real. It can't be.

"This makes no sense. The poisoning. Cole. Nothing makes any sense."

Maxwell grits his teeth, his eyes flashing. "I'm going to find the motherfucker and kill him."

"B-But Cole wouldn't do this. He couldn't. He was my friend." My chest throbs, thinking about my shelter buddy who used to cheer me up after dogs or kittens got euthanized, who was charming and funny…until recently.

"Plus, how would he poison me? I don't see him that often."

"I don't know and frankly, at this moment, I don't fucking care. I'm going to find that motherfucker and strangle the answers out of him before returning the favor tenfold."

A vein riots on his forehead and Maxwell trembles, his muscles locked in so much tension, I'm afraid he's going to hurt himself.

"Maxwell, promise me you won't do anything until we have all the answers. Promise me you won't make any decisions without me."

A muscle twitches in his jaw and he looks away.

Dread curls itself around my rib cage. *He won't look at me.*

"Please. Promise me. We make decisions together."

His breathing is heavy in the air, his intense gray eyes snaring on mine. I can see turbulent emotions swirling inside them, wanting to be unleashed. I clutch his hand tighter, begging him to let me in, to not lock me out again, but those dark pools only grow stormier.

Bang!

The door slams open and I see Taylor, Grace, and Millie rushing in, with Ryland, Steven, and Charles behind them.

"Belle! You're awake! We were so worried about you!" Millie rushes over and hugs me. "Ethan, Rex, and Lana were here earlier and your parents came by last night too."

"Shit, Belle. Don't ever do that to us again. My black heart can't take it," Taylor mutters, her eyes glistening with moisture. "Fuck, you're making me cry and I *never* cry!"

Grace bursts into tears, and Steven pulls her into his arms as she sobs against his shoulder. My own eyes burn and my lips tremble as I see my girlfriends so distraught over me.

"I'm okay, girls. I'll be fine."

Charles walks up and clasps his hand on my shoulder. He gives me a strained smile. "You gave your husband a heart attack. Thank God you're okay. Shit. Poisoning. What on earth is going on?"

The girls exchange a glance, and I shake my head. Please don't tell me they're buying into the curse now. *Come on Belle, with everything going on, the curse is a possibility, don't you think?* Fear grips me, and I shove the thought away. If I believe in it, then there won't be any hope for Maxwell and me to be together.

"We'll get to the bottom of this. Don't worry about anything, just focus on getting better," Ryland murmurs, his brows pinched. He sneaks a concerned glance at Maxwell, who is staring at my hand—the one with the IV in it.

Maxwell's face is mottled with anger, his lips parted in a snarl as he breathes rapidly. Tears prickle my eyes again.

He's so angry right now, and amid the confusion, the fear racing through me, I'm most concerned about him, about what's going through that beautiful mind of his.

Swallowing, I gently shift my hand with the IV under the blanket, out of view, and the motion snags his attention.

He releases a heavy exhale, his lips twisting in an unconvincing smile, and he leans down and presses a soft kiss on my forehead.

"Rest well, my little muse. Don't you worry about a thing."

He cups my face, his fingers trailing over my lips. Without another word, he stands up and strides out of the room, the men following him quietly.

As the girls converge by my bedside, I stare at the closed door, my pulse thundering in my ears, and the pit in my stomach grows. I have the strangest urge to cry, to run after him and tether him to me.

To tell him not to leave me. Panic clutches my chest, and I can't breathe. A sharp pain sears my chest and I touch the aching spot, noting a scabbed over wound. I must've nicked myself when I fell.

My eyes catch on a shiny object on the bedside table.

My locket—the one I haven't taken off since Maxwell put it on me that last night in Austria—glimmers under the florescent light.

The clasp on the jeweled chain is broken, the face of the locket is streaked with blood.

My blood.

CHAPTER 48

I NEED TO LEAVE her.

There's no other choice that won't endanger her life. Whether or not she believes in the curse, or if there's another nefarious reason for these incidents, the reality is simple.

She'll die if she stays with me.

And I'll die alongside her if she's gone from this world.

Perhaps that's why I've protected my heart behind steel bars, because I know deep inside, I'm an artist looking for his muse, a man roaming this earth missing a part of himself.

Once I find her, I'll give up everything for her.

I pause by the door of my studio and take out the locket I gave her—the one that had me mesmerized the moment I laid eyes on it on the website Lana sent over. Last night, after we came back home from the hospital, Belle asked me to fix the clasp for her.

Opening the locket, I swallow the lump in my throat and reread the masculine script.

Upon you, my dearest, my love rests for eternity and beyond, for anything less would be insufferable.

A shiver runs through me and I'm gripped with an unexplainable sensation that these words are specifically meant for Belle. From me.

A phantom echo foretold from the past.

My fingers tremble before I close the locket and walk out of the studio toward the stairs.

Toward Belle.

Because I have to leave her even though I love her. If one day I break the curse, I'll find her again and hope she'll take me back.

And if that day never comes, I'll spend the rest of my days loving her from afar, knowing that while I'm heartbroken, my better half is alive and hopefully thriving and moving on without me.

A heaviness sinks its talons into my chest, and I quietly walk toward the grand staircase, dread weighing down my feet like cement blocks.

"...I have everything handled. We'll get the money soon."

A furtive whisper interrupts my thoughts, and my hackles rise. My steps slow to a stop and I hold my breath.

"It's all your fault. If you could just stop your gambling, I wouldn't need to do this."

I hear a faint masculine voice, but it's too muffled for me to make out the words.

Suddenly, Agnes steps out of a room, her face flushed as she holds a cell phone up to her ear. She startles when she sees me and drops the phone.

Narrowing my eyes, I assess her before kneeling to pick up the phone from the floor. But before I can see who she's talking to, she snatches the phone from my grip.

"S-Sorry, Sir Maxwell, for disturbing you."

Her eyes dart behind me. She seems nervous.

"Is everything okay, Agnes?"

She nods. "Everything is fine. Excuse me, I need to tend to some things now that Ms. Belle is back."

She scurries away, her footfalls quick and loud before she banks a right and disappears from view.

Frowning, I continue my way to our bedroom. During Belle's stay in the hospital, I had an investigative crew come into the mansion and examine all the food, spices, and water sources in the kitchen to see if the cyanide somehow came from within these walls.

The team came up with nothing. They even searched the commonly used rooms, such as the staff's quarters and the bedrooms, but there were no signs of any illegal substances or poisons in the house. They concluded the poison must be from the outside, from her work, perhaps.

Elias has his people searching for Cole—the bastard disappeared without a trace after he left Belle to freeze in front of the emergency room entrance.

I hear Silas bark and howl as I approach Belle's room, and I grip the locket tighter in my clasp, dread curling around my heart, restricting every beat and flutter.

Forgive me, Belle.

I knock on the door.

"Come in," she hollers.

I find her propped up on the bed, her raven hair piled on top of her head. She's still too pale, her lithe frame too thin. Silas has commandeered my side of the bed, his body half on top of Belle as she giggles, trying to shift the fifty-pound dog off her chest.

My heart spasms as I stand at the doorway and stare at them, trying to commit every single second of this moment to memory—the way she closes her eyes as Silas smothers her with kisses, her hair falling out of her bun, but she doesn't seem to care. How a fire seems to light within her, even now, when she's still too frail and recovering, but the poison hasn't dimmed her spirits.

She's life and I'm death. Two people who never should've gotten together.

I rake in an inhale to steel myself.

At my silence, Belle looks up, her grin slipping off her face when she sees my expression.

"Maxwell? Is everything okay?"

My voice catches in my throat. The words I need to say are lodged in my throat, choking me to death. My body is fighting against my mind, refusing to let me speak.

Because we don't want to leave.

"Maxwell?" She sits up straighter.

Death has always been my dancing partner, and I used to be afraid—fearful of those dark shadows looming in the corners of the house, the whispering echoes warning me of more misfortunes if I step out of line. I hated him with every ounce of my soul for forcing me to live in the darkness and resigning myself to a life that was merely to survive.

I was afraid of death visiting my doorstep again. He had taken far too much from me already. From my family.

But now, I realize, I'm no longer afraid of him. Because living a lonely life isn't so bad anymore.

The worst thing in the world is to watch the one you love die in front of you, knowing you could've stopped it. It was a pain I saw on Dad's face when Mom passed away, an agony I suffered growing up in the shadows of the estate, constantly reminding myself this would be my future if I weren't careful. It was a pain I felt—a fragment of the real thing, I now understood—with Sydney, someone as I realized years later, wasn't the right person for me.

Staring at my wife, the woman who has filled my cavernous heart with light, whose presence has obliterated the restlessness and yearning I've felt all my life, I know one thing.

I would give up everything for her.

Everything, including my life and my happiness.

As long as she's safe and I can take death far away from her, I'll gladly be his dance partner for the rest of my life, confining myself in the dark shadows of loneliness forever, knowing somewhere out there, a rose is blooming brightly. Thriving. Happy. Imbuing the world with beauty.

And it's these thoughts that give me the strength to utter the next words.

"Belle, I want a divorce."

"What?"

My pulse thuds rapidly in my veins. A splitting pain stabs me in my chest. I shake my head. I must've misheard him. That can't be right.

"What did you say, Maxwell?"

He strides toward me, his muscles stretching against his fitted black suit—the frigid king in his full glory and what I now know is his armor against the world. He quietly sits down on the bed.

His jaw locks as he stares at my hand, at the wedding ring on my finger.

He won't look at me.

"You heard me, Belle."

Fury rages through my body, and I fist my hands. Silas lets out a growl, clearly sensing the change in my mood.

"*How dare you*, Maxwell? How dare you do this again? Bulldoze over me with your 'decision,'" I wiggle my fingers in air quotes, "and not talk over things with me. *Again!*"

Shaking my head, I add, "We aren't going to divorce. Unless you tell me it's because you don't love me anymore."

Maxwell swallows, his breathing heavy. He finally lifts his eyes and stares at me.

Intense. Passionate pools of gray.

"I don't love you anymore," he rasps.

I flinch, my chest flayed open by his words. Tears blur my vision as I grip my shirt, the spot over my heart, and try to breathe through the agony tearing me up inside, even though I know his words aren't true.

But they hurt so, so much.

"You're lying." I shake my head. "I can see right through you. You're lying."

Tears stream down my face, but I don't wipe them.

Maxwell's throat ripples, his piercing eyes reddening, shining with moisture.

"You don't know that." His voice is hoarse as he rakes in a ragged inhale.

"I do!" I cry, my face crumbling. I point to my chest. "I know it in here...I know it from your art, your kisses, your words. You love me, Maxwell. You told me yourself in Austria. You're lying."

My lips tremble as I whisper, "The least you can do is not lie to me while breaking my heart."

Maxwell stands up abruptly, his jaw clenching as he swipes his fingers over his eyes.

"It's *precisely* because I love you that I must leave you. I can't ignore everything that has gone on around us, all these accidents, all these threats against your life. *I can't lose you!* If we divorce, you'll no longer be married to me, and maybe, just maybe—"

"This is about that stupid curse again, isn't it? There are so many reasons why I could be getting poisoned. You're from a big family. Maybe you guys made some enemies. Heck, even my parents may have made some enemies, or I don't know, someone may have contaminated the water system at work."

Fury and sadness race through my veins, but I persist. "Why are you sabotaging us? Why aren't you fighting for us? For me?"

"*I'm fighting for you! This is me fighting for you!*" he roars.

A vein pulses angrily on his forehead and his reddened eyes meet mine. "We've been living in denial...on borrowed time, Belle. But fantasy, no matter how beautiful, isn't reality. I can't ignore the curse simply because you refuse to believe it. Even when the facts are right in front of us. You were dying...slowly, right in front of me, and I ignored the signs because I was selfish." He trembles, his voice breaking. "B-Because I wanted to keep you by my side."

His breathing is ragged as he rolls his lips inward and looks away.

"B-Belle, I can survive burning in the flames of hell knowing you're out here...alive and well." He turns toward me and the heartbreak in his face and voice robs me of my breath.

"But I can't survive if you're dead," he whispers.

He leans forward, his fragrance of amber and sandalwood cloaking my senses. Hovering over me, he whispers, "I love you, Belle. I'm sorry for hurting you. Despite everything, I'm the selfish bastard who wouldn't change a thing because I got to steal these moments with you, these moments I was never supposed to have. Because these were the happiest days of my life."

He presses a soft kiss on the whorl of my ear, and I shiver and close my eyes. He cups my face and tips his forehead to mine, much like that night at the pier when he was kissing me goodbye.

His breath catches in his throat. "My little muse, you're beautiful and perfect, just the way you are. Remember that. Please take care of yourself for me."

His shaking hand clasps mine as he puts something into my palm and closes my fingers around it.

Without another word, he stands up and slips out of the bedroom.

A sob chokes out of my mouth, followed by another. My heart pulverizes inside me, the pain eviscerating, far more painful than anything I've ever felt in my life.

Silas whines and licks the tears streaming down my cheeks.

Crying, I curl my arms around his soft fur and bury my face in his neck, and I slowly open my palm.

My broken necklace—repaired and as good as new.

But my heart lies in shreds, its bloody essence seeping into the very bones of this cursed estate, weaving itself into the cruel history of Wraithmoor Abbey.

CHAPTER 49

Belle

THE SKIES ARE FORLORN today. Lifeless. Like the colors have been leached from it, leaving behind ashes and gloom. The stack of papers crinkles in my hand, but I barely notice, my eyes drawn to the thick clouds looming in the horizon from my spot inside the sitting room. Maxwell told me Ryland loves storms, that they set him free, but he never liked them.

I never understood how he felt until now, when I'm feeling suffocated under the wrath of the dreary skies, when I can feel it stealing every remaining ounce of brightness inside me.

Maxwell left three days ago. The divorce papers I'm holding arrived this morning. Morris packed him a bag and wouldn't tell me where he went. My guess is, he's probably in one of the suites inside The Orchid. Morris told me Maxwell instructed the staff to take care of my needs.

As if that'll mend the gash in my heart. I want to be angry at him for once again making the decision without me. But I know he's doing it from a place of love and fear. He has experienced too many heartbreaking losses in his life, and while I'm willing to risk it all for him, I can't ask him to do the same.

If something were to happen to me, after all, there are no guarantees in life, I don't want him to blame himself for the rest of his life.

Silas lets out a mournful howl and stares at me with his deep blue eye. I rub his fur, thankful for his companionship.

The skeletal branches of the bushes in the rose garden twist in the cruel wind, nature intent on attacking them even when they have nothing more to give, their leaves and flowers, their beauty, long having shriveled to the ground. My eyes land on the patch of soil where nothing grows—the sign of the curse—and I wonder if it's time for me to explore the garden. If confronting that haunting sadness will help heal my broken heart.

I spent the last two days in the office, determined to drown myself in last minute preparations for the fashion show. I may have lost the only man I've ever loved in my life, but I won't lose my grandpa's legacy.

Swallowing the lump in my throat, I stare at the papers in my hand. Maxwell has left me with enough money to save McKenzie's if needed in the future, to get fertility treatments, to open humane shelters for abandoned animals. His only ask is for me to one day relinquish the estate back to his family.

He has given me all of my dreams—the dreams that drove me to accept this arrangement with him in the beginning. But doesn't he know my dreams have changed? Now, they contain a dark-haired man with beautiful scars on his body and soul, a man with the warmest touches and melting kisses, who fills the hole I've always felt inside my chest, the feeling I was missing a piece of me I couldn't identify.

Like I was waiting for him all this time and didn't realize it.

"Ms. Belle."

I jolt. Turning toward Morris, I muster up a smile.

The old butler lets out a sigh, the gloomy daylight illuminating every wrinkle on his face. He looks weary, like he has been fighting a long battle. For a moment, he looks as old as this estate—grand, stately, but having seen too much in his years.

"They say, before the curse claimed the life of another Anderson mistress, a tree branch would lodge itself through a window in the estate, scattering glass shards across the floors," he murmurs. "It was an omen."

My chest tightens, thinking back to the disturbance on the day of the gala and how my blood ran cold when Steven told us a branch blew into Maxwell's study even though there were no trees nearby.

"Rumor was, the first branch came in from the window next to you, all the way back in the eighteen hundreds."

"Silas," I whisper, the name slipping out of my lips automatically. I think back to the austere duke in the portrait gallery, the one with the sorrowful eyes.

My blood races. The missing journal, the curse, fragments of knowledge floating in my mind, a puzzle I'm almost certain I know the answer to but have inconveniently forgotten.

"Morris, curse or not, it doesn't matter anymore, right?" I look away and feel my eyes burning. "He left."

"What I'm trying to say is, perhaps it's for the best. I know it doesn't feel this way right now, but the pain...the pain will lessen over time. Even when you lose everything in the world and experience the most agonizing tragedy, time will go on and the wound will heal."

Something in his voice catches my attention and I glance at him, finding his blue eyes deepening, like he's seeing a ghost from his past. He must be talking about his family.

He clears his throat. "The curse has taken too many lives. Don't let it take yours. Focus the pain on something else and live. Live, because many others before you didn't get a chance to do so."

Our gazes hold, and he gives me a curt nod before bowing and disappearing back into the main hallways.

His words echo in my mind long after he left. I turn my attention to the lifeless landscape outside the window. A murder of crows is foraging in the patchy snow, their cries haunting but their spirits defiant.

Live. Even when the world seems empty.

My thoughts flit back to Maxwell's stormy painting of Lake Superior, the one he thought was soulless because it was missing hope, something I'd conveniently forgotten. *How could I forget hope? There's sunshine after the storm.*

Slowly, I stand up, resolve flooding inside me. The storm is temporary. This pain is temporary. Perhaps Maxwell and I aren't meant to be, but this won't be the end of me. My dreams are still out there, hidden behind the clouds, and I won't stop climbing until I reach them.

I'm Belle Law-McKenzie Anderson, and I won't go down without a fight, and if Maxwell comes to his senses one day, he'll have to prove he deserves me.

Because I deserve that and more.

Gritting my teeth, I speed down Houston Street toward FDR Drive, my heart throwing itself against my rib cage, begging to be let out so it can crawl back to its other half living in the mansion.

My little muse.

The lump forms in my throat as I shift gears, ignoring the honking cars, the dark expanse of the river beckoning me with its icy waters. Rain pelts against my face from the open window, the icy shards doing nothing to distract me from the scything pain that has been keeping me company since I walked away from her three days ago, knowing I was the reason for the tears and heartbreak on her face.

It felt wrong then, and it still feels wrong now. How could anything be right when I feel like my world has ended?

You took the choice away from her, you bastard. Our last conversation floats to my mind. I know I left her to save her, to buy me time to break the curse, if I can even break the curse. But my investigation hasn't turned up anything new. I'm still waiting for the medical examiner's report from Elias's contact.

In the past few days, I'd spent hours poring through scrapbooks and other relics hidden away in the attic. I'd even called up Wraithmoor Antiquities, since Belle mentioned thinking someone in the shop may know something about the curse. But the girl who answered didn't know anything, and she mentioned the owner was out of town.

I tried distracting myself from my constant anxiety by painting my portrait of Belle, the masterpiece I started but never finished. But the art that once brought me relief was now a burden, because every brushstroke reminded me of her—the soft streaks of black in her hair, the greens of her irises dotted by the lushest brown—the color of nature, as she used to remind me.

She saw beauty in everything.

She saw me.

She's the streak of red missing inside the teal of my atrovirens, and now, without her, I'm empty.

You took the choice away from her. The words echo in my mind. I think back to what she said before, how there were two people in a marriage, how we should make decisions together and I feel a slither of regret. *Did I make the wrong choice by walking away from her?*

I swerve to the right to overtake a slow car. I'd hope a damn drive would give me some clarity on the curse, but instead, I'm hit with the wisdom of Belle's words. Facing a reality that I might never break the curse, shouldn't I tell her everything and let her decide?

My phone blares, and without looking at the screen, I answer and put the call on the speakers. "Anderson speaking."

"Mr. Maxwell Anderson? I'm Dr. Greg Fenton, Elias's referral. I work at the county coroner's office."

My heart stutters as my attention snares on to the deep voice on the other line. *Elias's medical examiner.* "What do you have for me?"

"It took me a bit of time, but I went through all the photos and evidence gathered for the deaths of your late wife, mother, and grandmother. If I were the presiding examiner on the cases, I would've come to different conclusions."

My breath freezes. "What do you mean?"

"There were unexplained anomalies. It'd be easy to overlook them. With your family's influence, I'm sure there was a lot of pressure to close the cases quickly. Since the deaths occurred on your family's properties and there were plenty of circumstantial evidence and eyewitness testimonies pointing to accidents, I assume the examiner thought it was easier to conclude as such, but..."

He pauses and I can barely focus on the road ahead of me. He clears his throat and continues, "If these were random cases, not influenced by your family's name, please excuse me for being blunt, I'd be issuing a ruling of undetermined manner of death for all of them."

"Why?" I rasp.

"For your grandmother, there was a large-gauge needle mark in her neck that was unexplained, and the aspirator showed abnormal readings. The embolism that caused her fatal cardiac arrest could've been due to external trauma. For your mother, there was a bruise forming on her back. It was very fresh, the injury very close to the time of death. However, all the other injuries indicated she fell face forward. But I wouldn't be able to rule out if she was struck from behind and fell down the stairs."

My breathing comes out in quick pants, his findings echoing in my mind. *Their deaths could've been foul play.*

The curse isn't real. Belle's words reverberate in my mind. Could she have been right all along?

"And Sydney?" I ask, my heart racing a mile a minute.

"Your late wife had abnormal lab results, showing a low positive for Rohypnol and ketamine. There were traces of alcohol in her system, which was consistent with your family's testimony that she was intoxicated on the night of her death. My guess was, the examiner thought the results of the drug tests were false positives, since they coincided with a time when the county had a bad batch of test kits. And coupled with your family's testimony and influence, along with the alcohol in her system, the death was ruled as accidental. But again, if it were me..."

"It'd be undetermined," I whisper.

"Yes. Frankly, if this were Elias's investigation and he was asking me if the deaths were from foul play, I wouldn't rule that out at all. I'd frankly have him look into your family, to be honest, no offense." He chuckles at his morbid attempt at lighthearted banter.

My mind blanks from shock. I grip the steering wheel tighter as his words echo in my brain. I can barely see straight.

Their deaths were from foul play. A person was behind all of this, not a curse. The truth hits me in the gut. All these years of terror, of living my life in shadows, in fear…all this time wasted. My blood boils inside me as my lungs clamor for more oxygen. I recognize this sensation—anger. My entire life spent on believing this ridiculous curse and someone was behind this all this time?

This has to be it. I need to tell Belle. She was right all along. I need to find her and tell her everything.

The thought of Belle sends a torrent of water inside my charred insides. Belle. The woman I wasn't allowed to love because of the curse.

If a human is behind this, there's hope for us. I'll hire bodyguards for Belle, move us to another country, have a security team sweep through the house, perform background checks on everyone. I'll exhaust my entire fortune to keep her safe.

We can be together.

The thoughts jumble together, my mind disoriented by this turn of events. But just when life has given me a ray of hope, a car skids into my line of sight and I swerve, but the rain-slick roads betray me. I know the moment I lose control of my vehicle, when fate decides to deal an unyielding blow. The moments slow to flickering flashes.

The weightlessness of the car.

The shrill screeching and spinning of the wheels.

The blur of blinding headlights.

The guardrail suddenly appearing in front of me.

Everything comes to a head as I'm wrenched back in my seat. I swerve, my heart lurching, breath freezing, and everything…*everything* comes into startling clarity.

They say your life flashes before your eyes when you think you're going to die. But it isn't my life filling my mind right now.

It's visions of her. My Belle. Dancing with her in the cabin, listening to opera. Her lips trailing down my body, kissing the scars on my torso but healing the ones carved deep inside. Her in the rose garden, painting as I curled my arms around her, talking about dreams of Venice. A letter of heartbreak clenched in her hand as I cradled her broken body in the rain.

My chest seizes, the visions and memories blinding, and I squeeze my eyes shut as I hear the screeching of metal tearing against metal, the passenger side of my car caving in as it scrapes against the solid barrier.

Airbags explode, the force ripping the air out of my lungs, and the world spins around me as I slam forward.

My ears ring and every inch of my body throbs, the pain a latecomer to the violence. Blackness dots my vision, my lungs trying to draw in oxygen, but everything hurts so fucking much. A metallic taste bursts in my mouth and a sticky wetness seeps into my eyes.

A thick plume of smoke fills the cabin, death beckoning me to join him in another waltz as the sounds of the outside world finally filter in.

Screaming, yelling, chaos. I glance out the broken windows, finding bystanders getting out of their cars, their shadows looming like the monster I've seen all my life, its talons threatening to finish what the accident didn't.

As panic crashes through me with the force of a tsunami, I will my eyes to shut, to not look at the monster outside. I try to breathe, but the anxiety only rises, the waves smothering me from the inside.

I finally realize the truth Belle has been trying to tell me all along, but I was too blinded by fear.

If this were my last day on earth, I should've spent every single second with her in my arms. I should've fought my monsters, my anxiety, my fears, one by one, until my very last breath. I should've treated her as an equal partner and faced our challenges together.

I'm fighting for us, but I should've asked her to join the fight.

People pound on my car and nausea roils up my throat as everything becomes too much. Way too much.

With trembling hands, I reach for my phone and press a button.

"R-Ryland...I need help."

And much later, I realize...I've never seen Belle in the rose garden before.

CHAPTER 50

"I made the appointment. Dr. Lin will be here within the hour," Ryland comments as he settles into a chair in our reserved room inside the gentlemen's club at The Orchid.

He hands me a glass of water. I wince as I reach for it. Aside from a nasty gash on my forehead and bruised ribs, I was lucky I made it out alive from the crash two days ago.

I was such a damn fool.

A few mirthless chuckles slip from my lips, and I shake my head in self-derision.

"Why did you suddenly ask me to find a shrink for you?" he asks, his brows furrowed.

I stare at the lone ember in the fireplace, watching the dying spark glow before a sudden draft sweeps in, causing the small flame to twist and burgeon, the fire catching, fighting, winning against the cold air threatening to snuff it out.

The same fire is inside me now, and it only took a near-death experience for me to realize I couldn't live in fear anymore.

Of Belle getting hurt. Of my anxiety. Of all the unfortunate events I used to attribute to the damn curse.

"I don't want to hide anymore," I murmur, turning my gaze to my twin, my best friend. I filled him in on the medical examiner's findings.

When he went through his troubles with Millie months ago, I was angry he kept everything to himself, that he didn't confide in me. But I realize I'm the same way.

I haven't set a good example.

After taking a deep breath, I continue, "The curse took too much from me—I'd been a slave to it, scared shitless to be honest. It was easier to lock myself inside the mansion and avoid crowds, emotions, and human connection. We were raised to believe in it, and after Sydney, I never once considered it could be *anything* but the curse."

I swallow, my nose burning. "And so, I let it run my life. The more I hid, the more I convinced myself I was safe. From my anxiety, from more death and tragedy."

Ryland's eyes glitter and he locks his jaw.

"I thought—maybe if I didn't confront my anxiety, I'd have an excuse to hide forever. Maybe if I convinced myself I had flaws, whether they were the scars on my body, or," I tap my temple, "up here, I could continue avoiding human connection."

"Fuck," Ryland murmurs, his eyes downcast. "You got those gashes on your body because of me. If I was more careful when we were hunting—"

"No. I held onto those scars like a shield. Truth is, I never regretted what happened that day. I'd save you a thousand times over."

He knots his hands on his lap and stays silent.

"Belle actually taught me my scars were beautiful. There weren't flaws. She refused to stay away even when I hid from her and pushed her away."

My voice thickens. "And when I slammed into that guardrail the other night, when I thought those were my last moments on earth, I realized what an idiot I was."

Leaning forward, I release a ragged exhale. "If I'd died that night, my last actions to Belle would've been hurting her, not loving her, because dammit, I do. I fucking love her. She's it for me. I should've listened to her, talked to her, figured out a path forward together. Even if the medical examiner didn't call, I shouldn't have taken the choice away from her."

"Fuck, Maxwell," Ryland mutters, shaking his head. He lifts his face, his eyes shining with moisture. "Fuck. You were always the smarter man between the two of us."

I chuckle and shake my head. "No. I was the stupid one who got a second chance at life. And after I crashed my car and had another panic attack, I realized I needed to address this anxiety inside me, this fear that led me to hide from everyone. That's why I had you make the appointment, because you mentioned knowing a shrink."

"It was actually Steven who gave me the recommendation. His sister works with a therapist in LA, a Marybeth Connors, who had connections here as well, and Dr. Lin came highly recommended."

Ryland smiles, and I see the happy kid in the family portrait again—the boy who laughed a lot, the charismatic, popular guy at school, the one who became more stoic in the years after Sydney's death.

"There's also something else I want to tell you," I murmur, holding his gaze. It's time to pull out the thorn that has been buried in my side all these years.

He frowns and cocks his head.

"I knew Sydney loved you back then."

Blood drains from his face and he opens his mouth to speak.

I hold up my hand. "I overheard you two when she confessed to you outside our bedrooms. I never told you because I didn't want you to feel bad, because I knew you would've blamed yourself for getting in between us and would've piled a shitload of unnecessary crap on your conscience."

"Shit," he rasps. "I didn't...I was never with her—"

"I know. I know you wouldn't betray me that way. But she came in between us, didn't she? Even long after I fell out of love with her. She was a ghost that lingered behind, right?"

He swallows and nods. "I thought if you didn't know, I'd spare you more pain."

"We were both thinking of each other and not being honest. Just like I was with most of my life. Hiding. It didn't help shit."

Ryland chuckles and swipes his hand over his face. "Fuck man, I didn't know you were carrying this all by yourself the entire time."

"Just like I didn't know you felt burdened being the face of the company. Two fucking peas in a pod, asshole."

He snickers. "You're the asshole."

Knock. Knock.

"Come in," I call out.

The door opens and in strides a woman with glossy black hair and glasses, who I presume is Dr. Lin. She looks to be around Lana's age and is younger than I thought, but I trust Steven's judgment. Ryland slowly gets up and clasps my shoulder. "Brothers forever."

He holds up his wrist and flashes his bracelet. "I'm so proud of you for getting help."

I smile and nod. He quietly slips out of the room as I stand and extend my hand toward the doctor.

"Hi, I'm Maxwell Anderson, and I need your help." Acid roils in my gut and makes its way up my throat. I take a deep breath and force out the next words. "I have severe social anxiety and, quite possibly, PTSD."

I won't let the monsters inside me win again.

CHAPTER 51

THE WHISPERS OF THE crowd mingle with the haunting strains of the violin and cello from a live performance by a string quartet at the McKenzie Atelier fashion show, which will showcase our upcoming fall and winter collection. The space is dim, the dark ambiance stirring the excitement from the audience in the much-anticipated event of the season.

I shiver from the air conditioning, purposely set to a frigid forty-five degrees to simulate a late fall, early winter evening in a garden. A sense of dread snakes up my spine—the same restlessness growing inside me since three days ago, when I woke up in the middle of the night, my body bathed in sweat.

It was the same dark dream, but this time, the details were clearer and more vivid—me running in the rose garden, a place I still couldn't bring myself to visit, a place which seemed to be walled in with grief. He was there, the tall, dark-haired man dressed in the attire of a bygone era. The moon was high in the skies, the pale beam bathing him in an ethereal glow.

He hovered over an easel, a paintbrush in his hand, as sobs wracked his body.

I wanted to see what he was painting, what had him so devastated. A desperate need clawed inside me to comfort him. To tell him I was there and everything would be okay.

He whispered, "I miss you so much, my love. Why can't I paint you so I can keep your image with me always?"

My chest spasmed in pain and I broke into a run. But the distance between us seemed insurmountable. The faster I ran, the farther he was, the rose garden stretching endlessly, the thorns of the bushes prickling my skin. I screamed but nothing came out of my mouth, and I was helpless in my Sisyphean task, watching the blood prickling my arms, each scratch a dagger to my heart.

Normally, I'd wake up then. Breathless, heartache piercing my chest. But this time, I didn't.

I was still trying to run to the man, to save him because I knew he was very important to me. As if sensing my presence, the man turned around, his face illuminated by the eerie moonlight and the breath wrenched from my lungs.

It was Silas, the duke, dressed in his finest attire, like the one I saw in the portrait gallery. But he looked like Maxwell—the same glittering dark eyes, the soulful eyes that seemed ageless.

Tears streamed down his face, and I gasped, seeing a pool of blood spreading on his white shirt, the tendrils withering, curling its way up his body, but he didn't seem to notice as he sobbed into his hands.

Behind him was a portrait—a beautiful woman in a gray dress, her face blurry.

My heart splintered and the dream shattered.

It felt so real, unsettling, a ghostly memory or a vivid imagination.

"Belle? Hey, Belle!"

Grace's voice jolts me from my thoughts, and I rub my arms, trying to warm myself up.

"Sorry, I'm just nervous about the show."

"You'll do great. Didn't your boss say the pieces came out awesome? It's a huge accomplishment, having three pieces in the fashion show."

I strain a smile, my mind still reeling from the dream or nightmare that felt so devastatingly real.

"Fingers crossed the public likes it. It'll prove my talent as a designer...that I'm much more than my last name," I murmur, staring at the dark runway.

"You've won me over already, if your designs are anything like the vibe I'm getting here. Very gothic and dark, but romantic at the same time." Taylor crosses her arms, her black nails flashing under the dim lighting.

I won't be backstage for this fashion show, as Fiona and her senior designers have that covered. But if the show goes well and my pieces are well received, I may have a place on the go team next season.

"I wonder if he'll show up." I pinch myself. *Dammit. I'm moving on from him, my husband. Don't think about him.*

But I still can't bring myself to sign the divorce papers.

However, that doesn't mean I'm finished being angry at him. If he wants to be brave and face the so-called curse together, he can come find me. And even then, I'll have my reservations about him.

Millie nudges Taylor on the side and Taylor frowns before tugging on Grace's sleeve. The three are doing their silent communication thing again, and it's getting on my nerves. Heck, I'm still technically married and an Anderson.

"What are you guys keeping from me now?" I mutter.

Taylor grimaces. "Sorry. There's something you don't know—"

"Tay! He told us not to tell her!" Grace shoves her sister on the side.

"Ow!" Taylor nudges Grace back. "Look, girl code over bro code, even if the bro in question is related to us. And I *never* agreed with him. She *should* know!"

Alarm rings through me as the dread comes rearing back. "What happened? It's Maxwell, isn't it? Something happened to him? Tell me!"

Taylor grabs my hand, which is alarming in and of itself since the woman doesn't like to be touched. "Okay, don't freak out. Maxwell got into a bad accident a few nights ago. He was driving, but the roads were slick and he slammed into a guardrail."

My heart plummets to the ground and I get up, suddenly forgetting I'm angry at him, not caring the fashion show is about to start.

I need to see him, to see if he's fine.

To see if he has blood on his chest like that horrible dream.

That was a dream, Belle. A dream.

"He's fine," Millie whispers urgently. "He got really lucky. The car is totaled, but he left with some bruised ribs and cuts. He has been a mess since he left you, Belle."

Tears spring into my eyes, and I fan myself with my hand. I want to be by his side right now.

"He has to be the brave one this time. He needs to understand even if he's afraid, we're in a relationship and we need to make decisions together."

"He's just afraid for your life," Grace murmurs, throwing her arm around me.

"I know. That's why I don't hate him for it. I know he did it from a place of love." I look at my friends, my vision blurry with tears. "But I won't live my life in fear. Fear of accidents, curses, what-ifs. Year of yeses, right?"

Taylor nods and pats my leg. "Damn straight. Fearless badass bitch over here. Let him come to you."

The lights flicker off and the room plunges into darkness. The music increases in volume—an opera singer sings an eerie melody. The wrought iron chandeliers—relics in this historical building on the Upper East Side—turn on, the dim light casting serpentine shadows to the arched ceilings.

White smoke, backlit by strategic spotlights, blanket the runway, lending to an otherworldly atmosphere. Models pass through the gothic archway at the entrance of the stage, which is adorned in faux ivy and dark roses, all a nod to the theme tonight—Eternal Reverie.

Fiona told me this was to underscore the timeless beauty of McKenzie Atelier with an emphasis on sustainability. The outfits are all in a range of deep blues, forest greens, and dark burgundy with elements of nature woven in the designs.

The crowd gasps as model after model struts down the runway, gliding over the smoke as if they're ghosts moving in the ether, the luxurious fabrics glinting under the dark, romantic lighting.

I hear the frantic scribbles on notepads, see cell phones held up in the air as I watch with bated breath, waiting for my designs to show up, to see if the crowd will react to them.

The music transitions to a modern take of "Nessun Dorma" and my eyes immediately tear up as I think of him, the man who makes me feel too much of every emotion—love, anger, lust, sadness—someone who feels like home since the moment I laid eyes on him at the race.

The tenor sings the evocative aria and a lone spotlight falls on the next model gliding onto the runway. Shocked whispers erupt from the crowd as the model showcases the first of my designs—the shawl sweater lined with fleece. I've requested a special holographic thread to be woven into the organza that is part of the sweater. The end product is iridescent, the sweater glowing and changing between shades of navy and purple as the model moves effortlessly—a fallen angel owning the runway.

A quiet hush settles in the room as the tenor sings the high notes, his voice portraying the longing for his unrequited love, and another model steps into the spotlight wearing my coat, the light organza train fluttering behind her, rendering her into a ghostly apparition.

Shivers travel up my spine and Taylor murmurs, "Holy shit, Belle. This is amazing."

The crowd seems to agree as my third piece is shown and I hear a smattering of applause. My heart pulses in my chest, my eyes watering as I feel the ghost of my grandpa next to me, and I'm reminded of the kind man who braved his anxiety and created breathless wonders for the world—the man who taught me everything.

Grandpa, this is for you.

I wish he could be here to see me, to see my creations, to see me fighting for his legacy.

My thoughts drift back to the other man I wish were here. Maxwell. Regardless of my future at the company, whether Fiona lets me join her senior team, tonight feels like a pinnacle.

It's a success Maxwell took part in.

He calls me his little muse, but little does he know, *he* is my muse. He's the only person who truly understands me. He sees me as beautiful, not broken or flawed.

Perfect, just the way I am.

Swiping the tears off my cheeks, I'm suddenly overcome with emotions, a tidal wave of sadness for the men I've lost, one to the great beyond and one to a crippling fear of death.

Millie pulls me to her side. "Shh... I got you. I know how it feels," she whispers, her voice thick. She has had her share of losses in her life and I'm grateful she's here.

More models strut down the runway, the designs slowly shifting from fall to winter as the lighting on the stage slowly warms to highlight the lush green foliage on the runway that was hidden by the smoke before.

Hope within the stark winter. The ray of light shining behind the clouds on a dreary day at Lake Superior.

The fashion show ends with Fiona and her team walking down the runway to a standing ovation. Her eyes find mine as she beams at the crowd. She gives me the barest of nods—a public acknowledgment.

I dip my head in response, my smile tinged with grief—happiness amid grief. Life is strange this way, and I find myself oscillating between opposing emotions—love and hate, anger and calmness.

Fiona and her team stride back to the backstage and the room brightens, signaling the end of the event. Suddenly, a murmuring travels through the crowd, camera flashes aimed toward the entrance of the room.

And I see him.

CHAPTER 52

THE ROARING IN MY ears eclipses the shocked gasps and furtive whispers of the crowd. I was hoping to slip in undetected, to support Belle and the event she worked so hard to prepare for, but I should've known better. I should've known my anonymity went down the drain ever since the disastrous first press conference, the wedding, and the gala.

I'm suddenly transported back to Mom's funeral, when I stood frozen under the spotlight, trapped by the claws of fear, a helpless prey succumbing to the predators around me.

Flashes erupt, the blinding lights glaring assaults to my eyes, and sweat gathers on my forehead. The crowd morphs into the familiar monster who had haunted me my entire life—my inner demon.

My nostrils flare as my breathing quickens. I scan the blurry faces, my hands fisted at my sides.

Until I see her.

My little muse, standing in the shadows, her luscious hair piled on top of her head, her lips parted, eyes widening.

She clutches a notepad to her chest and shrinks into the dark.

As if I can't see her. As if she isn't the brightest beacon in this room, the beam of the lighthouse guiding my ship to shore in the turbulent seas.

I think back to what Dr. Lin told me in our meeting yesterday.

"We'll assemble a team for your treatment—talk therapy and medication," Dr. Lin concluded as she left me with a prescription of SSRIs, which would slowly take effect after a few weeks and benzodiazepines for panic attacks. We also had the next three appointments scheduled.

It isn't a magical bandage, no snap of the fingers to make everything go away.

But it's a start.

"Mr. Anderson! Are you here to support your wife?"

"There are rumors you've moved out of the estate. Is your marriage on the rocks?"

"An unnamed source told us you were in a car crash a few nights ago. Do you have any comment?"

Their questions are endless, bullets fired from an automatic weapon, as reporters converge around me, their phones thrusted into my face. But my eyes are only on her, my Belle, watching her throat rippling as emotions cloud her startling eyes.

While the beginning of an anxiety attack threatens to smother me, maybe because of the medication I took beforehand or the fact I'm making a choice to fight my inner demons, I'm able to keep the panic attack at bay.

I won't let it win this time.

"We came across a divorce filing. Is it true? Are you getting a divorce?"

Shocked gasps erupt from the crowd as more questions are thrown at me, the chaos adding to the rioting pulse hammering in my ears.

Closing my eyes, I take a deep breath and count to five before exhaling to a count of eight and repeat the process. Dr. Lin told me longer exhales than inhales help calm the nervous system. I rub my heirloom ring, focusing on the sharp corners and gilded edges.

I'm calm. I'm at peace. I accept myself.

This time, the affirmations finally feel true, not just lip service I've been giving myself all these years.

My eyes flutter open and I hold up my hand. I fix my gaze on Belle as she clasps a hand over her mouth.

"I-I want to say s-something," I murmur, but the crowd doesn't hear me.

More questions. More lights. More noises.

Heat rushes up my spine, my lungs working in overdrive, the dark monster looming before me again.

Not today.

"Be quiet! I want to say something!" I roar.

The room abruptly silences, clearly shocked at my outburst. I hear the furtive clicking of shutters and my heavy breathing.

"T-Thank you," I murmur. I stare at Belle as my next words tumble out of my lips. "I haven't been honest with you all."

More scratching of pens on paper as reporters take notes.

"When I first married my wife, it was done as a ruse to calm the media circus regarding my failed press conference. It was primarily a publicity stunt."

A few people gasp and raise their hands. Belle's eyes widen. Grace holds her hand in support.

I shake my head. "I'm not done. The truth is…" I tear my gaze away from the love of my life and stare into the eyes of the reporters in front of me, reminding myself they are human, just like me. Not monsters. "I have severe, debilitating, social anxiety. It prevents me from making speeches and it's also why I avoid crowds."

More murmurs erupt from the crowd, and I smell the headlines tomorrow.

"I don't care what you say or write about me tomorrow." I wipe my sweaty palms on my pants. "I'm not ashamed because it's just a medical condition many people deal with…like diabetes or heart disease. I only regret not treating it sooner and allowing it to rule my life for so long."

My eyes find Belle's again, every cell in my body clamoring for her, but I know I've hurt her too many times, and I need to make amends. "Yes, my marriage started as a sham. An arrangement. But I love her, my wife…my muse." My voice thickens at the end.

The fire that roared to life a few days ago is now burning hot in my veins, and I stare at her, the love of my life, hoping to convey the depths of my love for her, my sincerest regret for hurting her.

"She's taught me my scars are beautiful, that every step I take is a sign of courage. She's the better half of me, a woman I don't deserve. And I'd hurt her in the past by ignoring her feelings because I was too focused on mine."

Belle swipes her eyes, her lips trembling. Millie rubs her back as Taylor crosses her arms and frowns at me with clear disapproval.

"Belle," I call out, "I'm sorry for taking your choice away. I'm sorry for not listening to you. I'm sorry for any tears I've caused you to shed."

Thumping my chest, I let out a ragged breath. "This time, the choice is yours. Because I trust you, because you're the best person I know. Because with you, I'll be brave...and I'll fight my demons. I only wish you'll be by my side because I love you...so, so much."

Her face crumbles and she heaves in struggling breaths. The reporters turn toward her, clearly making the connection I'm talking directly to my wife. They take a few steps toward her.

"Please! Give her space, p-please," I murmur, and the press pauses, a few of them glancing at each other with uncertainty.

I love you, I mouth to Belle, who's being dragged away by Taylor and Grace, with Millie following fast behind. *I'll be waiting for you.*

Now and forever. This life and all the lifetimes thereafter.

CHAPTER 53

Belle

THICK CLOUDS ROLL IN from the distance, the color of a fresh bruise, swollen and festering. I take a seat on the lonely bench in the rooftop garden at the estate. Taking a page from Maxwell's book, I decided to face my discomfort and finally venture up here. In the past, I'd avoided this place along with the rose garden and blamed it on random reasons—bad weather, a fear of heights, a heaviness in my chest.

It felt like there was a loss buried deep in my soul, a hole I hadn't been able to fill until I met him. Considering Maxwell had avoided this place as well, perhaps he felt the same way.

I look at the wilted wildflowers and overgrown weeds, a rusted veranda barely standing. The forgotten rooftop garden is completely at odds with the well-kept grounds of the estate. This place appears frozen in time, a shrine for someone long having left this world.

But now, as I sit here, I get the distinct sensation I've been here before, a ghostly imprint I feel in the marrow of my bones, very much like the stirring of my heart when I first met Maxwell at the race. One look into his stormy eyes and I was instantly captivated.

I still can't believe Maxwell apologized so publicly yesterday. The headlines today are all about him—his brave acknowledgment of his anxiety, the press clearly sensing they have a heroic figure on their hands. Any lingering doubts about our marriage have faded away—the articles painting a devoted husband utterly obsessed with his wife.

His public declaration of love, his plea for me to choose him.

He's letting me decide this time.

He heard me.

I'm so proud of him, because I know it isn't easy—braving the world and their scrutiny, facing his fears.

Putting it all out there...for me.

I heave out a sigh, relief mixing with heartache as I rub the phantom soreness in my chest. I miss him so much.

The girls asked me last night if I'd accept his apology, if I'd take him back. My immediate impulse was to say yes, to run to him and throw myself in his arms. But I needed to think things through, to let my emotions settle, because I knew if I were to give him back my heart and he shatters it, I'd never feel whole again.

Standing up, I walk to the edge of the roof and look down at the rose garden, the thorny bushes gnarly, the small, lifeless patch of soil still there at the edge.

I remember my dream, the desperation of running toward Silas or Maxwell, as their figures blur together, the crushing agony when I never reach him. And I realize I want to forgive him and repair our relationship, knowing that it won't be a smooth journey ahead with his fears and anxiety.

But if he can be brave about it and take my hand, then so can I.

Mind made up, I breathe in the earthy scent carried by the blistering wind—the unmistakable smell of damp earth and thawing snow, cloying decay mixing with emerging life. I turn around and take a step toward the winding staircase when my eyes snag on something.

An iron placard hammered on the bench, long rusted, but the delicate carving is very much clear.

My heart is buried here with you, my love, resting alongside you for eternity and beyond.

I'll forever roam the land, searching for you, aching for you.

Missing you.

A sharp pain shoots through me, and images of Maxwell sobbing at the gardens flood my vision again, followed by me laughing, dancing with him in the rose garden I haven't stepped foot in, and furtive whispers about Venice and Aristotle.

There's so much happiness and sadness. But these are dreams. They aren't real, right?

What's happening to me?

My fingers tremble as I trace each carefully carved word, feeling and seeing the devastating heartbreak of the man behind this message who left a piece of his soul here.

It's a surety I feel deep in my gut.

I open the locket around my neck and stare at the near identical words inscribed inside.

It can't be...can it?

My pulse hammers in my veins and thunder rumbles in the skies, the wind picking up in speed and ferociousness, and wetness drops onto the wrought iron placard.

My tears.

Belatedly, I realize I'm crying for some unknown reason. Every atom inside me yearns to find Maxwell because he'll be able to soothe the ache. He'll be able to heal my heart.

My fingers trail over the writing one last time when suddenly—

A brick loosens from a leg of the bench.

My breath freezes, my hands shaking as I pull out the brick, and feel around the hollow inside until my fingers touch something solid.

Pulling it out, I stare at the nondescript brown package wrapped in twine, the size of a book, and lightning snakes across the skies.

Please tell me this is what I think it is.

I carefully pull loose the twine and unwrap the parchment, finding a brown leather book carefully preserved, the edges worn and pages yellowed.

A few loose leaves of paper are tucked inside, but I ignore them for now. Gingerly, I flip to the first page, finding an entry in immaculate masculine script.

January 2, 1860, Wraithmoor Abbey

I saw your smile today and I can't fathom why you were happy given you were ironing dresses and jackets at five in the morning. I should have been asleep were it not for the restlessness I felt inside me when I woke up lonely in my bedroom at the crack of dawn.

The house was cold, the fire long extinguished in the fireplace. But your smile was arresting—a flame brightening the dark crevices inside my chest. For the first time, I felt warmth.

"Silas," I whisper, my hand clutching the journal tightly. His missing journal, the one from the 1860s, the decade Maxwell suspected something happened that changed the duke from the hopeful man to the severe aristocrat with sorrowful eyes in the portraits.

He's writing about her...his Emma. I'm sure of it.

I want to know what happened to them; to him *and* to her. I need to know. I can't explain the desperation rushing through my veins.

I flip to the next page when a distant noise interrupts me.

Freezing, I look toward the stairwell, hearing the heavy pounding of shoes against the steps. Quickly, I wrap the journal back in its packaging and put it in its hiding place before replacing the brick. I don't want anyone to discover this journal, not before I finish reading it.

I know there are answers in there for the riddle I've been trying to solve since I stepped foot into these halls and felt like I was coming home.

Smoothing out my gray wool dress, I hurry to the staircase to head off whoever is coming up here because I don't want anyone to disturb this sacred shrine. Somehow, I know Silas wouldn't want anyone here.

A familiar blond head of hair and startling green eyes greet me as I make a turn in the stairwell, a dozen steps away from the fourth-floor entrance in the east wing.

"Cole?" I whisper, a chill sweeping through me.

"Belle. You need to come with me now. There's no time." His eyes are bloodshot, the dark circles under his eyes even more pronounced than last time. He has a full beard on his face and looks nothing like the charismatic friend I used to know.

Danger. Something's off.

Fear rips into me as I try to skirt around him and get to the fourth floor, where I can call for help.

"W-What are you doing here, Cole? How did you know where I was? How did you even get in?"

He lets me pass as I hurry down the rest of the stairs. I feel the heat of his eyes on my back and every instinct inside me tells me to run, that I'm in danger.

"I don't have time to explain right now. I snuck in and saw you up here from the ground. It's a long story. But you need to come with me."

"No. I won't go anywhere with you until you tell me what's going on. Why did you leave me in front of the ER the other day? Why did you disappear?"

I whirl around and face him, watching his handsome face darken, his nostrils flaring in the dim light. Slowly, I back away, my hand reaching for the doorknob of the stairwell door behind me.

Stay calm, Belle. Ask questions, but don't antagonize him.

Twisting my lips into a shaky smile, I add, "I-I've been worried about you, Cole. You can tell me what's going on, right?"

His face softens, and he swallows, his Adam's apple bobbing in his throat.

I grab hold of the doorknob and twist.

Thank God it isn't locked.

"Oh Belle, I have so much to tell you. It's not what you think it is, trust me. I'm just trying—"

His eyes widen in shock and I open my mouth to ask him what he's not telling me when I feel it.

A tight clamp on my shoulder followed by a sharp pinch of a needle jamming into my neck.

Everything fades into darkness.

CHAPTER 54

SOMEONE'S POUNDING ON MY door. The ruckus jolts my attention away from the canvas in front of me. Ever since the accident, I've been desperate to finish the portrait I started of her. Now, as I wait for her answer, to see if she'll give me a second chance, painting this portrait has been the only thing keeping me sane.

The doorknob rattles and I turn off the music playing from the surround sound system in my suite within The Orchid. The room falls into an eerie silence and unease curls in my gut.

Before I reach the marble foyer, the front door flies open and in strides Elias, his normally calm face flashing with rare emotion, his hair in disarray. He's clutching a thin metal rod in his hand and some electrical device.

"Did you just pick open my door? What the fuck is going on?" This is all off brand for him, the silent, unruffled assassin.

He storms in. "It was either that or breaking it down, and I didn't think you'd appreciate that. We need to leave. My men have spotted Cole."

"What?"

"Cole Whelan. They saw him sneaking into the estate just now and they called me. They haven't seen him leave yet, so I presume he's still there."

"Fuck!" My blood runs cold. For the past few days, I'd ask Elias to put men outside the estate just in case someone attempts to hurt Belle again.

I grab my keys and rush out the door, with Elias right behind me. I dial Belle's number, but it goes directly to voicemail. I try again three more times, then call Morris and the rest of the staff. All direct to voice-mail.

Fuck. Shit. Shit. Shit. I call the on-site security team and no one picks up. They always pick up—someone must've taken them out.

"Can you get your men inside?" I ask.

Elias shakes his head. "Someone set the alarms and locked the place up after Cole snuck in. My men tried to get in, and unless we use brute force, it'd be impossible. Your place is like a fortress. Can you disarm the alarm remotely?"

"No. We were going to do an upgrade for remote connection but we never got around to doing it." Breaking into a sprint, I dart into the nearest stairwell and fly down the steps as quickly as I can. All I can think about is Belle and the attempts at her life.

Please be okay.

"Did you find out anything about him?" I huff out.

"My people found emails on his server that were copies of your dad's correspondence to Belle's father a year and a half ago. I think he knew Belle was a top candidate for your arrangement and purposely inserted himself at the shelter to get close to her."

"Fuuuck!" *What does this man have against me? Why is he targeting Belle?*

I burst into the underground parking structure moments later, hop into my car, with Elias sliding into the passenger seat.

Fear and regret rush through my mind as we race toward the estate. Belle's smile. Her calming touch. Her rambling when she's nervous. The beauty mark underneath her eye. Every small quirk that fascinates me and makes me fall harder for her with each passing day.

I can't lose her. Fuck, I can't lose her.

I'll strangle him to death with my bare hands before he takes her.

Minutes later, I dart through the doors of the mansion and disarm the external alarms. Chills race down my spine. Elias mutters something on his phone, no doubt to call in reinforcements, but I don't pay any attention.

I need to get to her.

"Belle!" I roar, but no one responds.

A vase lies shattered on the floor, crimson coating the pieces. Blood.

My heart riots in my chest.

"Cole fucking Whelan," I holler, "if you hurt *one hair* on her head, I'll kill you!"

I move quickly from room to room, stopping by my gun safe on the first floor and take out a Glock, load it, and disengage the safety. I've never liked violence. The thrill of the hunt is something Ryland enjoys much more than me, but I'm deadly with a weapon.

I just hope I don't need to use it tonight.

"Belle! Cole!"

Muffled voices come from the direction of the family gallery. Elias gives me a hand signal, a gun gripped tightly in his hand as he steps to the side and wrenches open the door.

Darting in, I point my gun into the room, finding Agnes bound and gagged on the floor, her eyes widening in fright as she angles her head toward the far corner. Mora and Melody lie there—Mora unconscious, her face pale, and Melody barely holding on, sweat plastering her forehead.

"What happened? Where's Belle?"

Melody raises a shaky hand, her breathing rapid, voice weak. "R-Rose garden. P-Please help her." Her eyes flutter shut, and she slumps on the floor.

I hurry to Agnes and free her from her restraints. "Call the police commissioner."

Dashing toward the back entrance, I realize Elias is nowhere to be seen. But I don't give a fuck about that now.

Rain pours from the dreary skies, the storm unleashing its fury as dark clouds blanket the atmosphere in gloom. My clothes quickly soak through as I run past the barren trees and skeletal branches at the entrance of the rose garden.

I breathe heavily, my exhales coming out in plumes of white before merging with the mist from the rain. I can barely see the path in front of me, but I know these grounds like the back of my hand and I move quickly, my gun pointed down as I walk deeper into the garden, staying close to the towering hedges, keeping my ears peeled for any unusual sounds.

"Stop, please! You don't need to do this."

Belle. She's still alive. Fuck, she sounds terrified.

I hasten my steps, my heart digging its way out of my chest, desperate to find her.

I can't lose her. Not again. I can't lose her again. Flashes of another rainy day barrel into my mind.

Blood. So much blood. Belle lying stiffly in my arms, her body broken as she clutched a letter in her grip.

Not again. Take me instead.

The thoughts make no sense, and yet they ring true. Nausea churns inside me and I turn a corner, keeping my back against the hedge.

Then I see them.

Belle, tied to a chair, her eyes terrified and pleading. She digs her shoes into the mud, an attempt to break free, but it's no use. The ropes bind her too tightly.

Cole paces in front of her, tugging his hair. He looks distraught. He shakes his head. "I didn't agree to this. I didn't."

Click.

I freeze. The cocking of a gun, a hardness pressing onto my back—the unmistakable imprint of a metal barrel, and then a familiar, raspy voice.

"Maxwell, I was wondering when you'd show up."

"No!" Belle screams when she sees me.

I slowly raise my hands, shock tearing through me at the voice I've heard my entire life. Someone I've always considered...*family.*

"Morris? What the *fuck* are you doing?"

CHAPTER 55

EVERY MUSCLE IN MY body pulses at his voice. Memories barrel into my mind. The butler wrapping me in a hug when I came back home from Mom's funeral, completely distraught. Him fixing me a hot toddy whenever I'd gotten sick. Him making sure I didn't forget to eat when I was obsessing over my latest artwork.

I don't understand.

My heart clatters inside my chest like a runaway train, the sudden betrayal searing me. I hold Belle's terrified gaze, which is welling with tears as she struggles against the ropes once more.

It's okay, I mouth, giving her a curt nod.

Everything will be okay as long as she's unharmed.

A calmness settles over me—it doesn't matter what happens tonight as long as she escapes. That's my only goal. The fear that has accompanied me throughout my life is now a beam of focused energy.

To do anything to get her out alive. I don't care what happens to me.

"Morris," I rasp, turning my body around, only to be met with a sharp jab of the gun at my back again.

"Don't you think about it, son. Drop your gun."

"No!" Belle cries. "Don't do it, Maxwell."

She turns toward Morris, her voice frantic. "You wanted me all along, right? You got me. Let him go. He treated you like his family!"

"It's okay, Belle," I reply, keeping my voice calm even though my pulse is rioting and my breathing is uneven. Raising my hands, I slowly set the gun to the wet soil and stand back up.

"What do you want with us, Morris?"

Morris chuckles, the sound of his grandfatherly laughter now seeming sinister; so twisted I wonder how I had missed the darkness threaded in his voice all along. How could I have been so blind?

"What I want, you can't give, Maxwell. Because you can't bring back the dead!" he roars and gives me a surprisingly hard shove for an old man, sending me staggering a few steps toward Belle.

"Go. Tie up his hands and feet," he hollers at Cole.

"Fuck. Fuck. Fuck," Cole mutters under his breath. "Y-You need to stop. This is not what we agreed to."

"Shut up and do it before I put a bullet in between your eyes!"

Cole scrambles toward me, his hands shaking as he twists my arms behind my back and secures a rope tightly around my wrist. He presses something sharp into my palm. Then he fastens the rope around my ankles.

His eyes are frantic and guilt-ridden as they briefly meet mine, and he tugs at his hair and steps away.

"It's okay, Belle," I whisper, standing next to her, angling my body in front of her. "It's okay. Everything will be okay."

I'll die before letting anything happen to you.

"Maxwell," she whispers, "I'm so scared. He tranquilized me earlier and when I came to, I was already tied up here in the garden. I don't know what he wants."

Her trembling voice is a gut punch to my stomach and fury churns inside me. *How dare he hurt my wife? How could he betray us after my family treated him like one of our own?*

I knot my fists around the object Cole gave me. It's a shard from the broken porcelain vase I found earlier. "I'm here, little muse. Nothing will happen to you."

Turning back to Morris, I take in the old man clearly for the first time. The rain plasters his hair to his face and he holds the pistol tightly in his grip. He saunters toward us. *He isn't limping.*

Something must've given away my disbelief, and he chuckles, shaking his head. "All these years, you've never thought to look beyond the damn curse for the deaths. Never suspected maybe someone was behind all of this...like a sad, limping butler. You Andersons are *pathetic*."

"Deaths?" My blood freezes. The medical examiner's findings. He couldn't possibly mean—

Morris laughs. There's a madness in those normally calm eyes, his lips twisting in a snarl. "Your grandmother, your mom..."

He cocks his brow, and adds, "Sydney."

Belle gasps in horror. Morris's confirmation is a blow to my stomach. Of course, it had to be an inside job. I figured that was the case, but I'd never have thought it would be the man who was like a grandfather to me.

"W-Why?" I whisper.

Cole darts toward the old man. He bellows, "You killed Sydney? It was you all along? You fucking bastard! You led me to believe—"

Morris shoots him in the chest. Belle screams as I flinch, stepping in front of her, not wanting her to see this. Cole crumbles to the ground like a sack of potatoes, blood pouring out of his wound.

Cole groans, his shirt quickly darkening as he clutches his chest and wheezes, "I t-trusted you."

"No, you were desperate, and I gave you an in." Morris scoffs before turning to me. "Your family is cursed all right, but those deaths aren't supernatural. I killed them."

"But w-why? Why would you do this? We've treated you like family. We've done nothing to you. We've—"

"You've done *nothing* to me?" he yells and a flash of lightning flashes in the skies, illuminating the twisted darkness hiding inside him all along.

"I lost *everyone* because of your family!"

I shake my head. "No. You're wrong. Your sister died and your parents were depressed and killed themselves. We had nothing to do with it."

"She died because of your grandfather!"

His words ring out loudly in the barren garden and a brisk gale kicks up, sending torrents of rainwater across our bodies.

"My family gave everything to yours since my grandfather's generation. We lived, breathed, and died in service of the great Anderson family," he sneers. "And what did we get in return? Only death."

He paces in front of me and Cole groans on the ground, his eyes darting to my face, reminding me of the shard in my palm. Quickly, I work on the rope—the fucking bastard got in way over his head and is now trying to do the right thing.

Too late, you fucker.

Morris rambles, his tall frame shaking. "Your grandfather murdered my sister!"

What? I shake my head. "No. Your sister was killed in Central Park. It was a robbery; the murderer is still at large. That's what you told me before."

He scoffs. "Do you know why she was at Central Park that night? I bet you didn't know. Your *grandfather* was vile. He used her and broke her heart. He told her he didn't love her. My sweet sister was devastated when your grandfather turned her down and she ran away from the estate. He should've pursued her—I begged him to go after her. He knew it was dangerous for a woman to be out by herself at night. But he did nothing, and because of that, I lost my sister."

Morris steps toward me, his eyes welling with unshed tears. "I'm seventy-five years old, but my life ended at fifteen when Ruth died. My parents were heartbroken after her death and killed themselves shortly afterward. And do you know what your grandfather did?"

He throws his head back and laughs, the sound brittle. "He 'kept me on' like I should be grateful for him being so callous, for him murdering my entire family. Then he had the audacity to fall in love with another woman."

"Oh my God, he's crazy," Belle whispers behind me. Her breathing catches and I work the porcelain shard harder in my palm, feeling it cut into the thick rope.

"How could he fall in love and live a happy life when my sister never got a chance to do the same? How could your grandfather live his life as if my world didn't end? While he wasn't the one to plunge the knife into my sister's chest, he might as well have been the one to do it!" Morris blows out a deep breath, his nostrils flaring. "Do you know she was defiled before she was gutted?"

His gun shakes, the barrel aimed at my chest. "I identified her body because my parents couldn't bring themselves to go to the morgue. I saw all the cuts and bruises on her face and body as the coroner told me what happened. How she was battered, used in the worst ways and laid on the ground for *two hours* before she bled to death."

Morris pants, clearly out of breath from his unhinged tirade, his pale face now flushed. "Two hours, all alone! So no, I couldn't let your grandfather live his merry life with his wife, a woman he 'loved.' And conveniently, your family is rumored to be cursed."

He barks out another crazy laugh before his voice takes on a snotty tone. "'Should the firstborn son fall in love, the woman he loves dies.' I couldn't have asked for a better alibi for everything. A syringe filled with air took care of your grandmother—a random heart attack, out of the blue. It took everything in me not to celebrate when your grandfather almost drowned himself in his sorrows, blaming the curse for everything."

Shock rears through me at the callousness in his tone, as if he were talking about the weather and not about murder.

"But what about Granduncle Nathaniel?" I need to buy myself more time. I feel the rope giving, even as my fingers burn and a warm stickiness runs down my fingertips. Fuck, I must've pricked myself.

"That was just fate helping me out. You Andersons are so pathetically gullible. When Nathaniel's family died in that tragic, accidental drowning, you all just heaped it onto the curse, giving it more oxygen, letting it suck out all the joy in your house."

"But if you had issues with my grandfather, you already got your revenge. Why did you go after Mom, Sydney, and," I swallow, moving closer to my wife who is still sniffling behind me, "Belle?"

Belle whimpers and I step closer. My legs graze hers to tell her I'm here with her every step of the way, that I wouldn't let her go through this alone.

Morris snarls before answering, "My family didn't have descendants. My sister didn't get to marry, have children, have grandchildren. Why should your family get to do what was taken away from mine?"

Curling his lips in a sneer, he steps toward us and bares his teeth. "Sixty years! I've spent *sixty years* slaving away for your pathetic family when all I want to do is to kill each one of you. Every year when I visit my parents' and sister's graves, I vow to them I'll avenge their deaths. And I tormented you all, didn't I?"

He laughs. "Maybe your family *is* cursed after all, and I'm its messenger. After all, the firstborn Anderson is *never* supposed to fall in love. That's what the rumors said, right? So, when Linus stupidly did the same with Julianna after a decade of a 'cordial' relationship at best, I killed her, because your family should suffer like mine did. A swift push down the stairs, a few marbles scattered on the staircase, and no one suspected anything."

I clench my teeth, my blood boiling me from the inside at the nonchalance in his tone as he described how he murdered my mom, the wonderful woman who taught us to be kind, to appreciate life, the woman who left a permanent hole in our hearts.

"And Sydney?" I seethe. I struggle harder against my binds. *I'm going to kill this motherfucker with my bare hands.*

"Rohypnol and ketamine in her drink during dinner, and you did the rest, boy, when you argued with her afterward and left her alone. Another little push and she slipped right over the railing. Didn't even scream. And don't get me started on the useless cops. No one wants to piss off the mighty Anderson family, now do they? When everyone claimed it was an accident and she clearly drowned, no one cared to dig deeper."

He throws his head back and cracks open a satisfied smile, his eyes glazing over, spittle flying out of his mouth. It's like he's letting out all the poison he has bottled up inside him for all these years. "You and your family think you're all powerful, the mighty, impeccable Anderson family, but who ended up besting you all and driving each generation of you insane with fear...a curse, ha! I did it! And it's not enough... It'll never be enough!"

My nostrils flare, the fury obliterating my sanity.

He killed them all. He terrorized us all these years. He killed Sydney, an innocent girl who didn't even really know what love was. He killed Mom, Grandma, dooming our family into perpetual grief.

He let Rex, a six-year-old, take the fall for Mom's death.

The cold-blooded murderer. The true monster in our family.

I'm going to kill him before the night is over. But first, I need to save Belle.

"You've killed three people already. Your sister and family will never come back. Three lives for three lives. Just let Belle go. She didn't do anything. She's only been an Anderson for less than a year. Let her go. Take me instead. I'm the true Anderson. The eldest son."

"No!" Belle cries. "Maxwell, stop it. Don't do this."

Morris chuckles and shakes his head. The madness dims briefly in his eyes and he has the gall to look remorseful.

He looks at Belle and murmurs, "Belle, I've always liked you. You were kind to all of us, a joy to be around. You reminded me of Ruth. Her heart was pure, just like yours. But then, you had to fall in love with *him*."

He glares at me. "I saw you two cavorting late at night in the kitchen." His attention returns to Belle. "I tried warning you away, but you just didn't listen."

Belle gasps. "The strange sounds in the mansion. The masked man on the premises—"

"Your fall at BSUA. Cole here," he motions to the now unconscious man, "poured oil over the steps and gave you a small push. He thought you'd just tumble and hurt yourself a little. He convinced himself he was saving you in the long run because you'd leave Maxwell or he'd leave you because of the curse. That fool."

Morris *tsks*, kicking Cole's unmoving body with his foot. "He worked with me because, like me, his family was devastated when Sydney died. He was convinced Sydney was killed by dear Maxwell because she sent him a text message the night she died. She told him she cheated on Maxwell and she was going to confess."

Belle whispers, "Everything was premeditated—you and Cole. *Everything*." I can hear the shock and pain in her voice, the betrayal from two people she cared about.

"I approached him after I saw Maxwell and him arguing at the wedding reception. It was obvious there was something more to it than jealousy. Cole here, apparently, had revenge plans all along. He somehow found out you were on the shortlist as the candidate for the future Mrs. Anderson role and was hoping to use you to get close to Maxwell, but then the idiot fell in love with you instead."

Morris shakes his head. "He wanted to save you from Maxwell. He convinced himself he was doing the right thing, the pathetic fool. All I had to do was convince him we had the same goals, and he happily followed my plans instead—after all, I knew the Andersons the best."

He sighs and adds, "Sometimes, dear Belle, life is unfair. I would know that. You were in the wrong place, at the wrong time, loved by the wrong person."

Keeping the barrel of his gun steady, he turns toward me, his eyes taking on a dangerous glint. "I'm an old man. I'm not long for this earth. But I can't let the curse grow cold now, can I? You doomed Belle to death, son, by announcing your love to the world. You should've just left her alone...and maybe I would've spared her. After all, I'd grown rather fond of her myself."

Morris sneaks a glance behind me, no doubt looking at Belle. He says, "I wanted to let you go, my dear...that's why I never gave you a high dose of cyanide. I was hoping you'd feel sick enough to realize something was wrong, to believe the curse was real. But you were foolish...drunk on love. Stubborn to a fault."

The rope snaps in my hand, the broken shard finally slicing through the thick twine. Morris's frame stiffens, a calm lethality in his gaze as he clearly makes a decision.

For a moment, the world freezes around me—my chest stilling mid-inhale, the pouring rain battering my skin.

In this split millisecond, I know what he's going to do next, and I move automatically, acting only by impulse, by a surge of protectiveness toward the woman behind me.

The love of my life.

The world spins again, and Morris's arm moves, his aim shifting from my chest to the person behind me.

A thundering boom rings in the air, and I throw myself over Belle, my pulse roaring in my ears.

I hear her scream and feel a sharp burning impact on my back.

My breath rips from my lungs, and my vision blackens.

I've been shot.

CHAPTER 56

Belle

"Belle," Maxwell rasps as he collapses on top of me.

Another boom rings out and I scream, twisting my body on the chair and pushing us to the wet ground, the impact disorienting. The chair cracks and snaps, my bindings loosening, and I look up, finding Morris freezing in shock, a dark red stain blooming on his chest before he keels over.

Elias steps into sight from the hedges and lowers his gun, a few men following him. His eyes are cold with fury. "Fuck, I couldn't get a clear shot before."

He steps over Morris and aims his gun at his forehead. I squeeze my eyes shut as another shot rings out, followed by the loud cries of the crows nearby.

I crawl on top of Maxwell, who's lying so still on the ground, his chest is barely moving.

He took a bullet meant for me. He *sacrificed* his life for me.

"*Please*, Maxwell. Please don't die on me." Tears stream down my face as I lean over him, gasping when I see the blood pooling on the soil beneath him, crimson rivers of red.

"Here, press this on the wound. Keep the pressure firm. I'm going to get help." Elias rips the hem of his shirt and shoves it to me before darting off into the night, his men following him.

Another burst of lightning splinters across the skies, bathing the darkness in a brief flash of light, illuminating the sea of blood on the ground. The cry of thunder follows, mournful and filled with wrath as I press harder on the wound on his back.

The cloth soaks in a matter of seconds. *I can't stop the bleeding.* Tears stream down my face. I'm hit with the same dark dream I've had over the last few months—the bloody tendrils spreading on Silas's chest, his mournful sobs echoing in the air.

Dreams or visions, past or present, they all cease to make sense or matter.

Nothing matters except this man in front of me, who loves me so much, he threw himself in front of a bullet for me.

"Maxwell, please stay awake. For me, please. Stay with me," I sob, the agony in my chest eviscerating.

Maxwell's breathing is ragged, the color slowly leaching from his face, his gaze murky as his lips part. He reaches for my hand. He's so cold, so clammy, and I bury my face into his neck, my fingers clutching his tightly.

"I-I've always hated the r-rain," he whispers as the storm rages around us, a mist sweeping into the garden, cloaking the ground in a mystic fog. "It feels sad, haunting, like I can't breathe and the skies are crying with me."

He coughs and I shush him. "You'll be fine. Elias is getting help. You'll be okay. I'm here, Maxwell. I'm here with you always," I whisper.

I tilt my head up and look into his startling eyes. The intense pools of gray and charcoal, brimming with passion, with love, with heartache and pain. The very eyes that drew me to him that first night, the feeling of long-lost souls reuniting.

Kismet. Fated. Soulmates.

The light burning behind these beautiful eyes is fading fast and I shake my head, gripping his hand as sob after sob tears from my throat. *I can't lose him. Not again, not after he just found me.* The thoughts are scattered, chaotic, more clues to the riddle I still don't have the answer to.

But I don't care. All I know is, my Silas, *my Maxwell* found me, and my soul will forever be bereft if he leaves me again.

"I never knew why the rain made me feel this way," he whispers, his free hand trembling as he reaches for my face.

Gasping, I lean into his caress, my eyes fluttering close as he presses me toward him and softly kisses my forehead. An electric frisson flows through my body at his kiss, much like our first kiss that night at the pier, when I felt his heartbeat beating against mine.

"Perhaps I've lost you once before in the rain and ever since then, I've been wandering, lost, searching for you," he rasps in my ear. Those words sound so familiar, but I can't think straight.

His breathing weakens with each passing second. He murmurs, "But now I've found you again, my Belle. I'm no longer sad in the rain anymore. I'm complete."

I shake my head, tears blurring my vision. A scything agony radiates from my chest as I kiss the back of his icy hand before linking his long fingers with mine.

He's saying goodbye.

"You listen to me, you insane man. You aren't allowed to leave me, you hear me? You told me you'd let me make a choice this time. You promised me! You can't take that away from me!"

He lets out a rough chuckle, his pale lips twisting in a pained smile. "I'm s-sorry for not keeping my promise."

Maxwell's chest spasms and he coughs some more. This time, blood spews from his lips and drips down his chin. "D-Don't grieve for me, my little muse. You've given my life meaning. The c-colors are incandescent in my world ever since I met you. You are the streak of red in my atro-virens."

"No, no, no. You are *my* streak of red and stop talking like this! Because you're going to get better. Then I'll be *so mad* at you for doing this to me... for saving...saving—" The words are stuck in my throat and I clutch him tighter against me.

Moisture pools in his eyes as he strains a pained smile. He whispers, "Live. Bloom in the sun. Feel me in its warmth and I'll be waiting for you in the rain."

"No! Elias is getting help. You'll be okay. Fate didn't put us together just to tear us apart again! Don't you dare give up on me, Maxwell Angus Silas Anderson. Don't you fucking dare!"

He swallows and coughs and I feel more wetness seeping between my fingers, but I don't look down. I know it's his essence coating my hands, the bloody rivulets I can't seem to stop, no matter how hard I'm pressing on his wound. I can't stare at anything but his beautiful eyes and face in these moments I have with him.

Moments I'm not sure if I'll ever have any more.

"I-I love you, Belle. So, so much," he whispers, his eyes fluttering shut.

"No! Open your eyes, Maxwell, stay with me. *Please,* I can't do this without you," I cry, my hand caressing his face. "Please don't let me do life without you."

He blinks, the motion seeming taxing for him. His gaze is unfocused as he stares at me. It's like he has one foot in the ether and I'm the one keeping him tethered to this world.

And I won't let go.

"I love you most ardently and fervently," he rasps, his deep voice hoarse and filled with passion. "Yours forever...this lifetime and all the lifetimes thereafter."

The words are haunting, echoes of the same words Silas wrote to his Emma in my dream. I feel every single one of them in my soul. I can't compute what this all means. All I know is my heart had a hole in it ever since I could remember, a chasm only filled when I met him, a tapestry wrinkled and torn in the ages, only recently mended.

"Maxwell, I love you, so, so much. God, so much," I sob as I rain kisses on his face, my chest hollowing, my nose inhaling his sweet scent of amber and sandalwood, now tinged with the metallic smell of his blood. *"Please, don't leave me."*

"Perhaps in another life, we'll go to Venice, and we can paint the canals together," he whispers, his voice slurred. Delirious. "Hope is the dream of a waking man...and I-I'll see you in your dreams..."

His eyes roll back and close, his grip on my hand slowly loosening. I hear the shrill cries of sirens in the distance; the thundering sounds of footsteps pounding on wet soil as lightning coils against the dark skies again, the storm rioting around us, wrapping us in a tearful embrace.

"Maxwell!" I scream and cry in his chest.

Not again, please. I huddle him close to me, rocking his limp body in my arms. If there is a God, please let him stay with me this time.

Please.

CHAPTER 57

"We've packed up the rest of his things, Mrs. Anderson. The only item left is his art in the living room. Your housekeeper is en route with a carrying case for it."

I nod to the tall brunette, one of the staff members for the private suites here in The Orchid, and she closes the door softly behind her.

My chest is heavy as I amble into the living room of the suite Maxwell was staying in after he moved out of the estate. The drapes are drawn shut and only a sliver of daylight shows through from the gap.

Tears prickle my eyes when I see his leather jacket on the couch—the same one I kept from that night at the race, and brought back to the mansion when I moved in. With trembling hands, I bring it up to my nose and take a sniff of his scent.

"Maxwell," I whisper, burying my face into the jacket before clutching it to my chest.

I wish he were here with me, that he would wrap his arms around me and spin me around to the strains of Puccini's arias. Then, I'd cook for him, knowing he'd make fun of me before nudging me out of the way to whip up something far more delicious than the meals at fancy restaurants, because he made it with love.

I'd gladly spend my days hiding away with him in the estate, painting, sketching, reading, and they'd be the happiest days of my life because he'd be there with me, and I'd get to be the luckiest woman alive to love him.

I have a feeling I've loved him for a long, long time, and will continue to love him for the years to come.

He's been in a coma for the past week and the doctors don't know if he'll wake up. They said he not only suffered damage to his internal organs from the gunshot wound but also lost a lot of blood, and his brain was deprived of oxygen for too long when he coded in the ambulance on the way to the hospital.

I wouldn't have left his side if it weren't for the staff here contacting me, asking me if I'd like to keep his things here or move them back to the estate. I wanted to see where he lived these last days before the incident, to breathe the air he breathed, to touch the surfaces his fingers grazed.

A sob lodges in my throat as I drape his jacket over my shoulders, needing to surround myself with him as my soul feels bereft and lonely, the empty chasm inside me glaringly apparent.

But I won't give up on him. On us. Not when I've finally found him again.

My dreams have been a myriad of strange visions, echoes of what feel like memories that are so vivid, so true. I feel splintering heartache in my chest when I wake up. Some dreams are of Silas, the duke, his face brimming with joy, dimples flashing, as he twirls me around in the gardens at night before hauling me close and pressing kisses on my skin.

Kisses that felt like my Maxwell.

Other dreams are scattered memories from happier days when Maxwell was painting in his studio.

His brows furrowed as if displeased at his work, until his concentration broke and he looked up, seeing me staring at him. His grim face brightened, his brow cocking up arrogantly as he smirked.

The dimple on his cheek, identical to the one on his ancestor's face, the one I'd seen in my dreams even though I'd never seen it rendered in any of the paintings in the house.

Maxwell would beckon me to him and pat on his lap. "Sit, little muse. Maybe all I need is some inspiration to get through this artistic block."

He dipped his nose to my neck and sniffed and I giggled, the ticklish sensations sending heat to my core.

"Maxwell!" I swatted him away.

"Hmm?" He kissed a tender spot under my ear, his hand inching underneath my sweater before closing over my breast and tweaking the hard nipple. "Yes, little muse? I'm feeling rather inspired right now."

"Maxwell," I moaned, my head lulling to the side as he bit the tendered flesh of my neck before carrying me back to the bedroom, all work and art forgotten.

We were so happy. The clandestine moments in the Elysium, the whispered words of love and fleeting touches as we passed each other in the halls long before he said he loved me, because he later told me he didn't want the curse to hear us.

Perhaps Morris was the villain who set everything in motion. Perhaps there was a more nefarious force behind his actions, the mysterious curse that had tortured this family for generations.

It doesn't matter anymore. The result is still the same.

We're still torn apart, two souls standing on opposite sides of the abyss, hovering between life and death.

"You'll come back to me," I whisper to the darkness and clutch his leather jacket closer, taking another whiff of his fading scent.

I'll never give up on you. I'll be strong enough for both of us.

My fingers skim the plush couch as I walk past the Tiffany floor lamp toward the easel facing the windows. A dried-up paint palate lies on a side table, dirty brushes strewn on top of it, clearly in haste when he dashed out the door after Elias found him.

Slowly, I draw open the drapes and approach the canvas, the mysterious project I'd seen him working on but he'd never shown me when I'd asked before.

My breath catches at what I see, and a fresh wave of agony pierces my chest.

It's a portrait of me, with the rose garden as the backdrop. Unlike his painting of Lake Superior, with its harsh strokes and passionate sweeps of dark and moody colors, befitting of the turmoil and hopelessness he felt when he was there, this painting is imbued with light and hope.

I'm smiling, my eyes crinkling in the corners, the tawny greens vibrant like fresh blooms in spring. My face is tipped up toward the sun, the warmth of the golden rays seeming so real, I can almost feel them on my skin. He's captured every part of me in meticulous detail, including the mole under my eye. My black hair billows in the wind, full of life, and I appear to be laughing, smiling at the artist...at him, the roses in full bloom behind me.

Every tender stroke whispers of his abiding love. The brush marks a tender caress on my skin, like he's pouring his happiness and adoration into this canvas.

It's his love letter to me in his own language.

A language only I can understand. A language only I can feel. His answer to the question posed in his austere painting of Lake Superior, the painting that was missing a soul...missing hope. This one speaks of joy, of hope for the future, because we are together.

My eyes burn as my fingers hover over the art, careful not to touch it because I don't want to rub away any traces of him from the canvas.

"Maxwell, please come back to me," I whisper.

Ping.

I take out my phone from my pocket, noticing a text from an unknown number.

Unknown Number

> This is Liam Crenshaw, attorney for Cole Whelan. He's recovering in the hospital from his wound and I'm passing along a message from him.

A photo comes through—hastily scrawled writing on a slip of paper.

Belle,

I'm so sorry for hurting you, for lying to you, for the role I played in what happened to you and

Maxwell. There are no excuses for what I did, and I know nothing I say or do will make any difference.

But I just want to let you know I'm sorry. I hope Maxwell gets better and I wish you both nothing but happiness in the future.

Always,

Cole

Closing my eyes, I click off the phone, exhaustion weighing heavily on me. I don't have it in me to be angry at him or to hate him anymore. He was obviously led astray by Morris, who took advantage of Sydney's death and how it impacted Cole's family. I know he tried to right his wrong once he realized Morris was up to no good. He tried to take me away from the mansion—to save me multiple times without implicating himself. Regardless, his fate rests with the courts now.

Taking a deep breath, I swipe to my messages and type out my reply.

Belle

Please tell him I forgive him and I hope the answers have brought him and his family some closure. I don't want to talk to him or hear from him again, but I wish him peace.

Knock. Knock.

"Come in," I holler, and in strides Agnes, carrying a large black canvas case, followed by Taylor and Millie.

Agnes stands at the threshold, looking uncertain. Her fingers tightly clutch the handle of the case.

Maxwell and I've never finished our assessment of her performance in her probation period after he warned her about her attitude. And frankly, with everything that has gone on, I haven't given a crap about her.

Taylor and Millie stand next to me, their foreheads crinkled, clearly wondering the reason for this strange, silent standoff.

Finally, Agnes clears her throat. "I-I'm sorry, Ms. Belle."

"For?" I won't make this easy on her.

She swallows. "I've been unprofessional toward you and you didn't deserve my attitude. It was wrong of me...I see that now."

"How do I know you mean what you're saying when you've been anything but welcoming toward me? To be honest, I don't really want to talk about this with you right now." Not with everything going on. Not with Maxwell still in the hospital.

"Please!" she pleads. "It was misguided! I wanted to save you!"

My blood turns cold. *Please don't tell me she had anything to do with what happened.* Taylor stiffens next to me, clearly thinking the same thing.

"Were you a part of it, Agnes? Were you? Is this some ploy to get the inheritance? Because I swear if you were, I'll make you regret it and I—"

Agnes's eyes widen and she shakes her head vehemently. "No! Of course not! You might not see this, but I love the family. I watched Sir Maxwell and his siblings grow up."

Her voice chokes as her eyes glisten. "Ms. Juliana was one of my best friends when she was alive. She never treated me like staff. She never looked down at me for refusing to leave my gambler of a husband because I wasn't ready. She brought life to the estate...just like you."

My chest pinches at the sadness on her face, something that can't be faked.

She continues, "We all knew about the curse—the tree branch, the signs, the accidents—but Ms. Julianna didn't want to believe it. I couldn't say I blamed her," she looks up, her eyes pleading with me to understand, "by then she had fallen in love with her husband, who treated her like a queen."

Agnes shakes her head sadly. "But when she died, I lost a piece of me too—my best friend. And I blamed myself for not warning her, for not believing the curse and the signs. Of course, none of us suspected Morris was behind everything."

She steps forward, her fingers white-knuckled around the handle of the case. "Don't you see? When you arrived, I was hit with the strongest sense of déjà vu. I *knew* Sir Maxwell had feelings for you. I watched him grow up. That little boy didn't like to smile. He always seemed like he carried the weight of the world on his shoulders. But he smiled so much more these months, even when you two were fighting. There was a fire in his eyes I'd never seen before."

Her hand swipes the moisture pooling in her eyes. "I knew it was going to happen again. I was sure of it. And this time, I vowed to myself I wouldn't let anything happen. Not to Sir Maxwell. Not to you."

My heart pounds rapidly, listening to her ardent explanation. She was trying to save me. In her own twisted way?

"I now see that it was wrong of me to warn you away from the house. I thought—why would you listen to me, a stranger? Ms. Julianna and I were the best of friends, and she didn't listen to me. I knew I had to do something drastic this time—be cold toward you and chase you away. I was hoping you'd leave on your own and we wouldn't have to go through another tragedy. But I guess it didn't work." She shakes her head. "I still can't believe it was Morris...all these years, working side by side, I didn't know a thing."

A sob tears from my mouth, and I turn away. Millie hushes me, smoothing her hand over my back as I shake my head.

It's my fault. If I hadn't insisted Maxwell love me back, if I didn't ask him to fight for me, for us, would Morris have let us go? Would things still have turned out this way?

Agnes whispers, "Don't blame yourself, Ms. Belle. Perhaps everything is fated and we're all merely players in a game pre-planned for us. Sir Maxwell wouldn't want you to blame yourself. He loves you so much."

"Maxwell," I whisper, the hole in my chest feeling bigger than ever before.

Agnes sniffles. "Regardless of my intentions, I want to apologize. I shouldn't have treated you the way I did. Even if you don't keep me on, I just want to tell you the truth."

We stare at each other, united in the heaviness of sadness and slowly, I give her a nod, motioning to the canvas by the window.

A piece of him left for me.

"Please be careful," I whisper to her as her eyes widen in shock before she hustles over, getting to work and carefully wrapping up Maxwell's artwork.

My lips tremble and I turn to Millie, whose face crumbles as she wraps me in her arms.

"Oh Belle," she murmurs and I bury my face in her hair, tears slipping down my cheeks.

"I miss him, Millie," I sob, the pulverized pieces of my heart trying to flare back to life, but the effort is too painful. "God, I miss him so much."

"Let it out, Belle. We're here for you." I feel Taylor curling her arms around me, her hug light, but no less warm. Her voice is thick, like she has been crying too—the black-hearted ballerina has a warm, beating heart, hidden from everyone, but I know it's there.

"I don't know what to do," I whisper in our group hug as sobs wrack my body, the pain never-ending.

"One day at a time, Belle. One day at a time," Millie whispers, clutching me tightly. "Ryland, Grace, and the others are at the hospital, and they'll let us know if anything changes."

"You need to rest, Belle," Taylor murmurs when we disentangle ourselves from the hug. "You look like absolute shit. He won't recognize you when he wakes up." Her nose crinkles and lips twitch, like she's struggling not to cry.

"God, you suck at comforting people, Tay. But I love you anyway," I choke out before smiling, a rush of warmth flooding my insides.

My girls. My family. I'm not alone.

"Don't worry about me. I'm going to stay strong for him because I believe in him, in us." I sniffle and swallow the lump in my throat. "He'll come back to me. I know he will."

Just then, Taylor's phone rings, the shrill sound causing me to flinch.

She answers, her eyes widening as her mouth drops open.

"T-Thanks. I'll let her know."

She ends the call and stares at me.

"What? Tay, tell me." My heart races in my chest, the dying embers refusing to extinguish.

"It's Grace. H-He's awake."

CHAPTER 58

I keep having the same dream over and over again—Belle running through the gardens, the tall hedges hiding us from the rest of the world. Her eyes are dancing, her laughter a beautiful, tinkling sound I'll never get sick of hearing. Her hair floats behind her, like she's a fairy, imbuing my world with magic. The sunlight cascades over her features, bathing her in an otherworldly glow.

She squeals as I chase her and I laugh, my soul feeling light...like I can fly.

"Come and catch me, Maxwell!" She sticks out her tongue as she runs into the rose garden, the flowers in full bloom, the sweet scent toying with my senses. Her white sundress billows behind her.

Butterflies flit around the air and I feel so happy, so exhilarated.

But then the scene shifts.

Dark clouds sweep through the skies, blotting out the sun. The lush red blooms of the roses shrivel and melt, turning inky black as an icy gale hurls through the garden—aggressive and violent.

Belle is still laughing, seemingly oblivious to everything as panic takes root in my chest. Her dress turns dark gray, the hem dragging on the ground, gathering up muck and grime.

"Come catch me, Maxwell!"

But my feet are weighed down by cement blocks, and our distance grows. Desperation tears through me as I watch in horror the thorny bushes scratching her ivory skin, blood seeping out of the cuts, the droplets becoming macabre streams of art slithering down her body.

Then she crumbles in front of me, her body twisted and broken, and by the time I reach her, her beautiful tawny eyes are lifeless.

I'm too late.

My heart wrenches in pain as I collapse next to her when the first raindrops descend, the wind carrying the sound of her voice whispering, "Why didn't you find me, Silas?"

"My darling, sweet Emma." The words tumble out of my mouth.

Then the dreams will repeat themselves and each time, I'll begin my desperate chase again, trying to catch Belle before the weather turns, before disaster strikes.

To save her. To keep her with me. To find her once more.

"Come catch me, Maxwell," she cries as the skies turn sunny again.

My heart pounds rapidly inside my chest, the pain and heartbreak from moments ago not yet healed as desperation climbs up my spine and lodges itself in my throat.

She's running again, that same beautiful bright smile on her face.

Come back, Belle. Don't leave. Stay with me.

My feet give chase, my strides faster, adrenaline pulsing inside my veins.

Don't leave me.

The words echo in my mind, a desperate plea.

The skies turn black again, and I shake myself. *No. No. No. I can't do this again. I can't watch her die in front of me again. I can't—*

A sharp pain splinters inside my chest, an incessant beeping ringing in my ears.

Everything hurts. Everything fucking hurts.

A bright white light sears my eyes, adding to the splitting headache.

Pain, so much pain.

I knot my hands into fists.

"Did you see that?" the gale whispers, the hammering in my brain growing in intensity. "He moved!"

"Doctor!"

The strange voices disappear and I'm thrust into my dream again. The cycle repeats itself.

Again. And again. And again.

Belle is dashing into the rose garden once more. *I need to stop her. I need to stop her before she gets hurt. I need to stop her before she leaves me.*

Opening my mouth, I scream, expecting no sounds to come out much like all the times before, but this time, I hear it.

"Belle, Belle…"

Hands are on my body, dragging me away from her. *No. Stop it. I need to get to her.*

"Maxwell! Oh my God. Maxwell! Can you hear me?"

Belle. Her sweet voice pulls me in like the bright beam from the lighthouse.

"Maxwell! I'm here. Open your eyes. I'm here!" A slender hand grips my arm. Her hand. Her warmth. Her sweet scent of lilies.

With a lot of effort, I blink once…then twice…watching the dream flicker on and off like a broken television, until it disappears, and all I can see…is her.

Her beautiful smile, her cheeks wet with tears. Those breathtaking tawny eyes. The eyes of nature in bloom—vibrant and full of life.

"My little muse," I whisper, my voice raspy, like it hasn't been used for a while. The rest of the unfamiliar room slowly comes into focus. "W-Why are you crying? Who the fuck do I have to kill?"

Her face crumbles as she throws herself on top of me, her hair tickling my neck as she sobs into my chest.

Pain stabs through me and I groan. "Everything fucking hurts. What happened?"

Belle gasps, springing back, her teary eyes widening in panic as she moves her hands down my body, like she's checking for injuries. "Oh my God, did I hurt you? I'm so, so, sorry! How are you feeling? Are you okay? Oh fuck, that's a stupid question, of course you're not okay, you got shot and nearly died. What am I talking—"

"Shhhhhh." I lift my finger to her lips.

Even that motion seems to require a lot of effort. Her words finally sift through the haze, and bits and pieces of the most terrifying night of my life flash through my mind. Cole shot. Belle tied up in the rose garden. The storm. Morris pointing a gun at me then turning his aim toward her.

Me throwing myself in front of her, a bullet piercing my back because I couldn't let her die *again*. *What?* The dreams and visions meld together, blurring reality and imagination, but everything feels achingly real.

I remember my fevered words of love as the rain soaked our bodies, promising her I'll take her to Venice to paint the canals as if that was a promise I made her before. *We talked about Venice before, but she never mentioned anything about painting the canals. But why does this feel so real?*

I shake myself. It doesn't matter if nothing makes sense. I've survived, and she's here, alive and well.

With me.

I get a second chance with her. My love. Crushing relief floods through me, and I let out a shaky exhale.

I cradle her face, my fingers trailing over her silky skin. "I love you so much, Belle. So, so much." *It feels so good to say this without fear now.*

Her lips tremble and she shakes her head. "You insane, infuriating man. Mr. Bad Influence. God, I love you so much!"

She presses her lips to mine and I savor the gentleness of her touch, the sweetness of her taste, even as pain threatens to unmoor me.

"I'm here. I'm never leaving," I whisper against her lips as she pulls away.

The rest of the room slowly comes into focus. I see the teary eyes of Grace and Taylor standing by the corner. Steven is rubbing a hand over his weary face. Ryland is next to the bed, his hands gripping the railing, his nostrils flaring as moisture gathers in his eyes. Millie beams next to him, her cheeks already wet with tears. Rex is clutching a trembling Lana, with Ethan rubbing comforting circles on her back.

Charles mutters "fuck" over and over under his breath. He's by the window, sitting next to Dad, who looks like he hasn't slept in ages.

My family. They're all here. For me.

"How the fuck did you guys get the hospital to let you in here all at once?"

"You fucker," Ryland chokes out, his lips twisting into a relieved smile. "You fucking shit."

"You briefly woke up, but then you fell unconscious again." Lana lifts her head up from Rex's chest. "I was so worried!"

"Son, how are you feeling?" Dad edges closer, his throat working. He's clearly emotional and trying to stay calm—the bearing of the eldest Anderson son.

"I'm sorry, Dad, everyone, for scaring you all."

"This is why I never want to be a hero," Rex mutters, wiping his hand under his suspiciously red eyes. "Give me booze and pussy, but you won't find me trying to save the day any fucking time soon."

Taylor scoffs, her voice thick. "No one would ever mistake you as a hero, Rex."

Rex throws her a sarcastic glare.

"Aren't you a ray of sunshine, Taylor?" Charles mutters under his breath.

"Why the fuck are you in here, anyway? It's not like you're family." Taylor scowls.

Something niggles my consciousness. "What happened to Morris? Melody, Mora, and Agnes? Cole? Elias?"

My siblings take turns filling me in—Morris died from the two gunshot wounds, but mysteriously, the casings and bullets were never found, so the police had nothing to go on and no one implicated Elias, who, after calling for an ambulance, disappeared with his crew before the authorities arrived. Morris left behind a letter on his bed, detailing how he blamed my entire family for the tragedy that had befallen his and a journal that read like an unhinged manifesto.

It was a detailed confession to the multiple murders in our family, including the various accidents he engineered—the busted pipe incident at the shelter, hiring a driver to scare Belle in SoHo, giving a sedative to the security team the night he took me, among the other seemingly unrelated events in the past.

Melody and Mora are recuperating at home after they were treated for acute cyanide poisoning. Elias has disappeared somewhere, but I'm not worried about him. He's not the king of the underworld for no reason. Cole is rotting in lock up, awaiting trial. That motherfucker. If he didn't try saving Belle, I'd find him and gut him myself as soon as I get out of this hospital.

"What about Agnes? Is she part of this? I heard a strange phone call the other day," I ask.

Dad answers, "That was her husband. Agnes called me two days ago to tender her resignation. She said she would've contacted Belle, but she was too ashamed. Apparently, she stole a few heirlooms from us over the years and her husband was blackmailing her for his gambling habits. Anyway, I told her I'd hold on to her resignation until you woke up. I didn't even want to think about it then."

Knock. Knock.

"Okay, I need to check on the patient. May I please ask you to step outside? Even though we appreciate your generous donation for a new research wing," a slim woman wearing glasses and a doctor's coat says to Dad. "You're all drawing attention. Not the good kind."

Linus chuckles and walks toward the door, motioning for everyone to follow him. "Come on, kids. Let the doctor do her work."

"I'm staying, is that okay?" Belle asks, her fingers intertwining with mine.

The doctor nods. "That's fine."

She introduces herself as Dr. Jones, the primary intensivist in charge of my care, and runs a series of tests to check my pupils, motor function, and breathing. She asks me if I remember my name, age, the year, what happened, and a host of other questions.

"Things look promising, Mr. Anderson. You're very lucky. We'll have a team of specialists come in later for a more thorough cardiovascular check and respiratory assessment. Neurology will be here as well to assess your memory and cognitive function."

Dr. Jones smiles and pats my arm. "We'll give you some pain medication. Try to get some rest. You've been through a lot." She looks at Belle, who is still gripping me tightly. "Your wife barely left your side this past week. Maybe you can convince her to go home to get some rest." She nods and leaves the room, shutting the door quietly behind her.

I turn to Belle, taking her in fully for the first time. Her hair is in a messy bun, her face too frail and pale, dark circles rimming her bloodshot eyes. She looks like she hasn't slept in days.

But she's still the most beautiful person I've ever seen.

Slowly, I lift our intertwined hands and press a soft kiss on the back of her hand, relishing the pink flush blooming on her face.

"My little muse. You must've been so worried."

She nods vigorously. "I don't know how I would've gone on if I lost you."

"You would've been fine. You're strong. Perfect. Just the way you are," I rasp.

Belle wets her lips and sniffles. "Don't you *ever* do that again!"

I want to laugh but the movement causes too much pain. "I don't plan on getting shot for fun."

She presses kiss after kiss on my face, careful not to press her weight on my body.

"Does this mean you forgive me, Belle? For being a colossal idiot? For leaving you?"

Her lips curve into a tremulous smile, and she wipes her eyes. "I'm *so* angry at you, Maxwell. God, I'm so, so, so—"

Her throat works, the words seeming stuck inside her. I cradle her cheek with my hand, the other hand sliding up her nape, fingers tangling in her silky tresses.

I pull her head down and press her forehead to mine, feeling her soft breaths, her tears wetting my cheeks, our noses touching as we wrap ourselves in this intimate silence.

The artist and his muse.

Two halves of a soul torn apart, lost for centuries, roaming the earth, endlessly searching for each other.

Every tragedy in my life. Every heartache. The restlessness I'd felt before.

Everything led me back to her.

"I'll spend the rest of my life making it up to you, Belle," I whisper against her lips. "And if one lifetime isn't enough. I'll find you again in the next life and continue."

Her breathing quickens, and she leans into my touch. "Never," she murmurs. "One lifetime is too short."

She lifts her head, her brilliant eyes pinning me in place, stealing my breath. Her eyes darken into a smooth amber—a trick of the light, I'm sure—and for a moment it seems like I've waited my entire life to stare into these eyes again.

Belle whispers, "I love you most ardently and fervently."

I shiver. She's saying the same words I said to her when I thought I was dying, words that sounded foreign and yet ring true to the depths of my core. Tears mist her eyes as she smiles, her breath hitching.

I rasp, my voice joining hers in a vow—one that is far more powerful than any curse or omen—one I have a feeling I've been waiting lifetimes to say to her ears.

"I'm yours forever, this lifetime and all the lifetimes thereafter."

CHAPTER 59

My body is on fire and I feel his heated presence behind me.

The scent of amber and sandalwood wafts to my nose and I rake in a greedy inhale as my eyes flutter open, slowly adjusting to the darkness of our bedroom. I'm lying on my side on our bed, my skin sensitive and tingling as he presses up against me.

Everything feels taut. Achy. My breasts swollen and my pussy throbbing.

He rains hot kisses on my neck, his teeth nipping at the sensitive flesh as his fingers circle my swollen clit before dipping into my wet pussy. I whimper, my body coming alive for him.

"My little muse, I've missed this," he rasps. He grinds his hard body behind me, his thick cock thrusting against the cleft of my ass. "Fuck, I've missed this. Every night when we were apart, I'd wish I were by your side. Touching you. Kissing you. Making love to you."

"Maxwell," I moan, arching against him, suddenly realizing I'm already naked. He must've taken off my nightgown during the night.

The thought that he's so desperate for me has wetness seeping out of my core.

"Yes, my love." He grabs my breasts, kneading the soft mounds, and I whimper. "Fuck, I love your body."

"But your wounds. Are you sure?"

He has only been home for a few days, and while the doctor has given him the all clear, I've been hesitant, afraid I'll somehow hurt him. The image of him bleeding in my arms is still traumatizing.

"Yes, I'm sure. I'll to go crazy if I wait any longer."

Growling, he bites my neck, his fingers plucking my nipples, tugging the distended ends before flicking the tips.

Sharp pleasure shoots to my clit and I let out a lusty moan.

"So sensitive for me." He moves his hand up my body and slides a finger into my mouth.

I swirl my tongue around it before biting the tip, my other hand reaching between us to grip his cock, and he hisses. He's so hot and hard in my hands. My core clenches, needing him inside me. I pump his shaft, my thumb rubbing over the slit, and he trembles, his hips snapping into my body.

"Fuck, oh shit," he groans, his breathing loud. "Belle, I'm feral for you."

He flips me over, so I'm flat on my back. My fingers trail greedily over his body, feeling every pulse of his corded muscles, every ridge of his scars decorating his body like the most beautiful art.

His eyes glint in the tiniest sliver of moonlight shining in between the gap of the curtains. His gaze is smoldering, intense. Dark orbs of fire.

Maxwell hovers above me, his hard cock notched between my legs, grinding tortuously against my clit with each pass. I thrash underneath him, needing more connection, needing him inside me, needing to feel him come apart in my arms.

I almost lost him. Forever.

The thought slips in as desperation floods my insides. I dig my nails into his back and he growls.

"Little muse." His voice is urgent, like he senses my changing mood.

"I need you. Inside me. Around me." The words tumble out on choked gasps.

"Always." A vow. A tremor in his voice.

With a deep stroke, he thrusts his hard cock into the hilt and I scream in pleasure.

Maxwell slams his lips on mine as he twines our fingers together, pinning my hands above my head. Our hearts surrender to each other as our bodies do the same. We move our mouths in unison, tongues tangling, twisting in desperation, two souls lost in the arid desert, finally finding an oasis with life-sustaining water.

My senses are overloaded with him. His touch. His scent. His taste. *More. I need more.*

I grip his fingers tightly as I writhe underneath him, meeting him stroke for stroke, yielding yet fighting back—our bodies dueling in a transcendent dance.

Maxwell grunts as he hammers inside me, like he can't get close enough. The slapping sounds of our bodies coming together echo in the room.

"Yes. More. Please. I need you. I need everything," I moan and bite his lip, needing to mark him as mine somehow.

"Belle," he hisses, his movements quickening. "You're my everything."

His cock burrows deep, far deeper than ever before, and I feel myself blooming underneath him, my heart, my body opening for him, my soulmate.

My nerve endings spark, electricity coursing through my body, gathering between my legs, sharpening to an unbearable point. I arch my body, clamping my legs tightly around his back, moving underneath him to the melody of us coming together.

"Come for me, Belle. Let me feel you strangle everything out of me," he growls, his breathing loud against my ear.

The sparks alight into fireworks and I tremble beneath him, my body hovering on the brink of nirvana.

"Let me come so deep inside you, you'll always have a part of me with you. Forever."

His words send me into a tailspin. The thought of him melding himself with me so we'll never part. The pleasure bursts and sweeps through my body.

"Maxwell!" I scream, splintering into a thousand pieces.

He swallows my cries with his lips, our kisses fevered, desperate, our bodies merging. Over and over again.

"Belle," he grunts. His movements turn stilted, his hands gripping mine so tightly, like he's afraid I'll let go.

Never.

"I love you always," he rasps and I feel him swell and lengthen. "Fuck. Always."

My pussy pulses again, a fresh wave of sparks gathering where we're joined. My eyes roll back from the new onslaught of pleasure, the intense connection overwhelming.

"I'm yours," I cry as another orgasm crests inside me.

"Mine. Fuck yes. And I'm yours." He lets out a guttural roar, and I feel the streams of his cum bathing my insides, the pleasure blinding.

Our bodies are slick with sweat, our labored breathing loud in the dark room and minutes pass by before we slowly come down from our high.

He braces himself over me, his cock still semi-hard inside my pussy. Gently, he brushes my damp hair away from my face, his tenderness almost making me cry.

"My Belle," he whispers and rests his forehead on mine, just like all the times he has done in the past, like my mere presence soothes him.

My heart flutters and pulses and I feel the answering call of his heart nestled inside his chest. This soulful, deep connection—something I can't begin to explain—makes me want to laugh and cry at the same time.

Happy that I've found it. Scared that I'll lose it.

"I'll always be with you," he says, like he can read my mind.

My lips wobble and I nod, the movement so small I'm afraid he'll miss it. But of course he doesn't.

"Always. After all, I've been waiting for you... You're my missing piece," he murmurs and presses another gentle kiss on my lips.

After cleaning us up, he curls me into his arms and we listen to the gentle hooting of owls and the familiar howling of the wind outside. But it's comforting now. No longer scary.

He chuckles under his breath.

"What?"

"You make me behave like a caveman sometimes." His breath tickles my ear. "I think we might've created a baby just now, don't you think?"

The thought of me swollen with his child makes me smile—any child will be lucky to have him as a dad. *But what if I can't—*

"Shhh... Quiet those noises in your head. It'll happen one way or another. We'll be great parents, as long as that's something you still want to do."

The ache subsides as I burrow myself into his chest. "You're so good to me."

"What? I'm no longer Mr. Bad Influence?"

I laugh. "My soulmate. That's who you are."

He sobers, and I can feel his heated gaze on me.

"My soulmate," he repeats, "and you're perfect, your beautiful pieces, your ragged edges, all fitting next to mine, just the way it's meant to be."

I close my eyes and relish the strong thumping of his heartbeat against my ear.

"I dreamed about you when I was in a coma." I hear the rumble of his voice from his chest. "I was chasing you in the rose garden, but you were always out of reach and when I finally caught up to you, you were broken in my arms and I was devastated."

He sighs. "It was strange. The dreams felt so real. Like memories. Like I'd lost you before. But that doesn't make any sense. I've never seen you in the rose garden before."

The hairs on the back of my neck rise. His dreams are echoing visions of mine.

He continues, "The dreams would repeat and each time I'd grow more desperate, needing to save you. And that wasn't all... I'd been having similar dreams most of my life. Always a faceless woman in the rose garden. But now, I can finally make out her features."

He turns to me and whispers, "She's you. Your face. Your smile. I'd dream of you painting under the night skies, my arms around your waist.

You'd tell me you wanted to go to Venice to paint the canals. We'd be dancing, kissing. It felt so real."

My heart thuds wildly in my chest. How can this be? How are we dreaming the same things?

"I had dreams about you too." I swallow the lump in my throat and tell him about the ones I've had—him in the rose garden sobbing, blood spreading on his chest, visions of us waltzing in the gardens. I tell him about the letter I dreamed Silas wrote to a woman he loved—how I knew Silas had dimples on his face, just like Maxwell.

"Then there was the locket. When I saw it on the display, it was closed. But I knew what was inside. Maxwell, I-I don't understand how I could've known."

His body stills, his muscles coiling in tension as he listens to the strange stories, things that sound ridiculous and fantastical to my mind even as I say the words aloud.

But they feel like the truth, not figments of my imagination.
How can that be?

"I've always thought my dreams of you are vivid because I have the overactive imagination of an artist." He rakes in a sharp inhale. "But what if *it isn't?*"

"What do you mean?" It can't be...what he's implying. My mind spins to the stories I've read as a child—stories about reincarnation and ghosts, souls finding each other life after life.

I think back to what Mora told me in the basement kitchen when I asked her if she believed in the curse. She said there were many things science couldn't explain. I brushed her off then, but now...now I'm not so sure.

"Have you heard of the story of *Meng Po*?" I ask Maxwell, referring to a Chinese legend I read about when I was younger—all part of the Saturday Chinese school curriculum Mom signed me up for. She said it was a way for me to know my heritage.

Maxwell shakes his head.

"Meng Po is a goddess who serves a special soup in *diyu*, the realm of the dead, to the souls who are ready to be reincarnated. The soup wipes the memory of those who drink it, so they'll be cleansed of the burdens of their past lives before they're reborn."

I let out a shaky breath, feeling ridiculous for telling this story and yet, there aren't any other explanations that make sense either. "According to a variation of the legend, Meng Po was actually Lady Meng Jiang, who found herself so overcome with grief from the death of her husband, she couldn't reincarnate. So, she dedicated herself to creating this potion that'd save others from suffering the same fate. It was said some souls evaded the soup or didn't drink enough, and they'd go into their next lives with their memories of the past partially intact."

Maxwell stays silent, but I hear his breath hitching.

"It's a legend, of course. It has to be fake, right? I don't know why I just thought of it—"

"My family believed in a curse for generations. Of course, it turned out Morris was behind this crap all along. But still, after everything that happened, I find myself open to ideas that we once thought were impossible."

Something niggles in the back of my mind. I bolt up and turn to him. "Maxwell, but what about the branch? Morris's journals mentioned nothing about him engineering that. And the other deaths in your family before your grandmother?" I can't believe I'm even suggesting this since I was the one who kept telling him in the past that the curse wasn't real.

But what if?

He freezes, and I feel the tension mounting in his muscles. My heart races inside me and I ask, "Don't you feel like there's a piece of a riddle we're missing? An answer that has been evading us this whole time?"

I think about the missing journal hidden in the rooftop garden, the one I haven't shown him yet. The strong feeling of home whenever I'm in his presence.

Maxwell blows out a ragged breath. "Shit. I never thought of that. I was just so relieved when I learned the deaths were from foul play, because that meant I could be with you."

I open my mouth to speak. "Maxwell, we can still—"

"Shh," he holds his hand up, "Let me finish." He cups my face and looks me in the eye, his gaze intense. "I promise you, I won't run away this time. We'll face our future together. We'll find the damn answers together. *If* there is a curse, we *will* break it together."

CHAPTER 60

"Here it is, Wraithmoor Antiquities," I murmur to Maxwell as we duck under the awning, away from the light morning drizzle, which carries with it the clean, earthy smell of spring. I called this morning to make sure Eleanor was here before visiting.

"What if we don't get answers about the curse, if there is still one? Or the dreams?"

"Belle," Maxwell laces my fingers with his, "even if coming here is a waste of time, I'm happy because you're by my side. That's all that matters." He swallows and continues, "I'm not running away anymore. We'll figure this out together."

Heat swirls inside me, and I smile at him. "You're right."

"Come on, let's not keep her waiting."

He pushes open the door and pulls me into the shop. The same spicy aroma of incense hits my nostrils, and the door closes behind us with a soft click.

Eleanor looks up from where she stands behind the counter, her eyes widening as she sharply inhales a breath.

Something has obviously surprised her, given the way she's clutching the pearls around her neck. When I made the appointment to visit her, I didn't tell her Maxwell was coming with me.

"Eleanor, this is my husband, Maxwell." I glance at him, finding his brows furrowed in apparent confusion. "This is Eleanor. Her family owns this antiquities shop."

The old lady recovers and clears her throat. She motions for us to take a seat on the other side of the counter.

"You're ready," she murmurs, her eyes knowing. "I knew you'd come back."

"Yes, well, here I am. Can you tell us everything you know about the Anderson family and the locket?" I release a stale breath. Maxwell gives me a squeeze in reassurance.

She stares at us for a beat, her eyes skating over Maxwell's face again before she shakes her head in apparent disbelief.

"It's uncanny. The resemblance."

Hairs rise on the back of my neck.

Her lips tip in a secretive smile. She pulls open a drawer and takes out a yellowed parchment, her frail hands shaking as she slowly unfolds it before setting it on the countertop.

I gasp.

It's a beautiful drawing of a man cradling a woman in the rain, shriveled roses in the background. The woman's face is half-hidden, but I see the silhouette, a birthmark under her eye. *She looks like me.*

What on earth? My pulse races in my ears.

The man's features are also carefully drawn.

It's Silas. A devastated Silas.

I turn and stare at my husband, finding his face ashen. He shakes his head. "M-My dream... How? Tell me what's going on."

Eleanor sighs as she stares at the artwork. "I don't have all the answers, because everything I know has been passed down through the generations. They're stories told by the fireplace...stories that seem too far-fetched to believe. But now..."

She stares at him and lets out a rough exhale.

"I told Mrs. Anderson my ancestors were caretakers of Wraithmoor Abbey before it burned down. But I didn't tell her that years later, they ended up working for the Anderson family."

Maxwell snaps his gaze at her, his eyes piercing.

"Yes, your family. One of my great-grandfathers was a groundskeeper when your family rebuilt on top of the land. It was said he witnessed a tragedy so devastating; the image haunted him for the rest of his life."

She points to the drawing. "He drew multiple iterations of this scene—the devastated duke who found out the love of his life departed the earth."

Eleanor motions to the locket burning on top of my chest. "The guilt ate at him, I think. I didn't tell you before, but the Eternal Devotion locket was found on the estate grounds. My great-grandfather suspected it belonged to the duke, but he wasn't sure, and the duke was a different man after the tragedy—angry, depressed, volatile. So, he never asked but held onto it. It was then the rumors of a curse started. My great-grandfather thought the curse was borne from heartbreak, but no one could be sure."

Her words echo in my mind as I open the jeweled locket and read the inscription. Could it have been Emma's all along? Was it because the locket was imbued with tragedy that I felt an aching sadness when I first saw it? I remember the portrait of Silas in the estate, devastation in his eyes.

More clues and still no answers.

"But he firmly believed the locket would return to its owner one day. That should an Anderson come and claim it, we were supposed to give it back. Years went by and no one came looking for it, so we put it up online, thinking maybe that'd draw some attention to it."

She looks at me, her lips tipped up in a small smile. "It felt fated when the locket was purchased by an Anderson from *the* Anderson family. And when you came in asking for it, you looked so troubled, and you resembled..." Her voice trails off and she swallows.

"Her. Emma," Maxwell murmurs, his eyes still snagged on the drawing.

I gasp and grab his forearm. "H-How did you know her name? I-I never told you... That was the name I saw in the letter in my dream. The same name on the envelope in the secret room."

Maxwell freezes, his face leached of color. "I-I don't know. I just know the name. Fuck. What the hell," he whispers. He turns to Eleanor. "Do you know why this is happening?"

Eleanor shakes her head. "I don't have those answers." She turns to me. "When you came in, I saw how much you wanted the necklace, but I couldn't give it to you. And when you told me your husband asked you to pick up a gift…and he was the Anderson who purchased it, I knew it was fated. The necklace returning to its rightful owners."

Rightful owners.

My breathing is rickety as a chill sweeps through me. I glance up, finding Maxwell with a similar haunted expression on his face.

"This makes no sense," I whisper in disbelief.

Eleanor coughs as she taps her finger on the glass. "My family has always believed in destiny, that we all have a role to play in this world. And I now know it is my role to give you back the necklace and to tell you the story behind it."

"How can this be?" The locket, the curse, the visions. *Everything.*

"My dear, I've lived a long life, and there are many things we don't understand in this world. But we all end up where we're supposed to be. Every story will have an ending, even one you don't see coming."

She sits down, a soft smile on her wrinkly face. "I felt a lightness in my soul when you took back the necklace. And I feel even more certain now as I look at the two of you. My job is complete."

A burning fire sweeps through me—a sudden revelation. I know where the answers are. Where they had always been, hiding in plain sight, waiting for us to discover them.

I turn to Maxwell. "I need to show you something."

CHAPTER 61

"Where are you taking me?" I ask.

Belle is gripping my hand tightly as we approach the door to the stairwell leading to the rooftop garden in the estate. Silas howls in the background, probably chasing some poor creature on the grounds far below.

The ride home from our visit with Eleanor was filled with tense silence, with Belle gnawing on her lip and staring out the windows, clearly deep in thought.

"You'll see. Things will make sense. I know it. It's been there all along, waiting for us."

She huffs out a breath as we climb the spiral staircase, our hurried footsteps echoing against the stone walls.

My blood pulses inside me, a strange tingling appearing in my hands. My breathing quickens—it feels like I'm about to have the floor pulled out from under me. It's the moment before everything changes.

I've always avoided going to the rooftop garden—it has always been a place that seems more haunted, mournful, colder than the rest of the house. But right now, the discomfort from before has disappeared, and in its place I feel a breathlessness.

Anticipation.

Moments later, we step into the abandoned garden, a breeze brushing over our skin—a gentle caress. The weeds have grown taller than when I was here many years ago, but for the most part, it looks exactly the same—frozen in time.

Belle pulls me toward the edge of the roof, to the side facing the rose garden, and my pulse echoes in my ears, the rickety click I hear when sitting on a rollercoaster, ascending to the peak before plummeting down. Silently, she tugs me to the bench that has been there for as long as I can remember, her eyes wild, a desperate gleam in them.

"Look," she whispers urgently, pointing to a rusty placard I've never noticed before, because I've made it my business to avoid this place.

My heart is buried here with you, my love resting alongside you for eternity and beyond.

I'll forever roam the land, searching for you, aching for you.

Missing you.

Scything agony tears through my chest, the impact robbing my breath like a gut punch. I clutch the bench for support as the world spins around me and an inexplicable wetness gathers in my eyes.

Heartbreak. Traumatizing heartbreak that has teased the edge of my consciousness for my entire life; a hole inside me I've always thought was attributed to my role in the curse. Except now, the veil is pierced, and the pain rushes through, so potent it's disorienting.

"W-What?" I whisper, staring at the words that seem so familiar, yet I could've sworn I'd never seen before.

Visions of me clutching Belle in the rose garden below, the storm raging around us—a sepia-tinged slideshow that's becoming clearer by the minute.

"I know. I know," she whispers back before touching a spot on the placard and I hear a quiet click before a brick pops out.

Still reeling from the onslaught of grief, I stare at Belle as she takes out the brick and sets it aside. Then she reaches inside and takes out a parcel wrapped in paper and twine.

"I found this the day I was taken. It's Silas's missing journal from the time period when everything started."

She looks up, her eyes filling with sadness as she carefully flips opens the leather-bound cover.

January 2, 1860, Wraithmoor Abbey

I saw your smile today and I can't fathom why you were happy given you were ironing dresses and jackets at five in the morning.

I can see it. Her smile. *Belle's* smile brightening a dreary morning as she hovers over a table, hard at work with a pile of laundry gathered on the side.

A lump forms in my throat. I'm well educated, multiple degrees under my belt. Other than the curse that my family believed in for good reason, I'm a believer in science.

But nothing can explain this. Nothing except for... I take a deep breath and keep reading.

January 13, 1860, Wraithmoor Abbey

You came into the library tonight, looking for a specific book for Louisa, a Herculean task I heard her give you when I walked past her rooms earlier today.

My wife was temperamental and would most likely change her mind tomorrow, and all of us would suffer from her wrath. You didn't notice me as you bustled around the bookshelves, humming under your breath even though I knew you had been working since before dawn and must be exhausted.

I should've announced my presence, but I found myself transfixed, wondering what the source of your happiness was, and if you could find it in you to share it with me.

Curiously, instead of picking up only one volume, you started piling more and more books on your hand. The stack balanced precariously high, all the while you wore that beautiful smile on your face, like you were excited at the worlds you would find in the pages within your arms.

And when I finally couldn't resist anymore, and asked, "Which one of those books are you most looking forward to?" You let out a very unladylike shriek and the books dropped to the floor with an unfortunate volume or two joining the kinder in the fireplace.

Your first words to me were, "You are a serial murderer of books, Your Grace!"

But your lips twitched, the humor clear in your eyes, and I felt a spark of happiness in my chest.

I think back to Austria, when I saw Belle making a mess of the cooking, the strange sensation I felt when I called her a serial murderer of vegetables. How it felt familiar when she gave me a mock glare, an impish smile on her face.

Then there was the feeling of my heart stirring when she sat in my car for the first time, like it was finally awake after lying dormant in my chest for so long.

My breathing grows ragged and I stare at Belle, watching her eyes well with moisture as she looks at the diary—pages and pages of love and devotion from a man I feel a distinct kinship with to a woman who feels very much like her.

The same tugging of the soul. The same warmth on a dreary day. The same spark of light in the gloomy skies.

Belle whispers, "Do you sense it? The answer to the riddle?" She wrenches her gaze away from the journal and stares at me, her familiar tawny eyes darkening. She places her hand on her chest, and murmurs, "This feeling inside me...it's like...coming home. Do you feel it?"

The answering beating in my heart thuds louder in my ears, a rioting warmth spreading to every atom in my body, chasing away the emptiness and cold I've always felt my entire life.

Until her.

A crinkled piece of paper falls out. I pick it up, finding the ink on the surface marred by water marks. I set down the diary and read.

My Beloved Silas,

If you read this, then I and our unborn child have already departed this world. I have risked everything and given you my all—my love, my dignity, my reputation, and being the foolish woman I am, if we could rewind time, I'm not sure I would have had the strength to stay away from you.

It details the heartbreak of a desperate woman who endured un-speakable tragedies, who felt she had no other way out. A woman who thought she was abandoned.

I clasp my hand over my mouth, my eyes burning, chest heavy with grief. The scene from my dreams. The sketch from Eleanor. The broken woman in my arms, the letter in her grasp.

It's this one. I'm sure of it.

I get to the bottom of the letter.

I wish for your family to learn not to give love so cruelly, so selfishly. To learn the meaning of true sacrifice. Should a firstborn son of the Anderson name fall in love and marry, the person of his affections shall fall to an untimely demise lest the lesson be learned.

Yours, faithful in death,

Emma

"The curse," Belle gasps. "Does this mean what I think it means? That it exists?"

My heart thuds loudly in my ears, blood rushing swiftly to my head. I reread the words, my mind sifting through all the journals and letters

I've read in the past about the curse. All the deaths in the family before grandmother. The unexplained branch shattering the windows. The ardent belief in the curse by every Anderson generation since Grandfather Silas's time.

I look at Belle, suddenly fearful for her life again, but then the last few sentences of the letter echo in my mind.

True sacrifice. Lesson be learned.

And I feel a crushing sense of relief. One that feels as true as my love for Belle.

I look at my beloved and murmur, "I don't think we'll ever know definitively, Belle. But...*if* there was a curse, we've broken it. I know it deep inside." I point to the last lines of the letter.

Belle's eyes rove over the sentences. She murmurs, "Of course. Sacrifice. Y-You almost died for me. Y-You—" She chokes up, unable to continue.

"Shhh..." I tilt her face up and find her eyes shining with tears. "Everything worked out the way it was supposed to."

A breeze blows by, the pages of the diary fluttering, catching our attention, until it lands on a page.

October 2, 1863, Wraithmoor Abbey

My Beloved Emma,

I'm standing at the spot where you took your last breath, wondering what you saw before you closed your eyes three years ago. The hopelessness you must have felt. The agonizing betrayal. The desperation.

This is the same place where my lungs took their last breath, the last breath that filled my body with life, not merely life-sustaining oxygen.

Because my life ended when your soul left this earth.

The only reason I haven't joined you in the great beyond is because of the devastation I would bring to my family, who are innocent in all of this.

Not a day passes by where I don't think of you—your smile, your kindness, your laughter, your dreams of seeing the world—visiting my ancestral home in England, painting the canals in Venice. You're the first face I see when I wake up in the morning, and the last image in my mind before darkness overtakes me at night. I'd dream of you—running in the garden, beckoning me to find you once more.

Do you still hate me? Do you still love me?

I will find you again, and again, and again. One day, I'll make every one of your dreams come true and wipe away all the tears you've shed for me. Wait for me.

Yours eternally,

Silas

"Venice," Belle whispers, "I've always been waiting to go there with the right person..." Her voice trails off.

Me. She's waiting for me. My mind spins. The answers, however unbelievable, are battering me from all directions. *They don't have to make sense for them to be true, Maxwell.*

Shaking, I turn the page, finding a crumbled letter tucked inside.

My Beloved Emma,

In the next few days, you will see me behave like the role I was born into, a coldhearted duke. But let me reassure you, the man you love is still here, still very much in love with you with all of his heart.

"Oh my God," Belle whispers. She's shaking like a leaf next to me. "This letter..."

"Belle," I rasp, emotions clogging my throat. The letter, the dreams, the incomplete sketch by Silas in the gallery, the locket—all pieces of a tragedy from centuries ago.

A tragedy that kick-started everything.

"This was the letter I saw in my dream," Belle murmurs, tears flowing down her cheeks. She shakes her head. "But it wasn't a dream, was it?"

I don't know how to answer her. All I can do is to hold her tightly to me as we finish reading the letter.

We will escape and start a new life together. We will be free. While I won't have my wealth and influence, I know my life will be far richer because we'll be together. Bear with me and forgive me for the hurt I'm about to cause you.

I love you most ardently and fervently.

Wait for me.

Yours forever, this lifetime and all the lifetimes thereafter.

Silas

29th of September, 1860

"The curse... This is how it all started. But she never knew he didn't abandon her." Her eyes widen and she whispers, "I-I don't know what's happening, b-but I heard him in my dream. She never got the letter because the duchess took it. She wouldn't have killed herself if she'd known. She d-died thinking he didn't love her anymore. She never found out!" Belle cries, her face mottled, clearly overcome with emotions.

I pull her to me and wrap her in my arms, my hands smoothing over her back as she trembles in my embrace.

"Belle," my voice is thick and hoarse, "I think she knew. Maybe much, much later...but *she knew*." Perhaps Emma knew all those years ago when her soul lingered behind, looking after the man she loved, after she took her last breath on earth. Maybe that's why Belle has these dreams...these visions. It doesn't make sense and yet, it makes perfect sense.

Belle freezes, her sobs quieting. Her breath hitches as she pulls back and looks at me.

"I love you most ardently and fervently...this lifetime and all the lifetimes thereafter," I rasp, my body thrumming with crackling electricity.

These vows—I feel them in the depths of my soul, words I'll live and die by. Perhaps the impossible is possible.

"The words..." She shudders. "You said them the night you were shot and in the hospital." And they're the same words Silas wrote to his Emma.

"I remember. I remember it all." I breathe, my eyes catching hers.

"Belle," I wipe the tears on her face, "she knew. Whether it was back then and that's why you had those dreams or centuries later, but she finally knew."

Her face crumbles and tears fall down her cheeks again, sobs tearing out of her lungs.

"I love you so much." I hold her in my arms. A heady warmth sweeps through my body. The chains of the curse binding my family are broken. The deaths are solved.

We are finally free.

I hug her closer, tighter against me. *I'll never let go. Not again.*

Minutes pass by as we reel from the revelations, finally getting the answers we've been searching for all our lives.

"I think my soul recognized yours the moment we met, and I'm the lucky man who gets to fall in love with you all over again," I murmur, pressing a kiss to her hair.

A breeze blows by, bringing a scent of wildflowers—faint, a whisper of spring around the corner. The season of hope and new beginnings.

My voice leaves me as she flips to the next page of the journal, and what I see there has my heart thudding in a righteous rhythm.

A sketch—a dark silhouette of a woman wearing a locket, the jewelry rendered in the most intricate details. It's the same locket around Belle's neck. An inscription is dotted with watermarks. Tears, if I had to guess:

Once lost but destined to be found. My love for you transcends time and death.

Belle's eyes widen and I reach for the locket on her chest, the one I knew belonged around her neck the moment I laid eyes on the photo. Gently, I open it.

Images of the past meld with the present, of my fingers tracing the words when they were newly carved and again when I put the locket around Belle's neck centuries later.

To E.

Upon you, my dearest, my love rests for eternity and beyond, for anything less would be insufferable.

Your servant,

S

To Emma from her Silas, star-crossed lovers.

My heart churns and flutters as I stare at my wife, the woman I've been waiting for my entire life...and quite possibly longer, even if everything transcends logic and common sense.

I've loved her since before I can remember. Every moment with her just adds to the tapestry we've been weaving together since the dawn of time.

"Belle," I whisper, my hand gently clasping her nape.

"Maxwell." She looks up, her luscious lips parted, a pink swath blooming on her face. She looks like a wildflower in the snow. The beginning of spring.

Slowly, I lean down, watching her eyes flutter shut, and press my forehead against hers.

I breathe her in.

Her scent. Her warmth. Her vitality.

The wind caresses our bodies—a lover's embrace, and I angle Belle's face toward mine. My nose grazes her cheek, then to the hollow where her ear meets her neck, and every nerve ending inside me is on fire.

Burning for this woman in my arms.

Unable to withstand it any longer, I press kisses to her soft skin as I make my way back up to her lips.

A thousand kisses for all the years we were apart.

A thousand kisses for all the tears she had shed for me.

A thousand kisses to represent a tiny fraction of the love I feel for her.

Clasping her face in my hands, I seal my mouth over hers, my heart burgeoning and doubling in size.

Perhaps our bodies are transient in this world, but a soul is eternal, each lifetime leaving an indelible imprint behind, a familiar verse we've forgotten, but the feelings they evoke are permanent. That's why we roam this earth looking for the other half of our souls, seeking a connection that has been written in the grains of time.

We break apart for air and I tuck an errant lock of hair that has blown in front of her face.

Her lips curve into a bright teary smile, as beautiful as the golden sunlight breaking through the thick clouds behind us.

"I'm home," she whispers, moisture glinting in her eyes. "I love you, Maxwell Angus Silas Anderson."

"And I love you, Annabelle Charlotte Law-McKenzie Anderson," I reply. "This lifetime and all the lifetimes thereafter."

At the edge of my sight line, at the ground level where the rose garden lies, in the patch of soil where no life has ever taken root—a mark of the cursed land—the tender shoots of a new rose bush pierce the ground, their fragile green stems whispering of hope and new beginnings.

The locket is reunited with its owner, two lost souls reunited, and I am finally whole.

Finally home.

EPILOGUE

Belle

Six Months Later

"Thank y-you for coming tonight. The newly inaugurated Anderson Depression and Anxiety Research Center will greatly benefit from the proceeds of the sales this evening." Maxwell clears his throat and nods to the crowd gathered at a chic gallery in SoHo. It's not The Met, but I know he has no interest in being at such a high-profile place. This smaller setting is perfect for him.

His face is flushed, and I can hear the hitch in his breath as he stands *in front* of the stage.

Not on top of it, because he didn't want the spotlight shining on him.

He's drawn boundaries for himself, and I'm so proud of him for that.

Taking a deep breath, his eyes sweep the room until they land on me. A ghost of a smile appears on his lips. "M-May there be a day when the stigma of mental health conditions can be eradicated because we all deserve good health...both inside..." he points to his temple, "and outside."

Giving the crowd a terse nod, applause rings in the air as he hands the microphone over to an attendant. He then strides over, all tethered power and masculinity in his three-piece dark navy suit—a McKenzie's creation, of course—his hair artfully swept up, carefully groomed stubble on his chiseled jawline.

Pride swells in my chest, joining the undercurrent of excitement. *I can't wait to tell him the news.*

Heat sweeps through me as I watch my very handsome husband walking toward me, a lightness in his steps despite just having given a closing speech to the guests of his first-ever art show since he was in high school. I told him he didn't need to give a speech, that I could take care of it for him, but he said he wanted to.

"I'm a winner," he murmurs, his dark eyes glinting in our bedroom a week ago. "I'm not hiding behind my anxiety anymore."

I smile and touch his cheek. "You're a winner either way. Because you're battling your inner demons each day with bravery. On the good days, and the bad."

His voice hitches and his nostrils flare. "You're right. I'm the biggest winner in life already...because I have you by my side."

My chest warms at the memory as he reaches me, his comforting scent wafting to my nose. The guests are filtering out of the gallery as planned. When I finalized the schedule last week, I didn't want him to feel pressured to socialize for the entire night. Therefore, I slotted his speech as the closing remarks, so he could appear at the end of the evening on his own terms.

"I'm so proud of you." I loop my arms around his neck. "You did so well up there."

"Dr. Lin helped a lot." He's been seeing her weekly and diligently taking his medicine to help control his panic attacks. It hasn't been smooth sailing, but he's been so much happier.

It also helps that ever since we discovered Silas's journal and read Emma's parting words...words about sacrifice, much like what Maxwell did when he came in between the bullet and me, there have been no more strange accidents. The rose garden is in full bloom, including the patch of soil that grew nothing before. Maxwell was right. The curse, if there was one, has been broken.

Now, when I step in between the beautiful bushes and smell the lush scent of the flowers, I no longer feel sad. Instead, I feel a bone-deep peace and contentment. The estate also feels brighter, like all the missing parts have slid into place.

"All the pieces are sold. They love your work. A smart CEO and a brilliant artist. How did I get so lucky?" I gesture at the colorful canvases hung on the walls, all marked with orange stickers to indicate a sale.

He grins, his smile wolfishly handsome. Fleur's stock has rebounded and is higher than ever. The public is singing praises at how he has become a champion of mental health awareness.

Stepping on my tiptoes, I press a kiss on his lips. "My husband is so, so talented." I dip my tongue out and lick at the seam. "Just like his wife," I add, before giving him a saucy wink. Fiona called me into her office yesterday with a promotion to senior designer...all on my own merit.

He growls and hauls me flushed against him. "I can show you how talented I am." He gyrates his hips slightly, letting me feel his hardness for emphasis.

Heat unfurls between my legs and just as I'm about to ask him to show me his abilities in a supply closet, an angry voice penetrates the sexual haze.

"She was uncomfortable, you jackass."

Our heads whip toward the entrance, where Charles is in the face of a slim man. Taylor stands next to him, scowling while rubbing her forearm.

The man holds his hands up, clearly not wanting to anger the fuming god of thunder towering over him, and scurries away.

Taylor narrows her eyes and puts her hands on her hips. "I didn't need you to save me. I could've handled that myself. I'm very capable, you know."

"Didn't look like it from my angle. You were shivering like a leaf."

"Oh fuck you, Charles!"

"Not in a million years, even if you were to ask me," Charles growls as he stares Taylor down, who now has her arms crossed over her chest.

I can smell the hatred all the way from over here.

"You guys, what's going on? Is everything okay?" Grace hurries over to them. She looks at us and gives me a wink.

I've got this, she mouths. *Go enjoy your night.*

"Well, well, well, trouble in paradise, eh?" Rex grins, bringing with him Ryland, Ethan, and Steven. Lana and Millie are giggling over what probably is some gossip of the day.

"What paradise? More like hell," Charles mutters under his breath.

"The golden prince is ruffled by our black-hearted ballerina. I want to know all the details." Rex waggles his brows and everyone groans.

"Should we rescue them?" I ask Maxwell.

He chuckles, his deep voice sending shivers down my body as his finger draws circles over the triangle back cutout of my dress.

"No, they'll be fine," he murmurs and presses a kiss right under my ear where he knows I'm most sensitive.

"Maxwell," I moan, arching toward him. "We're in public."

"That's literally the only thing preventing me from ripping that dress off your body."

I shiver, the image of him having his way with me in public causing my pussy to clench.

"Ah, I forgot my wife is a slutty exhibitionist," he rakes his teeth down my neck, "but no one gets to see you naked except me. But maybe we can find a room here and everyone can hear how you scream for your husband's cock."

I think back to that night at The Lilith and how I fell apart in his arms with an audience on the other side of the glass. We may have reenacted that a few times in the last few months. My legs turn to jelly and I would've melted into a puddle on the floor if it weren't for him holding me upright.

Something flashes in my mind and the lustful haze clears.

I straighten. I completely forgot my surprise for him.

"Something wrong?" he asks, clearly sensing my mood change.

"I have something to show you."

I lace my fingers with his and tug him toward my destination, ignoring the curious glances of my friends and family. My heels click on the marble floors as we breeze through the white walls filled with Maxwell's art—pieces he has created over the years when he hid himself and his talent away from the rest of the world. Now, each of these paintings is sold, appreciated, and loved by others.

What's art if not to be loved and admired?

That's what he told me before, and I turn around as my legs pick up in speed, my hair floating behind me, hitting him in the face. He laughs, a rich, loud sound I'll never get sick of hearing.

Grinning, I break into a half jog, him matching my pace behind me, as my heart pounds in an excited rhythm. After a few turns in the convoluted maze of walls in the gallery, I come to a slow stop, my breathing coming out in quick pants. Squeezing his hand, I walk toward my destination, a singular portrait decorating a large, white wall, with a lone spotlight shining on it.

My favorite piece of his creations.

It's the painting of me smiling, with the rose garden behind me in full bloom. The painting he was working on when I was taken six months ago. The painting that made my heart hurt in sadness before, but now swells in joy because of the love in every stroke.

His love for me, captured on canvas. The essence of our story.

"I thought this one wasn't for sale," he says as we walk up to the painting.

"It isn't. But I want the world to see it, because it's so beautiful," I whisper, curling my arm around him and leaning my head against his shoulder. "Many people wanted to buy it, but I refused. Because this one is mine."

"Hmm..." He stares intently at the art.

I hold my breath, wondering if he'll see it. The subtle change I made. A glimmer of pale cream on the dress at the waist, so it looks like it's floating in the wind, molding to the subtle new curves of my belly. Just like the dash of hope I instilled in the turbulent skies in his painting of Lake Superior or the streak of red hidden in the blue-green of atrovirens.

A few moments of silence pass by as I'm breathless with anticipation.

Suddenly, he shifts, his muscles tensing at my side, and I smile inwardly.

He sees it.

He grips my hand tightly as his breath catches, and he slowly tugs me closer to the canvas.

"Did you... Is it? What?" Nonsensical words tumble out of his mouth and he turns to me, his eyes darting to my midsection, then to the painting, then back at me again.

"Belle... Are you? Is this what I think it means?"

Tears well in my eyes, and I press my lips together and nod as a choked sob slip out of my mouth.

"Yes, Maxwell." I throw my arms around his neck, pulling his head down so we are at eye level, his charcoal eyes glittering with moisture under the stark lighting.

His face blurs in front of me and I whisper in his ear, "You're going to be a dad."

His breath catches. Pulling back slightly, he cradles my face in his hands, his eyes shining with so much wonder and awe...and joy.

Complete elation.

We turned to IVF shortly after he recovered, since my egg reserves were much lower than expected. It had been months and months of pills, hormones, and shots—three egg retrievals, yielding only three viable embryos and the last two attempts had failed. I was a moody mess, my body reacting horribly to the procedures, and we promised each other if this last attempt failed, we would craft a different dream for ourselves.

Because we would be happy either way...even if the present was painful.

The last transfer was two weeks ago, and I got the call from the clinic yesterday with the good news. I then spent the next hour in the Elysium modifying his painting of me.

Maxwell's breathing grows ragged as he lifts my hand to his lips and kisses my fingertips with such reverence, my breath stalls in my throat.

He then leans forward and dips his forehead against mine, much like all the other times before, and he presses a kiss there.

Then he moves to my lips, searing me with a gentle kiss before whispering, "I love you so, so much, Belle."

Finally, he kneels down and cradles my belly. Tears slide down my face as I watch him smooth his hands over my nonexistent curves.

"Hello, baby. I'm your father, and I love you to the ends of the earth," he whispers before pressing a kiss there.

Another sob escapes my mouth, and he glances up at me, tears welling in his eyes.

Standing up, he curls his hand around my nape, the other angling my jaw before he crushes his lips to mine, making love to my mouth as I do the same to him.

Heat swirls over my chest and down my body, my heart pounding in an erratic rhythm as he deepens our connection before he pulls apart.

The beginning strains of Puccini's "Nessun Dorma" sound from the speakers. We smile at each other, and my heart skips a beat. I'm brought back to when I first heard this aria with him in his car, the night that is forever emblazoned in my mind.

How much things have changed since then...and yet, nothing has changed the way my heart pounds for him, an ancient rhythm created long before I walked this earth.

My lips curve up and I murmur, "I love you, husband."

He tucks me against him. "I love you, wife."

We stare at his masterpiece, the painting that captures me so perfect- ly, all the while listening to the evocative melody of hope and victory.

Silas's words float to my mind.

Your image dwells eternally in my mind, though I could spend the rest of my life attempting to capture your likeness on canvas, nothing will ever compare, for my skills can never do you justice.

Yet I vow, one day, when we are reunited in another life, when my heart is made whole, I shall attempt to portray you once more, my love. Perhaps then, I will finally be able to capture your essence.

Yes. He did capture my essence.
Completely, irrevocably, whole-heartedly.

———◆———

Thank you for reading WHEN HEARTS SURRENDER. Hope you've enjoyed Maxwell and Belle's story as much as I did writing it.

Bonus Epilogues: Want to go to Venice for Maxwell and Belle's babymoon? These are the bonus epilogues you don't want to miss! Sign up for my newsletter to get **TWO EXTRA BONUS CHAPTERS**, new release alerts, exclusive bonus material, and more. Just click on the "When Hearts Surrender Bonus Epilogues" on the website: https://www.victorialum.com/bonus

Read Charles's Story Next: Do you know Charles and Taylor's story is next? This is one angsty enemies to lovers, forced proximity billionaire romance with "Who did this to you?" and "I'll burn the world for you" vibes. Don't miss WHEN HEARTS AWAKEN. Read it here: https://geni.us/whenheartsawaken

Please Review: Please consider leaving a review on the retailer website and Goodreads https://www.goodreads.com/book/show/213326 289-when-hearts-surrender. Your reviews will really help this author out and will allow for more readers to find this book.

THANK YOU

THE IDEA FOR MAXWELL'S book came long before Steven's book (the first book of *The Orchid* series, *When Hearts Ignite*) was written. It stemmed from a coffee-fueled 2am discussion with my husband in our small hotel room in New York City. I wanted to write his story then. Desperate to get it on paper even. But I knew it had to wait, because I liked to work in order and I had Steven and Grace's story and Ryland and Millie's story to tell first.

Originally, Silas and Emma didn't exist. The prologue was supposed to showcase Morris's sister's last moments instead. But then, I knew it was missing something, that there was a bigger story for me to tell. And so, I sat down and wrote Silas and Emma's tragic love story instead.

I couldn't say goodbye to them. I couldn't end their story this way. Then came the "what if" moment. What if their story never ended? Many cultures believe in reincarnation and the wonderful thing about fiction is, whether you believe in it or not, you get to experience and interpret the story as you see fit. That was why I left the question of whether or not Maxwell and Belle were really Silas and Emma in present times open-ended.

A slight dash of magical realism, if you may.

But either way, their story was special to me and took a piece of me with it when I was writing it. I always believed in soulmates, in meeting that special someone who was meant to be your partner in this journey called life. And Maxwell and Belle were the definition of soulmates.

There were a few tough topics discussed in this book.

Infidelity was mentioned in Silas and Emma's story because unfortunately, it was common in the aristocracy during those times as many of their marriages were arranged.

Depression and anxiety were mental health issues important to me due to personal experiences and unfortunately, these were invisible conditions affecting far too many individuals in this world, regardless of their backgrounds.

If you are one of these individuals, know that help is out there and there is light at the end of the tunnel, even if you can't see it yet. Oftentimes, it's darkest before sunrise.

Belle also suffered from fertility struggles, which unfortunately also impacts many of us in the real world. I went through five years of secondary infertility including multiple heartbreaking losses and surgeries. Ultimately, thanks to science, I was able to conceive my youngest child. But there were many moments when I questioned my worth, when I couldn't bring myself to attend baby showers, when I wondered, why me? I ultimately decided to end their story with a viable pregnancy, which I knew could be triggering for individuals going through fertility struggles but I'm hoping it could also bring the same hope I held onto when I was reading success stories in the darkest of times. Everyone's experience is different, but I truly believe each and every one of you deserve your happily ever after, which could come in many forms—single, married, with children, without.

I hope you enjoyed Maxwell and Belle's story.

As always, thank you to everyone who has supported me, in no particular order:

My family: Thanks for putting with my long work hours. I couldn't do any of this without you all.

My editors: Theresa Leigh and Amy Briggs, thank you for your coaching and insights. Theresa, thank you for letting me slip in a loan shark and I'm glad we didn't add a trebuchet in the story.

Proofreader: Virginia Tesi Carey, thank you for being an eagle eye in catching all the tiny errors that slipped through.

My PA: Thank you to Nikki Johnson for keeping me on track with so many of the admin tasks!

Cover designer: To the awesome LK Farlow of Y'All That Graphic for these beautiful covers!

Beta readers: Malia, Jenn, Jess, Denny, Amy, and Isha, thank you so much for your prompt feedback and suggestions! You girls are the best beta readers an author could ask for.

My ilLUMinati girls: you know who you are! Thank you for everything! You are the best cheerleaders!

Fellow authors: So many authors have helped me on this journey—it is impossible to name everyone, but I appreciate each and every one of you.

PR Firms: Thank you to Literally Yours PR, Truly Yours PR, and Erica Anderson for your promotional efforts and helping me get the word out!

My Fellow Readers: I love you all so very much. I wake up each day feeling blessed that you have chosen my books to read. Thank you from the bottom of my heart.

With love,

Victoria

ALSO BY VICTORIA LUM

Catch up on Victoria's backlist! Don't miss these swoony, romantic stories with all the sizzling spice and angst. All stories are standalones and can be read out of order.

LA Hearts Series:

The Sweetest Agony (Friends to lovers – James and Jess)

The Coldest Passion (Single dad x nanny – Parker and Liz)

The Harshest Hope (Second chance, billionaire – Adrian and Emily)

The Brightest Spark (Dislike to like, unrequited love – Jack and Sarah)

The Orchid Series:

When Hearts Ignite (Boss x employee – Steven and Grace)

When Hearts Collide (Professor x student, primal play – Ryland and Millie)

When Hearts Surrender (Arranged marriage, family curse – Maxwell and Belle)

When Hearts Awaken (Enemies to lovers, forced proximity – Charles and Taylor)

About the Author

Victoria is a lover of all things romance, including movies, books, and television shows. A hopeless romantic since childhood, she is always dreaming up stories and happily ever afters. Caramel lattes are her fuel in the morning and she can usually be found reading anything she can get her hands on. She lives with her family and a beautiful Siberian husky in sunny California.

Keep in touch!
Sign up for her newsletter below:
Newsletter
Follow Victoria on social media:
Victoria Lum's Luminaries Facebook Group
Facebook Page
Instagram
Tiktok
Bookbub
Amazon
Goodreads
Scan the QR code below for all the links!